PRAISE FOR JULIE GARWOOD'S

THE PRIZE

". . . A DELIGHT . . . Mystery, betrayal, divided loyalties, gentle love, *The Prize* has it all, along with a heroine who will steal your heart."

—*Affaire de Coeur*

"Ms. Garwood brings to sparkling life an age when men had the opportunity to prove their mettle and women their wiles. . . . Engrossing, romantic, funny, adventurous . . . EXCELLENT."

—*Rendezvous*

THE GIFT

"Glorious . . . *The Gift* is a stunning achievement, full of warmth, humor, lovable characters . . . rich in emotion . . . You'll cherish this book."

—*Romantic Times*

"I am once again enthralled with the tale that flows from Ms. Garwood's pen. . . . *The Gift* belongs on my 'hands off or die!' shelf."

—*Rendezvous*

GUARDIAN ANGEL

"A treasure . . . with . . . a whirlwind pace and breathtaking sensuality, *Guardian Angel* is a tempting, delectable read . . . another surefire hit!"

—*Romantic Times*

"Ms. Garwood again proves herself to be a master storyteller. . . . Don't miss this one!"

—*Rendezvous*

BOOKS BY JULIE GARWOOD

Gentle Warrior
Rebellious Desire
Honor's Splendour
The Lion's Lady
The Bride
Guardian Angel
The Gift
The Prize
The Secret
Castles
Saving Grace
Prince Charming
For the Roses
The Wedding
Come the Spring
Ransom
Heartbreaker
Mercy

The Clayborne Brides
One Pink Rose
One White Rose
One Red Rose

PUBLISHED BY POCKET BOOKS

JULIE GARWOOD

The Secret

POCKET BOOKS

New York   London   Toronto   Sydney

Pocket Books
A Division of Simon & Schuster, Inc.
1230 Avenue of the Americas
New York, NY 10020

This book is a work of fiction. Names, characters, places, and incidents either are products of the author's imagination or are used fictitiously. Any resemblance to actual events or locales or persons, living or dead, is entirely coincidental.

This Pocket Books paperback edition June 2010

POCKET and colophon are registered trademarks of Simon & Schuster, Inc.

For information about special discounts for bulk purchases, please contact Simon & Schuster Special Sales at 1-866-506-1949 or business@simonandschuster.com.

The Simon & Schuster Speakers Bureau can bring authors to your live event. For more information or to book an event, contact the Simon & Schuster Speakers Bureau at 1-866-248-3049 or visit our website at www.simonspeakers.com.

Cover photo by Macduff Everton/© Corbis

Manufactured in the United States of America

10 9 8 7 6 5 4 3 2 1

ISBN 978-1-4391-9478-2

Prologue

England, 1181

They became friends before they were old enough to understand they were supposed to hate each other.

The two little girls met at the annual summer festival held on the border between Scotland and England. It was Lady Judith Hampton's first experience attending the Scottish games, her first real outing away from her isolated home in the west of England as well, and she was so overwhelmed by the sheer adventure of it all, she could barely keep her eyes closed during her mandatory afternoon naps. There was so much to see and do, and for a curious four-year-old, a good deal of mischief to get into, too.

Frances Catherine Kirkcaldy had already gotten herself into mischief. Her papa had given her a good swat on her backside to make her sorry she'd misbehaved, then carried her over his shoulder like a sack of feed all the way across the wide field. He made her sit on a smooth-topped rock, far away from the singing and the dancing, and ordered her to stay put until he was good and ready to come back and fetch her. She would use the quiet time alone, he commanded, to contemplate her sins.

1

Since Frances Catherine didn't have the faintest idea what the word "contemplate" meant, she decided she didn't have to obey that order. It was just as well, for her mind was already completely full, worrying about the fat, stinging bee buzzing circles around her head.

Judith had seen the father punish his daughter. She felt sorry for the funny-looking, freckle-faced little girl. She knew she surely would have cried if her uncle Herbert had smacked her bottom, but the redheaded girl hadn't even grimaced when her papa smacked her.

She decided to talk to the girl. She waited until her father had quit wagging his finger at his daughter and had strutted back across the field, then picked up the hem of her skirt and ran the long way around to sneak up on the rock from behind.

"My papa never would have smacked me," Judith boasted by way of introduction.

Frances Catherine didn't turn her head to see who was talking to her. She didn't dare take her gaze away from the bee now lingering on the rock next to her left knee.

Judith wasn't daunted by her silence. "My papa's dead," she announced. "Since before I was even borned."

"Then how would you be knowing if he would smack you or not?"

Judith lifted her shoulders in a shrug. "I just know he wouldn't," she answered. "You talk funny, like you've got something trapped in your throat. Do you?"

"No," Frances Catherine answered. "You talk funny, too."

"Why won't you look at me?"

"I can't."

"Why can't you?" Judith asked. She twisted the hem of her pink gown into a wrinkle while she waited for an answer.

"I have to watch the bee," Frances Catherine answered. "It wants to sting me. I have to be ready to swat it away."

Judith leaned closer. She spotted the bee flittering around the girl's left foot. "Why don't you swat it away now?" she asked in a whisper.

"I'm afraid to," Frances Catherine answered. "I might miss. Then it would get me for certain."

Judith frowned over that dilemma a long minute. "Do you want me to swat it for you?"

"Would you want to?"

"Maybe I would," she answered. "What's your name?" she asked then, stalling for time while she gathered her courage to go after the bee.

"Frances Catherine. What's yours?"

"Judith. How come you have two full names? I've never heard of anyone having more than one."

"Everybody always asks me that," Frances Catherine said. She let out a dramatic sigh. "Frances was my mama's name. She died birthing me. Catherine's my grandmama's name, and she died just the same way. They couldn't be buried in the sacred ground 'cause the Church said they weren't clean. Papa's hoping I'll start in behaving and then I'll get to Heaven, and when God hears my two names, he'll remember Mama and Grandma."

"Why did the Church say they weren't clean?"

"'Cause they were birthing when they died," Frances Catherine explained. "Don't you know anything, girl?"

"I know some things."

"I know just about everything," Frances Catherine boasted. "Leastways, papa says I surely think I do. I even know how babies get into the mamas' stomachs. Want to hear?"

"Oh, yes."

"Once they get married, the papa spits into his goblet of wine and then he makes the mama take a big drink. As soon as she swallows, she's got a baby in her stomach."

Judith made a grimace over that thrillingly disgusting information. She was going to beg her friend to tell her more when Frances Catherine suddenly let out a loud whimper. Judith leaned closer. Then she let out a whimper, too. The bee had settled on the tip of her friend's shoe. The longer Judith stared at it, the bigger it seemed to grow.

The talk about birthing was immediately put aside. "Are you going to swat it away?" Frances Catherine asked.

"I'm getting ready to."

"Are you afraid?"

"No," Judith lied. "I'm not afraid of anything. I didn't think you were, either."

"Why didn't you?"

"Because you didn't cry when your papa smacked you," Judith explained.

"That's because he didn't smack me hard," Frances Catherine explained. "Papa never does. It pains him more than me, too. Leastways, that's what Gavin and Kevin say. Papa's got his hands full with me, they say, and ruining me good for some pitiful man I got to marry when I'm all grown up because papa pampers me."

"Who are Gavin and Kevin?"

"Half my brothers," Frances Catherine explained. "Papa's their papa, too, but they had a different mama. She died."

"Did she die birthing them?"

"No."

"Then why'd she die?"

"She just got tuckered out," Frances Catherine explained. "Papa told me so. I'm closing my eyes real tight now if you want to swat the bee."

Because Judith was so determined to impress her new friend, she didn't think about the consequences any longer. She reached out to slap the bee, but as soon as she felt the flutter of its wings against the palm of her hand, it tickled her so, she instinctively closed her fingers.

Then she started wailing. Frances Catherine bounded off the rock to help the only way she knew how. She started wailing, too.

Judith ran around and around the rock, screaming so vigorously she could barely catch her breath. Her friend chased after her, screaming just as fiercely, though in sympathy and fear rather than in pain.

Frances Catherine's papa came running across the field. He caught hold of his daughter first, and when she'd stammered out her problem, he chased down Judith.

In a matter of minutes the two little girls had been properly soothed. The stinger had been removed from the palm of Judith's hand and cool wet mud applied. Her friend's papa gently mopped away her tears with the edge of his woolen plaid. He sat on the punishment rock now, with his daughter cuddled up on one side of his lap and Judith cuddled up on the other.

She'd never had anyone make such a fuss over her before. Judith turned quite shy because of all the attention she was getting. She didn't turn away from the comfort, though, and in fact edged a little closer to get even more.

"You two are a sorry pair," the papa announced when they'd quit their hiccuping and could hear him. "Screaming louder than the trumpets sounding the caber toss, you were, and running in circles like hens with your heads cut off."

Judith didn't know if the papa was angry or not. His voice had been gruff, but he wasn't frowning. Frances Catherine giggled. Judith decided her friend's papa must have been jesting after all.

"It was paining her considerably, Papa," Frances Catherine announced.

"I'm certain it did pain her," he agreed. He turned his gaze to Judith and caught her staring up at him. "You're a brave little lass to help my daughter," he praised. "But if there be a next time, try not to catch the bee. All right?"

Judith solemnly nodded.

He patted her arm. "You're a pretty little thing," he remarked. "What's your name, child?"

"Her name's Judith, Papa, and she's my friend. Can she have her supper with us?"

"Well now, that depends on her parents," her father replied.

"Her papa's dead," Frances Catherine announced. "Isn't that pitiful, Papa?"

"It surely is," he agreed. The corners of his eyes crinkled up, but he didn't smile. "She's got the prettiest blue eyes I've ever seen, though."

"Don't I have the prettiest eyes you've ever seen, too, Papa?"

"Aye, you do, Frances Catherine. You've got the prettiest brown eyes I've ever seen. You surely do."

Frances Catherine was so pleased with her father's praise, she scrunched up her shoulders and giggled again.

"Her papa died before she was even borned," Frances Catherine told him then. She'd only just remembered that information and was certain her papa would want to hear it.

He nodded, then said, "Now daughter, I want you to keep real quiet while I talk to your friend."

"Yes, Papa."

He turned his attention back to Judith. He found it a little unnerving, the way she was intently staring up at him. She was such a serious little thing, too serious for someone of her young age.

"How old are you, Judith?"

She held up four fingers.

"Papa, do you see? She's just my age."

"No, Frances Catherine, she isn't just your age. Judith's four in years and you're already five. Remember?"

"I remember, Papa."

He smiled at his daughter, then once again tried to talk to Judith. "You aren't afraid of me, are you?"

"She's not afraid of anything. She told me so."

"Hush, daughter. I want to hear your friend speak a word or two. Judith, is your mama here?"

She shook her head. She started twisting a lock of her white-blond hair around and around her finger in a nervous gesture, yet kept her gaze fully directed on the papa. The man's face was covered with red whiskers, and when he spoke, the bristles wiggled. She wished she could touch the beard to find out what it felt like.

"Judith? Is your mama here?" the papa repeated.

"No, Mama stays with Uncle Tekel. They don't know I'm here. It's going to be a secret, and if I tell, I won't ever be able to come back to the festival. Aunt Millicent told me so."

Once she started talking, she wanted to tell everything she knew. "Uncle Tekel says he's just like my papa, but he's only mama's brother and I never sit on his lap. I wouldn't want to if I could, but I can't so it doesn't matter, does it?"

Frances Catherine's father was having difficulty following the explanation, but his daughter wasn't having any trouble at all. She was filled with curiosity, too. "Why can't you if you wanted to?" she asked.

"He got his legs broke."

Frances Catherine let out a gasp. "Papa, isn't that pitiful?"

Her father let out a long sigh. The conversation was getting away from him. "Aye, it surely is," he agreed. "Now, Judith, if your mother's at home, how did you get here?"

"With Mama's sister," Judith answered. "I used to live with Aunt Millicent and Uncle Herbert all the time, but Mama won't let me anymore."

"'Cause why?" Frances Catherine asked.

"'Cause Mama heard me call Uncle Herbert 'Papa.' She was so fuming mad, she gave me a smack on the top of my head. Then Uncle Tekel told me I had to live with him and Mama for half the year long so I'd know who I belonged to, and my aunt Millicent and uncle Herbert would just have to do without me. That's what Tekel said. Mama didn't want me to go away even half the year, but Tekel hadn't started his after-supper drinking yet, so she knew he would remember what he told her. He always remembers when he isn't drunk. Mama was fuming mad again."

"Was your mama fuming mad because she was going to miss you half the year?" Frances Catherine asked.

"No," Judith whispered. "Mama says I'm a bother."

"Then why didn't she want you to go?"

"She doesn't like Uncle Herbert," Judith answered. "That's why she was being contrary."

"Why doesn't she like him?" Frances Catherine wanted to know.

"'Cause he's related to the damn Scots," Judith answered, repeating what she'd heard time and time again. "Mama says I shouldn't even want to talk to the damn Scots."

"Papa, am I damn Scots?"

"You most certainly are not."

"Am I?" Judith asked, her worry obvious in her voice.

"You're English, Judith," her friend's papa patiently explained.

"Am I damn English?"

Her friend's papa was clearly exasperated. "Nobody's damn anything," he announced. He started to say more, then suddenly burst into laughter. His big belly jiggled with his amusement. "I'd best remember not to say anything in front of you two little tarts I don't want repeated."

"'Cause why, Papa?"

"Never you mind," he answered.

He stood up, holding his daughter in one arm and Judith in the other. Both little girls let out squeals of delight when he pretended he was going to drop them.

"We'd best find your aunt and uncle before they start in worrying, Judith. Point me the way to your tent, lass."

Judith immediately became frightened inside. She couldn't remember where the tent was located. Since she didn't know her colors yet, she couldn't even give Frances Catherine's papa a description.

She tried not to cry. She bowed her head and whispered, "I don't remember."

She tensed in anticipation of his anger. She thought he'd shout at her for being ignorant, the way her uncle Tekel always did whenever he was drunk and pricked about something she'd inadvertently done that displeased him.

Frances Catherine's papa didn't get angry, though. She peeked up to look at him and caught his smile. Her anxiety completely vanished when he told her to quit her fretting. He'd find her relatives soon enough, he promised.

"Will they miss you if you don't come back?" Frances Catherine asked.

Judith nodded. "Uncle Herbert and Aunt Millicent would cry," she told her new friend. "Sometimes I wish they were my mama and papa. I do."

"'Cause why?"

Judith lifted her shoulders in a shrug. She didn't know how to explain why.

"Well now, there's nothing wrong with wishing," Frances Catherine's papa said.

Judith was so happy to have his approval, she put her head down on his shoulder. His warm plaid felt rough against her cheek. He smelled so nice, too, like the outdoors.

She thought he was the most wonderful papa in the whole world. Since he wasn't looking down at her now, she decided to appease her curiosity. She reached up to touch his beard. The bristles tickled and she let out a giggle over that notice.

"Papa, do you like my new friend?" Frances Catherine asked when they were halfway across the field.

"I surely do."

"Can I keep her?"

"For the love of . . . No, you can't keep her. She isn't a puppy. You can be her friend, though," he hastily added before his daughter could argue with him.

"Forever, papa?"

She'd asked her father that question, but Judith answered her. "Forever," she shyly whispered.

Frances Catherine reached across her father's chest to take hold of Judith's hand. "Forever," she pledged.

And so it began.

From that moment on, the two little girls became inseparable. The festival lasted three full weeks, with various clans coming and going, and the championship games were always scheduled on the last Sunday of the month.

Judith and Frances Catherine were oblivious to the competition, however. They were too busy telling each other all their secrets.

It was a perfect friendship. Frances Catherine had finally found someone who wanted to listen to what she had to say, and Judith had finally found someone who wanted to talk to her.

The two of them were a trial of patience for their relatives, however. Frances Catherine started using the word "damn" in every other sentence, and Judith was using the word "pitiful" just as often. One afternoon, while they were supposed to be napping, they cut each other's hair. When Aunt Millicent got a good look at the lopsided mess they'd made, she started in screeching and didn't let up until she'd slapped white caps on their heads to hide the sight. She was furious with Uncle Herbert, too, because he was supposed to be keeping his eye on the girls, and instead of being the least contrite over the catastrophe, he was laughing like a loon. She ordered her husband to take the imps across the field and set them on the punishment rock to think about their shameful behavior.

The girls did do a lot of thinking, but it wasn't about their behavior. Frances Catherine had come up with the wonderful idea that Judith should also have two full names so they'd be just alike. It took them a long while to settle on the name, Elizabeth, but once it was decided, Judith became Judith Elizabeth, and refused to answer anyone's summons unless they used both her names when they called to her.

A full year passed, and yet when they were reunited, it was as though they had only been apart an hour or two. Frances Catherine couldn't wait to get Judith alone, because she'd found another amazing fact about birthings. A woman didn't have to be married to have a baby after all. She knew that for certain because one of the Kirkcaldy women had grown a baby in her stomach and she wasn't wed. Some of the old women in the clan had thrown stones at the poor lass, too, Frances Catherine whispered, and her papa had made them stop.

"Did they throw stones at the man who spit in his drink?" Judith wanted to know.

Frances Catherine shook her head. "The woman wouldn't tell who'd done it," she replied.

The lesson was easy to understand, Frances Catherine continued. It had been proven that if a fully grown woman drank out of any man's goblet of wine, she would surely get a baby in her stomach.

She made Judith promise she would never do such a thing. Judith made Frances Catherine give her the same promise.

The growing years blurred together in Judith's memory, and the awareness of the hatred that existed between the Scots and the English was slow to penetrate her mind. She guessed she'd always known her mother and her uncle Tekel despised the Scots, but she believed it was because they didn't know any better.

Ignorance often bred contempt, didn't it? At least that's what Uncle Herbert said. She believed everything he told her. He was such a kind, loving man, and when Judith suggested that Tekel and her mother had never spent any time with a Scottish family and that was why they didn't realize what fine, good-hearted people they were, her uncle Herbert kissed her on her forehead and told her perhaps that was true.

Judith could tell from the sadness in his eyes that he was only agreeing with her to please her, and to protect her, too, from her mother's unreasonable prejudice.

When she was eleven years old and on her way to the festival, she found out the true reason her mother hated the Scots.

She was married to one.

Chapter 1

⌘

Iain Maitland was a mean son of a bitch when he was riled.

He was riled now. The black mood came over him the minute his brother Patrick told him about the promise he'd given his sweet wife, Frances Catherine.

If Patrick had wanted to surprise his brother, he'd certainly accomplished that goal. His explanation had rendered Iain speechless.

The condition didn't last long. Anger quickly took over. In truth, the ridiculous promise his brother had given his wife wasn't nearly as infuriating to Iain as the fact that Patrick had called the council together to render their official opinion on the matter. Iain would have stopped his brother from involving the elders in what he considered to be a private, family matter, but he'd been away from the holding at the time, hunting down the Maclean bastards who'd waylaid three unseasoned Maitland warriors, and when he'd returned home, weary but victorious, the deed had already been done.

Leave it to Patrick to take a simple issue and complicate the hell out of it. It was apparent he hadn't consid-

13

ered any of the ramifications of his rash behavior. Iain, as the newly appointed laird over the clan, would now be expected to put his duties to his immediate family aside, his loyalty, too, and act solely as the council's advisor.

He wasn't about to meet those expectations, of course. He would stand beside his brother no matter how much opposition came from the elders. He wouldn't allow Patrick to be punished, either. And if need be, he was fully prepared to fight.

Iain didn't share his decision with his brother for the simple reason that he wanted Patrick to suffer the uncertainty awhile longer. If the ordeal proved painful enough, perhaps Patrick would finally learn to use a little restraint.

The council of five had already gathered in the great hall to hear Patrick's petition when Iain finished his duties and made his way up the hill. Patrick was waiting in the center of the courtyard. He looked ready to go into battle. His legs were braced apart, his hands were in fists at his sides, and the scowl on his face was as fierce as the thunderstorm brewing overhead.

Iain wasn't at all impressed with his brother's bluster. He shoved Patrick out of his path when he tried to block his way, and continued on toward the steps to the keep.

"Iain," Patrick called out. "I ask you now, for I would know your position before we go inside. Do you stand beside me on this issue or against me?"

Iain stopped, then slowly turned around to look at his brother. The expression on his face showed his anger. His voice was deceptively mild, however, when he spoke. "And I would know, Patrick, if you deliberately try to provoke me by asking such a question?"

Patrick immediately relaxed his stance. "I meant no insult, but you're new as laird and still to be tested in such a personal way by our council. I hadn't realized until just now the awkward position I've put you in."

"Are you having second thoughts?"

"No," Patrick answered with a grin. He walked over to his brother. "I know you didn't want me to involve the council, especially now when you're battling to get them interested in forming an alliance with the Dunbars against the Macleans, but Frances Catherine was determined to gain their blessing. She wants her friend to be welcomed here."

Iain didn't remark on that explanation.

Patrick pressed on. "I also realize you don't understand my reasons for giving my wife such a promise, but someday, when you've met the right woman, all of this will make perfectly good sense to you."

Iain shook his head in exasperation. "Honest to God, Patrick, I'll never understand. There isn't any such thing as the right woman. One's just as good as another."

Patrick laughed. "I used to believe that, too, until I met Frances Catherine."

"You're talking like a woman," Iain said.

Patrick wasn't insulted by his brother's comment. He knew Iain couldn't understand the love he felt for his wife, but God willing, one day he would find someone to give his heart to. When that day arrived, he was going to thoroughly enjoy reminding Iain of this callous attitude.

"Duncan indicated they might want to question my wife," Patrick said then, turning the topic back to his main concern. "Do you think the elder was jesting with me?"

Iain didn't turn around when he gave his answer. "None of the council members ever jest, Patrick. You know that as well as I."

"Damn it, I'm responsible for this."

"Aye, you are."

Patrick ignored his brother's quick agreement. "I won't let the council intimidate Frances Catherine."

Iain let out a sigh. "I won't, either," he promised.

Patrick was so startled by that agreement, he lost his frown. "They think they'll be able to get me to change my mind," he said. "You'd better understand that nothing any of them do will make a difference. I've given Frances Catherine my word, and I mean to keep it. God's truth, Iain, I'd walk through the fires of Hell for my wife."

Iain turned and smiled at his brother. "A simple walk into the great hall will suffice for now," he drawled out. "Let's get it done."

Patrick nodded, then hurried ahead of his brother to open one of the double doors.

"A word of advice, Patrick," Iain said. "Leave your anger outside these doors. If they see how rattled you are, they'll go for your throat. Simply state your reasons in a calm voice. Let logic guide your thoughts, not emotion."

"And then?"

"I'll do the rest."

The door closed on that promise.

Ten minutes later the council sent a messenger to fetch Frances Catherine. Young Scan was given the duty. He found Patrick's wife sitting by the fire in her cottage and immediately explained she was to come to the keep and wait outside the doors for her husband to escort her inside.

Frances Catherine's heart started pounding. Patrick had told her there was a possibility she would be called before the council, but she hadn't believed him. It was unheard of for a woman to speak her mind directly to the council or the laird in any official capacity. And she wasn't consoled in the least by the fact that the new laird was her husband's older brother. No, that relationship didn't signify anything at all.

Her mind raced from one frightening thought to another, and in no time she'd worked herself into a fine state of agitation. The council obviously thought she was daft. Yes, she decided. By now Patrick had told them all about the promise he'd given her, and that was the reason she was being called to the great hall to give her own explanation. They wanted to make certain she really had lost her mind before damning her to isolation for the remainder of her days.

Her only hope rested in the hands of the laird. Frances Catherine didn't know Iain Maitland well. She doubted she'd exchanged more than fifty words with the warrior in the two years she'd been married to his younger brother, but Patrick had assured her Iain was an honorable man. He would see the fairness in her request.

She was going to have to get past the council first. Since it was an official meeting, four of the elders wouldn't speak directly to her. They would give their questions to their own leader, Graham, and he alone would have to suffer the indignity of conversing with her. She was a woman, after all, and an outsider, for she had been born and raised on the border and not the glorious Highlands. Frances Catherine was actually relieved that Graham would be the only one to question her, since she found him to be the least frightening of the elders. The old warrior was a soft-spoken man who was greatly admired by his clan. He'd been their laird for over fifteen years and had retired from that position of power just three months past. Graham wouldn't terrify her, at least not deliberately, but he'd use every other bit of trickery he possessed to get her to release Patrick from his promise.

She made a quick sign of the cross, and then prayed her way up the steep hill to the keep. She reminded herself she could get through this ordeal. No matter what, she wouldn't back down. Patrick Maitland had given her his promise the day before she agreed to marry him, and by God, he was going to see it carried through.

A precious life depended upon it.

Frances Catherine reached the top step of the keep and stood there waiting. Several women passed by the courtyard, curious at the sight of a woman lingering on the laird's doorstep. Frances Catherine didn't invite conversation. She kept her face averted, praying all the while that no one would call out to her. She didn't want the women in the clan to know what was going on until it was finished. They would surely start in making trouble then, but it would be too late to matter.

She didn't think she could bear the wait much longer. Agnes Kerry, the old biddy with her nose always up in the air because her pretty daughter was surely going to become the laird's bride, had already made two circles around the courtyard in an attempt to find out what was going on, and a few of her cohorts were also edging closer now.

Frances Catherine straightened the pleats of her plaid over her swollen stomach, noticed how her hands were shaking, and immediately tried to stop the telling show of fear. She let out a loud sigh. She wasn't usually feeling so timid and unsure of herself, but since she'd found out she was carrying, her behavior had undergone a dramatic change. She was terribly emotional now and cried over the most inconsequential things. Feeling big, awkward, and as fat as a well-fed mare didn't help her disposition, either. She was almost seven months into her confinement, and the weight of the babe slowed her movements considerably. Her thoughts weren't affected, though. They rushed through her mind like a whirlwind as she tried to guess what questions Graham would ask.

The door finally squeaked open and Patrick stepped outside. She was so relieved to see him, she almost burst into tears. He was frowning, but as soon as he saw how pale and worried she looked, he forced a smile. He took hold of her hand, gave it a little squeeze, and then winked at her. The unusual show of affection during daylight hours felt as soothing to her as one of his nightly back rubs.

"Oh, Patrick," she blurted out. "I'm so sorry to be putting you through this embarrassment."

"Does that mean you won't hold me to my promise?" he asked her in that deep rich voice she loved so much.

"No."

Her bluntness made him laugh. "I didn't think so."

She wasn't in the mood to be teased. She only wanted to concentrate on the ordeal ahead of her. "Is he inside yet?" she asked in a bare whisper.

Patrick knew who she was talking about, of course. Frances Catherine had a most unreasonable fear of his brother. He thought it might be because Iain was laird over the entire clan. The number of warriors alone reached well over three hundred. His powerful position would make him unapproachable to a woman, Patrick supposed.

"Please answer me," she pleaded.

"Yes, love, Iain's inside."

"Then he knows about the promise?" It was a foolish question to ask. She realized that fact almost as soon as the words were out of her mouth. "Oh heavens, of course he knows. Is he angry with us?"

"Sweetheart, everything's going to be all right," he promised. He tried to pull her through the open doorway. She resisted the gentle tug.

"But the council, Patrick," she rushed out. "How did they react to your explanation?"

"They're still sputtering."

"Oh, God." She went completely rigid on him.

He realized he shouldn't have been so honest with her. He put his arm around her shoulders and pulled her close. "It's all going to work out," he whispered in a soothing voice. "You'll see. If I have to walk to England to fetch your friend, I'll do it. You trust me, don't you?"

"Yes, I trust you. I wouldn't have married you if I didn't trust you completely. Oh, Patrick, you do understand how important this is to me?"

He kissed the top of her forehead before answering. "Yes, I know. Will you promise me something?"

"Anything."

"When your friend comes here, you'll laugh again?"

She smiled. "I promise," she whispered. She wrapped her arms around his waist and hugged him tight. They stood holding on to each other a long minute. He was trying to give her time to regain her composure. She was trying to remember the correct words to use when she was asked to give her reasons to the council.

A woman hurrying past with a basketful of laundry paused to smile over the loving couple.

Patrick and Frances Catherine did make a handsome pair. He was as dark as she was fair. Both were tall, though Patrick reached a full six feet in height, and the top of his wife's head barely reached his chin. It was only when Patrick stood next to his older brother that he appeared small, for the laird was several inches taller. Patrick was certainly every bit as wide through the shoulders, though, and had the same shade of black-brown hair. His eyes were a darker shade of gray than Iain's were, and he didn't have nearly the number of battle scars to mar his handsome profile.

Frances Catherine was as slight as her husband was muscular. She had pretty brown eyes that Patrick swore sparkled gold when she laughed. Her hair was her treasure, though. It was waist length, deep auburn in color, with nary a bit of curl to take away from the glorious shine.

Patrick had been drawn first to her appearance, for he was a man with a lusty appetite and she was a fair prize for the taking, but it was her wonderful wit that had snared him. She continually enchanted him. She had such a dramatic way of looking at life, and there was such a burning passion inside her to experience each new adventure. She never gave anything half measure, including the way she loved and pampered him.

Patrick felt her shiver in his arms and decided it was high time they went inside and get the ordeal finished so she could quit fretting. "Come inside now, love. They're waiting for us."

She took a deep breath, pulled away from him, and walked inside. He hurried forward to walk by her side.

They'd reached the steps leading down into the great hall when she suddenly leaned into her husband's side and whispered, "Your cousin Steven said that when Iain gets angry, his scowl can make a person's heart stop beating. We really must try not to make him angry, Patrick. All right?"

Because she sounded so serious and so worried, Patrick didn't laugh, but he couldn't quite contain his exasperation. "Frances Catherine, we really are going to have to do something about this unreasonable fear of yours. My brother—"

She grabbed hold of his arm. "We'll do something about it later," she rushed out. "Just promise me now."

"All right," he agreed with a sigh. "We won't make Iain angry."

She immediately relaxed her grip on his arm. Patrick had to shake his head over her behavior. He decided that just as soon as she was feeling better, he would find a way to help her get over this fear. He wouldn't wait to have a talk with Steven, however. No, he was going to take his cousin aside at the first possible opportunity and demand he quit telling the women such outrageous stories.

Iain was an easy subject for the exaggerated tales. He rarely spoke to any of the women, except on those rare occasions when as laird he was forced to give specific instructions, and his hard manner was often mistaken for anger. Steven knew most of the women were frightened of Iain, and he found it vastly amusing to stir up that fear every now and again.

His brother was unknowingly frightening Frances Catherine now. He stood alone in front of the hearth, facing them, with his arms folded across his massive chest. The stance was casual, the look in his piercing gray eyes anything but. The frown he wore made the fire in the grate behind him seem cold in comparison.

Frances Catherine had just started down the steps when she looked across the room and caught Iain's frown. She promptly lost her footing. Patrick reached out to grab her just in the nick of time.

Iain noticed her fear. He assumed she was afraid of the

council. He turned to his left, where the elders were seated, and motioned for Graham to begin. The sooner the inevitable fight was over, the sooner his sister-in-law could calm her fears.

The elders were all staring at her. In size, the five men resembled stair steps. The oldest, Vincent, was also the shortest. He sat at the opposite end of the line from Graham, their spokesman. Duncan, Gelfrid, and Owen took up the spaces in between.

Various amounts of gray streaked through the hair of each elder, and they had enough scars amongst them to cover the stone walls of the keep. Frances Catherine concentrated on Graham. The leader had deep lines around the corners of his eyes, and she wanted to believe he'd laughed those lines there over the years. That thought made it easier to imagine he would be understanding about her problem.

"Your husband has just shared an astonishing story with us, Frances Catherine," Graham began. "Tis the truth we're hard pressed to believe it."

The leader nodded to emphasize the last of his remarks, then paused. She wasn't certain if she was supposed to speak now or wait. She looked up at Patrick, received his encouraging nod, and then said, "My husband would only speak the truth."

The four other council members frowned in unison. Graham smiled. In a gentle tone of voice he asked, "Will you give us your reasons for demanding this promise be kept?"

Frances Catherine reacted as though Graham had shouted at her. She knew he'd used the word "demand" as a deliberate insult. "I'm a woman and would never demand anything from my husband. I would only ask, and now I ask that Patrick's word be honored."

"Very well," Graham conceded, his voice still smooth. "You don't demand, you ask. Now I would like for you to explain to this council your reasons for making such an outrageous request."

Frances Catherine stiffened. Outrageous indeed. She took a deep, calming breath. "Before I would agree to marry Patrick, I asked him to promise me that he would bring my dearest friend, Lady Judith Elizabeth, to me if and when I found I was expecting a child. My confinement is nearly over now. Patrick agreed to this request, and we would both like it carried out as soon as possible."

The look on Graham's face indicated he wasn't at all happy with her explanation. He cleared his throat and said, "Lady Judith Elizabeth is English, but that doesn't matter to you?"

"Nay, my lord, it doesn't matter at all."

"Do you believe that keeping this promise is more important than the disruption she'll cause? You would deliberately upset our lives, lass?"

Frances Catherine shook her head. "I would not deliberately do such a thing."

Graham looked relieved. She guessed he believed he now had a way to manipulate her into dropping the matter. His next remarks confirmed that suspicion.

"I'm pleased to hear this, Frances Catherine." He paused to nod to his four companions. "I never believed for one minute our lass would cause such an uproar. Now she'll forget this nonsense—"

She didn't dare let him finish. "Lady Judith Elizabeth won't cause any disruption."

Graham's shoulders slumped. Changing Frances Catherine's mind wasn't turning out to be such an easy task after all. He was frowning when he turned back to her. "Now lass, the English have never been welcomed here," he announced. "This woman would have to share her meals with us—"

A fist slammed down on the tabletop. The warrior named Gelfrid was responsible for that show of temper. Gelfrid stared up at Graham and said in a low, raspy voice, "Patrick's woman shames the Maitland name by asking this."

Tears filled Frances Catherine's eyes. She could feel herself beginning to panic inside. She couldn't think of a logical argument to give in response to Gelfrid's statement.

Patrick moved to stand in front of his wife. His voice shook with anger when he spoke to the council member. "Gelfrid, you may show me your displeasure, but you will not raise your voice in front of my wife."

Frances Catherine peeked around her husband to see Gelfrid's reaction to that command. The elder nodded. Then Graham waved his hand for silence.

Vincent, the eldest of the group, ignored the signal. "I've never heard tell of a woman having two full names before Frances Catherine came to us. I thought it was an oddity the border people shared. Now I'm hearing about another woman having two full names. What do you make of it, Graham?"

The leader let out a sigh. Vincent's mind tended to stray every now and again. It was an irritant everyone put up with. "I don't know what to make of it," Graham replied. "But that isn't the issue now."

He turned his attention back to Frances Catherine. "I ask you again if you would willingly disrupt our lives," he repeated.

Before giving her answer, she moved to stand next to Patrick rather than behind him, so she wouldn't appear to be a coward. "I don't know why you would think Lady Judith Elizabeth would cause any disruption. She's a kind, gentle woman."

Graham closed his eyes. There was a thread of amusement in his voice when he finally spoke again. "Frances Catherine, we don't particularly like the English. Surely you've noticed that in the years you've been with us."

"She was raised on the border," Gelfrid reminded his leader. The warrior scratched his whiskered jaw. "She might not know any better."

Graham agreed with a nod. A sudden sparkle came into his eyes. He turned to his companions, leaned down and spoke to them in a low voice. When he'd finished, the others were nodding agreement.

Frances Catherine felt sick. From the victorious look on Graham's face, she could only conclude he'd found a way to deny her request before asking the laird's counsel.

Patrick had obviously come to the same conclusion. His face turned dark with anger. Then he took another step forward. She grabbed hold of his hand. She knew her husband fully intended to keep his promise to her, but she didn't want him sanctioned by the elders. The punishment would be harsh, even for a man as proud and fit as Patrick was, and the humiliation would be unbearable for him.

She squeezed his hand. "You'll decide that because I cannot possibly know better, it therefore becomes your duty to know what's best for me. Isn't that right?"

Graham was surprised by her cleverness in knowing what was in his mind. He was about to answer her challenge when Patrick spoke up. "No, Graham would not decide he knows what's best for you. That would be an insult to me, wife."

The leader of the council stared at Patrick a long minute. In a forceful voice he commanded, "You will abide by the decision of this council, Patrick."

"A Maitland has given his word. It must be honored."

Iain's booming voice filled the hall. Everyone turned to look at him. Iain kept his gaze centered on the leader of the council. "Don't try to confuse this issue," he ordered. "Patrick gave his woman a promise and it must be carried out."

No one said a word for several minutes. Then Gelfrid stood up. The palms of his hands rested on the tabletop when he leaned forward to glare at Iain. "You are advisor here, nothing more."

Iain shrugged. "I'm your laird," he countered. "By your vote," he added. "And I now advise you to honor my brother's word. Only the English break their pledges, Gelfrid, not the Scots."

Gelfrid reluctantly nodded. "You speak the truth," he admitted.

One down and four to go, Iain thought to himself. Damn, he hated having to use diplomacy to get his way. He much preferred a battle with fists than with words. He hated gaining anyone's permission for his or his brother's actions, either. With an effort, he controlled his frustration and focused on the matter at hand. He turned his attention back to Graham. "Have you become an old man, Graham, to be so concerned about something as insignificant as this? Are you afraid of one English woman?"

"Of course not," Graham muttered, his outrage over the mere possibility apparent in his expression. "I'm afraid of no woman."

Iain grinned. "I'm relieved to hear this," he replied. "For a minute, I did begin to wonder."

His cunning wasn't lost on the leader of the oligarchy. Graham smiled. "You dangled your clever bait and my arrogance reached for it." Iain didn't remark on that truth. Graham's smile was still in evidence when he turned his attention back to Frances Catherine. "We are still confused by this request and would appreciate it if you would tell us why you want this woman here."

"Have her tell you why they both have two names," Vincent interjected.

Graham ignored the elder's request. "Will you explain your reasons, lass?"

"I was given my mother's name, Frances, and my grandmother's name, Catherine, because—"

Graham cut her off with an impatient wave of his hand. He continued to smile so she wouldn't think he was overly irritated with her. "No, no, lass, I'm not wanting to hear how you came by two names now. I'm wanting to hear your reasons for wanting this English woman here."

She could feel herself blushing over the misunderstanding. "Lady Judith Elizabeth is my friend. I would like her to be by my side when my time comes to deliver this baby. She has already given me her word that she'll come to me."

"Friend and English? How can this be?" Gelfrid asked. He rubbed his jaw while he worried over that contradiction.

Frances Catherine knew the elder wasn't deliberately baiting her. He looked genuinely puzzled. She didn't believe anything she could say would make the elder understand. In truth, she didn't believe Patrick truly understood the bond she had formed with Judith so many years ago, and her husband wasn't nearly as set in his ways as Graham and the other elders were. Still, she knew she was going to have to try to explain.

"We met at the annual festival on the border," she began. "Judith was only four years and I just five. We didn't understand we were . . . different from each other."

Graham let out a sigh. "But once you did understand?"

Frances Catherine smiled. "It didn't matter."

Graham shook his head. "'Tis the truth, I still don't understand this friendship," he confessed. "But our laird was correct when he reminded us that we do not break our pledges. Your friend will be welcomed here, Frances Catherine."

She was so overcome with joy, she sagged against her husband's side. She dared a quick look at the other council members then. Vincent, Gelfrid, and Duncan were smiling, but Owen, the elder she'd believed had slept through the questioning, was now shaking his head at her.

Iain noticed that action. "You don't agree with this decision, Owen?"

The elder kept his gaze on Frances Catherine while he answered. "I'm in agreement, but I think we should give the lass fair warning. She shouldn't be getting her hopes up for naught. I stand with you, Iain, for I too know from

27

my own experiences that the English can't keep their pledges. They follow their king's habits, of course. That scoundrel changes his mind every other minute. This English woman with two names might have given Patrick's wife her promise, but she won't be keeping it."

Iain nodded agreement. He'd wondered how long it would take for the council to come to that same conclusion. The elders were all looking much more cheerful now. Frances Catherine continued to smile, however. She didn't seem to be at all worried that her friend might not keep her promise. Iain felt a tremendous responsibility to protect each and every member of his clan. Yet he knew he couldn't protect his sister-in-law from the harsh realities of life. She would have to suffer this disappointment alone, but once the lesson was learned, she would surely realize she could only count on her own family.

"Iain, who will you send on this errand?" Graham asked.

"I should go," Patrick announced.

Iain shook his head. "Your place is with your wife now. Her time draws near. I'll go."

"But you're laird," Graham argued. "It's beneath your station—"

Iain wouldn't let him continue. "This is a family matter, Graham. Since Patrick can't leave his wife, I must see to this duty. My mind's set," he added with a frown, to discourage further argument.

Patrick smiled. "I've never met my wife's friend, Iain, but I can well imagine that when she sees you, she'll have second thoughts about coming here."

"Oh, Judith Elizabeth will be pleased to have Iain's escort," Frances Catherine blurted out. She turned to smile at her laird. "She won't be at all afraid of you. I'm certain. I thank you, too, for offering to go on this journey. Judith will feel safe with you."

Iain raised an eyebrow over that last remark. Then he let out a long sigh. "Frances Catherine, I'm just as certain she won't willingly come up here. Do you want me to force her?"

Because she was staring at Iain, she didn't see Patrick give his brother a quick nod. "No, no, you mustn't force her. She'll want to come to me."

Both Patrick and Iain gave up trying to caution her against getting her hopes up. Graham politely excused Frances Catherine from the meeting. Patrick took hold of her hand and started for the doors.

She was in a hurry to get outside so she could hug her husband and tell him how pleased she was to be married to him. He'd been so . . . magnificent when he'd stood up for her. She'd never doubted that he would, of course, but she still wanted to give him the praise she thought he'd want to hear. Husbands needed their wife's compliments every now and again, didn't they?

She had almost reached the top step to the entrance when she heard the name Maclean mentioned by Graham. She stopped to listen. Patrick tried to tug her along, and so she kicked off her shoe and motioned for him to fetch it for her. She didn't care if he thought she was clumsy. She was too curious to hear what the discussion was about. Graham had sounded so angry.

The council wasn't paying her any attention. Duncan had the floor. "I'm against any kind of an alliance with the Dunbars. We don't need them," he added in a near shout.

"And if the Dunbars form an alliance with the Macleans?" Iain asked, his voice shaking with fury. "Get your head out of the past, Duncan. Consider the ramifications."

Vincent spoke up next. "Why must it be the Dunbars? They're as slick as wet salmon and as sneaky as the English. I can't abide the thought. Nay, I can't."

Iain tried to hold on to his patience. "The Dunbar land sits between the Macleans and us, I would remind you. If we don't align ourselves with them, they could very well turn to the bastard Macleans for protection. We can't allow that. It's simply a choice between bad or worse."

Frances Catherine wasn't able to hear any more of the discussion. Patrick had put her shoe back on her foot and was once again nudging her along.

She forgot all about praising her husband. The minute the doors closed behind them, she turned to Patrick. "Why do the Maitlands hate the Macleans?"

"The feud goes way back," he answered. "Before my time."

"Could it ever be mended?"

Patrick shrugged. "Why do the Macleans interest you?"

She couldn't tell him, of course. She'd be breaking her promise to Judith if she did, and she would never betray that confidence. There was also the telling fact that Patrick would have heart palpitations if he ever found out Judith's father was Laird Maclean. Aye, there was that consideration as well.

"I know the Maitlands are feuding with the Dunbars, the Macphersons too, but I hadn't heard about the Macleans. That is why I was curious. Why don't we get along with any of the other clans?"

Patrick laughed. "There are a few we call friends," he told her.

She decided to change the topic around to the praise she wanted to give him. Patrick walked her back to their home, and after giving her a long kiss in farewell, he turned to go back to the courtyard.

"Patrick, you do realize my loyalty belongs to you, don't you?" his wife asked.

He turned back to her. "Of course."

"I've always considered your feelings, haven't I?"

"Yes."

"Therefore, if I knew something that would upset you, it would be better for me to keep silent, wouldn't it?"

"No."

"If I told, it would mean breaking a promise to someone else. I couldn't do that."

Patrick walked back to stand directly in front of his wife. "What are you trying not to tell me?"

She shook her head. "I don't want Iain to force Judith," she blurted out, hoping to turn his attention away from the talk about old promises. "If she can't come here, he mustn't use force."

She nagged Patrick into giving his word. He reluctantly agreed, just to please her, but he had no intention of keeping his pledge. He wasn't about to let the Englishwoman break his wife's heart. Lying to Frances Catherine didn't sit well, though, and Patrick frowned over it all the way back up the hill.

As soon as Iain came outside, his brother called out to him. "We have to talk, Iain."

"Hell, Patrick, if you're going to tell me about another promise you've given your wife, I'll warn you now, I'm not in the mood to hear it."

Patrick laughed. He waited until his brother reached his side, then said, "I want to talk to you about my wife's friend. I don't care what it takes, Iain. Drag her here if you have to, all right? I won't have my wife disappointed. She has enough to worry about with the baby coming."

Iain started walking toward the stables. His hands were clasped behind his back, his head bowed in thought. Patrick walked by his side.

"You are aware, aren't you, that if I force this woman, I could very well start a war with her family, and perhaps, if the king decides to take an interest, a war with England?"

Patrick glanced over to see what his brother thought about that remote possibility. Iain was smiling. Patrick shook his head. "John won't involve himself in this unless he can gain something from it. Her family's going to be the problem. They certainly won't just let her leave on such a journey."

"It could get messy," Iain remarked.

"Will that matter?"

"No."

Patrick let out a sigh. "When will you leave?"

"Tomorrow, at first light. I'll talk to Frances Catherine tonight. I want to know as much as possible about this woman's family."

"There is something Frances Catherine isn't telling me," Patrick said, his voice halting. "She asked me about the feud with the Macleans . . ."

He didn't go on. Iain was looking at him as though he thought he'd lost his mind. "And you didn't demand she explain whatever the hell it is she's keeping from you?"

"It isn't that simple," Patrick explained. "You have to be . . . delicate with a wife. In time she'll tell me what she's worrying about. I'll have to be patient. Besides, I'm probably jumping to conclusions. My wife's worrying about everything these days."

The look on Iain's face made Patrick sorry he'd mentioned Frances Catherine's odd behavior.

"I would thank you for going on this journey, but you'd only be insulted."

"This isn't a duty I embrace," Iain admitted. "It will take seven or eight days to reach the holding, and that means at least eight back with a complaining woman on my hands. Hell, I'd rather take on a legion of Macleans single-handedly than suffer this task."

Iain's bleak tone of voice made Patrick want to laugh. He didn't dare, of course, for his brother would only bloody his face if he so much as cracked a smile.

The two brothers walked along in silence for several more minutes, each caught up in his own thoughts.

Patrick suddenly stopped. "You can't force this woman. If she doesn't want to come here, then leave her be."

"Then why the hell am I bothering to go at all?"

"My wife could be right," Patrick rushed out. "Lady Judith Elizabeth might willingly come here."

Iain gave his brother a hard glare. "Willingly? You're out of your mind if you believe that. She's English." He paused to let out a weary sigh. "She won't willingly come here."

Chapter 2

$\mathcal{S}$he was waiting on her doorstep.

Lady Judith had been given advance warning, of course. Two days before, her cousin Lucas had spotted the four Scottish warriors just a stone's throw away from the border crossing near Horton Ridge. Lucas hadn't been there by chance, he had been diligently following his aunt Millicent's instructions, and after nearly a month of twiddling his thumbs and daydreaming the early summer evenings away, he'd spotted the Scots. He'd been so surprised to see the full-blooded Highlanders, he almost forgot what he was supposed to do next. Memory quickly returned, however, and he rode at a dust-choking pace all the way to Lady Judith's remote holding to tell her she'd best prepare herself for the visitors.

There hadn't been much for Judith to do to ready herself. Since the day word had reached her through the intricate gossip vine that Frances Catherine was expecting, she'd had most of her baggage packed and all of her friend's gifts wrapped in pretty pink lace ribbons.

Frances Catherine's timing certainly could have been

better. Judith had only just returned to her uncle Tekel's holding for her mandatory six-month visit when the message arrived. She couldn't pack up and go back to her aunt Millicent's and uncle Herbert's holding, for to do so would raise questions she wasn't about to answer, and so she hid her baggage and her gifts up in the loft of the stable and waited for her mother, who was home on one of her rare stopovers, to grow bored and leave again. Then she would broach the topic of her journey into Scotland with her guardian, Uncle Tekel.

Her mother's older brother was a soft-spoken, mild-mannered man, the complete opposite in temperament from his sister, Lady Cornelia, unless he was drinking. Then he'd turn as mean as a snake. Tekel had been an invalid for as many years as Judith could remember back, and in the early years he rarely lost his temper with her, even in the evenings when the pain in his misshapen legs became too much for him to endure. She'd know about his discomfort when he'd start rubbing his legs and ask one of the servants to fetch him a goblet of hot wine. From past experience, the servants had learned to bring along a full jug. Some nights Judith was able to sneak away to her own chamber before her uncle became abusive, but other nights he would demand that she sit by his side. He'd become quite melancholy and want to hold on to her hand while he talked about the past, when he'd been young and fit, a warrior to be reckoned with. An overturned cart had crushed his knees into grains of sand when he was but twenty and two years in age, and once the wine dulled his pain and loosened his tongue, he would rail against the injustice of that freak accident.

He'd rail against Judith, too. She didn't let him know how much his anger upset her. A knot would form in her stomach and wouldn't go away until she was finally dismissed for the night.

Tekel's drinking got much worse over the years. He began to demand his wine earlier and earlier in the day, and with each gobletful he consumed, his disposition would change more and more dramatically. By nightfall he would either be weeping with self-loathing or screaming incoherent insults at Judith.

The following morning Tekel wouldn't remember anything he'd said the night before. Judith remembered every word. She desperately tried to forgive him his cruelty to her. She tried to believe that his pain was far more unbearable for him than it was for her. Uncle Tekel needed her understanding, her compassion.

Judith's mother, Lady Cornelia, didn't have any compassion for her brother. It was a blessing that she never stayed home more than a month at a time. She had very little to do with Tekel or her own daughter even then. When Judith was younger and more easily hurt by her mother's cold, distant attitude, her uncle would comfort her by telling her she was a constant reminder of her father, and her mother had so loved the baron that she still, after all these many years, mourned his passing. When she looked at her daughter, he said, the ache of her loss would well up inside her, leaving little room for other emotions. Because Tekel hadn't been drinking so heavily back then, Judith had no reason to doubt his explanation. She didn't understand such love between a husband and wife, though, and she ached inside for her mother's love and acceptance.

Judith had lived with her aunt Millicent and uncle Herbert the first four years of her life. Then, on her first real visit with her uncle Tekel and her mother, she accidentally referred to Uncle Herbert as her papa. Judith's mother went into a rage. Tekel wasn't overly pleased, either. He decided she needed to spend more time with him, and ordered Millicent to bring Judith to his holding for six months each year.

Tekel was repelled by the idea that his niece would consider Herbert her father. For that reason he set aside an hour each morning, when his mind wasn't muddled with wine, and tell her stories about her real father. The long curved sword that hung over the hearth was the very sword her father had used to slay the dragons who dared try to snatch England away from the rightful king, and her noble father had died protecting his overlord's life, Tekel would tell her.

The stories were endless . . . and filled with fancy. In no time at all Judith had sainted her father in her mind. She'd been told he died on the first day of May, and on the morning of each anniversary of his passing she'd collect a skirt full of early spring flowers and cover her father's grave with the pretty blooms. She would say a prayer for his soul, though in truth she didn't believe her petition was necessary. Her papa was surely already in Heaven, pleasing his Maker now instead of the king he'd so valiantly pleased while on earth.

Judith was eleven years old and on her way to the border festival when she found out the truth about her father. He hadn't died defending England from infidels. The man wasn't even English. Her mother didn't mourn her husband; she hated him with a passion that hadn't dimmed at all through the years. Tekel had only told her one half-truth. Judith was a constant reminder to her mother, a reminder of the horrible mistake she'd made.

Aunt Millicent sat Judith down and told her everything she knew. Her mother had married the Scottish laird out of spite when the English baron she'd set her cap on was deemed unacceptable for her by her father and her king. Lady Cornelia wasn't accustomed to having her wants denied her. She married the Highlander a short two weeks after meeting him at court in London. Cornelia wanted to get even with her father. She wanted to hurt him, and she certainly accomplished that goal, but in the bargain she'd made, she hurt herself more.

The marriage lasted five years. Then Cornelia returned to England. She begged residence with her brother, Tekel, and at first refused to explain what had happened. Later, after it became apparent she was expecting a child, she told her brother that her husband had banished her as soon as he found out she was pregnant. He didn't want her any longer, and he didn't want her child.

Tekel wanted to believe his sister. He was lonely, and the thought of raising a niece or nephew appealed to him. After Judith was born, though, Cornelia couldn't stand having the infant in the keep. Millicent and Herbert were able to sway Tekel into letting them have Judith. The bargain they had to make was that they would never tell Judith about her father.

Millicent wasn't about to keep that promise, but she waited until she felt Judith was old enough to understand. Then she sat her down and explained everything she knew about her father.

Judith had a thousand questions. Millicent didn't have many answers. She wasn't even certain if the Scottish laird was still alive. She did know his name though. It was Maclean.

She'd never met the man and therefore couldn't offer a description of his appearance. Yet since Judith didn't look anything like her mother, she could only assume her blond hair and blue eyes came from her father's side of the family.

It was simply too much for Judith to take in. Her mind could only focus on all the lies she'd been told over the years. The betrayal was devastating to her.

Frances Catherine had been waiting for her at the festival. The minute the two friends were alone, Judith told her everything she'd learned. She wept, too. Frances Catherine held her hand and wept right along with her.

Neither one of them could understand the reasons behind the deceit. After days of discussing the topic, they decided the reasons weren't important now.

Then they formed their own plan. It was decided that Judith wouldn't confront her mother or her uncle Tekel with the truth. If they realized that Millicent had told her the truth about her father, they would very likely force her to permanently move in with them.

That real possibility was chilling. Aunt Millicent, Uncle Herbert, and Frances Catherine had become Judith's family. They were the only people she could trust, and she wouldn't allow her mother to keep her away from them.

No matter how difficult the task, Judith would have to hold on to her patience. She would wait until she was older. Then, if she were still inclined, she would find a way to go to these Highlands and meet the man who had fathered her. Frances Catherine promised to help.

The following years passed quickly, even for a young woman wishing to take on the world. Frances Catherine had been pledged to marry a border man from the Stewart clan, but three months before the wedding day the Kirkcaldys had a falling out with the Stewart laird. Patrick Maitland took full advantage of the fresh feud and offered for Frances Catherine a scant week after the contract to the Stewarts was broken.

When Judith heard that her friend had married a Highlander, she believed fate had taken a hand in helping her. She'd already given Frances Catherine her promise to come to her when she was expecting. While she was there, Judith thought, she would find a way to meet her father.

She would start her journey tomorrow. Frances Catherine's relatives were on their way to fetch her even now. The only problem was how to explain all this to Uncle Tekel.

At least her mother was back in London. The household was always in an uproar when Judith's mother was home, but she'd grown bored with the isolation of the country and had left for London the week before. Lady Cornelia loved the chaos and gossip of court life, the lax moral code, and most of all, the intrigue and secrecy that went along with the many liaisons. She currently had her eye on Baron Ritch, the handsome husband of one of her dearest friends, and had hatched a plan to get him into her bed within a fortnight. Judith had heard her mother make just that boast to Tekel and then laugh over his outraged reaction.

Nothing her mother did could surprise Judith. She was thankful she only had Tekel to contend with. She had waited until the night before her departure to tell him about her plans. She wasn't going to ask his permission, but she felt it would be dishonorable to simply leave without telling him where she was going.

She dreaded the confrontation. On the way up to his bedchamber, the familiar knot formed in the pit of her stomach. She said a prayer that the ale had made Tekel melancholy tonight and not god-awful mean.

The chamber was shrouded in darkness. A musty, damp odor permeated the air. Judith always felt as though she was being suffocated whenever she was inside the chamber. She felt that way now and took a deep breath to calm her nerves.

A single candle burned with light on the chest next to Tekel's bed. Judith could barely see her uncle's face in the shadows. The worry of fire from a forgotten candle was always a fear in the back of her mind, for often her uncle would pass into a drunken slumber before snuffing out the candle flame.

She called out to him. He didn't answer. Judith walked inside just as Tekel finally noticed her and called out to her.

His voice was slurred. He beckoned her forward with a wave of his hand, and after she'd hurried over to the side of the bed, he reached up to take hold of her hand.

He gave her a wobbly smile. She let out a sigh of relief. He was in a melancholy mood tonight.

"Sit beside me while I tell you a story I've just remembered about the time I rode into battle with your father. Did I tell you he used to sing the same ballad whenever the trumpets sounded the attack? He always kept right on singing the entire time he was fighting."

Judith sat down in the chair adjacent to the bed. "Uncle, before you continue this story, I would like to talk to you about an important matter."

"Hearing about your father isn't important?"

She ignored the question. "I have something I must tell you," she said.

"What is it?"

"Do you promise you'll try not to become angry?"

"When have I ever been angry with you?" he asked, completely unaware of the hundreds of nights he'd raged against her. "Now tell me what ails you, Judith. I'll smile all through this confesssion."

She nodded and folded her hands in her lap. "Each summer, your sister Millicent and her husband have taken me to the festival on the border. Uncle Herbert has relatives living there."

"I know he does," Tekel remarked. "Hand me my goblet and go on with this explanation. I'm wanting to know why you didn't tell me about these festivals."

Judith watched her uncle gulp down a large portion of his ale and pour himself another helping before she answered his question.

The pain in her stomach intensified. "Millicent thought it would be better if I didn't tell you or mother— she thought it would upset you to know I was associating with Scots."

"What you say is true," Tekel agreed. He took another long drink from his goblet. "I don't usually hold with such hatred, but I'll tell you your mother has good reason to feel the way she does. I can also understand why you kept quiet about attending these festivals, too. I know the fine time you must have had. I'm not so old I can't remember. Still, I must put a stop to it. You won't be going to the border again."

Judith took a deep breath in an effort to control her anger. "At the first festival I attended, I met a girl named Frances Catherine Kirkcaldy. She and I became good friends right away. Until Frances Catherine married and moved away from the border region, we renewed our friendship every summer at the festival. I gave her a promise, and now the time has come for me to keep it. I have to go away for a little while," she ended in a soft whisper.

Her uncle stared at her with bloodshot eyes. It was apparent he was having difficulty following her explanation. "What's this?" he demanded. "Where do you think you're going?"

"First I would like to tell you about the promise I gave when I was eleven years old." She waited for his nod before continuing. "Frances Catherine's mother died during childbirth and her grandmother died in just the same way."

"That isn't so extraordinary," he muttered. "Many women die doing their duty."

She tried not to let his callous attitude bother her. "Several years ago, I learned from Frances Catherine that her grandmother actually died sometime during the week after the birthing, and that was very hopeful news, of course."

"Why was it hopeful?"

"Because her death couldn't have been caused by narrow hips."

Judith knew she was making a muck out of her explanation, but Tekel's scowl was distracting to her concentration.

Tekel shrugged. "It was still the birthing that did her in," he said. "And you shouldn't be concerning yourself with such intimate topics."

"Frances Catherine believes she's going to die," Judith said. "For that reason, I did concern myself."

"Get on with the telling about this promise," he ordered. "But pour me a bit more of that sweet ale while you're explaining."

Judith emptied the last of the ale from the second jug.

"Frances Catherine asked for my promise to come to her when she was expecting. She wanted me by her side when she died. It was little enough to ask, and I immediately agreed. I made that promise a long time ago, but each summer I've told her I haven't changed my mind. I don't want my friend to die," she added. "And for that reason, I took it upon myself to learn as much as I could about the newest birthing methods. I've devoted a good deal of time to this project. Aunt Millicent was a wonderful help. Over the past two years, she has found quite a number of reputable midwives for me to interview."

Tekel was appalled by Judith's admissions. "Do you see yourself as this woman's savior? If God's wanting your friend, your interference could put a sin on your soul. You're a bit of nothing, you are, and yet you dare to think yourself important enough to make a difference?" he added in a sneer.

Judith refused to argue with him. She'd grown so accustomed to his insults, they barely stung anymore. She was proud of that accomplishment, but wished she could find a way to stop the ache in her stomach. She closed her eyes, took another deep breath, and then plunged ahead. "Frances Catherine's time is drawing near and her relatives are on their way to fetch me. I'll be perfectly safe. I'm certain there will be at least two women to accompany me and a fair number of men to see to my safety."

Tekel's head fell back on the pillows. "Good God, you're asking me if you can go back to the border? And what am I to tell your mother when she returns and finds you missing?"

Judith hadn't asked his permission, but decided not to point that out to him. Her uncle closed his eyes. He looked like he was hovering on the edge of sleep. She knew she was going to have to hurry if she wanted to get the rest said before he passed into a drunken slumber.

"I'm not going to the border region," she began. "I'm

going to a place called the Highlands, way up north, in an isolated area near the Moray Firth."

Her uncle's eyelids flew open. "I won't hear of it," he roared.

"Uncle—"

He reached out to slap her. Judith had already moved her chair out of his striking distance.

"I'm through discussing this," he roared. He was so upset, the veins in the side of his neck stood out.

Judith braced herself against his anger. "But I'm not through talking about this," she insisted.

Tekel was stunned. Judith had always been such a quiet, shy child. She'd never argued with him before. What had come over her? "Has Millicent been putting fancy ideas into your head?" he demanded.

"I know about my father."

He squinted at her a long minute before reaching for his ale. Judith noticed his hand shook.

"Of course you know about your father. I've told you all about the wonderful baron. He was—"

"His name is Maclean and he lives somewhere in the Highlands. He isn't an English baron. He's a Scottish laird."

"Who told you this nonsense?"

"Aunt Millicent told me a long time ago."

"It's a lie," he screamed. "Why would you listen to Millicent. My sister—"

"If it isn't true, why do you object to my going to the Highlands?"

He was too muddleheaded from the ale to think of a convincing answer. "You're not going and that's the end of it. Do you hear me?"

"The Devil himself won't keep me from going to Frances Catherine," she countered in a calm voice.

"If you leave, you won't be welcomed back here."

She nodded. "Then I won't come back here."

"You thankless bitch," he shouted. "I tried to do right by you. The stories I made up about your father . . ."

He didn't go on. Judith shook her head. "Why did you make up those stories?" she asked.

"I wanted to give you something to hold on to, especially since your mother couldn't stomach the sight of you. You knew that. I pitied you and tried to make it a bit better for you."

Judith's stomach coiled and tightened so intensely now that she almost doubled over. The room seemed to be closing in on her. "I heard mother say that Uncle Herbert was inferior because he had tainted blood running through his veins. She feels the same way about me, doesn't she?"

"I don't have any easy answers," he replied. He sounded weary, defeated. "I could only try to soften her influence over you."

"The sword hanging over the hearth . . . who does that really belong to?" she asked.

"It's mine."

"And the ruby ring I wear on this chain around my neck?" she asked. She lifted the ring from its resting place between her breasts. "Is this yours, too?"

He snorted. "The ring belongs to the bastard Maclean. The intricate design around the stone holds some meaning to the family. Your mother took it with her when she left just to spite him."

Judith let go of her death grip on the ring. "What about the grave?"

"It's empty."

She didn't have any more questions. She sat there another minute or two, with her hands fisted in her lap. When she next looked at her uncle, he was sound asleep. Within seconds he was snoring. She took the empty goblet out of his hand, removed his tray from the other side of the bed, blew out the candle flame, and then left the room.

She suddenly knew what she wanted to do. She could destroy one lie.

The sun was just setting when she ran across the

drawbridge and climbed the hill to the cemetery. She didn't slow down until she reached the empty grave. She kicked the wilted flowers away, then reached for the ornately carved headstone at the top of the mound. It took her a long while to tear the headstone out of the hard ground, longer still to destroy it completely.

The following morning she was ready to leave. She didn't return to her uncle's chamber to tell him good-bye.

All of the servants rushed around her, fighting for a chance to help. Judith hadn't realized until now that their loyalty belonged to her far more than to her uncle. She was humbled by their united show of support. Paul, the stable master, had already prepared the swaybacked pack mare with the baggages she would be taking with her. He was saddling her favorite steed, a speckle-legged mare named Glory, when Jane came rushing outside with another satchel full of food she promised would last the length of the journey. From the weight of the baggage and the way Jane was struggling to carry it to the stables, Judith concluded there was enough food packed inside to feed an army.

Samuel, the watch guard, shouted the arrival of the Scottish party. The drawbridge was immediately lowered. Judith stood on the top step of the keep, her hands at her sides, a smile of greeting on her face, forced though it was, for she was suddenly feeling extremely nervous.

When the warriors reached the wooden planks of the drawbridge and their horses thundered across, her smile faltered.

A shiver of worry passed down her spine. There weren't any women in the group. There were only warriors, four in all, and they looked like giant barbarians to her. Her worry moved into her stomach as soon as they rode closer and she got a good look at their faces. Not one of them was smiling. God's truth, they looked downright hostile to her.

They were all dressed in their hunting plaids. Each

clan, Judith knew, used two separate plaids. The muted colors of gold, brown, and green were preferred for hunting wild game . . . or men, for those colors blended into the forest more easily and hid them from their prey. The more colorful plaids were used for all other occasions.

Their bare knees didn't take Judith by surprise. She was used to their unusual dress, as all the men who attended the border games wore their knee-length plaids. She could even identify some of the clans by their colors. In England, a baron's banner carried his colors, but in Scotland, as Frances Catherine had explained, the laird and his followers were recognized by the colors of their dress.

What did surprise Judith was their angry expressions. She couldn't understand why they were so obviously cranky. Then she decided the journey must have made the men weary. It was a paltry excuse, but it was the best she could come up with.

None of the warriors dismounted when they reached her. Three of them formed a line behind the man she assumed was their leader. No one said a word for a long, long while. They all rudely stared at her. She couldn't stop herself from rudely staring back, though her attention was centered solely on their leader. She didn't think she'd ever seen such a magnificent sight in all her life. The man fascinated her. He was certainly the biggest of the lot. His broad shoulders fairly blocked out the sun shining down behind him, and only rays of light surrounded him, giving him an invincible, magical appearance.

He wasn't magical, though. He was only a man, a ruggedly handsome man at that, and surely the most muscular warrior in the group. The plaid he wore had opened on the side of his left thigh. The bulge of sleek muscle there looked as hard as roped steel. Since it wasn't proper for her to stare at such a private area, she turned her gaze back to his face. His expression didn't indicate he'd noticed her taking a little peek at his thigh, and she let out a sigh over that blessing.

Lord, she thought, she could be content to stare at the warlord for the rest of the day. His hair was a dark, rich brown in color, with just a little hint of curl to it. His bare arms were as bronzed as his face. He had a striking profile. Oh yes, he was a fit one all right, but in truth it was the color of his eyes that held her interest the longest. They were a beautiful, brilliant shade of gray.

The warrior's stare was intense, unnerving. There was such an aura of power radiating from him, it almost took her breath away. The intensity in the way he was staring at her made her want to blush, but she couldn't imagine why. Dear God, she hoped this one wasn't Frances Catherine's husband. He seemed to be a terribly rigid man, controlled too. Judith didn't think he was a man given to much laughter.

Yet there was definitely something about him that pulled at her heart, something that made her want to reach out to him. It was an odd reaction to the Scotsman, yet certainly no more odd than the fact that the longer she stared up at him, the more her worry dissipated.

She was going to have a wonderful adventure. That realization popped into her mind all of the sudden. It didn't make any sense to her, but she was too confused by her reaction to the warrior to try to sort it out now. She only knew that she was suddenly feeling completely free of all her worries. Safe, too. The look on the warlord's face indicated he had little liking for the duty he'd undertaken, but she was certain he'd protect her on this journey to his home.

She didn't even care that there weren't any ladies riding escort for decency's sake. Hang convention. She couldn't wait to get started. She was going to leave the lies, the hurt, the rejection, all the betrayals behind her. She made a promise to herself then and there. She would never come back here. Never. She wouldn't even agree to a visit, no matter how brief. She would stay with her aunt Millicent and Uncle Herbert, and by God, if she wished, she would call them Mother and Father, too, and no one was going to stop her.

Judith felt an almost overwhelming urge to shout with laughter just to give sound to the happiness she was feeling. She suppressed that desire, knowing full well the Scots wouldn't understand. How could they? She barely understood herself.

It seemed the silence had gone on for hours, yet she knew only a few minutes had actually passed. Then Paul pushed open the stable doors. The noise of the old hinges squeaking and groaning for fresh oil drew the warriors' immediate attention. All but the leader turned to look in that direction. Two, Judith noticed, reached for their swords. It dawned on her then that the warriors considered themselves to be in hostile territory and would naturally be on their guard against attack.

No wonder they were all so cranky. Their frowns made good sense to her now. Judith turned her attention back to the leader. "Are you Frances Catherine's husband?"

He didn't answer her. She was about to repeat her question in Gaelic when the warrior directly behind the leader spoke up. "Patrick's with his wife. We're his relatives."

There was such a burr in his voice, she had difficulty understanding him. The warrior nudged his mount forward. When he reached his leader's side, he spoke again. "Are you Lady Judith Elizabeth?"

She smiled. No one but Frances Catherine ever added Elizabeth to her name. It was a sweet reminder to her of days gone by. "I am," she answered. "Though you may call me Judith. Please tell me, sir. How is Frances Catherine?"

"Fat."

She laughed at his curt reply. "She's supposed to be fat," she said. "But she's also feeling well?"

He nodded. "Madam, we've come a long way to hear

you tell us you won't come back with us. Kindly give us your refusal now and we'll be on our way."

Her eyes widened in surprise. The one who had so casually insulted her had dark auburn-colored hair and pleasing green eyes.

She turned to look at the others. "Do you all believe I won't go back with you?" she asked, her voice incredulous.

Every single one of them nodded.

She was astonished. "You came all this way just to hear me tell you no?"

They all nodded in unison again. Judith couldn't contain her amusement. She burst into laughter.

"Do you laugh at our Frances Catherine because she innocently believed you would keep your word?" one of the warriors asked.

"Nay, sir," she blurted out. "I'm laughing at you."

She decided she shouldn't have been so honest with the Scot. He was looking like he wanted to throttle her now.

She forced herself to quit smiling. "I do apologize if I've offended you, sir," she said. "I was laughing at you, but only just a little. Your comments, you see, took me by surprise."

He didn't look placated by her apology.

Judith let out a little sigh over the sorry beginning of the conversation and decided to start over. "What is your name, sir?"

"Alex."

"I'm pleased to meet you, Alex," she announced with a quick curtsy.

He rolled his eyes heavenward in exasperation. "Madam, you're wasting our time," Alex returned. "If you'll only give us your refusal, we'll take our leave. You don't have to go into your reasons for declining. A simple no will suffice."

They immediately all nodded again. She thought she might strangle on her laughter.

"I'm afraid I won't be able to give you what you're so obviously hoping for," she began. "I have every intention of keeping my word to my friend. I'm most anxious to see Frances Catherine again. The sooner we leave, the better, to my way of thinking. I will of course understand if you would like to refresh yourselves before we depart."

She had astonished them with that little speech, she decided. Alex looked stunned. The others, save for the leader, who still hadn't shown any outward reaction at all, looked only mildly ill. Judith didn't laugh, but she did smile. She'd deliberately spoken in Gaelic, too, just to impress them, and from the way they were staring at her, she assumed she'd accomplished that goal.

Judith decided she must be certain to remember every one of their expressions so she could recount every single detail of this initial meeting to Frances Catherine. Her friend would surely find this just as amusing as she did.

"You really mean to come with us, lass?" Alex asked.

Hadn't she just said as much? Judith hid her exasperation. "Yes, I really do mean to come with you," she answered in a forceful, no nonsense tone of voice. She turned her gaze to the leader again. "You had better understand that it doesn't matter if you want my company or not. Nothing's going to stop me from keeping my promise. If I have to walk to Frances Catherine's home, then by all that's holy, I will. Now then," she added in a much softer voice. "Have I made myself clear enough for you?"

The leader neither nodded nor spoke, but he did raise one eyebrow. Judith decided to take that reaction as a yes.

Paul drew her attention with a long whistle. She motioned for him to bring out the horses. She lifted the hem of her blue gown and hurried down the steps. She was just passing the line of warriors when she heard one mutter, "I can already tell she's going to be difficult, Iain."

She didn't even pretend she hadn't heard that remark.

"Tis the truth I probably will be difficult," she called out as she continued on toward the stables. Her laughter trailed behind her.

Because she didn't turn around, she didn't catch their smiles over her boast.

Iain couldn't seem to take his gaze off the woman. He was certainly astonished she meant to keep her word, of course, but damn it all, he hadn't expected to be attracted to the woman. It took him by surprise, this appalling response, and he wasn't at all certain what he could do about it.

Her long wheat-colored hair was lifted by the breeze as she hurried over to the stable master. Iain couldn't help but notice . . . and appreciate the gentle sway of her hips. There was such grace in her every movement. Aye, she was beautiful, all right. Her eyes were the prettiest violet he'd ever seen, but it was the wonderful sound of her laughter that had truly affected him. It was filled with such joy.

Iain had already made the decision to force the woman to come home with him, a decision he hadn't shared with his companions. When the time came, they would do what he ordered. Lady Judith had certainly surprised him, though. She was a woman of her word. And yet she was English. He shook his head over the contradiction.

"What do you make of her?"

Iain's second cousin, Gowrie, asked that question. He stared after the Englishwoman while he scratched his dark beard in a rhythmic motion, as if that repetitive action might help him come to some important conclusion. "She's a pretty little thing, isn't she? I'm thinking I'm warming to the lass."

"I'm thinking you talk too much," Alex muttered. "Hell, Gowrie, you warm to anything wearing a skirt."

Gowrie smiled. He wasn't the least offended by his friend's insulting remarks. "She's keeping her word to our Frances Catherine," he said. "And that's the only reason I'd ever warm to an Englishwoman."

Iain had heard enough of the idle chatter. He was in a hurry to get started. "Let's get the hell out of here," he ordered. "I can't breathe when I'm in England."

The other warriors were in full agreement. Iain turned in his saddle to look at Brodick. "She'll ride with you," he said. "Tie her satchel behind your saddle."

The blond-haired warrior shook his head. "You ask too much, Iain."

"I'm not asking," Iain countered, his voice as hard as sleet. "I'm giving you an order. Now try telling me no."

Brodick backed away from the threat. "Hell," he muttered. "As you wish."

"She can ride with me," Gowrie suggested. "I won't mind."

Iain turned to glare at the soldier. "Aye, you won't mind. You aren't touching her, either, Gowrie. Not now, not ever. Understand me?"

He didn't wait for Gowrie's agreement, but turned his gaze back to Brodick. "Move," he commanded.

Judith had just mounted her steed when the warrior reached her side. "You're riding with me," he announced. He paused when he saw the number of baggages tied on the mount's back. Then he shook his head. "You'll have to leave—"

He never got to finish his explanation. "Thank you so much for offering, sir, but there really isn't any need for me to ride with you. My mare's quite strong. She's certainly fit enough for this journey."

Brodick wasn't accustomed to being contradicted by a woman. He didn't know how to proceed. He started to reach for her, then stopped in mid action.

Iain noticed the soldier's hesitation. Then Brodick turned to look at him and he saw the confusion in his expression.

"She's being difficult," Alex muttered.

"Aye, she is," Gowrie agreed with a chuckle. "I was wrong, Alex. She isn't pretty. She's damn beautiful."

Alex nodded. "Aye, she is," he admitted.

"Will you look at Brodick?" Gowrie said then. "If I didn't know better, I'd guess he was about to swoon."

Alex found that remark vastly amusing. Iain shook his head and nudged his mount forward. Judith hadn't noticed Brodick's discomfort. She was occupied smoothing her skirts over her ankles. She adjusted the heavy cloak over her shoulders, tied the black cord into a bow, and finally reached for the reins Paul was patiently holding for her.

Iain motioned Brodick out of the way, then edged his mount closer to Judith's side. "You may take only one bag with you, lass."

His voice didn't suggest she argue with him. "I'm taking every one of them," she countered. "Most are presents I've made for Frances Catherine and the baby, and I'm not about to leave them behind."

She thought she was acting very courageously, considering the fact that the huge warrior was trying to glare her soul right out of her body. It was apparent he liked getting his own way. She took a quick breath, then added, "I don't wish to ride with that young man, either. My horse will carry me just as well."

He didn't say anything for a long minute. She was matching him frown for frown, too, until he pulled out his sword from the sheath at his side. She let out a little gasp then. Before she could move out of his path, he'd raised the sword, shifted his position in his saddle, and then used the blade to slice through the ropes holding her precious baggage.

Her heart was pounding inside her chest. She calmed down when he put his sword away. He motioned for his friends to come forward, and then ordered them to each take one of her satchels. Judith didn't say a word while the disgruntled-looking soldiers secured her baggage behind their saddles, but she let out another startled gasp when the leader tried to snatch her out of her saddle. She slapped his hands away.

It was a puny defense against such a big man, and it

was obvious to her that he was vastly amused by her action, too. The sparkle in his eyes said as much. "It will be a hard ride up the mountains, lass, and it would serve you better if you rode with one of us."

She shook her head. The idea of being so close to the handsome man wasn't actually dispeasing, but she didn't want him to think of her as inferior. She'd had enough of that in the past to last her a lifetime.

"I'm very fit for this journey," she boasted. "You needn't worry about me keeping up."

Iain held his exasperation. "There will also be times when we'll have to ride through hostile territory," he patiently explained. "Our mounts are trained to be quiet—"

"My horse will be just as quiet," she interjected.

He suddenly smiled at her. "Will she be as quiet as you are?"

She immediately nodded.

He let out a sigh. "I suspected as much."

She didn't realize he'd given her an insult until he reached for her again. He didn't give her time to push his hands away, either. The man was determined, all right. He wasn't overly gentle when he lifted her from her saddle and settled her on his lap. He hadn't considered the indecency of the position. Her legs straddled his saddle in just the same way a man's would when he was riding, and if that wasn't an embarrassment, the fact that the backs of her thighs were plastered on top of his certainly was. She could feel her face turning pink with a blush.

He wouldn't let her correct the shameful position. His left arm was tightly wrapped around her waist. She couldn't move at all, but she could breathe, and she guessed that would have to be enough. Judith waved farewell to the servants watching the spectacle.

She was a little irritated with the warrior for using such high-handed tactics to get his way. She still noticed how warm she was feeling in his arms, though. She noticed his scent, too, and found the faint masculine aroma extremely pleasing.

Judith leaned back against his chest. The top of her head was just below his chin. She didn't try to look up at him when she asked him to give her his name.

"Iain."

She bumped his chin when she nodded to let him know she'd heard his gruffly whispered reply. "How are you related to Frances Catherine?"

"Her husband is my brother."

They'd crossed the drawbridge now and were climbing the hill adjacent to the family cemetery. "And his name is Patrick?"

"Yes."

It was apparent he wasn't in the mood to talk. Judith pulled away from him and turned to look at him. He was staring straight ahead, ignoring her. "I've only one more question to ask you, Iain," she said. "Then I promise to leave you to your thoughts."

He finally looked down at her. Judith's breath caught in her throat. Dear Lord, he had beautiful eyes. It was a mistake, asking him to give her his full attention, she decided, because his penetrating gaze robbed her of her concentration.

It was perfectly safe to find him attractive, she decided. Nothing could ever come of it, of course. She was going to his home, yes, but she was going to be an outsider, a guest. Once there, he probably wouldn't have anything to do with her, or she with him.

Besides, she was English. No, nothing could ever come from this harmless attraction.

"Are you married?" She'd blurted out that question. She seemed more surprised than he was.

"No, I'm not married."

She smiled.

He didn't know what to make of that. She'd asked her question and now he could ignore her. The problem, unfortunately, was that he couldn't take his gaze off her.

"I've one more question to ask you," she whispered. "Then I'll leave you to your thoughts."

They stared into each other's eyes a long minute. "What is this question you wish to ask me?"

His voice was whisper soft. It felt like a caress to her. That reaction confused her and she had to take her gaze away from the handsome devil so she could sort out this bizarre reaction.

He noticed her hesitation. "This question of yours must not be very important."

"Oh, it is important," she countered. She paused another minute while she tried to remember what the question was. She stared at his chin so she could concentrate. "Now I remember," she announced with a smile. "Is Patrick kind to Frances Catherine? Does he treat her well?"

"I imagine he's kind to her," he answered with a shrug. Almost as an afterthought he added, "He would never beat her."

She looked up into his eyes so he could see her amusement over that comment. "I already knew he wouldn't beat her."

"How would you know?"

"If he ever raised a hand against her, she'd run away from him."

It was such an outrageous thing to say, Iain didn't know how to respond. He quickly regained his wits. "And where would she run?"

"To me."

Since she'd sounded so sincere, he knew she believed what she'd just told him. Iain had never heard of anything so preposterous. A wife simply did not leave her husband, no matter what the reason.

"None of the Maitlands would ever touch a woman in anger."

"Iain, what do you make of this?"

Alex shouted that question, interrupting their discussion. Judith turned just in time to see the warrior motion to the grave she'd destroyed the evening before. She immediately turned her gaze to the line of trees at the top of the ridge.

Iain felt her tense in his arms. "Do you know who did this?"

"Yes," she answered, her voice whisper soft.

"Who does the grave—"

She didn't let him finish. "It was my father's grave."

They'd reached Alex's side when she made that remark. The green-eyed warrior glanced over at Iain, then back to Judith. "Would you like us to put the headstone back before we go, lass?"

She shook her head. "I'd only have to knock it down again if you did, but I do thank you for offering."

Alex couldn't hide his astonishment. "Are you telling us you did this?"

There wasn't a hint of embarrassment on her face when she answered him. "Yes, I did this. It took me a good hour. The ground was as hard as rock."

The Scot looked appalled. Then Iain drew her attention. He nudged her face up to his with the back of his thumb. "Why would you do such a thing?"

She lifted her shoulders in a dainty shrug. "It seemed appropriate at the time."

He shook his head. The atrocity she'd just admitted to seemed completely out of character with what he'd already surmised about her. He'd guessed she was a sweet-tempered, innocent woman. Stubborn, too. The way she'd argued over riding her own mount indicated that flaw. Still, she didn't seem the type of woman who would desecrate holy ground.

"This is your father's grave?" he asked again, determined to get to the bottom of this intriguing puzzle.

"Yes," she answered. She let out a little sigh. "You needn't be concerned about this. The grave's empty."

"Empty."

"Yes."

She wasn't going to explain further. He decided not to prod. She'd gone completely rigid in his arms. It was obvious the topic was distressing to her.

Iain motioned for Alex to take the lead again, then nudged his mount into line behind him. Once the cemetery was well behind them, Judith visibly relaxed.

They didn't speak again until the sun was setting and it was time to make camp for the night. They'd ridden long hours. The men were in a much more jovial mood now that they'd crossed the border and were once again back in Scotland.

Judith was exhausted by the time they finally stopped. Iain noticed when he helped her dismount. She could barely stand up on her own. His hands spanned her waist to hold her steady until she regained the strength in her legs.

He could feel her trembling. He stared at the top of her head while she stared at the ground. Since she didn't mention her obvious problem, he didn't, either. She was holding on to his arms, but as soon as she let go, he released his grip on her waist.

He immediately turned to his stallion. She slowly made her way around his horse and continued on toward the stream she'd glimpsed halfway hidden behind the line of trees adjacent to the small clearing. Iain watched her walk away and was again struck by her regal bearing. She moved like a princess, he thought to himself.

Lord, she really was a beauty. Damn innocent, too. The way she blushed over every little thing was telling. She was enchanting, too.

This one could get to his heart. Iain was so stunned by that sudden realization, he almost blanched. He continued to stare at the trees where Judith had disappeared, but he was frowning now.

"What's got you so riled?" Alex asked from behind.

Iain rested his arm on the saddle of his mount. "Foolish thoughts," he replied.

His friend glanced over to the trees where Judith had gone, then turned back to Iain. "Foolish thoughts about a beautiful Englishwoman, perchance?"

Iain shrugged. "Perhaps," he allowed.

Alex knew better than to pursue the topic. His laird didn't look at all happy over his confession. "It's going to be a long journey home," he predicted with a sigh before turning back to take care of his own steed.

Judith had been able to maintain her dignified walk until she was safely hidden by the trees. Then she all but doubled over and grabbed hold of her lower back. Lord, she ached. Her backside and thighs felt as though someone had taken a whip to her.

She walked around in circles until she'd worked the stiffness out of her legs. Then she washed her face and hands in the cold water. She felt better, hungry too. She hurried back to the clearing. She could hear the men talking, but as soon as she came into their view, they all closed their mouths.

Iain, she quickly noticed, wasn't there. She felt a moment of pure panic. It made her stomach lurch, so quickly did the feeling come upon her. Then she spotted his stallion. The fear immediately eased. The Scottish warrior might very well leave her, but he'd never leave his faithful steed, would he?

She was alone in the forest with four men who were virtual strangers to her. If word of this circumstance ever reached anyone in England, her reputation would be tattered. Her mother would probably want to kill her, too. Odd, but that last thought didn't bother Judith much at all. She couldn't seem to feel anything toward her mother now. Uncle Tekel had excused his sister's cold attitude toward her only daughter with the lie that Judith was a constant reminder of the man she'd loved and lost.

Lies, so many lies.

"You'd best get some rest, lass."

Judith jumped a foot when Alex's deep voice sounded

behind her, and her hand flew to her breast. She took several deep breaths before she answered him. "We must have our supper before we rest. What have you done with the baggage?"

Alex motioned to the opposite side of the clearing. Judith immediately hurried across the area to set out the food. Jane had packed a pretty white cloth at the top of the satchel. She spread that on the hard ground first, then covered it with her offerings. There was thick, crusty black bread, triangles of red and yellowed cheeses, fat strips of salted pork, and fresh, tart green apples.

When everything was ready, she invited the men to join her. Then she waited. After a long moment she realized they didn't have any intention of eating with her. She could feel herself turning red with embarrassment. She sat on the ground, her legs tucked under the hem of her skirts, her hands folded together in her lap. She kept her head bowed so none of them would see her humiliation.

It had been a stupid mistake, offering to share her food with them. She was English, after all, and they probably couldn't stomach the thought of eating a meal with her.

She told herself she had nothing to feel embarrassed about. She wasn't acting like a rude barbarian. They were.

Iain walked back into the clearing and came to a quick stop. One look at Judith told him something was wrong. Her face was flaming red. He turned to look at his men next. Alex and Gowrie sat on the ground on the opposite side of the clearing with their backs resting against tree trunks. Alex was wide awake, but Gowrie looked as though he'd fallen asleep. Brodick, as silent as usual, was already fast asleep. He was so completely wrapped in his plaid, only the top of his white-blond hair was visible.

Iain noticed the mound of food in front of Judith and guessed what had happened. He let out a sigh, then clasped his hands behind his back and walked over to stand next to her. She wouldn't look up at him. As soon as she spotted him coming toward her, she turned her attention to repacking the food. She was stuffing the containers back into her satchel when he sat down across from her.

He picked up one of the apples. She snatched it out of his hand. He snatched it back. She was so surprised by that boldness, she looked up at him. His eyes sparkled with laughter. She couldn't imagine what he found so amusing. She continued to stare at him while he took a bite out of the apple. He leaned forward and offered the apple to her. She took a bite before she realized what she'd done.

Alex suddenly appeared at her side. Without a word he sat down and reached into the satchel. He pulled out all the containers she'd just repacked. After tossing a piece of bread to Iain, Alex popped a triangle of cheese into his mouth.

Then Gowrie joined them. Judith put one of the apples in her lap and shyly explained that she would save it for the sleeping warrior to eat in the morning.

"Brodick must be terribly weary to miss his supper," she remarked.

Alex snorted with amusement. "Brodick's not weary, just stubborn. He won't eat your apple tomorrow either, you being English and all. No, he—"

Judith's frown stopped his explanation. She turned to look at Brodick, judged the distance in her mind, then picked up the apple from her lap. "If you're really certain he won't eat the apple tomorrow, he must want to eat it now."

She had every intention of hurling the apple at the surly Scot, but just as soon as she leaned back to take aim, Iain grabbed hold of her hand.

"You don't want to do that, lass," he said.

He wouldn't let go of her hand. Judith struggled with him for a second or two before giving up. "You're right," she said. "It would be a waste of a perfectly good apple, a superior English apple, I might add, on a mean-tempered

Scot." She paused to shake her head. "I cannot believe he's related to Frances Catherine. You really can let go of my hand now, Iain."

He obviously didn't trust her. He did let go of her hand, but he kept the apple. Judith was too surprised by his sudden smile to argue with him.

"You don't want Brodick for an enemy, Judith," Alex said.

"But he's already my enemy," she replied. She had difficulty taking her gaze off Iain when she answered his friend. "Brodick made up his mind to dislike me even before we met, didn't he?"

No one answered her. Then Gowrie turned the topic. "If you retaliate each time you think someone dislikes you, you'll be throwing apples all day long once we reach the Highlands."

"Superior Scottish apples," Alex teased.

Judith turned to frown at the warrior. "I don't care if I'm liked or not," she said. "Frances Catherine needs me. That's all that really matters. My feelings certainly aren't important."

"Why does she need you?"

Brodick called out that question. Judith was so surprised the man had spoken to her, she turned and smiled at him.

Before she could form an answer, he said, "She has Patrick."

"And all of us," Alex said. "We're her relatives."

She turned around again. "I'm certain she's comforted by such loyalty, but you are men, after all."

Iain raised an eyebrow over that statement. He obviously didn't understand what she was talking about. He wasn't alone in his confusion, either. Gowrie and Alex looked just as puzzled.

"Frances Catherine has relatives who are women, too," Gowrie said.

"I would imagine she does," Judith agreed.

"Then why does she need you?" Gowrie asked. He

reached down to take a third helping of the pork strips, but kept his gaze on her while he waited for her answer.

"For the birthing," Iain guessed aloud.

"Then she thinks she's going to have trouble?" Gowrie asked his laird.

Iain nodded. "It appears so."

Alex snorted. Judith took exception to that response. "Frances Catherine has every right to be worried. She isn't a coward, if that's what you're thinking. Why, she's one of the most courageous women I've ever known. She's strong and—"

"Now don't get yourself all worked up," Alex interrupted with a grin. "We are all aware of Frances Catherine's many fine qualities. You don't have to defend her to us."

"Does she think she's going to die?" Gowrie asked. He looked startled, as if he'd only just worked out that possibility in his mind.

Before Judith could answer him, Brodick called out, "If Patrick's woman thinks she's going to die, why did she send for you, English?"

She turned around to glare at the plaid cocoon. Then she turned around again. She decided to ignore the rude man. He could shout a hundred questions at her, but she wasn't going to answer any of them.

Everyone waited a long minute for Judith to explain. She occupied herself by once again gathering up the containers of food to put away.

Brodick's curiosity proved to be greater than his dislike for her. The rude man didn't just join the group, either. Nay, he elbowed his way in next to her, shoving Alex out of his way. She moved over to make room for the big man, but his arm still rubbed against hers when he was finally settled. He didn't recoil away. She looked at Iain to judge his reaction. His expression didn't tell her anything, though. He picked up the apple and tossed it to Brodick. She still refused to look at the warrior, guessing he was still scowling, but she heard him take a loud bite of the offering.

Then Iain winked at her. She smiled back.

"Are you going to make me ask you again, English?" Brodick muttered around a mouthful of apple.

She decided she was. "Ask me what, Brodick?" she asked, trying to sound sincere.

His sigh was fierce enough to knock over the containers. Judith bit her lower lip to keep herself from laughing.

"Are you pricking my temper on purpose?" he asked. She nodded.

Alex and Gowrie both laughed. Brodick glared. "Just answer my question," he commanded. "If Frances Catherine thinks she's going to die, why in thunder did she send for you?"

"You won't understand."

"Because I'm Scots?"

She let him see her exasperation. "Do you know, I was always told the Scots could be mule-headed. I never believed such nonsense, of course, but now that I've met you, I believe I'll have to rethink my position on that issue."

"Don't get him riled," Alex warned with a chuckle.

"Aye, Brodick gets downright surly when he isn't in a good mood," Gowrie told her.

Her eyes widened. "Do you mean to say he's happy now?"

Both Gowrie and Alex nodded at the same time. Judith burst into laughter. She was certain they were jesting with her.

They were just as certain she'd lost her mind.

"We're all curious as to why Frances Catherine sent for you," Alex said once she'd controlled herself.

She nodded. "Since you don't know me at all well, I'll have to confess to a few of my considerable flaws so you'll understand. I'm extremely stubborn, arrogant too, though in truth I have absolutely nothing to be arrogant about. I'm sinfully possessive . . . did I mention that flaw?"

Everyone but Iain shook his head at her. Judith stared at their leader, though. His eyes had taken on such a warm glint. It was a little unnerving to have such a handsome man give her his full attention. She had to force herself to turn her gaze away so she could concentrate on what she was saying.

She stared at her lap. "Well, I am possessive," she whispered. "Frances Catherine is well aware of my many imperfections, too. Tis the truth she's counting on them."

"Why?" Brodick asked.

"Because she thinks she's going to die," Judith explained. She let out a little sigh before adding, "And I'm too stubborn to let her."

Chapter 3

They didn't laugh at her. Iain smiled, but none of the others showed any reaction to her sinful boast. She could still feel herself blushing. She hid that telling show of embarrassment by turning her attention to repacking the containers.

There wasn't any food left to put away. Once Brodick started eating, he didn't stop until the last morsel was gone.

Judith excused herself and went back to the stream to wash the sticky apple juice off her fingers. She sat down on the grassy slope near the water and brushed her hair until her scalp tingled. She was exhausted, yet was enjoying the beauty and the peaceful solitude of her surroundings too much to move.

When the sun had almost disappeared from the sky, and only streaks of golden-orange shadows remained, Iain came to fetch her.

Her smile of greeting took him by surprise. He reacted by being a bit more gruff than usual. "You should get some sleep, Judith. Tomorrow will be a difficult day for you."

"Will it be difficult for you, too?" she asked. She stood up, patted the wrinkles out of her gown, and then started down the slope. In her haste she forgot about her brush. It got caught up in her feet, tripping her, and she went flying toward the ground. Iain moved with amazing speed for such a giant of a man. He grabbed her before she could pitch forward.

She was horrified by her clumsiness. She turned her gaze up to his to thank him for his assistance, but the words got caught in her throat and she could only stare up at him in confusion. The intensity of his gaze made her tremble inside. Her reaction to the warrior didn't make any sense to her, and because she couldn't reason it through, she couldn't control it.

"No."

He'd whispered that reply. She didn't have the faintest idea what he was talking about. "No, what?" she whispered back.

"No, tomorrow won't be difficult for me," he explained.

"Then it won't be difficult for me, either," she said.

His eyes sparkled with amusement. He smiled, too. Her knees went weak. Lord, he was a handsome devil. She had to shake her head because she'd noticed. She forced herself to turn away from him. He bent down to pick up her brush. She had the same intention. Their foreheads bumped. Her hand reached the brush first. His hand covered hers. The warmth of his fingers startled her. She stared down at his hand, marveling at the sheer size of it. It was at least twice the size of hers. His strength was so apparent to her. He could crush her if he wanted to, she thought to herself. The power radiating from him was fairly overwhelming, yet the gentleness in his touch was evident, too. She knew she could pull her hand away if she wanted to.

She stood up when he did, but she still didn't pull her hand away. Neither did he. They stayed that way for what seemed an eternity to Judith, yet she knew only a minute or two had actually passed.

Iain was staring down at her with a puzzled look on his face. She didn't know what to make of that. Then he suddenly jerked his hand away. The abruptness of that action embarrassed her.

"You confuse me, Iain."

She hadn't realized she'd spoken those words out loud until she'd said them. She backed away from him, then hurried down the hill.

Iain watched her leave. His hands were clasped behind his back. When he realized how rigid his stance was, he forced himself to relax.

"Hell," he muttered to himself. He wanted her. Iain accepted that fact without flinching. He excused his behavior by telling himself any man with healthy appetites would be drawn to her. She was a damn beautiful woman, after all, incredibly soft and feminine, too.

What shook Iain was the fact that he'd only just realized she was also attracted to him. He wasn't at all pleased by that realization, either. He knew he could control his own desires, but he didn't have any idea how he could control hers.

This simple errand had already become complicated.

Iain decided it would be best if he separated himself from her as much as possible for the duration of the journey. He would ignore her, too.

After forming that plan of action, he felt better. He went back to the camp and saw that Judith had already gone inside the tent Alex and Gowrie had built for her. Iain went over to the tree next to Brodick, sat down and leaned back against the trunk. Alex and Gowrie were already sound asleep. Iain thought Brodick was too, until Brodick turned and spoke to him. "She's English, Iain. Try to make that matter."

Iain glared at his friend. "Meaning?"

"You want her."

"How the hell would you know what I want?"

Brodick wasn't intimidated by Iain's angry tone of voice. The two men had been friends for long years. Besides, Brodick had Iain's best interests at heart, and knew his friend understood that his motives were good-hearted.

"If you don't hide your feelings, Alex and Gowrie will soon know about this attraction."

"Damn it all, Brodick—"

"I want her, too."

Iain was astonished. "You can't have her," he commanded, before he could stop himself.

"You're sounding possessive, Iain."

His friend didn't answer that statement of fact. Brodick let out a long sigh.

"I thought you hated the English, Brodick," Iain remarked after several minutes of silence.

"I do," Brodick answered. "But when I look at her, I forget. Her eyes . . . it's an affliction . . ."

"Get over it."

Iain's voice had gone hard.

Brodick raised an eyebrow over that ferocious command. Iain was finished with the discussion. He closed his eyes and took a deep breath. He couldn't understand his reaction to Brodick's admission that his friend also wanted Judith. He'd been furious. Hell, he still was. Why did he care if Brodick wanted the woman or not? No, it shouldn't have mattered to him, yet the mere thought of anyone touching her—anyone but him, he qualified to himself—set his blood boiling.

Iain didn't go to sleep for a long, long while. He kept trying to sort out his irrational thoughts.

His mood didn't improve the following morning. He waited until the last possible minute to wake Judith. She hadn't moved at all during the night. He knew that for a fact because he'd spent the night watching her. The tent concealed most of her body, and only her feet and ankles were visible to him, but they hadn't moved at all during the dark hours.

Only after the horses were readied did Iain go over to the tent to wake Judith. He tossed the furs covering the posts to Alex, then knelt down on one knee and gently touched Judith's shoulder. He called her name, too.

She didn't move. Iain nudged her again, more forcefully.

"Lord, she's a sound sleeper, isn't she?" Gowrie made that remark. He'd walked over to stand next to Iain. "Is she breathing?"

Judith finally opened her eyes. She stared up at the giants looming over her and almost screamed. She caught herself in time and only a startled gasp escaped.

Iain noticed her fear. He noticed she'd grabbed hold of his hand, too. He stood up, then helped her stand.

"It's time to leave, Judith," he said when she continued to stand there. "Why don't you go to the stream and wash the sleep away."

She nodded.

She finally started moving. Brodick caught her from behind. His hands rested on her shoulders as he slowly turned her around so that she was facing in the right direction. Then he had to nudge her to get her moving again.

The men were vastly amused by Judith's stupor, but none of them smiled until she was out of sight.

"Think she'll walk into the water?" Alex asked.

"She might wake up before then," Gowrie said with a chuckle.

Judith was wide awake by the time she reached the water's edge. The water was refreshing, too. She took care of her personal tasks as quickly as possible, then hurried back to the camp.

Everyone but Iain was mounted and waiting. Judith didn't know who she was supposed to ride with today. Both Alex and Gowrie motioned to her to come to them.

Iain was on the opposite side of the clearing. She watched him mount his stallion's back, and when he still didn't look her way, she decided that since Alex was closer, she'd ride with him.

Iain had made the decision the night before to distance himself from Judith. That intention was completely forgotten, however, when he saw her walking toward Alex.

She was just taking hold of the soldier's hand when she was intercepted. Iain's stallion didn't pause in his gait. He had his arm wrapped around her waist and lifted her up onto his lap without breaking stride.

She didn't even have time to grab hold. Iain took the lead. She heard someone laugh behind her, but when she tried to turn around to see which one of the soldiers was making all the racket, Iain pulled her up against his chest and wouldn't let her move.

His hold was downright painful. She didn't have to tell him to let up on his grip, though. As soon as she touched his arm and relaxed against him, he lessened his hold.

The next several hours proved to be an exhausting ordeal for Judith. They had veered away from the broken north road and ridden as though they had a legion of devils chasing them. The pace was grueling until they reached the rugged steep mountain terrain. They had to slow down then.

Iain finally allowed a short respite. They stopped in a small clearing surrounded by thick thistle. The prickly plant was filled with vibrant purple and yellow flowers. Judith thought the area was beautiful. She walked around the lovely paradise, careful not to step on any of the blooms while she worked the ache out of her legs. She wanted to rub the sting from her backside, too, but didn't dare because the men were watching her every move.

They weren't a very talkative group, and so she spent her time touching the surprisingly durable flowers and sniffing their unusual fragrance.

Judith walked to the pond Gowrie told her about and

drank a fair amount of cold water. When she returned to the clearing, Alex handed her a square of cheese and a huge helping of thick bread.

She sat by herself on a smooth-topped boulder, her nooning meal in her lap. Iain came back to the clearing and joined the other men. The four warriors stood near their horses, talking to each other. Every now and then Iain would turn to look at her, as if making certain she was still where she was supposed to be.

She took her time finishing her food, staring at Iain most of the time. It occurred to her that she really didn't know much about any of the men, except that they were all in some way related to Frances Catherine. They were loyal to her too. She hoped that her dear friend realized how fortunate she was to have so many caring people around her. Of course, they were damn lucky to have Frances Catherine in their family now too.

She suddenly remembered the very first time they met. She had been too young at the time to remember all the details of that day, but over the years since then, Frances Catherine's papa had liked to recall the first time he'd met Judith. She'd heard about the story of the stinging bee from him so many times that she no longer knew which details she remembered and which ones she'd been told.

She thought about that incident now. According to Frances Catherine's papa, there was this bothersome bee . . .

"What has you smiling, lass?"

Judith had closed her eyes and was so intent on her recollection, she didn't hear Alex's approach. She opened her eyes and found him standing just a foot away from her.

"I was remembering the first time I met Frances Catherine," she answered.

"When was that?" Alex asked.

He seemed genuinely interested. She assumed he wanted to hear about Frances Catherine's childhood. She told him how she met her friend, and by the time she'd finished the story, Gowrie and Iain had joined in to listen. Alex asked her several questions, too. Judith didn't embellish on her answers until the topic of Frances Catherine's father came up. She lingered over the explanation of how she'd met that wonderful man, even described his appearance. Her voice had taken on a soft, loving tone. Iain noticed the change, noticed too that she had mentioned three times how kind Frances Catherine's father had been to her. It was as though she was still, after all these years, surprised by that realization.

"Did Frances Catherine take to your father the way you took to hers?" Gowrie asked.

"My father wasn't there."

The smile had left her voice. She stood up and walked toward the privacy of the trees. "I'll just be a few minutes," she called over her shoulder.

Judith was quiet the rest of the day. She was subdued during supper, too. Gowrie, the most outspoken of the group, asked her if something was wrong. She smiled, thanked him for inquiring, and then excused her behavior by telling him she was just a little weary.

They slept outdoors that night, the following four nights as well, and by the sixth day of the journey, Judith had reached the point of real exhaustion. The cold nights didn't help. The farther north they rode, the more frigid the wind became. Sleeping was an almost impossible task, and when she did doze off, it was only for a few minutes at a time. The tent offered little protection against the fierce wind, and there were times during those dark hours when she felt as though the cold was slicing through her bones.

Iain had become just as withdrawn. He still insisted she ride with him, but he barely spoke a word to her.

She'd learned from Alex that Iain was the newly appointed laird over the clan, and she wasn't at all surprised by that news. He was a born leader of men, which she thought was a blessing because he was far too arrogant to follow orders. He liked to have things his way. Oh, she'd noticed that flaw quick enough.

"Are there problems at home that have you worrying?" she asked when the silence of the long ride started to grate on her nerves.

They were riding through a difficult mountain pass and the pace was slow. Judith turned to look up at him while she waited for his answer.

"No."

He didn't expound on that answer.

Another hour passed in silence. Then Iain leaned down and asked, "Do you?"

She didn't know what he was talking about. She turned to look up at him again. His mouth was only inches away from hers. He abruptly pulled back. She quickly turned around. "Do I what?" she asked in a tight whisper.

"Do you have problems at home that have you worrying?"

"No."

"We were surprised your family allowed you to leave with us."

She shrugged. "Will it get warmer during the summer or is it always this cold up here?" she asked in an attempt to change the topic.

"It's as warm now as it's ever going to be," he answered. The amusement in his voice confused her. "Is there a baron back home who has spoken for you, Judith? Are you pledged to anyone?"

"No."

The man wouldn't let up on his personal questions. "Why not?"

"It's complicated," she answered. In a rush she added, "I really don't wish to discuss this. Why aren't you married?"

"There hasn't been time or the inclination."

"I don't have the inclination either."

He laughed. She was so surprised by that reaction, she turned to look at him again. "Why are you laughing?" she asked.

Damn, he was appealing when he was happy. The corners of his eyes crinkled with his merriment, and his eyes fairly sparkled silver. "Then you weren't jesting with me?" he asked.

She shook her head. He laughed all the louder. She didn't know what to make of him. Neither did Gowrie. He turned in his saddle to see what was going on. He looked a little stunned too. Judith decided the soldier wasn't used to hearing his laird laugh.

"In the Highlands, it doesn't matter if a woman is inclined or not," Iain explained. "I assumed it was the same in England."

"It is the same," she said. "A woman doesn't have a voice in the matter of her future."

"Then why—"

"I've already explained," she said. "It's complicated."

Iain relented. He quit his questions. Judith was immensely thankful. She didn't want to talk about her family. She'd really never given the matter of her future much thought. She doubted a marriage could be arranged by her mother, though. It was a fact that both mother and daughter were still the property of the laird Maclean . . . if he was still alive. If he'd died, then Uncle Tekel would become her guardian . . . or would he?

Aye, it really was complicated. She decided she was simply too tired to think about it. She leaned back against Iain and closed her eyes.

A little while later, Iain leaned down and whispered, "In an hour or so, we'll be riding through hostile territory, Judith. You must be silent until I give you permission to speak again."

Her safety was in his hands, and for that reason she immediately nodded agreement. She fell asleep minutes later. Iain adjusted her in his arms so that both her legs were drapped over one of his thighs. The side of her face rested against his shoulder.

He motioned both Gowrie and Alex ahead of him and left Brodick to protect the rear from attack.

The secluded area they rode through was thick with foliage and summer blooms. The sound of the falls roaring down into a gigantic gorge drowned out the sound their horses made.

Gowrie suddenly reined in his mount and raised one fist into the air. Iain immediately turned to the east and nudged his stallion into a thick cluster of trees. The others followed his lead now and hid themselves in the surrounding forest.

A shout of laughter came from the broken path not twenty feet away from where Judith and Iain waited. Other laughter joined in. Iain strained to hear over the thundering of the falls. He calculated that at least fifteen Macphersons were in the area. His hand itched to reach for his sword. Damn, he wished he could take the enemy by surprise. The odds were in his favor. With Gowrie, Alex, and Brodick fighting by his side, fifteen or twenty inept Macphersons wouldn't even provide a victory large enough to talk about.

Judith's safety came first, however. Iain instinctively tightened his hold around her waist. She snuggled closer, then started to let out a little sigh. His hand clamped down over her mouth. That action woke her up. She opened her eyes and looked at him. He shook his head. He still didn't remove his hand. She realized then that they were in enemy territory. Her eyes widened for just a second or two over that worry. Then she forced herself to relax.

She was safe as long as she was with him. Judith didn't understand why she had such confidence in his ability, but in her heart she knew he wouldn't let anyone harm her.

A good twenty minutes passed before he finally removed his hand from her mouth. His thumb slowly rubbed across her lower lip and she couldn't imagine why he'd done that, even as shivers of pleasure coursed through her body. He shook his head at her again; a signal, she guessed, that she was to remain silent. She nodded to let him know she understood.

She simply had to quit staring at him. Her stomach was fluttering, her heart as well, and she knew she'd be blushing in no time at all if she didn't control her thoughts. She thought she'd die if he had any inclination of his effect on her. Judith closed her eyes and rested against him. Both his arms were wrapped around her waist. It would be easy for her to pretend he wanted to hold her, easy to dream impossible dreams about the handsome laird too.

She told herself she wouldn't allow such nonsense. She was made of stronger stuff and could certainly control her emotions, and her thoughts.

The wait continued. When Iain was finally certain the Macphersons were well away from their shelter, he let go of his fierce hold on her. He gently nudged her face up, to look at him, with his thumb under her chin.

He'd meant to tell her the threat was over, but he forgot his intention the second her gaze met his. Desire such as he'd never experienced before gained his full attention. His discipline deserted him. He felt powerless against this attraction. He couldn't stop himself from tasting her. He slowly leaned down, giving her plenty of time to pull away from him if she wanted to, but Judith didn't move. His mouth gently brushed over hers. Once. Twice. And still she didn't pull away.

He wanted more. His hand clasped her jaw and his mouth settled possessively on top of hers. He captured her gasp, ignored it. He thought to end this attraction with one thorough kiss. He told himself his curiosity would then be appeased. He'd know the taste of her, and the feel of her soft lips too, and then it would be finished. He would be sated.

It didn't work out that way. Iain recognized that fact soon enough. He couldn't seem to get enough of her. Damn, she tasted good. And she was so soft, so warm and giving in his arms. He needed more. He forced her mouth open, and before she guessed his intent, his tongue swept inside to mate with hers.

She did try to pull away from him then, though only for the briefest of seconds. Then she wrapped her arms around his waist and clung to him. His tongue rubbed against hers until he was shaking with his need. She certainly wasn't acting shy now. Nay, she was actively kissing him back.

He growled low in his throat. She whimpered. Passion raged between them. His mouth slanted over hers again and again, and when he realized he wasn't going to be content until he was resting between her thighs, he forced himself to stop.

Iain was stunned, furious too, though only with himself. His lack of discipline was appalling to him. She was staring up at him with such a confused expression on her face. Her lips looked swollen . . . he wanted to kiss her again.

He shoved her head down on his shoulder, then jerked on the reins of his mount to get them moving back to the main path.

Judith was thankful for his inattention now. She was still shaking from the kisses he'd given her, astonished too by her own passionate response. It was the most wonderful and the most frightening experience she'd ever had.

She wanted more. She didn't think Iain did, though. He hadn't said a word to her, but the way he'd abruptly pulled away from her and the anger she'd glimpsed in his eyes were both sound indications he'd been displeased.

She suddenly felt very inadequate and horribly embarrassed. Then she felt like shouting at the brute for injuring her feelings and her pride. Her eyes filled with tears. She took a deep breath in an effort to regain her composure. After a few minutes her trembling subsided a little, and she was beginning to think she'd won this battle with her own confusing emotions, when Iain injured her feelings again. He stopped his mount next to Alex's brown stallion, and before Judith had an inkling of what he was planning to do, the rude man had dumped her into Alex's lap.

So be it. If he didn't want to have anything more to do with her, she would retaliate in kind. She refused to even glance his way. She carefully adjusted her skirts, keeping her gaze downcast all the while, and prayed to her Maker that Iain wouldn't see her blush. Her face felt like it was on fire.

Iain took over the lead. Gowrie nudged his mount into position behind his laird, then she and Alex joined the procession. Brodick was once again left to protect the rear.

"Are you cold, lass?"

Alex whispered that question close to her ear. The concern in his voice was most apparent.

"No," she answered.

"Then why are you trembling?"

"Because I'm cold."

She realized the contradiction in her answers and let out a little sigh. If Alex thought she wasn't making any sense, he was kind enough not to mention it. He didn't speak another word to her that long afternoon, and she didn't speak to him.

She couldn't seem to get comfortable in his arms, either. Her back brushed against his chest several times, but she couldn't relax enough to lean back against him.

By nightfall she was so exhausted she would barely keep her eyes open. They stopped at a beautiful stone cottage with a thatched roof, nestled in the side of the mountain. Thick ivy covered the south side of the structure and a stone path led all the way from the barn adjacent to the front door of the cottage.

A gray-haired man with a thick beard and wide shoulders stood in the entrance. He smiled in greeting and hurried outside.

Judith saw the woman hovering in the doorway. She had been standing behind her husband, but when he moved forward, she backed into the shadows.

"We'll be spending the night here," Alex said. He dismounted, then reached up to assist her. "You'll have a roof over your head and a good night's rest."

She nodded. Alex, she decided, was a truly compassionate man. He'd helped her to the ground, but he didn't let go of her. He knew she'd fall on her face if he did. He didn't mention her pitiful condition, and even allowed her to hold on to his arms until she could make her legs quit shaking. His hands held her by her waist and she knew he could feel her trembling.

"Get your hands off her, Alex."

Iain's hard voice came from behind Judith. Alex immediately let go. Her knees buckled. Iain caught her from behind just as she was falling forward. His left arm was tightly wrapped around her waist and he wasn't at all gentle when he pulled her to his side. Alex backed away from his laird's glare, then turned to walk toward the cottage.

Iain continued to stand there holding Judith for several more minutes. Her shoulders were pressed tightly against his chest. She kept her head bowed. She was so weary she wanted to close her eyes and let him carry her inside. That wouldn't have been proper, of course.

How could a man smell so wonderful after such a long day's ride? Iain's scent was a combination of the clean outdoors . . . and male. Heat radiated from him. She was drawn to his warmth, and when she realized that fact, she knew she should pull away.

He was as distant as the storm brewing in the south. Judith knew he was only holding her because she needed his assistance. He felt responsible for her and was simply doing his duty.

"Thank you for your help," she said. "You may let go of me now. I've recovered."

She tried to push his arm away. He had other intentions. He half turned her in his arms, then nudged her chin up.

He was smiling. She didn't know what to make of that. He'd been acting like a disgruntled bear just minutes before, though she admitted to herself that Alex had been his target.

"I'll let go of you when I want to," he explained in a soft whisper. "Not when you give me permission to, Judith."

His arrogance was outrageous. "And when do you suppose that will be?" she asked. "Or am I allowed to ask?"

He raised an eyebrow over the irritation in her voice. Then he shook his head at her. "You're angry with me," he said. "Tell me why."

She tried to push his hand away from her chin but gave up when he squeezed her jaw.

"I'm not letting go until you tell me why you're upset," he told her.

"You kissed me."

"You kissed me too."

"Yes, I did," she admitted. "I'm not sorry either. What think you of that?"

The challenge was there, in her voice and her eyes. A man could forget his every thought if he allowed himself to be captured by her beauty. That thought settled in his mind even as he answered her. "I'm not sorry either."

She gave him a disgruntled look. "Perhaps you weren't sorry at the time, but you're sorry now, aren't you?" He shrugged. She felt like kicking him. "You'd better not touch me again, Iain."

"Don't give me orders, lass."

His voice had taken on a hard edge. She ignored it. "When it comes to kissing me, I can give all the orders I want to. I don't belong to you," she added in a much softer tone of voice.

He was looking like he wanted to throttle her. She decided she'd been a little too high-handed with him. Iain seemed to have a prickly nature.

"I didn't mean to sound surly," she began. "And I know you must be used to getting your way, because you're a laird and all. Still, as an outsider, I really shouldn't have to obey any of your commands," she continued in a reasonable tone of voice. "In this instance, as a guest—"

She stopped trying to explain when he shook his head at her. "Judith, do you agree that while you're in my brother's home, you'll be under his protection?"

"Yes."

He nodded. He smiled too. He acted as though he'd just won an important argument, and she wasn't even certain what the topic had been.

He let go of her and walked away. She chased after him. When she reached his side, she grabbed hold of his hand. He immediately stopped.

"Yes?" he asked.

"Why are you smiling?"

"Because you just agreed with me."

"How?"

She wasn't deliberately trying to bait him. He could see the confusion in her gaze. "Until you return to England, I'm responsible for you. You will follow all my commands," he added with a nod. "That's what you just agreed to do."

She shook her head. The man was daft. How in heaven's name had her announcement that he couldn't kiss her ever again led to this twisted conclusion?

"I agreed to no such thing," she said.

She hadn't let go of his hand. He doubted she realized she was still holding on to him. He could have pulled away. He didn't.

"You told me I'd be under Patrick's protection," she reminded him. "Therefore, he would be responsible for me, Iain, not you."

"Yes," he agreed. "But I'm laird and Patrick therefore answers to me. Now do you understand?"

She pulled her hand away. "I understand you think that both you and Patrick can give me orders," she replied. "That's what I understand."

He smiled. He nodded, too. She burst into laughter. He couldn't imagine what had caused that response.

He wasn't left guessing long.

"Does that mean that you and Patrick are both accountable for all my actions?"

He nodded. "My transgressions become yours?" He clasped his hands behind his back and frowned down at her. "Do you plan to cause mischief?"

"Oh, no, of course not," she answered in a rush. "I'm really very thankful to you for allowing me to come to your home, and I certainly don't wish to cause any problems."

"Your smile makes me wonder about your sincerity," he remarked.

"I'm smiling for a different reason altogether," she explained. "I've just realized what an illogical man you are," she added with a nod, when he looked so incredulous.

"I'm not in the least illogical," he snapped.

She didn't realize she'd insulted him. "Yes, you are," she countered. "Unless you can explain how my decision not to let you kiss me again led to this bizarre conversation."

"The issue of my kissing you isn't relevant enough for discussion," he replied. "It holds no importance."

He might as well have slapped her. The hurt from his casually spoken words stung just as much. She wasn't about to let him know he'd injured her feelings, though. She nodded, then turned and walked away from him.

He stood there watching her for a long minute.

Then he let out a weary sigh. Judith didn't understand, but she was already causing problems. His men couldn't keep their gazes off her. Damn, neither could he.

She was a beautiful woman, and any man would notice. Yes, that made sense. That was logical. Yet the raw possessiveness he felt toward her was another matter altogether. That wasn't at all logical.

He told her that ultimately he was responsible for her . . . until she returned to England. Hell, he'd almost choked on the words. The thought of taking her back didn't sit well at all. What in thunder was wrong with him?

How was he ever going to let her go?

Chapter 4

She couldn't wait to be rid of him. Judith knew she wasn't thinking like a reasonable person now. The long, endless journey had worn her out so thoroughly, her mind had turned to mush. She was admittedly overreacting to Iain's harsh words. She couldn't seem to sort anything out because her feelings kept getting in her way. She was still feeling the sting of his rejection, she supposed.

"Judith, come and meet Cameron," Alex called out.

Everyone turned to look at her. She hurried over to stand in front of their host. She made a quick curtsy and forced a smile. It was a difficult undertaking, for Cameron was staring at her as though she'd just turned into a demon . . . or worse. The expression on his face didn't leave any doubt as to what he was thinking. He was apparently appalled by her very existence.

Oh Lord, she really didn't have the strength to endure this nonsense. She let out a little sigh, then said, "Good eve to you, sir."

"She's English."

Cameron roared that statement of fact with such force,

the veins in his forehead stood out. Judith had spoken in perfect Gaelic, but she hadn't been able to conceal the English accent. Her clothes were another clue as to her heritage, of course. While she well understood the shameful distrust that existed between the Scots and the English, Cameron's hostility was so unreasonable and so filled with loathing, he frightened her. She instinctively took a step back in an attempt to protect herself from his wrath.

She bumped into Iain. She tried to move to his side, but he waylaid that intent when he put his hands on her shoulders. He tightened his hold and pulled her back until she was pressed against him.

Iain didn't say a word for a long minute. Alex walked over to stand next to his laird. Then Gowrie strolled over to stand on the opposite side. Brodick was the last to move. He stared at Iain, waiting for permission, and when his laird finally took his gaze off Cameron and turned to give him a nod, Brodick walked over to stand directly in front of Judith.

She was literally pressed between the two warriors. She tried to peek around Brodick's back, but Iain tightened his hold so she couldn't move at all.

"We've already noticed she's English, Cameron," Brodick announced in a low yet forceful voice. "Now I would like you to notice that Lady Judith is under our protection. We're taking her home with us."

The elderly man seemed to shake himself out of his stupor. "Yes, of course," he stammered out. "It was just a surprise, you see, hearing her . . . voice and all."

Cameron didn't like the look in Laird Maitland's eyes. He decided he had better smooth over this breach of manners as quickly as possible. He took a step to his left so that he could look directly at the Englishwoman when he made his apology.

Brodick moved with him, effectively blocking his intent. "Are we all welcome here?"

"Of course you are," Cameron replied. His fingers

threaded through his stock of white hair in a nervous gesture, and he fervently hoped the laird didn't notice how his hand was shaking. He'd really made a muck of this greeting. The last thing he wanted to do was offend such a powerful, ruthless man . . . and if he had offended Iain, he knew it probably would be the very last thing he'd ever do on this sweet earth.

Cameron resisted the nearly overwhelming urge to make the sign of the cross. He couldn't hold Iain's hard stare long, and turned his full attention to Brodick. He cleared his throat, then said, "Since the day your brother married my only daughter, you and every other member of the Maitland clan are welcome here. Laird Maitland's woman, too, of course," he hastily added. He half turned, then bellowed to his wife, "Margaret, put the supper on the table for our guests."

Judith had wondered why Iain hadn't spoken up, but as soon as Cameron mentioned that Brodick's brother was married to his daughter, she understood why Iain had given him the duty of sorting out the awkward situation.

Cameron beckoned everyone inside. Judith reached out and grabbed hold of the back of Brodick's plaid. He immediately turned around. "Thank you for speaking up for me," she whispered.

"You needn't thank me, Judith." His voice was gruff with embarrassment.

"Yes, I must," she argued. "Brodick, will you please explain to your relative that I'm not Iain's woman. He seems to misunderstand."

Brodick stared at her a long minute without saying a word, then glanced up to look at Iain.

Why was he being so hesitant? "I'm only asking that you set the man straight," she said.

"No."

"No?" she asked. "Why in heaven's name not?"

Brodick didn't actually smile, but the corners of his

eyes crinkled together in what she decided was amusement. "Because you are Iain's woman," he drawled out.

She shook her head. "Where did you get that ridiculous notion? I'm only a guest—"

She quit trying to explain when Brodick turned and walked inside the cottage. She watched the obstinate man leave. Alex and Gowrie followed. Those two were openly grinning.

Judith stayed where she was. Iain finally let go of her shoulders and gave her a little prod.

She didn't budge. He moved to stand beside her. His head was bent down toward hers. "You may come inside now."

"Why didn't you say something when Cameron called me your woman?"

He shrugged. "I didn't feel like it."

He wasn't telling her the truth, of course. Cameron had been wrong; Judith wasn't his woman, but he had liked the sound of it too much to take exception. Lord, he was weary to be thinking such foolish thoughts. "Come inside," Iain ordered again, his voice a bit more gruff than he'd intended.

She shook her head and turned her gaze to the ground.

"What's this?" he demanded. He forced her face up with the back of his hand under her chin.

"I don't wish to go inside."

She'd sounded downright pitiful. He tried not to smile. "Why not?" he asked.

She shrugged. He gently squeezed her jaw. She knew he wouldn't let up on her until she'd given him a proper answer. "I just don't want to go where I'm not wanted," she whispered. His smile was filled with tenderness. She suddenly felt like crying. Her eyes were already getting misty. "I'm overly exhausted this evening," she excused.

"But that isn't the reason you wish to stay out here, is it?"

"I just explained . . . I was humiliated," she blurted

out. "I know I shouldn't take his dislike personally. All the Highlanders hate the English, and most of the English hate the Scots, even the border Scots . . . and I hate all the hatred. It's . . . ignorant, Iain."

He nodded agreement. Some of the bluster went out of her. It was difficult to stay outraged when he wasn't arguing with her.

"Did he frighten you?"

"His anger did," she admitted. "It was most unreasonable. Or am I overreacting again? I'm too weary to know."

She was exhausted. He hadn't paid enough attention, or he certainly would have noticed the dark smudges under her eyes before now. She had taken hold of his hand when she'd admitted she'd felt humiliated, and she still hadn't let go.

Yes, Judith looked tired, defeated too, and utterly beautiful to him.

She suddenly straightened her shoulders. "You must go inside. I'll be happy to wait out here."

He smiled as he pulled his hand away from hers. "But I'd be happier if you went inside with me," he announced.

He was through discussing the topic. He threw his arm around her shoulders, gave her a little squeeze, and then dragged her along with him toward the doorway.

"You said you might be overreacting once again," he remarked as he hauled her along. He was deliberately ignoring the fact that she was acting like a stiff board. The woman had a stubborn streak in her nature. That flaw amused him. No other woman had ever appeared to be disgruntled with him, but Judith was quite different from all the women he'd known in the past. She was glaring at him every other minute, or so it seemed. He found her reactions refreshingly honest. She didn't have to try to impress him, and she sure as hell didn't have it in her nature to cower away from him, either. Odd, but her uninhibited behavior freed him. He didn't have to act the laird over a submissive subject with Judith. The fact that she was an outsider seemed to break the bindings of traditions pressed upon him as leader of his clan.

Iain had to force himself back to the question nagging him. "When was the first time you overreacted?" he asked.

"When you kissed me."

They'd reached the opening when she whispered that admission. He came to a dead stop and grabbed hold of her. "I don't understand," he said. "How did you overreact?"

She could feel her face heating up. She shrugged his arm away from her shoulder. "You were obviously angry with me . . . after, and that made me angry, too. I shouldn't have cared," she added with a firm nod.

She didn't wait to gain his reaction to her outburst of honesty. She hurried inside. The older woman she'd noticed standing in the shadows came forward to greet her. Her smile seemed genuine to Judith, and some of the tension went out of her shoulders when she smiled back.

Margaret was a pretty woman. The creases edged in her brow and around the corners of her mouth didn't take away from her appeal. She had lovely green-colored eyes with flecks of gold in them, and thick brown hair streaked through with strands of gray. She'd fashioned a braid at the nape of her neck. Although the woman was a good foot taller than Judith, she wasn't at all intimidating. Kindness radiated from the woman.

"Thank you for allowing me to come into your home," Judith said after she'd completed a curtsy.

Margaret wiped her hands on the white apron she wore around her middle before returning the curtsy. "If you'll take your seat at the table, I'll finish getting our supper ready."

Judith didn't want to sit with the men. Iain had already joined the group, and Cameron was leaning across the table pouring him a gobletful of wine. Judith's stomach immediately tightened. She took a quick breath to calm herself. A single cup of wine wasn't going to turn Iain mean . . . was it? This reaction was absolutely ridiculous, she told herself. And uncontrollable. Her stomach was aching as though she'd swallowed fire. Iain wasn't at all like Tekel. He wouldn't turn ugly. He wouldn't.

Iain happened to glance up. He took one look at Judith and knew something was terribly wrong. The color had left her face. She looked as though she was in a panic about something. He was about to get up from the table to find out what was troubling her when he realized she was staring at the jug of wine.

What in God's name had gotten into her?

"Judith? Did you wish to drink some—"

She vehemently shook her head. "Wouldn't water be more . . . refreshing after such a long day's journey?"

He leaned back. What they drank seemed damned important to her. He didn't have the faintest idea why, and he guessed that didn't really matter. She was obviously upset. If the woman wanted them to drink water, then they would drink water.

"Yes," he agreed. "Water would be more refreshing."

Her shoulders slumped with relief.

Brodick noticed her reaction too. "We'll be getting up early, Cameron," he said, though his gaze was locked on Judith. "We won't drink wine until we're home."

Margaret had heard the conversation, too. She hurried over to the table with a pitcherful of fresh spring water. Judith carried over more goblets.

"Sit yourself down and rest," Margaret told her.

"I would rather help you," Judith replied.

Margaret nodded. "Fetch that stool and sit by the hearth. You can stir the stew while I see to cutting the bread."

Judith was relieved. The men were in discussion now, and from the frowns they wore, she assumed it was an important topic. She didn't want to interrupt. More importantly, she didn't want to sit next to Cameron, and the only empty stool was at the end of the table, on Cameron's left.

Judith carried the stool from against the wall over to the hearth to follow Margaret's instructions. She noticed that the woman kept giving her covert glances. She obviously wanted to speak to her, but must have been concerned about her husband's reaction. She kept glancing over to the table to see if Cameron was paying them any attention.

"We rarely get company," Margaret whispered.

Judith nodded. She watched Margaret peek over at her husband again, then turn back to her.

"I'm curious as to why you're wanting to go to the Maitlands' home," she whispered next.

Judith smiled. "My friend married a Maitland and requested that I come for the birthing of her first child," she answered, keeping her voice as whisper-soft as Margaret's had been when she asked her question.

"How did you ever meet?" Margaret wanted to know.

"At the festival on the border."

Margaret nodded. "We have the same festivals in the Highlands, though it comes in the fall and not the spring."

"Have you ever attended?"

"When Isabelle still lived with us we went," Margaret answered. "Cameron's been too busy to go since," she added with a shrug. "I always had a fine time."

"I understand Isabelle's married to Brodick's brother," Judith said. "Was it a recent wedding?"

"No, over four years ago now," Margaret answered.

The sadness in Margaret's voice was most evident. Judith quit stirring the meaty stew and leaned back from the fire so she could give Margaret her full attention. Odd, but although they were virtual strangers, she felt the urge to comfort the woman. She seemed to be terribly lonely, and Judith well understood that feeling.

"Haven't you had time to go and visit your daughter?"

"Not once have I seen my Isabelle since she wed," Margaret answered. "The Maitlands stay to themselves. They don't take to outsiders."

Judith couldn't believe what she was hearing. "But you're certainly not an outsider," she protested.

"Isabelle belongs to Winslow now. It wouldn't be proper to ask that she come to visit us, and it wouldn't be proper either to ask to go to her."

Judith shook her head. She'd never heard of anything so preposterous. "Does she send messages to you?"

"Who would bring them?"

A long minute passed in silence. "I would," Judith whispered.

Margaret looked over at her husband, then turned her gaze back to Judith. "You would do that for me?"

"Of course."

"I'm worrying it wouldn't be proper," Margaret said.

"Of course it would be proper," Judith argued. "It wouldn't be difficult, either, Margaret. If you have any messages you'd like me to give Isabelle, I promise I'll find her and give them to her. Then, on my way back to England, I'll give you her messages. Perhaps there will even be an invitation to visit," she added.

"We're going outside to see about the horses, wife," Cameron announced in a booming voice. "Shouldn't take us any time at all. Supper almost ready?"

"Aye, Cameron," Margaret answered. "It will be on the table when you come back inside."

The men left the cottage. Cameron shut the door behind them. "Your husband sounded angry," Judith remarked.

"Oh, no, he's not angry," Margaret rushed out. "He's a little nervous, though. It's quite an honor to have the Maitland laird in our home. Cameron will be boasting about this for a good month or two."

Margaret set the treachers on the table, then added

another jug of water. The bread was sliced into wedges. Judith helped her ladle the stew into a large wooden bowl and put it in the center of the long table.

"Perhaps, during our supper, you could ask Brodick how Isabelle is doing," Judith suggested.

Margaret looked appalled. "It would be an insult for me to ask," she explained. "If I ask if she's happy, then I'm suggesting Winslow isn't making her happy. Do you see how complicated it is?"

It wasn't complicated, it was ridiculous in Judith's estimation. She could feel herself getting angry on Margaret's behalf. The Maitlands were being cruel-hearted with such an attitude. Didn't any of them have any compassion for relatives like mothers and fathers?

She didn't know what she would do if someone told her she could never see her aunt Millicent and uncle Herbert again. She got all misty-eyed just thinking about it.

"If you were to ask . . ." Margaret smiled at Judith while she waited for her to catch on.

Judith nodded. "Brodick might think that because I'm English, I don't know any better."

"Yes."

"I'll be happy to ask, Margaret," she promised. "Are all the clans in the Highlands like the Maitlands? Do they all isolate themselves from outsiders?"

"The Dunbars and the Macleans do," Margaret answered. "When they aren't fighting with each other, they stay to themselves," she explained. "The Dunbar holding sits between the Maitlands and the Macleans, and Cameron tells me they're constantly fighting over land rights. None of them attend the festivals, but all the other clans do. Are all the English like you?"

Judith tried to concentrate on what Margaret was asking. It was a difficult task, for she was still reeling from the woman's casual remark that the Macleans were the Maitlands' enemies.

"Milady?" Margaret asked. "Are you feeling ill?"

"Oh, I'm feeling very well," Judith replied. "You asked me if I was like all the other English, didn't you?"

"I did," Margaret replied, frowning over the notice that her guest's complexion had turned so pale.

"I don't know if I'm like the others or not," Judith answered. "'Tis a fact I've led a rather sheltered life. Margaret, how in heaven's name do the men ever find mates if they never mingle with the other clans?"

"Oh, they have their ways," Margaret answered. "Winslow came here to barter for a speckled mare. He met Isabelle and took to her right away. I was set against the union because I knew I'd never see my daughter again, but Cameron wasn't going to listen to me. Besides, you don't say no to a Maitland, leastways I've never heard of anyone trying, and Isabelle had her heart set on marrying Winslow."

"Does Winslow look like Brodick?"

"Aye, he does. He's much more quiet, though."

Judith burst into laughter. "Then he must be dead," she remarked. "Brodick rarely speaks a word."

Margaret couldn't stop herself from chuckling. "They're a strange breed, the Maitlands are, but in their defense I'll tell you that if ever Cameron came under attack or needed any true assistance, he would only have to send word to Laird Iain.

"Before the marriage, every now and again a couple of our sheep would disappear. The thievery stopped as soon as word went out that our Isabelle married a member of the Maitland clan. Cameron's gained new respectability, too. Of course, his initial reaction to meeting you might have changed that status."

"Do you mean his surprise to find out I was English?"

"Aye, he was surprised all right."

The two women looked at each other and suddenly burst into laughter just as the men returned to the cottage. Iain was the first to walk inside. He nodded to

Margaret, then paused to give Judith a frown. She guessed he didn't think her amusement was proper behavior. That possibility made her laugh all the more.

"Go and take your place at the table," Margaret instructed.

"Aren't you joining us?"

"I'll serve first, then I'll join you."

Whether she realized it or not, she'd just given Judith an excuse not to sit next to Cameron. The men had all taken their same positions. Judith picked up the stool near the hearth and carried it over to the other side of the table. Then she nudged her way between Iain and Brodick.

If the warriors were surprised by her boldness, they didn't let on. Brodick even moved over so she wouldn't be crowded.

They ate in silence. Judith waited until the men had finished before bringing up the topic of Isabelle's welfare.

She decided to ease into the discussion. "Margaret, this was a fine stew."

"Thank you," Margaret replied with a faint blush.

Judith turned to Brodick. "Do you see your brother very often?"

The warrior glanced down at her, then shrugged.

"Do you see his wife, Isabelle?" she prodded.

He shrugged again. She nudged him under the table with her foot. He raised an eyebrow over that boldness. "Did you just kick me?"

So much for trying to be subtle, Judith thought. "Yes, I did kick you."

"Why?"

Iain asked that question. She turned to smile at him. "I didn't want Brodick to shrug at me again. I want him to talk about Isabelle."

"But you don't even know the woman," Iain reminded her.

"I wish to learn about her," Judith argued.

Iain looked like he thought she'd lost her mind. She let out a sigh. Then she started drumming her fingertips on the tabletop.

"Tell me about Isabelle, please," she asked Brodick again.

He ignored her.

She let out a sigh. "Brodick, would you please step outside with me for just a minute? I wish to say something terribly important to you in private."

"No."

She couldn't restrain herself. She kicked him again. Then she turned to Iain. She missed Brodick's quick grin. "Iain, please order Brodick to step outside with me."

"No."

She drummed her fingertips on the tabletop again while she considered her next ploy. She looked up, caught Margaret's pitiful expression, and determined then and there that even if she looked the fool, she would get her way.

"All right then," she announced. "I'll just have to talk to Brodick tomorrow on our journey. I'll ride with you," she added with an innocent smile. "I'll probably talk from sunup to sundown, too, Brodick, so you'd better get your rest tonight."

That threat carried substance. Brodick shoved himself away from the table and stood up. The scowl on his face was scorching. He made it apparent to everyone at the table that he was angry.

Judith wasn't angry. She was furious. God's truth, she couldn't wait to get the insensitive clod outside. She forced a smile and even managed a curtsy to her host before turning and walking out the doorway. She kept right on smiling, too, when she turned and pulled the door closed behind her.

In her haste to blister Brodick, she forgot about the two windows on either side of the door.

Margaret and Gowrie were seated with their backs to

the door, but Iain and Alex had a clear view of the grassy area outside the windows.

Needless to say, everyone's curiosity was caught. Gowrie half turned on his stool to see what was going on.

Iain kept his attention centered on Brodick. The warrior faced him. He stood with his legs braced apart and his hands clasped behind his back. He wasn't trying to hide his irritation from Judith, either. Brodick had a fierce temper. Iain knew the warrior wouldn't touch Judith, no matter how angry she made him, but he could hurt her with a few cruel remarks.

Iain waited to see if he needed to intervene. The last thing he needed tonight was a weeping woman on his hands, and Brodick was almost as good at intimidating tactics as he was.

A sudden smile caught him by surprise. He couldn't believe what he was seeing. Neither could Alex. "Will you look at that?" he whispered.

"I'm looking," Gowrie announced. "I'm just not believing. Is that our Brodick backing away?" He snorted with amusement. "I've never seen that particular expression on his face before. What do you think she's saying to him?"

She was giving the warrior hell, Iain decided. Judith's hands were settled on her hips, and when she'd started toward her adversary, she didn't stop. Brodick was literally backing away from her. He looked . . . astonished, too.

Her voice was muffled by the wind and the distance, but Iain knew she wasn't whispering. Nay, she was shouting, all right, and every now and then Brodick actually flinched.

Iain turned to look at Margaret. Her hands covered her mouth, and when she realized he was watching her, she immediately turned her gaze to the tabletop. She wasn't quick enough. He caught the look of worry in her eyes and knew that she was somehow involved.

The door opened. Judith forced a smile and hurried

back to the table. She sat down, folded her hands in her lap, and let out a sigh. Brodick took his time following. When he was once again settled on his stool, the attention turned to him. Judith felt it safe enough to nod to Margaret. She winked, too.

Iain caught that action. His curiosity intensified.

Brodick cleared his throat. "Isabelle and Winslow have a cottage almost this size." He'd muttered that comment.

"Well now, that's fine to hear," Cameron replied.

Brodick nodded. He acted terribly uncomfortable. "She's due to have her baby any time now."

Margaret let out a happy gasp. Tears filled her eyes. She reached out and took hold of her husband's hand. "We're going to have a grandchild," she whispered.

Cameron nodded. His eyes, Judith noticed, were getting misty, too. He turned his attention to his goblet.

Iain finally understood what Judith's game had been. She'd thrown a tantrum, embarrassed herself, too, and all because she wanted to help Margaret find out how her daughter was doing. Judith was such a gentlewoman. It had never dawned on him to think Isabelle's parents might want news about their daughter, but an outsider had seen the obvious and had set out to help.

"Were there any specific questions you would like to ask about your daughter?" Brodick asked.

Margaret didn't just have one question. She had hundreds. Alex and Gowrie even answered a few of them.

Judith couldn't have been more pleased. It did chafe to know that the only reason Brodick was cooperating was because she had threatened to ride with him. The thought of having to touch her was more repulsive than talk about private family matters. Still, what did her feelings matter? The look of joy on Margaret's face was adequate compensation for Brodick's surly attitude.

The cottage was wonderfully warm, almost toasty. Judith tried to pay attention to the conversation, but exhaustion made that a difficult task. She noticed Cameron had tried to refill Brodick's goblet with more water, but the pitcher was empty.

Judith put the stool she'd been sitting on back against the wall near the hearth and carried another pitcher of water over to the table. Cameron nodded his thanks to her.

Lord, she was weary. The men swallowed up the space she'd occupied, and her back was aching too much to sit there anyway. She went over to the stool by the hearth, sat down and rested her shoulders against the cool stone wall. She closed her eyes and was sound asleep less than a minute later.

Iain couldn't take his gaze off her. She was so lovely. Her face looked angelic. He stared at her a long, long while, until he realized she was slumping herself off the stool.

He nodded to Brodick to continue the story he was telling, then went over to stand next to Judith. He leaned against the wall, folded his arms across his chest in a relaxed stance and listened to the tale Brodick was telling about Winslow and Isabelle. Margaret and Cameron were hanging on his every word. They both smiled when Brodick made mention that Isabelle was generous to a fault.

Judith lost her balance. She would have pitched forward if Iain hadn't reached down to steady her. He pushed her back against the wall, then nudged her head toward him. The side of her face rested against the lower portion of his thigh.

A good hour passed before Iain called a halt to the conversation. "We'll leave at first light, Cameron. We've still two full days ahead of us before we reach home."

"Your woman can have our bed," Cameron suggested. His voice started out loud, but then he turned and saw that Judith was sleeping, and his voice dropped to a whisper.

"She'll sleep outside with us," Iain replied. He softened his denial. "Judith wouldn't want you to give up your bed for her."

Neither Margaret nor Cameron argued over the laird's decision. Iain leaned down, transferred Judith into his arms, then stood up.

"The lass is dead to the world," Alex remarked with a grin.

"Would you like extra blankets? The wind's biting tonight," Margaret warned.

Gowrie opened the door for Iain. "We have everything we need."

Iain carried Judith through the opening, then suddenly stopped. He turned around. "Thank you for the supper, Margaret. It was a fine meal."

The compliment sounded awkward to him, but Margaret looked pleased. Her blush was as bright as the fire in the hearth. Cameron acted as though he'd been given the praise, too. His chest swelled until it was in jeopardy of bursting.

Iain continued on toward the trees across from the barn. The foliage would give them protection against the wind, privacy too. He held Judith while Alex fixed a shelter for her, then knelt down and placed her on the plaid Gowrie had spread inside the small fur-lined tent.

"I promised the lass she would have a warm bed inside tonight," Alex remarked.

Iain shook his head. "She stays with us," he announced.

No one argued over that statement. The men turned and walked away just as Iain was covering Judith with a second plaid. She never opened her eyes. The back of his hand deliberately brushed against her cheek.

"What am I going to do about you?" he whispered.

He hadn't expected an answer and didn't get one. Judith snuggled under the blankets and let out a little moan.

He was reluctant to leave her. He forced himself to stand up, and grabbed one of the plaids Alex offered him on his way over to the nearest tree. He scratched his shoulders against the bark, sat down, leaned back and closed his eyes.

A sound he'd never heard before awakened him in the dead of the night. The other men heard it, too.

"What in God's name is that noise?" Brodick muttered.

Judith was making all the racket. She was wide awake, miserable too. She thought she was in jeopardy of freezing to death. She couldn't quit shivering. Her teeth were chattering, and that was the sound the men were hearing.

"I didn't mean to wake you, Brodick," she called out. Her voice literally trembled with each word. "I was moaning over the cold."

"You're really cold, lass?" Alex asked. The surprise in his voice was evident.

"I just said that I was," she answered.

"Come here," Iain commanded, sounding a bit surly. Judith responded in kind. "No."

He smiled in the darkness. "Then I'll have to come to you."

"You stay away from me, Iain Maitland," she commanded. "And if you think to order me to quit being cold, I'm warning you now—it won't work."

He walked over to stand in front of the tent. She could only see the tips of his boots until he tore the furs away. He destroyed the cocoon in seconds.

"That helped," she muttered. She sat up so she could glare at him.

Iain pushed her back and stretched out on the ground beside her. He rested on his side, giving her the heat from his back.

Brodick suddenly appeared on her other side. He stretched out on his side with his back toward her. Judith instinctively wiggled closer to Iain. Brodick followed her, until his back was pressed against hers.

She was certainly warm enough now. The heat radiating from the giant warriors was amazing.

It felt wonderful.

"She feels like a block of ice," Brodick remarked.

Judith started laughing. The sound made both Iain and Brodick smile.

"Brodick?"

"What is it?"

He sounded mean again. She didn't let that bother her. She was finally catching on to his ways, and knew the bluster was all for show. Underneath that gruff exterior beat a kind heart. "Thank you."

"What for?"

"For taking the time to talk about Isabelle."

The warrior grunted. She laughed again.

"Judith?"

She snuggled closer to Iain's back before answering him. "Yes, Iain?"

"Quit wiggling and go to sleep."

She felt like obeying him. She fell asleep almost immediately.

A long while passed before Brodick spoke again. He wanted to be certain Judith really was asleep and wouldn't hear what he was going to say. "Each time she's given a choice, she turns to you."

"How's that, Brodick?"

"She's glued to your back now, not mine. She prefers riding with you, too. Didn't you notice the pitiful expression on her face when you made her ride with Alex today? She looked damn forlorn."

Iain smiled. "I noticed," he admitted. "But if she prefers me, it's only because I'm Patrick's brother."

"There's a hell of a lot more to it than that."

Iain didn't respond to that comment.

Several minutes passed before Brodick spoke again. "Let me know, Iain."

"Let you know what?"

"If you're going to keep her or not."

"And if I'm not?"

"Then I am."

Chapter 5

It took two more days to reach the Maitland holding. They spent the last night in a beautiful forest called Glennden Falls. Birch, pine, and oak trees were so thick in the area, the horses could barely get through the narrow path. A mist, more white than gray, and nearly waist high in some spots, floated around the greenery, giving an air of magic to the paradise.

Judith was enchanted. She walked into the mist until it completely surrounded her. Iain watched her. She turned around, caught him staring at her, and whispered in a voice filled with awe that this was surely the most beautiful spot in all the world.

"This is what I envision Heaven to be, Iain," she told him.

He seemed surprised, took a good look around him, and then, in his arrogant way, said, "Perhaps."

It was evident the man had never taken the time to appreciate the beauty around him. She told him so. He gave her a long, thorough look that started at the top of her head and ended at the tips of her boots. He moved forward, gently touched the side of her face, and then said, "I'm noticing all right."

She could feel herself blushing. He was referring to her, of course. Did he truly find her beautiful? She was too embarrassed to ask. He turned her attention, however, with his announcement that she could have a proper bath.

She was thrilled. The water cascading down the gentle slope was frigid, but she was too happy to have the opportunity to thoroughly scrub herself to mind the cold. She even washed her hair. She had to braid it damp, but that didn't bother her, either.

She wanted to look her best when she was reunited with her friend. Judith was a little apprehensive about seeing Frances Catherine again. It had been almost four years since their last visit. Would her friend think she'd changed very much . . . and if so, would she think the changes were for the better or the worse?

Judith didn't allow herself to fret over the reunion long. In her heart she knew it would be all right. Her excitement grew as soon as she pushed the silly worry aside, and by the time they'd finished their supper, she was literally pacing around the campfire.

"Did you know Cameron's wife stayed up all night cooking for us?" she asked no one in particular. "She sent Isabelle her favorite sweet biscuits, but she made enough for us as well."

Alex, Gowrie, and Brodick were all sitting around the fire. Iain leaned against a fat birch, watching her. No one replied to her comments about Margaret.

She wasn't daunted. Nothing could dampen her enthusiasm. "Why do we have a fire tonight? We haven't had one before," she remarked.

Gowrie answered her. "We're on Maitland land now. We weren't before."

She let out a gasp. "This wonderland belongs to you?"

Alex and Gowrie both smiled. Brodick frowned. "Will

106

you quit your pacing, woman? You're making my head ache watching you."

She threw Brodick a smile when she strolled past him. "Then don't watch," she suggested.

She wanted to nudge his temper a bit, but he surprised her with a grin.

"Why are you pacing?" Iain asked.

"I'm too excited about tomorrow to sit still. It's been a long while since I've seen Frances Catherine, and I have so many things I want to tell her. My mind's cluttered with them. I wager I won't be able to sleep a wink tonight."

Iain secretly wagered she would. He won. Judith was dead to the world as soon as she closed her eyes.

When morning arrived, she refused to be rushed. She warned them she was going to take her time, and when she returned to the camp where Iain and the others impatiently waited on horseback for her, she looked as magical as her surroundings. She was dressed in a brilliant blue gown that perfectly matched the dramatic color of her eyes. Her hair was unbound, and the thick curls floated around her shoulders when she moved.

A tightness settled in Iain's chest. He couldn't seem to take his gaze away from her. His lack of discipline appalled him. He shook his head over his own shameful behavior and scowled at the woman driving him to distraction.

Judith reached the clearing and then stopped. Iain didn't understand why she was hesitating until he turned and noticed his men had all extended their hands to her. Each was beckoning her forward.

"She's riding with me."

His voice didn't suggest anyone argue. She thought he was irritated because she'd taken so long to get ready this morning.

She slowly made her way over to his side. "I did warn you I'd need more time today, so you really don't have anything to frown about."

He let out a sigh. "It isn't ladylike to speak to me in that tone," he explained.

Her eyes widened. "What tone?"

"Demanding."

"I wasn't demanding."

"You really shouldn't argue with me, either."

She didn't even try to hide her exasperation. Her hands settled on the sides of her hips. "Iain, I understand that because you're laird, you're used to ordering people around. However—"

She didn't get to finish her explanation. He leaned down, grabbed her around the waist, and lifted her up into his lap. She let out a yelp. He hadn't hurt her, though. Nay, it was his amazing quickness that caught her off guard.

"You and I are going to have to come to some sort of understanding," he announced in a hard, no nonsense tone of voice.

He turned to his companions. "Go ahead," he ordered. "We'll catch up."

While he waited until his men had left, she tried to turn in his lap so she would be facing the front. He squeezed her around the waist, a silent message to stay where she was.

She pinched his arm to get him to let up on his hold. He watched his men take their leave, waiting for privacy so he could speak to her without being overheard, but he did let up on his grip. She immediately quit squirming.

She turned to look up at him. He hadn't shaved this morning. He looked a little disheveled and very, very masculine.

Abruptly, he turned his full attention to her. They stared into each other's eyes a long minute. He wondered how in God's name he was ever going to be able to leave her alone once they reached his home. She wondered how he'd come by such a fine, unblemished profile. She turned her attention to his mouth. She couldn't seem to catch her breath. Heaven help her, she really wanted to be kissed.

He wanted to kiss her. He took a deep breath in an effort to control his wayward thoughts. "Judith, this attraction between us is probably due to the fact that we've been forced to endure each other's company for over a week now. The closeness—"

She took immediate exception to his poor choice of words. "You feel you've been forced to endure my company?"

He ignored her interruption. "When we reach the holding, everything will change, of course. There's a specific chain of command, and everyone in the Maitland clan adheres to the same rules."

"Why?"

"So there won't be chaos."

He waited for her to nod before continuing. He was trying not to look at her sweet mouth.

"The rule we all follow . . . or rather, the chain of command, was put aside during this journey for necessity's sake, but once we reach our destination, we will not have such an unstructured relationship."

He paused again. She assumed he was waiting for her agreement. She dutifully nodded. He looked relieved until she asked, "Why is that?"

He let out a sigh. "Because I'm laird."

"I already knew you were laird," she replied. "And I'm certain you're a fine one, too. Still, I do wonder what this talk is about. I believe I mentioned before, I'm not a member of your clan."

"And I'm certain I explained that while you're a guest on my land, you'll obey the same rules as everyone else."

She patted his arm. "You're still worried I'll cause trouble, aren't you?"

He suddenly felt like throttling her.

"I'm really going to try to get along with everyone," she whispered. "I won't make any problems."

He smiled. "I'm not certain that's possible. As soon as they realize you're English, their minds will be set against you."

"That isn't fair, is it?"

He wasn't in the mood to argue with her. "Fairness isn't the issue. I'm simply trying to prepare you. When everyone gets over their initial surprise—"

"Do you mean to tell me no one knows I'm coming?"

"Don't interrupt me when I'm speaking to you," he commanded.

She patted his arm again. "I do beg your pardon," she whispered.

She didn't sound the least bit contrite to him. He let out a sigh. "Patrick, Frances Catherine, and the council members know you're coming. The others will find out when you get there. Judith, I don't want you to have a difficult . . . adjustment."

He was truly worried about her. And trying to hide his concern with a gruff voice and a hard frown. "You're a very kind man," she said, her voice husky with emotion.

He acted as though she'd insulted him. "The hell I am."

Judith decided then and there she was never going to understand him. She brushed her hair back over her shoulder, let out a sigh, and then said, "Exactly what are you so concerned about? Do you think they'll find me inferior?"

"Perhaps, at first," he began. "But once—"

She interrupted him again. "That attitude won't bother me. I've been considered inferior before. Nay, it won't bother me at all. My feelings won't be so easily injured. Do quit worrying about me, please."

He shook his head at her. "Aye, your feelings will get injured," he countered, remembering the look on her face when his men hadn't immediately sat down with her to eat her supper that first night. He paused, trying to remember what he wanted to tell her, then said in a near shout, "Who the hell thinks you're inferior?"

"My mother," she answered before she thought better of it. "I'm not in the mood to talk about my family," she added with a firm nod. "Shouldn't we get started?"

"Judith, I'm merely trying to tell you that if you should run into any substantial problems, tell Patrick. My brother will find me."

"Why can't I simply tell you? Why must I involve Frances Catherine's husband?"

"The chain of command—" Her sudden smile stopped him cold. "Why are you amused?"

She lifted her shoulders in a dainty shrug. "I'm pleased to know you're concerned about me."

"How I feel about you has nothing to do with this discussion," he told her, his voice downright mean. He was being deliberately harsh because he wanted her to understand the importance of what he was telling her. Damn it, he was trying to protect her from hurt. Women had such fragile feelings, if Patrick's comments were to be taken seriously, and he didn't want Judith upset. He wanted her adjustment to be as peaceful as possible, and he knew that if she didn't behave in an appropriate manner, the members of the clan would make her life miserable. Her every movement would be scrutinized. Judith had been correct. The immediate dislike wasn't fair. How like an innocent to think in such terms. Iain was a realist, however, and knew that fair didn't matter. Survival did. He was almost overwhelmed by his need to protect her any way he knew how, and if that meant intimidating her to get her to understand her tenuous position, then by God he would intimidate.

"I really don't care for the way you're frowning at me, Iain. I haven't done anything wrong."

He closed his eyes in surrender. She couldn't be intimidated. Lord, he felt like laughing. "Talking to you is an extremely trying experience," he remarked.

"Because I'm an outsider or because I'm a woman?"

"Both, I suppose," he answered. "I haven't had much experience conversing with many women."

Her eyes widened in disbelief. "Why not?"

He shrugged. "It hasn't been necessary," he explained.

She couldn't believe what he was telling her. "You make it sound like a chore."

He grinned. "It is."

He'd probably just insulted her, but she didn't mind. His smile softened the comment. "Aren't there women at home who you enjoy talking to on occasion?"

"That isn't the topic now," he countered.

He was about to return to the original subject but she beat him to it. "I know, I know," she muttered. "Even though your rules shouldn't apply to me, I promise to try to fit in while I'm a guest on your land. There, does that ease your mind?"

"Judith, I won't allow insolence."

His voice was soft and without a hint of anger in it. He'd simply made a statement of fact. She responded in kind. "I wasn't being insolent," she said. "At least not on purpose."

Her sincerity was very apparent. He nodded, satisfied. Then he tried to explain her position again. "While you're on *my* land, you will obey *my* orders, because ultimately I'm responsible for you. Do you understand?"

"I understand you're sinfully possessive," she replied. "And Lord, I am weary of this conversation."

His scowl told her he didn't care for that bit of truth.

She decided to turn the topic. "Iain, you don't get much company, do you?"

Was she being flippant with him? He didn't think so. "Very few outsiders are allowed on our land," he admitted.

"Why is that?"

He didn't have a ready answer. In truth, he didn't even know why outsiders weren't allowed. He'd never taken the time to think about it. "It's just the way it's always been," he remarked.

"Iain?"

"Yes?"

"Why did you kiss me?"

That switch in subjects gained his full attention. "Damned if I know," he replied.

A faint blush colored her cheeks. "Will you be damned if you know again?" He didn't understand what she was asking. The look in his eyes said as much. She pushed her embarrassment aside. She thought the moment of privacy would probably be the last they would share, and she meant to take blatant advantage. She reached up to stroke the side of his face with her fingertips.

"What are you doing?" He captured her hand but didn't push her away.

"Touching you," she answered. She tried to sound nonchalant, yet knew she hadn't managed that feat. The intensity in his expression made her heart take notice. "I was curious to know what your whiskers felt like." She smiled. "And now I know." She pulled her hand away from his and let it drop back into her lap. "They tickle."

She felt like a fool. Iain didn't ease her discomfort, either. He looked at a loss for words. Her boldness had surprised him, all right. She let out a little telling sigh. He probably thought she was just a shameless wench without any morals. She was certainly acting like one. What was the matter with her? She wasn't usually so aggressive.

She was stroking his upper arm with the tips of her fingers while she mulled over his probable opinion of her. She wasn't even aware she was caressing him. He was. The gentle, soft as a butterfly's touch was driving him daft.

She stared at his chin when she gave him her roundabout apology. "I'm not usually so curious or so aggressive."

"How would you know?"

She was so startled by that question, her gaze flew up to his. The amusement in his eyes was evident. Was he mocking her?

She looked as though he had just crushed her heart. "It was a serious question, Judith." His fingers now stroked the side of her face. Her reaction pleased him too. She leaned into his touch, instinctively wanting to gain more, like a kitten would lean into the hand that was stroking, caressing.

"I keep remembering the way you kissed me, and I would like for you to kiss me again. It's a shameful confession, isn't it? I've led a very sheltered—"

His mouth stopped her explanation. The kiss was very gentle, undemanding too, until she put her arms around his neck and turned all soft and willing on him. He couldn't control himself. The kiss turned hard, hot, consuming. Wonderfully arousing. She felt as though she were melting in his arms. She loved the taste of him, the feel of his tongue rubbing against hers, the way his mouth slanted over hers again and again. She loved the low growl that came from the back of his throat, and the rough gentleness in the way he held her in his arms.

But she hated the way he looked at her when he pulled away. It was the same expression he'd worn the first time he'd kissed her. Iain was angry he'd touched her, probably disgusted as well.

She didn't want to see that expression. She closed her eyes and collapsed against him. Her heart was slamming inside her chest. So was his. She could hear the thundering beat against her ear. He had been affected by the kiss, perhaps as much as she had. Was that why he was angry? He didn't want to like touching her.

She was saddened by that possibility. Embarrassed too. She suddenly wanted to put some distance between them. She turned in his lap until her back rested against his chest. She tried to edge off his lap. He wouldn't let her. His hands settled on the sides of her hips and he roughly pulled her backside up tight against him. "Don't move like that," he ordered. His voice was harsh, angry.

She thought she'd hurt him. "I'm sorry," she replied. She kept her gaze downcast. "I shouldn't have asked you to kiss me. I won't ever ask again."

"You won't?"

He sounded like he was about to laugh. Her spine straightened in reaction. Iain felt as though he were holding a block of ice. "Judith, tell me what's wrong," he commanded in a gruff whisper.

She might have been able to explain if he hadn't leaned down and rubbed the side of her face with his jaw. Shivers of pleasure raced across her shoulders. Lord, she was disgusted with herself. Why couldn't she control her reaction to him?

"Answer me."

"I know a future together isn't possible," she began. Her voice trembled. "I'm not a complete fool, even though I realize I've been acting like one. My only excuse is that I felt safe with this attraction for you, because of that very reason." She wasn't making any sense. She was getting all riled up, though. She was gripping her hands together in real agitation.

"Explain this 'very reason,'" he asked.

"The very reason that I'm English and you're not," she answered. "I don't feel safe now."

"You don't feel safe with me?"

He sounded appalled. "You don't understand," she whispered. She kept her gaze downcast so he wouldn't see her embarrassment. "I thought my attraction for you was safe because you're a laird and I'm English, but now I've come to the conclusion that it's dangerous. You could break my heart, Iain Maitland, if I allow it. You must promise to stay away from me. It's . . . impossible."

His chin rested on top of her head. He inhaled her sweet light scent and tried not to think about how good she felt in his arms. "Not impossible," he muttered. "Damned complicated, though."

He didn't realize the significance of what he was saying to her until he had actually spoken the thought aloud. He immediately considered all the ramifications. The problems were staggering. He decided he needed time, and distance, away from Judith, so he could think the matter through.

"I believe it would be easier if we just ignored each other," she suggested. "When we reach your holding, you'll go back to your important duties and I'll keep busy with Frances Catherine. Yes, it will be easier that way, won't it, Iain?"

He didn't answer her. He took the reins in his hands and goaded the mount into a full gallop. His arm blocked the branches as they made their way through the narrow opening. He felt her tremble, and once they were in the fields at the base of his home, he pulled her cloak from behind his saddle and covered her with it.

Neither spoke a word to the other for the next several hours. They rode across a magnificent field of rape; the dazzling yellow was so brilliant to the eye, she had to squint against the sheer beauty of it all. Cottages nestled intimately between the proud pines covering the hills beyond. Flowers of every color in the rainbow spilled down the hillside, surrounded by a thick carpet of grass as green as emeralds.

They rode across an arched bridge atop a sparkling clear stream, then started up the steep climb. The air was thick with the scent of summer. The aroma of the flowers mingled with that of the clean earth.

Scots, both men and women, came outside their cottages to watch the procession pass by. The clan members all wore the same colors, their plaids identical to Iain's, and for that reason she knew they'd finally reached his home.

She was suddenly so excited to see Frances Catherine, she could barely sit still. She turned to smile at Iain. He stared straight ahead, ignoring her.

"Are we going directly to Frances Catherine's home?"

"They'll be waiting in the courtyard at the top of the crest," Iain answered.

He hadn't even spared her a glance when he'd explained. She turned around again. She wasn't going to let his sour mood ruin her excitement. She was enchanted with the rugged beauty around her and couldn't wait to tell Frances Catherine.

Then she got a good look at Iain's keep. Lord, it was ugly. The huge stone structure was on the very top of the crest. There wasn't a wall surrounding the building, either. Iain must not have been worried about the enemy breaching his home. She guessed he'd have plenty of time to become alerted, as an outsider would have quite a climb to reach the top.

A gray mist hung down over the roof of the mammoth structure. The main building was square in shape, and as gray and dreary as the skies above.

The courtyard wasn't any better. It was more dirt than grass, and as worn-out as the scarred double doors leading into the keep.

Judith turned her attention to the crowd gathered before her. The men nodded to Iain, but the women didn't show any outward reaction to their arrival. Most stayed behind the men, silent, watching, waiting.

Judith looked for Frances Catherine. She really wasn't at all apprehensive until she spotted her friend and got a good look at her face.

Frances Catherine looked close to tears. Her face was deathly pale. She was obviously frightened. Judith didn't understand the reason for that reaction, but her friend's worry immediately became her own.

Iain forced his mount to a stop. Gowrie, Alex, and Brodick immediately did the same. Frances Catherine took a step forward. The man standing next to her grabbed hold of her arm and forced her to stay where she was.

She turned her attention to Patrick Maitland. She had little doubt he was Frances Catherine's husband. He looked very like Iain, and though he was slighter in build, his frown was every bit as fierce as Iain's was.

He looked worried too. When he glanced down at his

wife, Judith realized his concern was for Frances Catherine.

Her friend was wringing her hands together. She stared up at Judith for a long minute, then took another hesitant step forward. Patrick didn't stop her this time.

It was an incredibly awkward moment because of the large crowd watching so intently. "Why is Frances Catherine frightened?"

She'd whispered that question to Iain. He leaned down close to her ear and answered her question with one of his own. "Why are you?"

She was about to deny that accusation, but Iain drew her attention by gently prying her hands away from his arm. Lord, she'd had a death grip on him.

He gave her a little squeeze before dismounting. He nodded his greeting to Patrick, turned and assisted Judith to the ground.

She didn't spare him a glance now. She turned and slowly walked over to her friend. She stopped when she was a few feet away.

She didn't know what to say to make Frances Catherine's fear go away. Or her own. She remembered that when they were little, when one cried, the other immediately joined in. That memory led to another, and she suddenly knew exactly what she wanted to say in greeting to her dear friend.

Her gaze was centered on Frances Catherine's swollen stomach. She took another step forward and looked up into her eyes. In a low whisper she was certain only her friend could hear, she said, "I specifically remember we both promised never to drink from any man's goblet of wine. From the looks of you, Frances Catherine, I'm thinking you broke your word."

Chapter 6

Frances Catherine let out a low gasp. Her eyes widened in surprise. Then she burst into laughter and threw herself into Judith's arms. She remembered how she had been so certain and so full of authority when she'd told Judith a woman could only get pregnant if she drank out of a man's goblet.

She all but swallowed Judith up when she hugged her. The two women were laughing and crying at the same time, and to the crowd gathered around them, they appeared to have lost their senses.

The tension and the worry eased out of Patrick's shoulders. He turned to look at Iain and slowly nodded. His brother nodded back.

The journey had been well worth the trouble, Patrick decided. He clasped his hands behind his back and waited for his wife to remember her manners. The joy in her expression more than made up for her inattention. And Lord, how he had missed the sound of her laughter. A part of him wanted to take this Englishwoman into his own arms and hug her just as fiercely as his wife was doing, to let her know how much he appreciated her loyalty.

He had to wait another five minutes or so before his wife remembered he was there. The two women were talking at the same time, asking and answering their own questions. They created a whirlwind of happy chaos.

Iain was just as pleased as Patrick with the reunion. He was a bit surprised, too, for until this very minute he hadn't realized that women could actually be trusted friends with each other. The strength of the bond between Judith and Frances Catherine was unique. It intrigued him. He remembered Judith had told him they'd become friends before they were old enough to understand they were supposed to be enemies, and he found he admired the two of them all the more for continuing to give each other loyalty even after they had learned the lessons of distrust . . . and hate.

Judith remembered her audience before Frances Catherine did. "We have so much to catch up on," she said. "But now I must thank Iain and the others for bringing me to you."

Frances Catherine grabbed hold of her hand. "First, I must introduce you to my husband," she said. She turned to smile up at Patrick. "This is Judith."

Patrick's smile was a replica of Iain's. "I gathered as much," he told his wife. "I'm pleased to meet you, Judith."

She would have made a nice curtsy if Frances Catherine had let go of her hand. She smiled instead. "And I'm pleased to be here, Patrick. Thank you for inviting me."

Her attention turned to Iain. He'd taken the reins of his mount and started toward the stables. She tugged her hand away from Frances Catherine, promised to come right back, and then hurried after her escort. "Iain, please wait," she called out. "I wanted to say thank-you."

He didn't stop, but he did look back over his shoulder. He gave her an abrupt nod and continued on. She said thank-you to Alex, Gowrie, and Brodick as they filed past her. They reacted in the very same manner. They were abrupt, distant.

Judith told herself she shouldn't have expected anything more. They'd done their duty and were finally rid of her. She held on to her smile and turned around. As she was passing a group of women, she heard one whisper, "Dear God, I'm thinking she's English, but that can't be, can it?" If Judith's clothing hadn't given her away, she knew her accent certainly had.

She continued to walk toward Frances Catherine, but smiled at the women gawking at her. "Aye, I am English."

One woman's mouth actually dropped open. Judith suppressed the urge to laugh, because she felt it would be terribly rude to show amusement over someone else's obvious distress.

When she reached her friend, she said, "Everyone seems quite thrilled to have my company."

Frances Catherine laughed. Patrick reacted in just the opposite way. He evidently thought she'd been serious when she made that remark. "Judith, I don't believe thrilled is the proper word. Actually, I would wager they're . . ."

He looked at his wife for help in softening the truth. Frances Catherine didn't give him any assistance, however. She couldn't quit laughing.

Judith smiled up at Patrick. "Would 'appalled' be a better word?"

"Nay," Frances Catherine said. "Outraged, disgusted, or perhaps—"

"Enough," Patrick interrupted with a low growl. The sparkle in his eyes indicated he wasn't really angry. "Then you were jesting with me when you suggested—"

Judith nodded. "Yes, I was jesting. I know I'm not welcome here. Iain warned me."

Before Patrick could comment on that remark, an elderly warrior called out to him. He bowed to Frances Catherine and Judith, then walked over to the cluster of men standing near the steps to the keep. Frances Catherine linked her arm through Judith's and started walking down the slope.

"You'll be staying with Patrick and me," she explained. "It might be a little cramped but I want you close by."

"Is there more than one room in this cottage?"

"No. Patrick wants to add another after the baby's born."

Patrick came down the hill to join them. The frown on his face made Judith believe he'd already had to defend her presence to the warriors.

"Is it going to be difficult for you, Patrick, because you invited me to come here?"

He didn't give her a direct answer. "They'll become accustomed to having you around."

They reached the cottage. It was the first along the pathway. Flowers bordered the front of their home, some pink, others red, and the stone had been thoroughly whitewashed until it was pristine clean.

There was a wide square window on each side of the door. The interior was just as inviting as the exterior. A stone hearth took up the center of one wall. A large bed covered with a beautiful multicolored quilt was positioned against the opposite wall, and a round table surrounded by six stools took up the rest of the space. The washstand was near the door.

"We'll bring a cot inside before nightfall," Frances Catherine promised.

Patrick nodded agreement, but he didn't look very happy about the arrangement. Nay, he looked resigned.

It was a delicate topic, but one that needed to be settled as soon as possible. Judith went over to the table and sat down. "Patrick, please don't leave yet," she called out when he started back out the doorway. "I would like to talk to you about this sleeping arrangement."

He turned, leaned against the door, folded his arms across his chest and waited for her to explain. He thought she was going to suggest that he find someplace else to stay while she was there, and he was already preparing himself for his wife's disappointment when he told Judith no. Although it wasn't possible to be physically intimate with Frances Catherine now, he still enjoyed holding her close during the night, and by God, he wasn't going to give that up.

Unless Frances Catherine got all teary-eyed on him again, Patrick admitted. He'd give up anything just to ease her distress.

Judith was taken aback by the intense frown Patrick was giving her. Frances Catherine's husband was turning out to be as gruff-natured as Iain was. She still liked him, of course, and all because she could tell from the way he watched his wife that he loved her.

She folded her hands together. "I don't feel it's appropriate for me to stay with you. You both should have your privacy each night," she added in a rush when Frances Catherine looked like she was going to argue. "Please don't take offense," she said. "But I think a husband and wife should have time alone. Isn't there someplace I could stay that's close by?"

Frances Catherine was vehemently shaking her head when Patrick spoke up. "The cottage two down is empty. It's smaller than ours, but I'm certain it would do."

"Patrick, I want her to stay with us."

"She just explained she doesn't want to, love. Let her have her way."

Judith was embarrassed. "It isn't that I don't want to stay—"

"There, do you see? She does want to—"

"Frances Catherine, I'm going to win this argument," Judith announced. She nodded to her friend when she made that prediction.

"Why?"

"Because it's my turn," she explained. "You may win the next argument."

"Lord, you're stubborn. All right. You may stay in Elmont's cottage. I'll help you make it comfortable."

"You will not," Patrick interjected. "You're going to rest, wife. I'll see to your friend's comfort."

Patrick was looking much happier now. Judith guessed he was relieved she was going to be sleeping somewhere else. He even smiled at her. She smiled back. "I do assume Elmont isn't living there anymore and won't mind."

"He's dead," Patrick told her. "He isn't going to mind at all."

Frances Catherine shook her head at her husband. He winked at her, then left the cottage. "My husband didn't mean to sound so callous, but Elmont was very old when he died, and his passing was peaceful. Patrick was just making a little jest. I think he's taken with you, Judith."

"You love him very much, don't you, Frances Catherine?"

"Oh, yes," her friend answered. She sat down at the table and spent a good hour talking about her husband. She told Judith how they'd met, how he relentlessly pursued her, and finished by mentioning just a hundred or two of his special qualities.

The only thing the man wasn't capable of was walking on water . . . yet. Judith made that comment when her friend paused for breath.

Frances Catherine laughed. "I'm so happy you're here."

"You don't have hurt feelings because I want to sleep somewhere else?"

"No, of course not. Besides, you'll be close enough to hear me shout if there's need. I must be careful not to exclude Patrick. My husband does get his feelings hurt quite easily if he thinks I'm not paying him enough attention."

Judith tried not to laugh. Patrick was such a big brute of a man. The idea that he could have injured feelings was vastly amusing, and terribly sweet.

"He looks like his brother."

"Perhaps just a little," Frances Catherine agreed. "Patrick's much more handsome, though."

Judith was of the opinion that it was really just the opposite. Iain was much better-looking than Patrick was. Love really must color one's perception, she decided.

"Patrick's incredibly gentle and loving."

"So is Iain," Judith remarked before she could stop herself.

Her friend immediately latched on to that comment. "And how would you know if Iain's loving or not?"

"He kissed me." She'd whispered that confession, felt herself blush, and immediately lowered her gaze. "Twice."

Frances Catherine was stunned. "Did you kiss him back . . . twice?"

"Yes."

"I see."

Judith shook her head. "No, you don't see," she argued. "We were attracted to each other. I'm not at all certain why, but it doesn't really matter. The attraction's over now. Really," she added when she saw her friend's reaction.

Frances Catherine didn't believe her. She was shaking her head. "I know why he was attracted to you," she said.

"Why?"

Frances Catherine rolled her eyes heavenward. "Honest to God, you don't have a bit of vanity inside you. Don't you ever see yourself in the looking glass? You're beautiful, Judith." She paused to let out a dramatic sigh. "No one's ever taken the time to tell you that."

"That's not true," Judith argued. "Millicent and Herbert gave me plenty of compliments. They let me know how much they loved me."

"Yes," Frances Catherine agreed. "But the one you most needed acceptance from turned her back on you."

"Don't start in, Frances Catherine," Judith warned. "Mother can't help the way she is."

Frances Catherine snorted. "Is Tekel still roaring drunk every night?"

Judith nodded. "He's drinking during the day now, too," she said.

"What do you suppose would have happened to you if you hadn't had your aunt Millicent and uncle Herbert protecting you when you were so young and vulnerable? I think about such things now that I'm expecting my own child."

Judith didn't know what to say to those remarks. Her silence told her friend to ease up.

"Did you have difficulty leaving?" Frances Catherine asked. "I worried because I knew you would probably be at Tekel's holding. You always have to stay with him for six months at a time, and I couldn't remember exactly when you would move back. I've been fretting over it."

"I was with Tekel but I didn't have any trouble leaving," Judith replied. "Mother had already left for London and the king's court."

"And Tekel?"

"He was sotted when I told him where I was going. I'm not certain he even remembered the next morning. Millicent and Herbert will tell him again if there's need."

She didn't want to talk about her family any longer. There was such sadness in Frances Catherine's eyes, and Judith was determined to find out the reason.

"Are you feeling well? When is the baby due to arrive?"

"I feel fat," Frances Catherine answered. "And I'm guessing I have about eight or nine more weeks before it's time."

Judith took hold of her friend's hand. "Tell me what's wrong."

She didn't have to explain that gentle order. Her friend

understood what she was asking. "If it weren't for Patrick, I would hate it here."

The vehemence in Frances Catherine's voice told Judith she wasn't exaggerating her misery. "Do you miss your father and your brothers?"

"Oh, yes," she answered. "All the time."

"Then ask Patrick to go and fetch them for a nice long visitation."

Frances Catherine shook her head. "I can't ask for anything more," she whispered. "We had to go to the council to get permission for you to come here."

With Judith's prodding, she explained all about the council's power. She told Judith how Iain had interfered when the oligarchy was getting ready to deny her request, and how frightened she'd been during the entire ordeal.

"I don't understand why you would have to go through the council to get permission," Judith remarked. "Even though I'm English, I still don't see the need to have their approval."

"Most of the Maitlands have good reason to dislike the English," Frances Catherine explained. "They've lost family and friends in battles against the English. They hate your King John, too."

Judith lifted her shoulders in a shrug. "Tis the truth most of the barons in England dislike the king." She resisted the urge to make the sign of the cross so she wouldn't burn in purgatory for defaming her overlord. "He's self-serving and has made some terrible mistakes, at least that's what Uncle Herbert tells me."

"Did you know your king was pledged to marry a Scot and then changed his mind?"

"I hadn't heard, but I'm not surprised. Frances Catherine, what did you mean when you said you couldn't ask Patrick for anything more? Why can't he fetch your father?"

"The Maitlands don't like outsiders," she answered. "They don't like me either."

She sounded like a child when she blurted out that

remark. Judith thought that perhaps her delicate condition was the reason for her emotional turmoil. "I'm just as certain everyone likes you."

"I'm not making this up in my mind," she argued. "The women think I'm spoiled and accustomed to having my own way."

"How do you know that?"

"One of the midwives told me so." Tears started down Frances Catherine's cheeks. She wiped them away with the backs of her hands. "I'm so scared inside. I've been scared for you, too. I knew it was selfish of me to ask you to come here."

"I gave you my word years ago that I would come," Judith reminded her. "I would have been hurt if you hadn't sent for me. Don't talk such nonsense."

"But the promise I made you give me . . . that was before I knew I'd end up here," she stammered out. "These people are so . . . cold. I worried they might offend you."

Judith smiled. How like her friend to be so concerned about her well-being. "Frances Catherine, have you always felt like this or did you begin to hate it here after you found out you were expecting?"

Her friend had to consider the question a long minute. "I was happy at first, but it soon became clear to me I didn't fit in. I feel like an outsider. I've been married for over three years now and they still don't consider me a Maitland."

"Why not?"

"Perhaps because I was raised on the border," she answered. "At least that might be part of their reasoning. Patrick was supposed to marry someone else. He hadn't offered for her, but it was assumed he would. Then he met me."

"Have you discussed your unhappiness with Patrick?"

"I did mention it a few times," she said. "My unhappiness was very upsetting. My husband can't make the women like me. I don't want to die here. I wish Patrick would take me back to Papa before the birthing and stay with me until it's over."

"You aren't going to die." Judith nearly shouted that denial. "After all the trouble and embarrassment I've gone through, you damn well better not die."

Frances Catherine was comforted by the anger in her friend's voice. "Tell me about the trouble you've gone through," she demanded, her voice filled with enthusiasm.

"I've spoken to at least fifty midwives in the past two years, and I swear I've memorized every single word they've told me. Millicent was as determined as I was, of course, and she had servants scour the countryside looking for these women. I don't know what I would have done without her assistance."

"Millicent's a dear woman."

"Aye, she is," Judith agreed. "She sends you her love, of course."

Frances Catherine nodded. "Tell me what you learned from all of these midwives."

"To be completely honest with you, at first I heard so many conflicting opinions, I almost lost heart. One would tell me the chamber had to be as hot as purgatory during the laboring, and another would be vehemently in favor of just the opposite. Aye, it was frustrating, Frances Catherine. Then a miracle came about. One morning a midwife named Maude marched into the keep, acting very like she owned the place. She was old, terribly fragile-looking, with stooped shoulders and gnarled hands. She was a sight, all right. I'll confess I had immediate misgivings about her knowledge. I quickly realized how foolish that conclusion was. Frances Catherine, she is the dearest of women. She was full of insight, too, and told me that most of her opinions were based on just plain sense. She's been a midwife for ages and ages, but her methods are really quite modern. She's kept up with all the changes and says she's always interested in hearing about the newest techniques. She's a dedicated midwife. If she hadn't been so old and fragile, I would have begged her to come here with me. The journey would have been too much for her."

"The women would never have allowed her interference," Frances Catherine said. "You don't understand, Judith."

"Then help me understand. Have you spoken to the midwives here about your fears?"

"Good Lord, no," Frances Catherine answered in a rush. "If I told her I was frightened, she'd only make it worse. Her name's Agnes, and I don't want her near me when my time comes. She and another woman named Helen are the only two midwives here. They're both very high- and mighty-acting. Agnes's daughter, Cecilia, is supposed to marry Iain when he gets around to asking, and I think that's the reason Agnes always has her nose in the air. She thinks she's going to become the laird's mother-in-law."

Judith's heart felt as though it had just dropped to the bottom of her stomach. She turned her gaze to the tabletop so Frances Catherine wouldn't notice how upset she was by this news.

Her friend didn't notice. She continued right along with her explanation. "The marriage isn't certain in anyone's mind but Agnes's, and Patrick doesn't believe Iain has any intention of offering for Cecilia."

"Then why does Agnes believe he will?"

"Her daughter is a beautiful woman. Tis the truth she's probably the prettiest woman in the whole clan. It's a shallow reason, but Agnes thinks that because her daughter is so appealing, Iain will eventually want her. Cecilia's dim-witted and can't hold a thought longer than a flea."

Judith shook her head. "Shame on you for saying such cruel things about this woman." She tried to sound as though she meant what she had just said, but ruined the effect completely by bursting into laughter. "A flea, Frances Catherine?"

Her friend nodded. Then she started laughing. "Oh, Judith, I'm so happy you're here."

"I'm just as happy to be here."

"What are we going to do?"

Frances Catherine's change in mood happened so quickly, Judith was quite astonished. She had been laughing just a moment before and was now looking like she was going to cry again.

Maude had told Judith that expectant mothers were prone to emotional outbursts. She had also said that a calm, peaceful frame of mind was imperative for an uncomplicated delivery. Whenever the mother became upset, she was to be soothed as much as possible.

Judith followed that dictate now. She patted Frances Catherine's hand and smiled at her. She tried to act confident. "Do about what? Everything's going to be fine, Frances Catherine."

"Agnes won't let you assist me when my laboring starts. And I won't have that vile woman near me. So what are we going to do?"

"You mentioned another midwife named Helen? What about her?"

"Agnes taught her everything she knows," Frances Catherine replied. "I don't believe I want her near me, either."

"There have to be more midwives here," Judith said. "From the number of cottages and the crowd I spotted when I arrived, I guessed there were nearly five hundred men and women living here."

"I'd guess twice that number," Frances Catherine estimated. "You didn't see all the cottages along the back side of the mountain. Only the warriors are counted, and their number swells to over six hundred at the very least."

"Then there have to be other midwives here," Judith said again.

Frances Catherine shook her head. "Agnes runs things," she explained. "And because I'm the laird's sister-in-law, she will insist on delivering the babe. If there are other midwives, they keep quiet about it. They wouldn't want to get Agnes riled."

"I see."

Judith suddenly felt sick. Panic was beginning to take hold inside. Dear heavens, she wasn't qualified to take on this duty alone. Yes, she had gathered information about the latest birthing methods, but she'd never been allowed to witness an actual delivery, and she felt completely inadequate overseeing Frances Catherine's care.

Why wasn't anything ever easy? Judith had pictured herself mopping her friend's brow during the pains, holding her hand, too, and occasionally whispering "There, there," while the experienced midwife took care of the more necessary duties.

Tears were once again streaming down Frances Catherine's face. Judith let out a little sigh. "Only one thing is certain," she announced. "You're going to have this baby. I'm here to help you, and surely between the two of us, we can solve any problem, no matter how impossible it seems."

Her matter-of-fact tone of voice soothed Frances Catherine. "Yes," she agreed.

"Is it possible to win Agnes over or do we give up on her?"

"We give up," Frances Catherine answered. "She won't change her ways. She's cruel-hearted, Judith. Every chance she gets, she makes horrid remarks about the pain I'm going to have to endure. She likes to tell stories about other difficult birthings, too."

"You mustn't listen to her," Judith said. Her voice shook with anger. She had never heard of anything so appalling. Agnes did sound cruel-hearted. Judith shook her head while she thought about this bleak situation.

"I know what you're doing," her friend whispered.

"You're trying to understand Agnes, aren't you? Once you come up with a reason for her behavior, you'll set out to change it. It won't matter to me," she added. "I don't care if she turns into an angel. She isn't coming near me."

"No, I'm not trying to understand her. I already know why she acts the way she does. She's after power, Frances Catherine. She uses fear and a woman's vulnerability to get what she wants. She feeds on their weakness. Maude told me there are women like her. Nothing I can do will change her attitude, either. Don't you worry. I won't let her near you. I promise."

Frances Catherine nodded. "I don't feel so alone any longer," she confessed. "Whenever I try to talk to Patrick about the birthing, he gets very upset. He's afraid for me, and I always end up comforting him."

"He loves you," Judith said. "That's why he's worried."

"I can't imagine why he loves me. I've been so difficult lately. I cry all the time."

"There isn't anything wrong with that."

Frances Catherine smiled. Judith had always been her champion. She felt very fortunate to have her for her friend. "I've talked long enough about my problems. Now I want to talk about yours. Are you going to try to see your father while you're here?"

Judith shrugged. "It has become a little more complicated. First, I didn't realize how large these Highlands are," she said. "And second, I heard the Macleans were feuding with the Maitlands."

"How did you find that out?"

Judith explained about the discussion she'd had with Isabelle's mother. Frances Catherine was frowning when she finished.

"What she told you is true. The Macleans are enemies."

"My father might be dead."

"He isn't."

"How do you know?"

"I asked Patrick to tell me what the Maclean laird was like, pretending only mild curiosity, of course, and he said he was an old man who had ruled his clan for many years."

"What else did he tell you?"

"Nothing else," Frances Catherine said. "I didn't want to prod him. He'd ask me why I was so interested in the Macleans if I asked too many questions. I gave you my promise never to tell anyone who your father was, and since I made that promise before I married Patrick, I can't tell him. Besides, he'd have heart palpitations. Judith, no one must ever know, not while you're here. It would be dangerous for you."

"Iain would protect me."

"He doesn't know about Maclean," she argued. "I don't know what he would do if he found out."

"I think he would still protect me."

"Lord, you sound certain."

Judith smiled. "I am certain," she said. "But it doesn't matter, does it? Iain's never going to find out. I'm not even sure I want to meet my father. I had hoped to see him from a distance, though."

"And what would that accomplish?"

"My curiosity would be appeased."

"You should talk to him," Frances Catherine insisted. "You don't know if he banished your mother or not. You need to find out the truth. You certainly can't believe your mother's story, not after all the lies you've been told."

"I know for certain he never came to England to get us," Judith argued. Her hand instinctively went to her bosom. Her father's ring was nestled between her breasts on the gold chain, hidden beneath her gown. She should have left the ring at home, but she hadn't been able to do that. She couldn't understand why. Lord, it was a confusion.

She let her hand drop back to the tabletop. "Promise

me that if a way doesn't present itself, you'll let this go. All right?"

Frances Catherine agreed just to placate her friend. She could tell this was a painful discussion for Judith. She decided to change the subject, and began to reminisce about some of their adventures at the festivals.

In no time at all, both women were laughing.

Patrick could hear the sound of his wife's laughter outside. He smiled in reaction. Her friend was already helping. Brodick walked by Patrick's side. He also smiled. "Frances Catherine is pleased to have Judith here," he remarked.

"Aye, she is," Patrick replied.

He was still smiling when he walked into the cottage. His wife remembered her manners this time. She immediately stood up and walked over to her husband. Judith also stood up. She folded her hands together and called her greeting to both warriors.

Brodick carried three of her satchels inside. Patrick carried two. The men dropped the baggage on the bed. "Exactly how long are you planning to stay, lass?" Patrick asked.

He sounded worried. Judith couldn't resist teasing him. "Just a year or two," she answered. He tried not to blanch. She laughed. "I was jesting," she told him then.

"Brodick, you must stay for supper," Frances Catherine said. "Judith, don't jest with Patrick. You've made the color drain from his face."

Both women thought that fact was vastly amusing. They were still laughing when Alex and Gowrie appeared in the opened doorway. The two warriors looked a little sheepish. Frances Catherine immediately invited them to supper too.

Patrick seemed surprised to have visitors. Judith helped her friend finish the preparations for the meal. Frances Catherine had made a thick lamb stew and had baked round loaves of rich, black bread.

The men crowded around the table. Judith and

Frances Catherine served them before squeezing in next to Patrick to eat.

Neither Judith nor Frances Catherine had much of an appetite. They talked to each other all through the supper. Alex did more staring at Judith than eating, Patrick noticed, and when he realized Gowrie hadn't touched his food, either, the reason for their spontaneous visit became clear.

They were both taken with Judith. Patrick had to restrain himself from laughing. The ladies were oblivious to the men. They excused themselves from the table and went over to the bed. Judith gave her friend all the presents she'd made, then blushed with pleasure over Frances Catherine's joy. All but one of the gifts were for the baby, but Judith had also made her friend a beautiful white nightgown with pink and blue roses embroidered along the neckline. It had taken Judith a full month to finish the garment. The work had been worth the effort, for Frances Catherine thought the gown was exquisite.

Since the women weren't paying the men any attention, the men didn't find it necessary to hide their interest. Their gazes were centered on Judith. Patrick noticed that whenever she smiled, so did the soldiers. Brodick's interest surprised Patrick the most because he was usually quite good at keeping his emotions under tight rein.

"What are you grinning about?" Brodick suddenly asked him.

"You," Patrick answered.

Before Brodick could take exception to that honest reply, Judith called out, "Brodick, I've forgotten to take the sweet biscuits over to Isabelle."

"I'll see she gets them," Brodick said.

Judith shook her head. "I want to meet her," she explained. She stood up and walked over to the table. "I have messages to give her from her mother."

"I'll be happy to show you the way," Alex volunteered.

"I'll do it," Gowrie announced in a much firmer voice.

Brodick shook his head. "Isabelle is my sister-in-law," he snapped. "I'll show Judith the way."

Iain had opened the door, and stood there listening to the argument. He was having difficulty believing what he was hearing . . . and seeing. His warriors were acting like lovesick squires while they argued over who would escort Judith.

She didn't have a clue as to their real motives, however. Judith looked confused by all the attention she was getting.

Alex drew Iain's notice. He planted his hands on the tabletop and leaned forward to glare at Brodick. "Isabelle's cottage is close to my uncle's and I was going to stop by there anyway. Therefore, I'll see to this chore of showing Judith the way."

Patrick did laugh then. Everyone seemed to notice Iain at the same moment. Judith's reaction was the most telling to Patrick's way of thinking. The joy in her expression was more than evident.

Iain looked irritated. He barely spared Judith a glance before turning his full attention to his brother. "Now do you understand my reasons?"

Patrick nodded.

Judith and Frances Catherine shared a look. "What reasons, Laird Iain?" Frances Catherine asked.

"Laird Iain?" Judith repeated before Iain could answer the question. "Why don't you just call him Iain?"

Frances Catherine folded her hands together in her lap. "Because he's our laird," she explained.

"He's still your brother," Judith countered. "You shouldn't have to be so formal with him."

Her friend nodded. She looked up at Iain and forced a smile. The warrior was intimidating to her and it took a great deal of effort to stare into his eyes. The man took up the entrance. He ducked under the door overhang, and once he was fully inside, leaned against the corner of the wall and folded his arms across his chest, his stance casual.

"Iain," Frances Catherine began again, grimacing inside over the shiver in her voice. "What reasons do you mean?"

Iain realized his sister-in-law was actually afraid of him. He was quite astonished by that revelation. He forced a mild voice in an effort to ease her fear when he answered her. "Patrick asked that Judith be allowed to stay in the vacant cottage. I've denied his request. Your husband understands my reasons."

Frances Catherine immediately nodded. She wasn't about to argue with her laird. Besides, the arrangement suited her just fine. She wanted Judith to stay with her and Patrick.

"Your guests are leaving now," Iain told his brother.

Alex, Gowrie, and Brodick immediately filed out of the cottage. Iain moved out of their way, then resumed his place near the door. He'd said something to the warriors as they walked past, but his voice was so low, neither Judith nor Frances Catherine could overhear. Patrick heard, though, and his sudden smile indicated he was amused by his brother's remarks.

"Iain, may I please speak to you in private for just a moment?" Judith asked.

"No."

Judith wasn't daunted. There was more than one way to flay a fish. "Patrick?"

"Yes, Judith?"

"I have need to speak to your laird in private. Would you arrange it please?"

Patrick looked as though she'd lost her senses. Judith let out a sigh. She tossed her hair back over her shoulder. "I'm following the chain of command around here. I'm supposed to ask you and you're supposed to ask the laird."

Patrick didn't dare look at Iain. He knew his brother was already riled. The look in his eyes when he'd seen Alex, Gowrie, and Brodick gawking at Judith was one

Patrick had never seen before. If he didn't know better, he would think his brother was actually jealous.

"Iain—" Patrick began.

"No." Iain snapped that denial.

"Lord, you're difficult," Judith muttered.

Frances Catherine let out a sound somewhere between a snort and a gasp. She was still sitting on the side of the bed. She reached up to touch Judith's arm. "You really shouldn't criticize Laird Iain," she whispered.

"Why not?" Judith whispered back.

"Because Ramsey says Iain's a mean son of a bitch when he gets riled," Frances Catherine replied.

Judith burst into laughter. She turned around to look at Iain again, and immediately knew he'd heard Frances Catherine's remark. He wasn't angry, though. Nay, the sparkle in his eyes indicated just the opposite. Patrick looked quite appalled by his wife's loudly whispered comment.

"For the love of God, Frances Catherine—" Patrick began.

"It was a compliment Ramsey was giving," his wife replied. "Besides, you weren't suppose to hear it."

"Who is Ramsey?" Judith asked.

"An incredibly handsome devil," Frances Catherine replied. "Patrick, don't frown at me. Ramsey is handsome. You'll easily recognize him, Judith," she added with a glance in her friend's direction. "He's always surrounded by a crowd of young ladies. He hates the attention, but what can he do? You'll like him, too."

"No, she won't."

Iain made that prediction. He took a step forward. "You'll stay away from him, Judith. Do you understand me?"

She nodded. She didn't care for his surly tone of voice one bit, but she decided not to take issue with him now.

"How do we keep Ramsey away from her?" Patrick wanted to know.

Iain didn't answer him. Judith remembered the chore she wanted to complete before night was full upon them, and picked up Margaret's satchel filled with the sweet biscuits.

"Patrick, would you please ask Iain to show me the way to Isabelle's cottage? I must give her this gift from her mother and relay messages."

"Judith, the man's standing right in front of you. Why don't you ask him?" Frances Catherine asked.

"It's this chain-of-command thing," Judith answered with a wave of her hand. "I have to follow it."

"Come here, Judith."

His voice was soft, chilling. She forced a serene smile and walked over to him. "Yes, Iain?"

"Do you deliberately try to provoke me?"

He waited for her denial. An apology, too. He didn't get either.

"Yes, I do believe I am trying to delibcratcly provoke you."

The look of astonishment on his face was slowly replaced with a fierce frown. He took a step closer to her. She didn't back away. God's truth, she took a step closer to him.

They were just a breath away from touching. She had to tilt her head all the way back to meet his stare. "In all fairness, I think I should point out the fact that you actually provoked me first."

The woman was a temptress. Iain was having difficulty following her explanation. His concentration was centered on her mouth. His own lack of discipline was more appalling to him than her impudent behavior.

He couldn't stay away from her. The woman hadn't even settled in his brother's cottage and he was already looking in on her.

Judith really wished he'd say something to her. His expression didn't give her a hint of what he was thinking. She was suddenly feeling very nervous. She told herself it was only because Iain was such a big man, he seemed to swallow up all the space around him. Standing so close to him didn't ease her discomfort, either.

"I did ask you to please give me a private moment of your time, and you were most abrupt in your denial. Yes, you did provoke me first."

Iain couldn't make up his mind if he wanted to strangle the woman or kiss her. Then she smiled up at him, a sweet, innocent smile that made him want to laugh. He knew he could never touch her in anger, never ever raise a hand against her.

She knew it, too.

She wished she knew what he was thinking. She never should have started this baiting game, either. It was dangerous to tease a mountain wolf, and in her mind Iain, for all his gentle ways, could be even more dangerous than a wild animal. The power radiating from him was nearly overwhelming to her.

She turned her gaze to the floor. "I'm most grateful for all you've done for me, Iain, and I apologize to you if you believe I was trying to rile your temper."

She thought she'd sounded properly contrite. When she glanced up to see his expression, she was surprised to find him smiling.

"You were trying to rile my temper, Judith."

"Yes, I was," she admitted. "But I'm still sorry."

She realized, then, she was clutching the satchel in her arms. Before Iain realized her intent, she skirted her way around him and walked out the doorway.

"She'll knock on every door along the path until someone tells her where Isabelle lives." Frances Catherine made that prediction. "Patrick, would you please go and—"

"I'll go," Iain muttered.

He didn't wait for an argument. His sigh was as loud as the slam of the door when he pulled it closed behind him.

He caught up with Judith just as she was starting down the hill. He didn't say a word to her, but took hold of her arm to force her to stop.

"I made a promise to Margaret, Iain, and I'm going to see it carried through."

Her bluster wasn't needed. Iain was already nodding agreement. "You're going the wrong way. Winslow's cottage is on the other side of the courtyard."

He took her satchel from her and started walking back up the second hill. Judith walked by his side. Their arms brushed against each others, but neither moved apart.

"Iain, now that we're alone—"

His laughter stopped her question. "Why are you amused?"

"We aren't alone," he answered. "I would wager at least twenty of my clan are watching us."

She looked around but didn't see a single person. "You're certain?"

"Yes," he answered in a clipped voice.

"Why are they watching?"

"Curiosity."

"Iain, why are you angry with me? I've already apologized for trying to provoke your temper."

She sounded upset to him. He let out a sigh. He wasn't about to explain his reasons for being angry. Hell, her nearness was damn disturbing to his peace of mind. He wanted to touch her. He wasn't about to admit that, either.

"I'm not angry with you. You place too much importance upon yourself if you believe I would feel anything other than duty to my brother when I watch out for you."

He might as well have struck her. She didn't know what to say in response to his cruel piece of honesty. She realized he was right. She had placed too much importance upon herself to think he would be concerned about her. A puny attraction was one thing; caring was quite another.

Tears filled her eyes. Thankfully, the fading sunlight hid her expression from him. She kept her head bowed and deliberately edged away from his side until there was enough room for two horses between them.

Iain felt lower than a snake's belly. He damned himself for sounding so harsh, even as he wished to God she wasn't so tenderhearted.

He started to apologize, then immediately discarded the idea. Not only was he sure he'd muck that up, too, but also, warriors didn't apologize. Women did.

"Judith . . ."

She didn't answer him.

That quickly, he gave up trying. He had never told anyone, man or woman, he was sorry for his actions, and by God he wasn't about to start now.

"I didn't mean to hurt you."

He couldn't believe he said the words until he'd muttered them. He had to shake his head over his own inexplicable behavior.

Judith didn't acknowledge his apology, and he was thankful for that consideration. She must have guessed from the strangled sound of his voice how difficult it had been for him.

But Judith didn't believe he meant one word of his apology. There wasn't anything for her to forgive anyway, she told herself. He had hurt her feelings, yes, but he had been telling her exactly how he felt.

Iain was acutely relieved when they reached their destination. Yet he hesitated at the threshold. Both he and Judith could hear Isabelle weeping. They heard Winslow's voice as well, and though the words weren't clear, his soothing tone of voice certainly was.

Judith thought they should come back in the morning, but before she could suggest as much, Iain had already knocked on the door.

Winslow opened it. The look of irritation on his face indicated he wasn't happy with the interruption. As soon as he saw Iain, however, his surly look vanished.

Brodick's brother didn't look at all like him, save for the color of his eyes. They were the same intense shade of blue. He was shorter than Brodick, and not nearly as

143

handsome. His hair was a darker blond, unruly with curls, too.

Iain explained his reasons for the visitation, and when he'd finished, Winslow shrugged, then opened the door wide to invite them inside.

The cottage was similar to Patrick's in size, but was filled with clutter of clothes strewn about, and forgotten treachers stacked on top of each other on the table.

Isabelle wasn't much of a housekeeper. The pretty woman was in bed, propped up by a mound of pillows behind her. Her eyes were swollen from crying.

Judith thought she was ill. Her brown hair hung limp around her shoulders and her complexion was as pale as the moon.

"I don't wish to disturb you," Judith began. She took the satchel from Iain and was about to put it on the table when she realized there wasn't room. Since the two stools were also covered with clothing, she settled on placing the satchel on the floor. "Your mother sent a gift for you, Isabelle, messages too, but I'll be happy to come back when you're feeling better."

"She isn't ill," Winslow remarked.

"Then why is she in bed?" Judith asked.

Winslow looked surprised by that question. She thought it was because she'd been impudent asking.

"She's going to have my son any time now," Winslow explained.

Judith turned back to Isabelle. She saw the tears in her eyes. "Are you in labor now?"

Isabelle vehemently shook her head. Judith frowned. "Then why are you in bed?" she asked again, trying to understand.

Winslow couldn't understand why the Englishwoman was asking such foolish questions. He forced a patient voice. "She's in bed so she can conserve her strength."

The midwife Judith put such faith in would have had palpitations over that twisted bit of logic. She smiled at Isabelle before turning to look at her husband again.

"Then why doesn't a warrior conserve his strength before going into battle?"

Winslow raised an eyebrow. Iain smiled. "A warrior must always train for battle," Winslow answered. "He becomes weak and ineffective if he doesn't constantly train. Don't the English follow this dictate?"

Judith shrugged. Her attention had already moved on, for she'd just spotted the birthing stool in the corner near the door. She immediately walked over to get a better look at the contraption.

Winslow noticed her interest and was reminded of a duty he needed to complete. "Iain, would you help me get this outside? It's upsetting to Isabelle," he said in a low whisper. "I'll take it back down to Agnes's home in the morning."

Judith was intrigued by both the design and the craftsmanship. The birthing stool was actually a horseshoe-shaped chair. The circular back was tall, sturdy-looking. The seat of the stool was only a narrow ledge fashioned to support the woman's thighs. Both the wooden handles and the sides were inlaid with gold, and the craftsman had used a clever hand to draw angels along the sides.

She tried to hide her curiosity. "Would you like to see what your mother sent to you, Isabelle?" she asked.

"Yes, please."

Judith carried the satchel over to the bed. She stood by the side, smiling over Isabelle's pleasure.

"Both your mother and your father are feeling well," she said. "Margaret wanted me to tell you your cousin Rebecca is marrying a Stuart in the fall."

Isabelle mopped at the corners of her eyes with a linen square. She made a grimace, clutched the covers with both hands and then let out a low sigh. Beads of perspiration appeared on her brow. Judith picked up the linen cloth she'd dropped, leaned over the bed and mopped the sweat away.

"You aren't feeling well, are you?" she whispered.

Isabelle shook her head. "I ate too much of Winslow's supper," she whispered back. "It was terrible but I was very hungry. I wish he'd let me out of bed. Why are you here?"

The question, asked so casually, caught Judith by surprise. "To give you your mother's gifts and tell you the news from home."

"No, I mean to ask you why you're here in the Highlands," she explained.

"My friend, Frances Catherine, asked me to come," Judith replied. "Why are you whispering?"

The pretty woman smiled. Then Winslow inadvertently ruined her budding good mood.

Iain had opened the door, and Winslow was carrying the birthing chair outside. Isabelle immediately got teary-eyed again. She waited until Iain had pulled the door closed and then said, "Frances Catherine's afraid, too, isn't she?"

"Isabelle, every woman becomes a little frightened before the birthing. Does the chair upset you?"

Isabelle nodded. "I won't use it."

She was getting as worked up as Frances Catherine had been when she talked about the birthing. Judith barely knew Isabelle, but she still felt terribly sorry for her. Her fear was so apparent.

"The chair isn't used for torture," Judith said. "Maude says the birthing mothers are happy to have such comfort. You're fortunate to have one here."

"Comfort?"

"Yes," Judith replied. "She says the chair is made in such a way that the woman's back and legs are nicely supported."

"Who is this Maude?"

"A midwife I know," Judith answered.

"What else did she say?" Isabelle asked. She quit twisting the top of the quilt.

"Maude stayed with me for a good six weeks," Judith

explained. "She gave me a great deal of advice for Frances Catherine."

The clutter in the cottage was driving Judith to distraction, and while she repeated some of the midwife's suggestions, she folded the clothing and put the garments in a neat stack on the foot of the bed.

"You should be up and about," Judith said as she turned to tackle the mess on the table. "Fresh air and long walks are just as important as a peaceful mind."

"Winslow worries I'll fall," Isabelle said.

"Then ask him to walk with you," Judith suggested. "Being cooped up inside all day long would make me daft, Isabelle."

The sound of Isabelle's laughter filled the cottage. "It's making me daft too," she admitted. She pulled back the covers and swung her legs over the side.

"Are you a midwife in England?"

"Good heavens, no," Judith answered. "I'm not even married. I just made it my purpose to get as much information as possible from experienced midwives so I could help Frances Catherine."

"Do you mean to say that in England an unmarried woman can openly discuss this intimate topic?"

Isabelle sounded stunned. Judith laughed. "Nay, it isn't discussed at all, and my mother would be most unhappy if she knew what I was learning."

"Would she punish you?"

"Yes."

"You took quite a risk for your friend."

"She would do the same for me," Judith answered.

Isabelle stared at Judith a long minute, then slowly nodded. "I don't understand such friendship between women, but I envy the trust you have in Frances Catherine. You put yourself at risk for her and tell me she would do the same for you. Yes, I do envy such loyalty."

"Didn't you have friends when you were growing up?"

"Only relatives about," Isabelle answered. "And my

mother, of course. She was sometimes like a friend to me, when I was older and more of a help to her."

Isabelle stood up and reached for her plaid. The top of her head only reached Judith's chin, and her middle seemed to be twice the size of Frances Catherine's.

"Do you have friends here?"

"Winslow is my dearest friend," Isabelle answered. "The women here are kind to me, but we're all kept busy with our chores and there really isn't time to socialize."

Judith watched in amazement as the woman deftly wrapped the long narrow strip of material around and around herself. When she was finished, she was wearing a plaid from shoulders to ankles, with perfectly even pleats that widened over her swollen belly.

"You're very easy to talk to," Isabelle remarked in a shy whisper. "Frances Catherine must be happy to have your company. She needs someone besides Patrick to talk to," she added. "I think she's had a difficult time making her place here."

"Why do you suppose that is?" Judith asked.

"Some of the older women think she's uppity," Isabelle said.

"Why?"

"She keeps to herself," Isabelle explained. "I think she's homesick for her family."

"Are you homesick for your family?"

"At times I am," Isabelle admitted. "But Winslow's aunts have been most kind to me. Would you tell me what other suggestions this midwife had? Does she believe in using the birthing hook?" Isabelle turned to straighten the covers on the bed, but not before Judith saw the fear in her eyes.

"How would you know about such a thing?"

"Agnes showed it to me."

"Good God," Judith whispered before she could stop herself. She took a deep breath to rid herself of her anger. She wasn't there to cause trouble, and knew it wouldn't be at all appropriate to criticize the methods the midwives used here. "Maude doesn't believe in using the birthing hook," she said. She kept her voice even, almost pleasant. "She says it's barbaric."

Isabelle didn't show any reaction to that explanation. She continued to ask Judith questions. Every now and again she'd bite on her lower lip and sweat would break out on her brow. Judith thought the discussion was upsetting her.

Winslow and Iain still hadn't come back inside. When Judith made that mention to Isabelle, she laughed again. "My husband is probably enjoying the peace outside. I've been difficult to get along with lately."

Judith laughed. "It must be a common affliction, Isabelle. Frances Catherine said the exact same thing to me not an hour ago."

"Is she afraid of Agnes?"

"Are you?"

"Yes."

Judith let out a weary sigh. God's truth, she was beginning to be afraid of the woman, too. Agnes sounded like a monster. Did she have no compassion in her heart?

"How much time do you have before your laboring begins?"

She wouldn't look at Judith when she answered. "A week or two."

"Tomorrow we will talk about this again. Would you come to Frances Catherine's home? Perhaps the three of us can find a way to solve this worry about Agnes. Isabelle, I'm completely without experience. I've never even seen a birthing, but I do know that the more information we have, the less chance fear has to catch hold. Isn't that true?"

"You would help me?"

"Of course," Judith answered. "Why don't we go outside now? The fresh air will do you good."

Isabelle was in full agreement. Judith was just reaching for the door when Winslow opened it. He nodded to Judith, then turned to frown at his wife.

"Why are you out of bed?"

"I have need for some fresh air," she answered. "Have you taken the birthing chair back to Agnes yet?"

He shook his head. "I will in the morning."

"Please bring it back inside," she requested. "It will be a comfort for me to have it near."

She smiled at Judith when she gave her husband that explanation. Winslow looked confused. "But you didn't want to look at it," he reminded her. "You said—"

"I've changed my mind," Isabelle interrupted. "I've remembered my manners as well. Good evening, Laird Iain," she called out.

Judith had already walked outside and now stood next to Iain. She refused to look at him. She bowed to Isabelle and Winslow and then started walking back to Frances Catherine's cottage.

Iain caught up with her at the crest. "Winslow and Isabelle both want you to know they're thankful for bringing Margaret's gifts. You cleaned their cottage, didn't you?"

"Yes."

"Why?"

"It needed cleaning." Her words were clipped, cold.

Iain clasped his hands behind his back and continued to walk by her side. "Judith, don't make this more difficult than it already is," he said in a harsh whisper.

She was walking so fast she was almost running. "I don't mean to make anything difficult," she replied. "I'll stay away from you and you'll stay away from me. I'm already over this insignificant, puny, inconsequential attraction. I don't even remember kissing you."

They had reached the cluster of trees in front of the courtyard leading to Frances Catherine's cottage when she told him that outrageous lie.

"The hell you have forgotten," he muttered. He grabbed hold of her shoulders and forced her to turn around. Then he took hold of her chin and pushed her face up.

"What do you think you're doing?" she demanded.

"Reminding you."

His mouth came down on hers then, sealing off any protest she might have wanted to make. And Lord, how he kissed her. His mouth was hot, hungry, and his tongue thrust inside with gentle insistence. She went weak in her knees. She didn't fall down, though. She sagged against him; he wrapped his arms around her waist and pulled her up against him. His mouth slanted over hers again and again, and God help him, he couldn't seem to get enough of her. She returned his kiss with equal passion, perhaps even more, and the last coherent thought she had before his kiss completely robbed her of the ability to think at all was that Iain certainly knew how to rid her of her anger.

Patrick opened the door and let out a snort of laughter at the sight before him. Iain ignored his brother, and Judith was oblivious to everything but the man holding her so tenderly in his arms.

He finally pulled back and looked down with arrogant pleasure at the beautiful woman in his arms. Her mouth was swollen, rosy as well, and her eyes were still misty with passion. He suddenly wanted to kiss her again.

"Go inside now, Judith, while I still have enough discipline to let you."

She didn't understand what he meant by that remark. She didn't understand his frown either. "If you dislike kissing me so much, why do you continue to do so?"

She looked thoroughly disgruntled. He laughed.

She took exception to that reaction. "You may let go of me now," she ordered.

"I already have."

Judith realized she was still clinging to him, and immediately pulled away. She patted her hair back over her shoulder and turned to walk inside. Spotting Patrick lounging against the open doorway, she felt her face heat to a full blush.

"You mustn't make anything out of what you've just

seen," she announced. "Iain and I don't even like each other."

"You could have fooled me," Patrick drawled out.

It would be impolite for her to kick her host, she supposed, and so she gave him a frown instead as she walked past him.

Patrick wasn't finished teasing her yet. "Aye, it seemed to me you two were liking each other a whole lot, Judith."

Iain had turned to go back up the hill. He heard Patrick's remark and immediately turned back. "Let it go, Patrick."

"Wait up," Patrick called out. "I've something to discuss with you," he added as he hurriedly pulled the door closed behind him.

Judith was thankful for the privacy. Frances Catherine was already sound asleep. She was even more thankful for that blessing. Her friend would have plied her with questions if she'd been awake and seen Iain kissing her, and Judith simply wasn't up to answering.

Patrick had placed a tall screen at an angle in the corner of the room behind the table and chairs. There was a narrow bed with a pretty forest-green quilt on top. Her satchels were neatly stacked against one wall next to a narrow chest. A white porcelain pitcher and matching bowl were on top of the chest next to the wooden vase filled with fresh wildflowers.

Frances Catherine had had a hand in arranging the make-do bedchamber. Patrick never would have thought to add flowers. He wouldn't have unpacked her brush and looking glass, either, and both were within easy reach on the corner of the stool on the other side of the bed.

Judith smiled over her friend's thoughtfulness. She didn't realize her hands were still shaking until she tried to undo the latches at the top of her gown. Iain's kiss had done that, she realized, and dear God, what was she going to do about him? From what Frances Catherine had told her about the hatred between the Maitlands and the Macleans, Judith doubted Iain would have touched her if he'd known she was his enemy's daughter.

She remembered she'd told her friend Iain would protect her. Now she felt a desperate need to protect herself from him. She didn't want to love him. Oh, it was all so impossible for her to sort out. She wanted to weep, but she knew crying wouldn't solve any of her problems.

She was too exhausted from the long day and the journey here to think the matter through logically. Problems were always easier to solve in the morning light anyway, weren't they?

Sleep eluded her for a good long while, however. When she was finally able to push the worry about her growing attraction for Iain aside, her mind immediately turned to the worry about Frances Catherine.

Judith kept seeing the look of fear in Isabelle's eyes when she mentioned the midwife's name, and after Judith finally drifted off to sleep, she was locked in a nightmare about birthing hooks and screams.

She was awakened in the dead of the night. When she opened her eyes, she found Iain kneeling on one knee at her side. She reached up, touched the side of his face with her fingertips, and then closed her eyes again. She thought she was having an incredibly realistic dream.

Iain wouldn't quit prodding her. The next time she opened her eyes, she noticed that Patrick was also in the little room. He stood behind Iain. Frances Catherine stood by her husband's side.

Judith turned her attention back to Iain. "Are you taking me home now?"

The question didn't make any sense, but then neither did his presence.

"Winslow asked me to come and get you," Iain explained.

She slowly sat up. "Why?" she asked. She slumped against him and closed her eyes again.

"Judith, try to wake up," Iain commanded in a much stronger voice.

"She's exhausted." Frances Catherine stated the obvious.

Judith shook her head. She pulled the covers up to her chin and held them there. "Iain, this isn't proper," she whispered. "What does Winslow want?"

He stood up before explaining. "Isabelle asks that you come to her. She just started her laboring. Winslow said you have plenty of time. The pains aren't strong yet."

Judith was suddenly wide awake. "Are the midwives there yet?"

Iain shook his head. "She doesn't want them to know."

"She wants you, Judith," Frances Catherine explained.

"I'm not a midwife."

Iain's smile was gentle. "It appears you are now."

Chapter 7

He thought she was going to faint. The color left her face. In a matter of seconds her complexion had turned as white as the gown she wore. She threw the covers off, got out of the bed, and then her knees buckled. He caught her just as she was sinking back to the bed.

Judith was so stunned by his outrageous announcement, she completely forgot about her lack of clothing. The quilt was on the floor. She was wearing only a thin sleeping gown.

The garment had a low scooped neck that wasn't overly revealing, yet was still very provocative to him. Hell, the woman could wear a wheat sack and he'd think she looked appealing. He felt like a cad for noticing. But damn it all, he was a man, and she was a beautiful woman. The gentle swell of her breasts distracted his concentration, and the only reason he reached for the chain she wore around her neck was to try to take his mind off her body.

He lifted the chain and stared down at the gold and ruby ring a long minute. There was something familiar about the design, but Iain couldn't remember if and when he'd ever seen it before. Only one thing was certain in his mind. It was a man's ring and she was wearing it.

"This is a warrior's ring," he said in a low whisper.

"What . . ." She couldn't concentrate on what he was saying to her. She was too busy reeling from his suggestion she become a midwife. The man was daft, but she was still determined to try to make him understand her limitations. "Iain, I can't possibly—"

He interrupted her. "This is a warrior's ring, Judith."

She finally realized he was holding her father's ring. She quickly snatched the piece of jewelry out of his hand and let it drop back down between her breasts.

"For the love of God, who cares about the ring now? Will you please listen to what I'm trying to tell you? I can't be Isabelle's midwife. I don't have any experience."

She was so desperate to make him listen to her, she grabbed hold of his plaid and started pulling on it.

"Who gave you this ring?"

Dear Lord, he wouldn't let up. She wanted to shake some sense into him. Then she realized she was already trying to do just that, and Iain wasn't moving. She gave up. She let go of his plaid and took a step back.

"You told me there wasn't anyone pledged to you back in England. Were you telling me the truth?"

He took hold of the ring again and twisted the chain around his fingers. His knuckles brushed against the side of her breast, once, then again, and he didn't seem at all inclined to stop that intimacy, even when she tried to pry his fingers away.

"Answer me," he commanded.

The man was furious. She was stunned when she realized that fact. "My uncle Tekel gave me the ring," she said. "It belonged to my father."

He didn't look like he believed her. His frown didn't ease at all.

She shook her head. "It doesn't belong to a young man waiting to marry me. I didn't lie to you, so you can quit glaring at me."

Judith didn't feel at all guilty. She hadn't told him the full truth, but Tekel had given her the ring, and Iain never really needed to know he was holding Laird Maclean's prized possession in his hand.

"Then you may keep it."

She couldn't believe his arrogance. "I don't need your permission."

"Yes, you do."

He used the chain to pull her forward. He leaned down at the same time and kissed her hard, thoroughly. When he lifted his head back, she had a bemused look on her face. He was pleased by that reaction.

The sudden sparkle in his eyes was more confusing to her than his ridiculous inquisition about the ring. "I've told you that you can't kiss me whenever you want."

"Yes, I can."

To prove his point, he kissed her again. Judith hadn't recovered from that surprise when he suddenly pushed her behind his back.

"Patrick, Judith isn't dressed for company. Leave."

"Iain, you happen to be inside his home, not yours," Judith reminded him.

"I know where I am," he replied, his exasperation obvious in his voice. "Patrick, get out of here."

His brother didn't move fast enough to suit Iain. He was grinning, too, and that didn't suit Iain at all. He took a threatening step forward. "Do you find my order amusing?"

Judith grabbed hold of the back of Iain's plaid to keep him from going after his brother. It was a puny effort against a man of his size. It was ridiculous behavior on her part, too. She started pushing him instead.

Iain didn't budge. Patrick did. He put his arm around his wife and led her to the other side of the room. She was about to say something to him, but Patrick shook his head.

He softened the order with a wink, then motioned toward the screen with the tilt of his head, a silent message to his wife that he wanted to hear the argument going on. Frances Catherine put her hand over her mouth to keep herself from laughing.

"I would like you to leave," Judith ordered. "Now." Iain turned around to look at her. She snatched the quilt up and held it in front of her. "This isn't proper."

"Judith, it isn't at all proper for you to take that tone with me."

She wanted to scream. She sighed instead. "I'm not happy with your tone either," she announced.

He looked astonished. He almost laughed, but caught himself in time. The woman really needed to understand her position. "I'll wait outside," he announced in a hard voice. "Get dressed."

"Why?"

"Isabelle," he reminded her. "Remember?"

"Oh, God, Isabelle," she cried out. "Iain, I can't—"

"It's all right," he interrupted. "There's plenty of time."

He walked away from her before she could make him understand. Judith muttered a very unladylike expletive. She guessed she was going to have to get dressed so she could go outside and make him listen to her. The ignorant man obviously believed one woman was just as good as another when it came to assisting with a birthing. She was going to set him straight so that Isabelle could get experienced help.

Frances Catherine helped her get dressed. As soon as that chore was completed, she wanted Judith to sit down so she could brush her hair for her.

"For the love of God, Frances Catherine, I'm not going to a festival. Leave my hair alone."

"You heard Iain," her friend replied. "You have plenty of time. A woman's first baby takes long, long hours of pain, and Isabelle has only just begun her laboring."

"How would you know?"

"Agnes told me."

Judith pulled her hair back over her shoulder and

secured it with a ribbon at the base of her neck. "What a lovely bit of information to share with an expectant mother," she muttered.

"The blue ribbon would be prettier," Frances Catherine told her. She tried to substitute it for the pink ribbon Judith had used.

Judith felt as though she was living a nightmare and even her dear friend was part of it. "For heaven's sake, Frances Catherine, if you don't quit poking at me, I swear you won't have to worry about giving birth. I'll strangle you first."

Frances Catherine wasn't at all offended by that empty threat. She let go of Judith's hair and smiled. "Should I wait up for you?"

"Yes . . . no, oh, I don't know," Judith muttered as she headed for the door.

Patrick and Iain were standing in the courtyard. Judith came rushing outside the entrance. She stepped on a stone, muttered something under her breath, and then hurried back inside. She found her shoes under the bed, put them on, and then ran back outside again.

"She seems a little rattled," Patrick remarked.

"Aye, she does," Iain agreed.

"Tell Isabelle I'll be praying for her," Frances Catherine called out.

Iain waited until Judith reached his side, then turned his attention to his brother. "Winslow doesn't want anyone to know about this until it's over."

Patrick nodded agreement.

The mockery had gone far enough. Judith stood there smiling until Patrick pulled the door closed and Frances Catherine couldn't see her. She turned on Iain then.

"I can't do this," she blurted out. "I don't have any experience. You have to understand, Iain."

In her panic to make him listen, she grabbed hold of his plaid and started to tug on it.

"Judith, how did you plan to help Frances Catherine if you—"

She wouldn't let him finish his question. "I was going to mop her brow, damn it, and pat her hand, and whisper 'There, there,' and—"

She couldn't go on. Iain wrapped his arms around her and held her tight. He didn't know what to say to her to help her get over this worry.

"Iain?"

"Yes?"

"I'm scared."

He smiled. "I know."

"I don't want to do this."

"It will be all right."

He took hold of her hand and led the way to Isabelle's cottage. It was so dark she could barely see the path ahead of her.

"I supposed the midwives would do all the work," she whispered as she was being dragged along in his wake. "And I was going to give suggestions. Oh God, how arrogant I am."

They continued along for several more minutes before Judith spoke again. "I won't know what to do."

"Isabelle will know what to do when the time comes. She wants you with her."

"I don't understand why."

Iain smiled. "I understand. You're a very gentle woman, compassionate too. Isabelle needs both right now. Aye, you'll do fine."

"What if it gets complicated?"

"I'll be right outside the door."

Odd, but that promise comforted her. "And you'll come inside if need be and take over? You'll deliver this babe?"

"Hell, no."

He sounded appalled by the very idea. She would have laughed if she hadn't been so frightened.

Judith still didn't understand why Isabelle had chosen her. "If you were going into battle and could only choose one other warrior to go with you, would you take your squire?"

He knew the parallel she was going to make. "Yes."

"Isabelle is like a warrior going into battle and she needs . . . you said yes? You'd really choose an inexperienced squire?" she asked, her voice incredulous.

He laughed. "I would."

She smiled. "You're lying to me to make me feel better. It's all right. It's working. Now tell me another lie. Tell me once again that it's going to be all right. I might believe you this time."

"Judith, if it does become complicated, I'll send someone to get Agnes."

"God help Isabelle then," Judith whispered. "Iain, don't you wonder why she hasn't already sent Winslow to get the midwife?"

He nodded. "I did wonder," he admitted.

Judith told him what she'd learned about the midwife and her assistant. Then she gave him her opinion. Her voice was shaking with fury by the time she'd finished.

She wanted to know what Iain thought about Agnes's conduct, but they'd reached the narrow courtyard in front of Isabelle's cottage and there wasn't time now for a discussion.

Winslow opened the door before Iain had even raised his hand to pound on it. A wave of heat, so intense it felt like it was scorching Judith's face, poured through the opening. Perspiration covered Winslow's brow and fat drops of sweat rolled down from his temples.

It was so unbearably hot inside the cottage, Judith could barely catch her breath. She walked inside the doorway and came to an abrupt stop. She spotted Isabelle sitting on the side of the bed. She was doubled over, huddled beneath several thick quilts, and even from across the room Judith could hear her softly weeping.

In that moment while she stood there staring at

Isabelle, she knew without a doubt that she couldn't walk away from this. She would do whatever was needed to help the woman.

Isabelle's terror tore at Judith's heart.

Iain put his hands on Judith's shoulders. She realized then that he was standing right behind her.

"Winslow, Judith doesn't feel that—"

She stopped him. "I don't feel that the heat in here is helping," she announced. She turned around and looked up at Iain. "Don't worry so," she whispered. "It's going to be all right."

The change in her astonished Iain. There wasn't a hint of panic in her expression or her voice. Judith looked serene . . . and in command.

She slowly walked across the room to stand in front of Isabelle.

"Good Lord, Isabelle, it's as hot as purgatory in here," she announced with forced cheerfulness.

Isabelle didn't look up at her. Judith knelt down on the floor in front of her. She slowly removed the cocoon of covers from Isabelle's head and shoulders. Then she gently tilted her face up so she could look at her.

Tears streamed down Isabelle's cheeks. Her hair was dripping wet too, and hung in limp clumps around her shoulders. Judith brushed her hair back over her shoulder, then mopped her cheeks dry with the edge of the quilt. When she was finished with that motherly task, she took hold of Isabelle's hands.

The fear in Isabelle's eyes made Judith want to weep. She didn't, of course, because her new friend needed her strength now, and Judith was determined to see that she got it. She could weep later, after the two of them had gotten through this frightening experience.

She squeezed Isabelle's hands. "I want you to listen carefully to what I'm going to say to you," she instructed. She waited for Isabelle's nod, then continued. "We're going to do just fine."

"You'll stay with me? You won't leave?"

"I'll stay," she answered. "I promise."

Isabelle nodded.

"How long have you been having these pains?" Judith asked.

"Since early morning," Isabelle answered. "I didn't even tell Winslow."

"Why did you wait?"

"I was hoping the pains would go away," she answered in a low whisper. "And I was worried he wouldn't listen to me and insist on going to get Agnes to help me. It took me a long time to convince my husband to ask Iain for permission to get you."

Tears started down Isabelle's cheeks again. She gripped Judith's hands now.

"Thank you for coming."

"I'm pleased to be here," Judith answered, hoping God would understand and forgive her for not wanting to come here at all. She was still so worried inside, her stomach was aching, and the heat in the room was draining her of her strength.

"Isabelle, it's all right for you to be a little afraid, but you should also be very excited and joyful, too. You're about to bring a new life into this world."

"I would rather Winslow do it."

Judith was so surprised by that remark, she started laughing. Isabelle smiled.

"We'd better get organized," Judith said then. "Is the heat in here comforting to you?"

Isabelle shook her head. Judith stood up and turned to the two men standing at the door. She smiled when she saw the look on Iain's face. The poor man was very ill at ease. He was trying to leave the cottage. Winslow wasn't letting him. Isabelle's husband was blocking the door while he frowned at Judith.

She smiled at him. "Winslow, please pull the furs back from the windows. We need fresh air now."

163

She turned to Iain next. He was reaching for the door latch. She stopped him with her question. "Is that beam of wood above strong enough to hold your weight?"

"It should be sturdy enough," he answered.

He tried to leave again. "Wait," she called out. She hurriedly looked through the piles of linen stacked on the foot of the bed but couldn't find anything long enough to suit her purposes. Then she remembered the plaid. The material was quite long, narrow in width, and perfect for her needs. She took the plaid over to Iain. "Will you please loop this over the beam for me? Test your weight against it, too. I wouldn't want the wood to come crashing down on Isabelle."

"You think to tie her?" Winslow blurted out.

She shook her head. "I want to give Isabelle something to hold on to when she's standing," she explained. "This is for her comfort, Winslow."

The warrior wasn't convinced until his wife nodded. Then he helped Iain see to the chore. When they were finished, the narrow strips of the plaid hung down at equal lengths on both sides of the beam.

Winslow wanted to add another log to the fire. Judith wouldn't let him. She excused both men from the cottage. Winslow hesitated. "I'll be standing right outside the door, wife. If you want me to get Agnes, just call out. I'll hear you."

"I won't be sending for her," Isabelle replied, her voice an angry shiver.

Winslow let out a weary sigh. His worry for his wife was evident. So was his frustration. He threaded his fingers through his hair, took a step toward Isabelle, then stopped. Judith thought he wanted a moment of privacy. She quickly turned around and pretended to be busy poking at the fire with the prod.

She heard whispering behind her. A moment later the sound of the door closing reached her. She went back to Isabelle to get to the chore of preparing her for the birthing. She tried to pull the quilts away, but Isabelle held tight. She was trying to hide under the covers, too.

"Isabelle, are you having a pain now?"

"No."

"Then what is it?"

It took Isabelle a long time to gather enough courage to tell Judith what was wrong. She whispered her confession that her water had broken and she'd ruined the bedding. She sounded ashamed, humiliated. And after she had finished explaining, she burst into tears.

"Please look at me," Judith asked in a gentle voice. She waited until Isabelle finally turned her gaze up to hers, then forced a very matter-of-fact tone of voice. "Giving birth is a miracle, Isabelle, but it's also messy. You're going to have to put your embarrassment aside and be practical about this. Tomorrow you can blush all day long if you want to, all right?"

Isabelle nodded. "You aren't embarrassed?" she wanted to know.

"No," Judith answered.

Isabelle looked relieved. Her face was still bright red, and Judith wasn't certain if it was from blushing or from the horrible heat inside the cottage.

The next hour was spent on necessary preparations. Judith kept up a constant chatter while she stripped the bed, bathed Isabelle from head to foot, washed and dried her hair, and helped her into a fresh nightgown. All those duties were performed in between the growing contractions.

Maude had told Judith that she'd learned over the years to give the mothers as many instructions as possible. She even made some up just to keep them occupied. She explained that if the woman had plenty to do, she felt more in control of the situation, and the pain. Judith followed that advice now, and it really did seem to help Isabelle. The contractions were strong, and coming close together. Isabelle found she preferred standing during the pains. She wrapped the ends of the hanging plaid around her waist and held on tight. She had moved from whimpers to low, gut-wrenching groans. Judith felt completely helpless during the pains. She tried to soothe her with words of praise, and when Isabelle asked, she rubbed her lower back to ease the ache.

The last hour was the most grueling. Isabelle became extremely demanding. She wanted her hair braided, and she wanted it braided now. Judith didn't even think about arguing with her. The sweet-tempered woman turned into a raving shrew, and when she wasn't bellowing orders, she was blaming Winslow for causing her this unbearable pain.

The unreasonable storm didn't last long. Judith's prayers were answered, too. The delivery wasn't complicated. Isabelle decided to use the birthing stool. She let out a blood-chilling scream, then another and another, while she beared down. Judith knelt on the floor in front of her, and when Isabelle wasn't gripping the leather handles built into the sides of the stool, she was gripping Judith's neck. She would have strangled Judith without even noticing, and Lord, she was a strong woman. It took all Judith's strength to pry her fingers away so she could draw a breath.

A fine baby boy was born minutes later. Judith suddenly needed five extra pairs of hands. She wanted to call to Winslow to come inside to help. Isabelle wouldn't hear of it. Between her laughter and her tears, she explained she wasn't about to let her husband see her in such an undignified position.

Judith didn't argue with her. Isabelle was weak but radiant. She held her son in her arms while Judith took care of the other necessary matters.

The baby appeared to be healthy. His cries were certainly lusty enough. Judith was in awe of the little one. He was so tiny, so perfect in every way. She counted to make certain he had all his fingers and toes. He did, and she was nearly overcome with emotion over that miracle.

She wasn't given time to fully react to the wonderful event, however, as there was still work to be done. It took Judith another hour to get Isabelle cleaned up and settled in bed. Both she and her son had been bathed. The infant was wrapped in a soft white blanket and then covered with his father's woolen plaid. He was sound asleep by the time she finished taking care of him. She placed him in the crook of Isabelle's arm.

"Before I fetch Winslow, I have one more instruction to give you," Judith said. "I want you to promise you won't let anyone . . . do anything to you tomorrow. If Agnes or Helen want to put packing inside, you mustn't let them."

Isabelle didn't understand. Judith decided she would have to be more blunt. "Some of the midwives I spoke to in England believed in packing the birthing canal with ashes and herbs. Some even used dirt to form a paste. Maude convinced me that the packing does more damage than good, but the ritual is dictated by the Church, and what I'm asking you could get you into trouble. . . ."

"I won't let anyone touch me," Isabelle whispered. "If anyone asks, perhaps it would be better for me to pretend that you've already taken care of the matter."

Judith let out a sigh of relief. "Yes," she said. "We'll pretend that I've already taken care of the chore," she added as she adjusted the covers at the bottom of the bed.

She glanced around the room to make certain she had everything cleaned up, nodded with satisfaction, and then went to fetch Isabelle's husband.

Winslow was waiting outside the door. The poor man looked horribly ill. "Is Isabelle all right?"

"Yes," Judith answered. "She's ready to see you."

Winslow didn't move. "Why are you weeping? Is something wrong?"

Judith hadn't realized she was crying until he'd asked her that question. "Everything's fine, Winslow. Come inside now."

She moved out of his way in the nick of time. Winslow was suddenly overcome with eagerness to get to his family. The initial meeting between father and son should be a private affair, and Judith wasn't going to linger. She pulled the door closed and leaned against it.

She was suddenly overcome with exhaustion. The emotional ordeal she'd been through had drained her of her strength and her composure. She was shaking like a leaf in a windstorm.

"Are you finished here?"

Iain asked that question. He was standing at the end of the narrow walkway, leaning against the stone ledge. His arms were folded across his chest in a relaxed stance. He looked rested to her.

She thought she probably looked like hell. "I'm finished here for the time being," she answered. She started walking toward him. The night breeze felt wonderful against her face, but it was making her trembling increase. Her legs were shaking so much they could barely support her.

Judith felt like she was falling apart inside, and took a deep breath in an effort to regain control. The only saving grace was that Iain would never know how close she was to breaking down. Such weakness, even in a woman, would surely disgust him. It would be a humiliation for her, too, to weep in front of him. She did have some pride after all. She'd never needed to lean on anyone else, and she wasn't about to lean on anyone now.

She took a deep, cleansing breath. It didn't help. The shivers increased. She told herself she was going to be all right; she wouldn't disgrace herself. She'd gone through a frightening ordeal, yes, but she had gotten through it, and she could certainly get back to her own bed before she completely lost her dignity and started in sobbing and gagging and God only knew what else.

It was a logical plan to Judith, but her mind was telling

her one thing and her heart was insisting upon another. She needed privacy now, yet at the same time she desperately wanted Iain's comfort, his strength. She'd used all hers up tonight. Heaven help her, she needed him.

It was an appalling realization. She hesitated for the barest of seconds. And then Iain opened his arms to her. She lost the battle then and there. She started running. To him. She threw herself against his chest, wrapped her arms around his waist and burst into uncontrollable sobs.

He didn't say a word to her; he didn't have to. His touch was all she needed now. Iain was still leaning against the ledge. Judith stood between his legs with her head tucked under his chin, crying without restraint until she'd soaked his plaid. She muttered incoherent phrases between her sobs, but he couldn't make any sense out of what she was saying to him.

He thought the storm was almost over when she started hiccuping. "Take deep breaths, Judith," he instructed.

"Please leave me alone."

It was a ridiculous order, considering that she had a death grip on his shirt. Iain rested his chin on the top of her head and tightened his hold on her.

"No," he whispered. "I'm never going to leave you alone."

Odd, but that denial made her feel a little better. She mopped her face with his plaid, then sagged against him again.

"Everything went well, didn't it?" Iain already knew the answer to that question. The radiant smile on her face when she'd opened the door for Winslow had told him all was well, but he thought that if she was reminded of the happy outcome, she might calm down enough to get rid of this unreasonable reaction.

Judith didn't want to be reasonable yet. "As God is my

witness, Iain, I'm never going through that again. Do you hear me?"

"Hush," he replied. "You'll wake England."

She didn't appreciate his jest. She did lower her voice, though, when she told him her next vow. "I'm never going to have a baby. Never."

"Never's a long time," he reasoned. "Your husband might want a son."

She shoved herself away from him. "There isn't going to be a husband," she announced. "I'm never getting married, either. By God, she can't make me."

He pulled her back into his arms and shoved her head down on his shoulder. He was determined to comfort her whether she wished it or not. "Who do you mean when you say she can't make you?"

"My mother."

"What about your father? Won't he have something to say about a marriage?"

"No," she answered. "He's dead."

"But the grave was empty, remember?"

"How would you know about the grave?"

He let out a sigh. "You told me."

She remembered then. She'd torn the headstone down and hadn't had enough sense not to boast about it to the Scots. "In my heart, the man's as good as dead."

"Then I needn't be concerned about that complication?"

She didn't answer him because she didn't have the faintest idea what he was talking about. She was too weary to think straight now, too.

"Judith?"

"Yes?"

"Tell me what this is really all about."

His voice was soft, coaching. She started crying again. "I could have killed Isabelle. If there had been any problems, I wouldn't have known what to do. She was in such terrible pain. No woman should have to go through that. And the blood, Iain," she added, her words tripping over themselves now. "There was so much blood. Dear God, I was scared."

Iain didn't know what to say to her. They had all asked an incredible amount from her. She was such an innocent, too. Hell, she wasn't even married, and yet they'd demanded she deliver a baby. He wasn't even certain if she knew how Isabelle had conceived the babe. Judith had risen to the challenge thrust upon her, however. She'd shown compassion, strength, and intelligence, too. The fact that she was so frightened made her victory all the more amazing in Iain's mind.

Her unhappiness bothered him, and he felt it was his duty to help her get through this upset.

He decided to try praise first. "You should be very proud of what you accomplished tonight."

She gave him an inelegant snort.

He tried logic next. "Of course you were frightened. I would imagine that would be a normal reaction for one of your inexperience. You'll get over it."

"No, I won't."

He tried intimidation as a last resort. "Damn it, Judith, you are going to get over this and you are going to have sons."

She pushed herself away from him again. "How like a man not to mention daughters."

Before he could respond to that remark, she poked him in the chest. "Daughters aren't important, are they?"

"I would make room for daughters, too."

"Would you love a daughter as much as a son?" she asked.

"Of course."

Because he'd answered her so quickly, without wasting any time at all to think about it, she knew he meant what he said. The bluster went out of her anger. "I'm pleased to hear this," she said. "Most fathers don't feel the same way."

"Does yours?"

She turned around and started walking back to Frances Catherine's cottage. "As far as I'm concerned, my father's dead."

He caught up with her, grabbed hold of her hand, and then took over the lead. She glanced up at him, saw his frown, and immediately asked, "Why are you angry?"

"I'm not angry."

"You're frowning."

"Damn it, Judith, I want you to admit you'll marry."

"Why?" she asked. "My future isn't any concern of yours. Besides, my mind's set, Iain Maitland."

He stopped abruptly and turned to her. He grabbed hold of her chin, leaned down and whispered, "My mind's set, too."

His mouth covered hers. She grabbed hold of him so she wouldn't fall over. Her mouth opened for him. He growled low in his throat and deepened the kiss. His tongue thrust inside to mate with hers. He wanted to devour her softness.

He didn't want to stop with one kiss, either. When he realized that fact, he immediately pulled away. Judith was too innocent to realize her own jeopardy. He wouldn't take advantage of the trust she had in him. That truth didn't stop him from thinking about it, though.

He shook his head to clear it of the erotic fantasies going through his mind, then grabbed hold of Judith's hand again and dragged her behind him.

She had to run to keep up with his long-legged stride. He didn't say another word to her until they'd reached his brother's home. Judith had her hand on the latch, but he blocked it with his arm. She decided then that he wasn't quite through confusing her.

"No matter how horrible this birthing was, in time you'll get over it." She looked up at him with the most astonished expression on her face. He nodded to let her know he meant what he'd just said. "That's an order, Judith, and you will obey it."

He nodded again while he opened the door for her. She didn't move. She continued to look up at him in confusion. "Horrible? I never said it was horrible."

It was his turn to look confused. "Then what the hell was it?"

"Oh, Iain, it was beautiful."

Her face was radiant with joy. Iain shook his head in confusion. He didn't think he was ever going to understand her.

He took his time walking home. His thoughts were centered on Judith. What was he going to do with her?

He'd reached the doors of the keep when the picture of the warrior's ring she wore popped into his mind.

Where the hell had he seen it before?

Chapter 8

There was hell to pay for her interference. The priest arrived on Frances Catherine's doorstep the following afternoon and requested an immediate audience with the Englishwoman.

Both the seriousness in Father Laggan's voice and the look on his face indicated trouble was brewing. He shifted to the side of the stoop while he waited for her agreement to fetch Judith. Frances Catherine spotted Agnes standing a little distance behind him. She understood the reason for the audience then.

Agnes looked quite smug. Frances Catherine's worry increased tenfold. She stalled for time so she could find her husband. Patrick would stand up for Judith, and from the look on Agnes's face, she knew Judith would need someone in her corner.

"My friend was up most of the night, Father, and is still sleeping. I'll be happy to wake her, but she will need a few minutes of privacy to get dressed."

Father Laggan nodded. "If you would ask her to meet me at Isabelle's cottage, I'll go on along now."

"Yes, Father," Frances Catherine whispered. She made an awkward curtsy before shutting the door in his face.

She shook Judith awake. "We're in trouble," she announced. "God, Judith, roll over and open your eyes. The priest was here . . . with Agnes," she stammered out. "You have to get dressed now. They're waiting for you at Isabelle's home."

Judith let out a groan and finally rolled onto her back. She brushed her hair out of her eyes and sat up. "Is Isabelle ill? Is she bleeding again?"

"No, no," Frances Catherine rushed out. "I'm guessing she's fine. She . . . Judith, you sound horrible. What's the matter with your voice? Are you coming down with something?"

Judith shook her head. "I'm all right."

"You sound like you swallowed a frog."

"I haven't," Judith replied. "Quit worrying about me," she added with a yawn.

Frances Catherine nodded. "You have to get dressed now. Everyone's waiting for you at Isabelle's home."

"You already told me that," Judith replied. "I'm waiting to find out why. If Isabelle isn't ill, why do they want me?"

"Agnes," Frances Catherine announced. "She's bent on making trouble. Get up now. I've got to find Patrick. We need his assistance."

Judith caught her friend just as she was opening the door. "You can't go running after Patrick in your condition. You'll fall down and break your neck."

"Why are you so calm about this?"

Judith shrugged. She opened her mouth to yawn again. That action made her throat hurt. Puzzled, and still half asleep, she walked across the room and picked up Frances Catherine's looking glass. Her eyes widened in astonishment when she saw the dark bruises covering her throat. No wonder it hurt to move her neck. Her skin was swollen and looked as though it had been painted with black and blue oil.

"What are you doing?"

Judith immediately pulled her hair forward to hide the marks from Frances Catherine. She didn't want her to know Isabelle had done the damage. She would demand details then, and Judith would have to mention the pain the woman was enduring at the time. No, it was best to cover the bruises until they faded away.

She put the looking glass down and turned to smile at Frances Catherine. "After I get dressed, I'll go find Iain," she explained.

"Aren't you at all worried?"

"Perhaps just a little," Judith admitted. "But I'm an outsider, remember? What can they do to me? Besides, I haven't done anything wrong."

"That might not matter. Agnes is good at twisting things around. Since she dragged our priest into this, I think she's going to make trouble for Isabelle, too."

"Why?"

"Because Isabelle asked for you to attend her," Frances Catherine explained. "Agnes will want to get even over that insult." She started pacing in front of the hearth. "I'll tell you what they can do. They can go before the council and ask that you be sent back home. If they do, and the council agrees, by God, I'm going with you. I swear I am."

"Iain won't let them send me home before you have your baby," Judith answered. She felt quite certain of that fact. He'd be breaking his word to his brother if he took her back now, and Iain had too much integrity to ever do that. "You mustn't get upset, Frances Catherine. It isn't good for the baby. Now sit down while I get dressed."

"I'm going with you."

"To England or to find Iain?" Judith called out from behind the screen.

Frances Catherine smiled. Her friend's calm attitude soothed her own. She sat on the side of the bed and folded her hands together over her stomach. "We always did get into trouble when we were together," she called out. "I should be accustomed to it by now."

"No," Judith returned. "We didn't get into trouble. You got me into trouble. I'm the one who got my bottom pounded all the time. Remember?"

Frances Catherine laughed. "You've got it all upside down in your mind. I'm the one who got pounded, not you."

Judith put on her pale gold gown because the neckline was higher than the other gowns she'd packed. The bruises on her neck were still visible, though.

"Do you have a shawl or a lightweight cloak I could borrow?"

Frances Catherine gave Judith a pretty black shawl and she used that to hide the marks. When she was finally ready to leave, her friend walked outside with her.

"Try not to worry about this," Judith instructed. "I shouldn't be gone too long. I'll tell you everything that happened, too."

"I'm going with you."

"No, you're not."

"What if you can't find Patrick or Iain?"

"Then I'll go to Isabelle's by myself. I don't need a man to speak up for me."

"You do here," Frances Catherine replied.

The argument was interrupted when Frances Catherine spotted Brodick coming up the hill. She waved to the warrior, and when he didn't notice her, she put two fingers in her mouth and let out an ear-piercing whistle. Brodick immediately turned his mount toward them.

"Patrick hates it when I whistle," Frances Catherine confessed. "He doesn't think it's ladylike."

"It isn't," Judith said. "It's effective, though," she added with a smile.

"Do you still remember how? My brothers would be disappointed if they thought you'd forgotten their important training."

Judith laughed. "I still remember how," she said.

"Brodick's a handsome man, isn't he?" she remarked then. The surprise in her voice indicated she had only just realized that fact.

"You were in the man's company for almost ten days and you're only just noticing he's handsome?"

"Iain was also with me," Judith reminded her. "And he tends to overwhelm everyone else around him."

"Aye, he does."

"What a magnificent horse," Judith announced, hoping to turn the topic away from Iain. She wasn't ready for Frances Catherine to question her about her relationship with the laird, for in truth she didn't understand her own feelings well enough to answer any questions.

"The horse belongs to Iain, but he lets Brodick drive him every now and again. The stallion has a horrible disposition, and that's probably why they like him. Don't get too close, Judith," she shouted when her friend hurried forward to greet Brodick. "The surly mount will stomp on you if he gets a chance."

"Brodick won't let him," Judith called back. She reached the warrior's side and smiled up at him. "Do you know where Iain is?"

"He's up at the keep."

"Will you please take me to him?"

"No."

She pretended she didn't hear his denial. She put her hand up to his and kept right on smiling for Frances Catherine's benefit while she whispered, "I'm in trouble, Brodick. I need to speak to him."

She hadn't even gotten the words out of her mouth before she was settled on his lap. He goaded the stallion into a full gallop. Minutes later he was assisting her to the ground in the center of the barren courtyard in front of the huge keep.

"Iain's with the council," Brodick told her. "Wait here, I'll go get him."

He tossed her the reins to his mount and then went inside.

The stallion really was surly-natured. It was a struggle to keep him from bolting away. She wasn't intimidated by his snorts of bluster, though, for she had been taught how to handle a horse from a very early age by a man she considered to be the finest stable master in all of England.

Judith waited a long while before her patience ran out. In the back of her mind was the worry that the priest would have his mind set against her because she hadn't hurried to do his bidding.

She didn't want Isabelle to fret, either. Isabelle might think she was going to leave her to face the inquisition alone.

She decided she couldn't waste any more time. She soothed the horse with honeyed words of praise as she mounted him, then nudged him into a trot back down the hill. She made one wrong turn, had to backtrack, and reached Isabelle's cottage a few minutes later. There was a crowd gathered outside the door. Winslow stood on the doorstep. He looked furious . . . until he spotted her. Then he looked quite stunned.

Didn't he believe she would answer the priest's summons? She decided he didn't. That chafed her pride a little, which really was a ridiculous reaction, she told herself, because Winslow didn't know her well enough to form any kind of opinion of her.

The stallion didn't like the crowd any better than she did. He tried to rear up and sidestep at the same time. Judith's concentration was focused on calming the stubborn beast.

Winslow took over the task. He grabbed hold of the reins and forced the horse to stop misbehaving.

"Iain actually allowed you to ride this mount?" he asked, his voice incredulous.

"No," she answered. She adjusted the shawl around her neck, then dismounted. "Brodick was riding him."

"Where is my brother?"

"He went inside the keep to fetch Iain. I did wait, Winslow, but neither one came back out."

"Only Iain and Brodick have ever been able to ride this spirited horse," he said. "You'd best be prepared to catch hell when they hunt you down."

She couldn't tell if he was jesting with her or giving her a worry. "I didn't steal the horse, I just borrowed him," she said, defending herself. "Am I about to catch hell from the priest as well?" She added her question in a low whisper.

"It appears someone's going to," he answered. "Come inside. Isabelle will worry until this is resolved."

The warrior took hold of her elbow and escorted her through the silent crowd of onlookers. The group was openly staring at her, but they didn't seem hostile to her, only curious. She kept her expression as serene as possible. She even managed to smile.

She had trouble maintaining that cheerful facade when the priest came into the doorway. He was frowning at her. She prayed his irritation was due to the fact that she was tardy and not because he had already made up his mind to make trouble.

Father Laggan had thick silver hair, a hawklike nose, and a complexion that had weathered into deep creases over his years of outdoor living. He was as tall as Winslow, but as thick as a board. He wore a black cassock and a wide strip of plaid across one shoulder. The material was secured by a rope belt around his waist. The colors of his plaid were different from the Maitland colors, indicating the priest hailed from another clan. Didn't the Maitlands have their own cleric in residence? Judith decided to put that question to Frances Catherine.

As soon as the priest appeared in the doorway, Winslow let go of her elbow. She rushed forward and stopped at the bottom of the stoop. She bowed her head in submission and made a curtsy. "Pray forgive me for taking so long to get here, Father. I know how valuable your time must be, but I had difficulty finding my way here. There are so many pretty cottages along the hill and I took a wrong turn."

The priest nodded. He looked pleased with her apology. He didn't smile, but he quit frowning. Judith took that as a good sign.

"Winslow, perhaps it would be better if you waited outside until this is finished," the priest suggested in a voice raspy with age.

"Nay, Father," Winslow replied. "My place is with my wife."

The priest agreed with a slow nod. "You will try not to interfere," he ordered.

He turned his attention to Judith again. "Please come inside with me. I would like to ask you a few questions about what took place here last night."

"Certainly, Father," she answered. She lifted the hem of her skirt and followed him through the doorway.

She was surprised to see how many people were gathered inside the cottage. There were two men and three women seated at the table, all elderly, and two more women standing together in front of the hearth.

Isabelle was sitting on a stool next to the bed. She held her son in her arms. Judith hadn't been too worried about her audience with the priest until she saw the look on Isabelle's face. The poor woman looked terrified.

Judith hurried over to her. "Isabelle, why are you out of bed? You need your rest after the ordeal you went through last night." Winslow stood right beside Judith. She took the baby from Isabelle and then moved back a step. "Please help her get back into bed, Winslow."

"Did Isabelle go through an ordeal, then?" Father Laggan asked.

Judith was so taken aback by the question, she didn't soften her reply. "She bloody well did, Father."

The priest raised his eyebrows over the vehemence in her tone of voice. He lowered his head, but not before Judith detected a look of relief on his face.

She didn't know what to make of that. Was the priest

on Isabelle's side? Lord, she hoped so. Judith looked down at the beautiful infant in her arms to make certain she hadn't awakened him, then turned her gaze back to Father Laggan. In a much softer voice she said, "I mean to say, Father, that Isabelle should really be resting now."

The priest nodded. He quickly introduced Winslow's relatives seated at the table, then motioned to the two women standing side by side in front of the hearth.

"Agnes be the one on the left," he said. "Helen stands next to her. They are your accusers, Lady Judith."

"My accusers?"

She'd sounded incredulous. She couldn't help that. She was incredulous. A slow anger began to seethe inside her. She was able to hide that reaction, however.

Judith turned to look at the two troublemaking women. Helen took a step forward and gave Judith a quick nod. She wasn't a very attractive woman. She had brown hair and eyes to match. She seemed nervous, if her fisted hands were any indication, and she couldn't meet Judith's stare long.

Agnes was a surprise to Judith. From the horror stories she'd heard about the midwife, she expected her to look like a shrew, or at the very least an old hag with a wart on the end of her nose. She wasn't either of those, however. In truth, Agnes had the face of an angel, and the most magnificent green eyes Judith had ever seen. The color was as brilliant as green fire. Age had treated her kindly. There were only a few paltry wrinkles on her face. Frances Catherine had told Judith that Agnes had a daughter ready to marry Iain, and that meant the midwife had to be as old as Judith's own mother. Yet Agnes had been able to retain a youthful skin and build. She hadn't spread at all around her middle the way most older women did.

Out of the corner of her eyes Judith saw Isabelle reach up and take hold of Winslow's hand. Her own anger intensified. A new mother shouldn't have such turmoil.

Judith carried the baby over to Winslow, transferred him into his father's arms, and then turned and walked back to the center of the room. She faced the priest, deliberately giving her back to the midwives.

"What are these questions you have for me, Father?"

"We didn't hear any screaming."

Agnes blurted out that announcement. Judith refused to acknowledge her outrageous remark. She kept her attention on the priest and waited for him to explain.

"Last night," Father Laggan began. "Both Agnes and Helen have let it be known they didn't hear any screaming. They live close by, Lady Judith, and believe they should have heard something."

He paused to clear his throat before continuing. "Both midwives sought me out to voice their concern. Now then, as you most certainly know, according to the teaching of our Church, and your Church as well, as your King John still follows the rules set down by our holy fathers—"

He suddenly stopped. He seemed to have lost his train of thought. Several minutes passed in silence while everyone waited for him to continue, and finally Agnes stepped forward. "The sins of Eve," she reminded the priest.

"Yes, yes, the sins of Eve," Father Laggan said in a weary voice. "There you have it, Lady Judith."

She didn't have a clue as to what he was talking about. Her confusion was evident in her gaze.

The priest nodded. "The Church holds that the pain a woman endures during the birthing is a necessary and a fitting retribution for the sins of Eve. Women are saved through this pain and suffering. If it is decided Isabelle didn't have sufficient pain, well then . . ."

He didn't go on. His pained expression told her he didn't want to expound on that point of Church law.

"Well then what?" she asked, determined to make him give her the full explanation.

"Isabelle will be condemned by the Church," Father Laggan whispered. "The babe as well."

Judith was so sickened by what she was hearing, she could barely think straight. And Lord, she was furious. It all made sense to her now. The midwives weren't out to get her; nay, they wanted Isabelle punished and were cleverly using the Church to accomplish their goal. It wasn't just a question of dented pride, either. It was far worse. Their position of power over the women in the clan had been shaken, and this condemnation by the Church would serve as a chilling message to the other expectant mothers.

Their vindictiveness was so appalling to Judith, she wanted to scream at them. Such behavior wouldn't help Isabelle, however, and for that reason alone she kept silent.

"You are familiar with the Church's ruling concerning the sins of Eve, aren't you, Lady Judith?" the priest asked.

"Yes, of course," she answered. It was a blatant lie, but Judith couldn't be bothered about that now. She wondered what other rules Maude had failed to mention to her, even as she struggled to hold on to what she hoped was a very serene expression.

The priest looked relieved. "I ask you now, Lady Judith, if you did anything last night to mitigate Isabelle's pain?"

"No, Father, I did not."

"Then Isabelle must have done something," Agnes shouted. "Or the Devil had a hand in this birthing."

One of the two men seated at the table started to stand. The look of fury on his leathered face was frightening.

Winslow took a step forward at the same time. "I will not allow such talk in my house," he bellowed.

The elderly man at the table nodded, obviously satisfied Winslow had spoken up, and then sat down again.

The infant let out a shrill cry of distress. Winslow was in such a rage he didn't seem to notice Isabelle was trying to take the baby out of his arms. He took another step toward the midwives.

"Get the hell out of my house," he ordered in another bellow.

"I don't like this any more than you do," Father Laggan announced. His voice was heavy with sadness. "But it needs to be resolved."

Winslow was shaking his head. Judith walked over to him. She put her hand on his arm. "Winslow, if you will allow me to explain, I believe I can clear up this nonsense in quick time."

"Nonsense? You dare call this serious matter nonsense?"

Agnes asked that question. Judith refused to acknowledge her. She waited until she'd received Winslow's nod of agreement before turning back to the priest. Winslow walked back over to the side of the bed and gave his son to Isabelle. The infant was ready to be soothed back to sleep, and immediately quit crying.

Judith faced the priest again. "Isabelle was in terrible pain," she announced in a hard voice.

"We didn't hear her," Agnes called out.

Judith continued to ignore her. "Father, do you think to condemn Isabelle because she tried to be so courageous? She did scream, several times in fact, but not with every pain, because she didn't want to distress her husband. He was waiting right outside the door and she knew he could hear her. Even in her misery, she was thinking of him."

"Are we to take this Englishwoman's word on this?" Agnes challenged.

Judith turned to the group of relatives seated at the table. She addressed her next remarks to them. "I only met Isabelle yesterday, and I therefore admit to you that I don't know her very well. Yet I judged her to be an extremely sweet-tempered woman. Would you say that judgment was a fair evaluation?"

"Aye, it was," a dark-haired woman announced. She

turned to glare at the midwives when she added, "She's as kind and gentle as they come. We're blessed to have her in our family. She's God-fearing, too. She wouldn't deliberately do anything to soften her pain."

"I also would agree Isabelle is a very gentle woman," the priest interjected.

"That doesn't have anything to do with this question," Agnes snapped. "The Devil—"

Judith deliberately interrupted when she addressed the group at the table again. "Would it also be fair to say Isabelle wouldn't deliberately hurt anyone? That her sweet disposition wouldn't allow such conduct?"

Everyone nodded. Judith turned back to Father Laggan. She removed the shawl from around her neck. "Now I will ask you, Father, if you believe Isabelle suffered enough."

She lifted her hair back over her shoulders and tilted her head to one side so the priest could see the swelling and the marks on her neck.

His eyes widened in surprise. "Holy Mother of God, did our sweet Isabelle do this to you?"

"Yes," Judith answered. And thank God she did, she thought to herself. "Isabelle was in such agony during the birthing, she grabbed hold of me and wouldn't let go. I doubt she even remembers. I had to pry her fingers away, Father, and try to make her take hold of the handles on the birthing stool."

The priest stared at Judith a long minute. The relief in his gaze warmed her heart. He believed her.

"Isabelle suffered enough for her Church," the priest announced. "We'll have no more talk about this."

Agnes wasn't about to give up so easily. She hurried over with a linen cloth she'd pulled from the sleeve of her gown. "This could be trickery," she said in a near shout. She grabbed hold of Judith's arm and tried to wipe the marks away from her throat.

Judith winced against the pain. She didn't try to stop

the torture, however, guessing that if she did, the woman would start the rumor she had used trickery, such as colored oils, to stain her skin.

"Get your hands off her."

Iain's roar filled the cottage. Agnes jumped at least a foot. She bumped into the priest; he jumped, too.

Judith was so happy to see Iain, tears filled her eyes. The urge to run to him fairly overwhelmed her.

He kept his gaze on her when he ducked under the overhang and walked inside. Brodick was right behind him. Both warriors looked fighting mad. Iain stopped when he was just a foot or two away from Judith. He slowly looked her over from head to feet to satisfy himself she hadn't been injured.

She was immensely thankful she'd been able to hold on to her composure. Iain would never know how upsetting this audience had turned out to be. Judith had already humiliated herself quite thoroughly last night when she had wept all over the man, and just looking at him in the light of day was embarrassment enough for her. She wasn't ever going to let him see such vulnerability again.

He thought she looked like she was about to weep. Her eyes were misty, and it was very apparent to him that she was struggling to maintain her dignity. Judith hadn't been physically injured, but her feelings had certainly been trod upon.

"Winslow?" Iain's voice was hard, furious.

Isabelle's husband took a step forward. He knew what his laird was asking and immediately gave his explanation of what had happened in a quick, concise manner. Winslow still hadn't gotten over his anger, either. His voice shook.

Iain put his hand on Judith's shoulder. He could feel her trembling. That notice made him even more furious. "Judith is a guest in my brother's home."

He waited until everyone inside the cottage had acknowledged that statement of fact, then added, "But she is also under my protection. If there is trouble, you will bring it to me. Is that understood?"

The rafters shook from the fury in his voice. Judith had never seen Iain this angry. It was a little overwhelming. Frightening, too. She tried to remind herself that he wasn't upset with her, that he was actually defending her, but logic didn't help much. The look in his eyes still made her shiver.

"Laird Iain, do you realize what you're implying?"

The priest whispered his question. Iain stared at Judith when he gave his abrupt answer. "I do."

"Hell," Brodick muttered.

Iain let go of Judith and turned around to confront his friend. "Do you want to challenge me?"

Brodick had to think the question over a long minute before shaking his head. "No. You have my support. God knows you're going to need it."

"You have my support as well," Winslow called out.

Iain nodded. The muscle in the side of his jaw quit flexing. Judith thought his friends' show of loyalty was calming his anger.

Why the man needed their support was beyond her understanding. In England, hospitality was offered by all the members of the family to a guest, but here it was obviously very different.

"The council?" Winslow asked.

"Soon," Iain answered.

A gasp came from behind Judith. She turned to look at the midwives. She was surprised to see Helen's expression. The woman seemed to be relieved about the outcome of the inquisition. She was trying hard not to smile. That notice didn't make any sense to Judith.

Agnes's expression didn't leave her guessing, however. Her eyes blazed with anger. Judith turned away from the woman. Father Laggan, she noticed, was watching her intently.

"Father, do you have any other questions to ask me?"

He shook his head. He smiled, too. Since no one was paying the two of them any attention now, she moved forward to ask the priest a question. Winslow, his brother Brodick, and Iain were in deep discussion, and the relatives at the table were all talking at once.

"Father, may I ask you something?" she whispered.

"Of course."

"If there hadn't been any bruises, would you have condemned Isabelle and her son?" Judith adjusted the shawl around her neck while she waited for his answer.

"No," he answered.

She felt better. She didn't want to think a man of the cloth would be so rigid. "Then you would have taken my word alone as proof enough, even though I'm an outsider here?"

"I would have found a way to support your claim, perhaps by calling on all of Isabelle's relatives to speak up on her behalf." He took hold of Judith's hand and patted her. "The bruises made my task much easier."

"Yes, they did," she agreed. "If you'll excuse me now, Father, I would like to leave."

She hurried outside as soon as he'd given her permission. It was probably rude of her to leave without saying good-bye to the others, especially their laird, but Judith couldn't stomach the idea of staying in the same room with Agnes a minute longer.

The crowd had more than doubled in size since she'd gone inside. Judith wasn't in the mood for their curiosity now. She held her head high as she made her way over to the tree where she had left her mount.

She wasn't in the mood for the stallion's skittish behavior, either; she gave the animal a good swat on his left flank to get him to settle down long enough for her to gain the saddle.

Judith was still too upset by the ordeal she'd just gone through to go directly back to Frances Catherine. She needed to calm down first. She didn't have a destination in mind but goaded the stallion up the path toward the crest. She would ride until she'd gotten rid of her anger, no matter how long it took.

Father Laggan came outside Isabelle's cottage a scant minute after Judith had left. He raised both hands into the air to gain the crowd's attention. His smile was wide. "It has all been resolved to my satisfaction," he called out. "Lady Judith cleared up the matter in quick time."

A loud cheer went up. The priest moved to the side of the stoop to allow Brodick to pass by. Iain and Winslow followed.

The gathering moved out of Brodick's way as he strode over to the trees where Judith had left his horse. He had almost reached his destination before he realized his mount was gone.

Brodick had an incredulous look on his face when he whirled around. "By God, she's done it again," he roared to no one in particular. He couldn't seem to make sense out of the insult Judith had given him by taking his horse. The fact that the stallion actually belonged to Iain didn't make any difference, either.

"Lady Judith didn't steal your horse," Winslow called out. "She only borrowed it. Those were her words to me when she arrived here, and I imagine she still believes—"

Winslow couldn't go on. His laughter got in his way. Iain had more discipline. He didn't even smile. He gained his mount, then put his hand down to Brodick. The warrior was about to swing himself up behind his laird when Bryan, an older man with hunched shoulders and bright orange hair, took a step forward. "The woman didn't steal your mount and you shouldn't be thinking she did, Brodick."

Brodick turned around to glare at the man. Then another soldier shoved his way to the front of the crowd. He took his position next to Bryan. "Aye, Lady Judith was probably just in a hurry," he said.

Yet another and another came forward to offer their

reasons for Lady Judith taking the mount. Iain couldn't have been more pleased. The issue wasn't really the borrowing of the horse, of course. The men were letting it be known to their laird that Judith had won their support . . . and their hearts. She'd stood up for Isabelle and they were now standing up for her.

"She didn't have to help our Isabelle last night and she didn't have to come back here today to answer Father Laggan's questions," Bryan stated. "You won't be speaking ill of Lady Judith, Brodick, or you'll answer to me."

A stiff wind would have knocked Bryan over, so feeble was he in strength, yet he courageously challenged Brodick.

"Hell," Brodick muttered, his exasperation obvious.

Iain did smile then. He nodded to Judith's champions, waited until Brodick had swung up behind him, and then goaded his mount forward.

Iain assumed Judith would go directly back to his brother's home. The horse wasn't out front, however, and he couldn't imagine where she'd gone.

He stopped his mount so Brodick could drop to the ground. "She might have ridden back up to the keep," Iain remarked. "I'll look there first."

Brodick nodded. "I'll look down below," he said. He started to walk away, then suddenly turned around again. "I'm giving you fair warning, Iain. When I find her, I'm going to give her hell."

"You have my permission."

Brodick hid his grin. He waited for the catch. He knew Iain well enough to understand how his mind worked. "And?" he prodded when his laird didn't qualify his agreement.

"You may give her hell, but you can't raise your voice while you're at it."

"Why not?"

"You might upset her," Iain explained with a shrug. "I can't allow that."

Brodick opened his mouth to say something more, then changed his mind. Iain had just taken all the bluster out of his indignation. If he couldn't yell at the woman, why bother lecturing her at all?

He turned around and started down the hill, muttering under his breath. Iain's laughter followed him.

Judith wasn't waiting for him at the keep. Iain backtracked, then took the path to the west that led up to the next ridge.

He found her at the cemetery. She was walking at a fast clip along the path that separated the sacred ground from the trees.

She had thought that a brisk walk would help her get rid of some of her anger over the ordeal she'd just gone through for Isabelle, and had come upon the cemetery quite by chance. Curious, she'd stopped to have a look.

The burial ground was really a very pretty, peaceful place. Tall wooden slats, newly whitewashed and standing as straight as lances, surrounded the cemetery on three sides. Ornately carved headstones, some arched, others square-topped, filled the interior in neat rows. Fresh flowers covered almost every other plot. Whoever had been given the task of looking after this final resting place had done his duty well. The care and attention was very evident.

Judith made the sign of the cross as she walked along the path. She left the cemetery proper and continued on up the narrow climb, past the line of trees blocking the sight of the valley below. The wind whistled through the branches, a sound she found quite melancholy.

The ground reserved for the damned was directly ahead of her. She came to an abrupt stop when she reached the edge of the stark burial ground. There wasn't any whitewashed fencing here, or any ornately carved headstones. Only weathered wooden stakes had been used.

Judith knew who was buried here. They were the poor

souls the Church had decided belonged in Hell. Aye, there were robbers, and murderers, and rapists, and thieves, and traitors, of course . . . and all the women who had died during childbirth.

The anger she'd hoped to get rid of grew until it was a burning rage inside her.

Wasn't there any fairness in the afterlife, either?

"Judith?"

She whirled around and found Iain standing no more than a few feet away. She hadn't heard him approach.

"Do you think they're all in Hell?"

He raised an eyebrow over the vehemence in her voice. "Who are you talking about?"

"The women buried here," she explained with a wave of her hand. She didn't give him time to answer her. "I don't believe they're in Hell. They died doing their sacred duty, damn it. They suffered with the laboring and died fulfilling their obligation to their husbands and their priests. And for what, Iain? To burn in Hell for eternity because the Church didn't think they were clean enough for Heaven? It's all rubbish," she added in a harsh whisper. "All of it. If that opinion makes me a heretic, I don't care. I cannot believe God would be so cruel."

Iain didn't know what to say to her. Logic told him she was right. It was rubbish. In truth, he had never taken the time to think about such matters.

"A woman's duty is to give her husband heirs. Isn't that so?"

"Yes," he agreed.

"Then why is it that from the moment she finds out she's carrying his child, she isn't allowed to go inside a church? She's considered unclean, isn't she?"

She asked him another question before he could respond to the first. "Do you believe Frances Catherine's unclean? No, of course you don't," she answered. "But the Church does. And if she gives Patrick a son, she need wait only thirty-three days before she undergoes the cleansing ritual and can return to church. If she gives him a daughter, she must wait twice as long . . . and if she dies during her laboring or any time before she's received the blessing, she'll end up here. How fitting for Frances Catherine to be buried next to a murderer and a—"

She finally stopped. She bowed her head and let out a weary sigh. "I'm sorry. I shouldn't have railed against you. If I could just force myself not to think about such matters, I wouldn't become so angry."

"It's in your nature to care."

"How would you know what's in my nature?"

"The way you helped Isabelle is one example," he replied. "And there are many other examples I could give you."

His voice was filled with tenderness when he answered her. She felt as though she'd just been caressed. She suddenly wanted to lean into him, to wrap her arms around him and hold him tight. Iain was so wonderfully strong, and she was feeling so horribly vulnerable now.

She hadn't realized until that moment how much she admired him. He was always so certain about everything, so sure of himself. There was an air of quiet authority about him. He didn't demand respect from his followers. Nay, he'd earned their loyalty and their trust. He rarely raised his voice to anyone. She smiled then, for she'd just realized he had raised his voice to her several times. He wasn't as disciplined when she was around, she guessed. She wondered what that meant.

"If you don't like something, isn't it your duty to try to change it?" he asked.

She almost laughed over his suggestion until she realized from his expression he was quite serious. She was flabbergasted. "You believe I could take on the Church?"

He shook his head. "One whisper, Judith, added to a thousand others will become a roar of discontent even the Church can't ignore. Start with Father Laggan. Put your questions to him. He's a fair man. He'll listen to you."

He smiled when he said the word "fair." She found herself smiling back. He wasn't mocking her. Nay, he was really trying to help. "I'm not significant enough to make any changes. I'm only a woman who—"

"As long as you believe that nonsense, you won't accomplish anything. You'll defeat yourself."

"But Iain," she argued, "what difference could I make? I would be condemned if I openly criticize the teachings of the Church. How would that help?"

"You don't begin by attacking," he instructed. "You discuss the contradictions in the rules. If you make one other person aware, and then another and another . . ."

He didn't go on. She nodded. "I must consider this," she said. "I can't imagine how I could make anyone pay any attention to my opinions, especially here."

He smiled. "You already have, Judith. You made me realize the contradictions. Why did you stop here today?" he asked.

"It wasn't on purpose," she replied. "I wanted to walk for a little while, until I'd gotten rid of my anger. You probably didn't notice, but I was really very upset when I left Isabelle's cottage. I was ready to scream. It was all so unfair, what they put her through."

"You could scream here and no one would hear you." There was a sparkle in his eyes when he gave her that suggestion.

"You would hear," she said.

"I wouldn't mind."

"But I would mind. It wouldn't be proper."

"It wouldn't?"

She shook her head. "Nor ladylike," she added with a nod.

She looked terribly earnest. He couldn't resist. He leaned down and kissed her. His mouth brushed over hers just long enough to feel her softness. He pulled back almost immediately.

"Why did you do that?"

"To get you to quit frowning up at me."

She wasn't given time to react to his admission. He took hold of her hand. "Come along, Judith. We'll walk until your anger is completely gone."

She had to run to keep up with him. "This isn't a race, Iain. We could walk at a more leisurely pace."

He slowed down. They walked along for several minutes in silence, each caught up in his own thoughts.

"Judith, are you always proper?"

She thought it was an odd question to ask her. "Yes and no," she answered. "I'm always very proper the six months of each year I'm forced to live with my mother and my uncle Tekel."

He caught the word "forced," but decided against questioning her now. She was being unguarded, and he wanted to learn as much as he could about her family before she closed up on him again.

"And the other six months of each year?" he asked, his tone casual.

"I'm not proper at all," she answered. "Uncle Herbert and Aunt Millicent let me have quite a bit of freedom. I'm not at all restricted."

"Give me an example of not being restricted," he requested. "I don't understand."

She nodded. "I wanted to find out all I could about childbirth. Aunt Millicent allowed me to pursue my goal and helped every way she could."

She continued to talk about her aunt and uncle for several more minutes. The love she felt for the couple came through in each remark. Iain kept his questions to a minimum and slowly worked his way around to her mother.

"This Uncle Tekel you mentioned," he began. "Is he your father's brother or your mother's?"

"He's my mother's older brother."

He waited for her to tell him more. She didn't say

another word. They turned back to where the horses were secured, and had passed through the cemetery before she spoke again.

"Do you think I'm different from other women?"

"Yes."

Her shoulders slumped. She looked terribly forlorn. He felt like laughing. "It isn't bad, it's just different. You're more aware than most women. You aren't as accepting."

"It will get me into trouble some day, won't it?"

"I'll protect you."

It was a sweet pledge, arrogant as well. She didn't think he was really serious. She laughed and shook her head.

They reached the horses. He lifted her into her saddle. He brushed her hair back over her shoulder and gently prodded the bruised skin on the side of her neck. "Does this pain you?"

"Just a little," she admitted.

The chain drew his attention. He pulled the ring from her gown and once again looked at it.

She immediately snatched the ring away and hid it in her fist.

And it was the fist that prodded his memory at last.

He took a step back, away from her. "Iain? Is something the matter? You've turned gray."

He didn't answer her.

It took Judith a long while to give Frances Catherine all the details of the inquisition. The retelling was made more difficult because her friend kept interrupting her with questions.

"I think you should go with me to see Isabelle and the baby," Judith told her.

"I would like to help her," Frances Catherine replied.

"And I would like for you to become Isabelle's friend. You have to learn to open your heart to these people. Some of them are certainly as sweet as Isabelle is. I know you'll like her. She's very kind. She reminds me of you, Frances Catherine."

"I'll try to open my heart to her," Frances Catherine promised. "Oh God, I'm going to be so lonely after you leave. I only see Patrick during the evenings, and I'm so sleepy by then I can barely concentrate on what he's saying to me."

"I'll miss you, too," Judith replied. "I wish you lived closer to me. Perhaps then you could come to see me every now and then. Aunt Millicent and Uncle Herbert would love to see you again."

"Patrick would never let me go into England," she said. "He'd think it was too dangerous. Will you braid my hair for me while we wait?"

"Certainly," Judith replied. "What are we waiting for?"

"Patrick made me promise to stay home until he finished an important duty. He'll be happy to walk with us over to Isabelle's."

She handed Judith her brush, sat down on the stool, and asked about Isabelle's laboring again.

The time got away from them, and a good hour passed before they realized Patrick still hadn't returned. Since it was almost the supper hour, they decided to put off the visit until the following morning.

They were in the midst of preparing the dinner when Iain knocked on the door. Frances Catherine had just made an amusing remark, and Judith was still laughing when she opened the door.

"Oh heavens, Iain, you aren't going to tell me Father Laggan has thought of another question to put to me, are you?"

She was jesting with him, and fully expected a smile at the very least. She got a curt answer instead. "No."

He walked inside, gave Frances Catherine a quick nod, then clasped his hands behind his back and turned to Judith.

She couldn't believe this was the same man who had

been so sweet and kind to her not two hours ago. He was as cold and distant as a stranger.

"There won't be any other questions from the priest," he announced.

"I knew that," she replied. "I was only jesting with you."

He shook his head at her. "Now isn't the time for jests. I've more important matters on my mind."

"What pressing matters?"

He didn't answer her. He turned to Frances Catherine. "Where is my brother?"

His abruptness worried Frances Catherine. She sat down at the table, folded her hands together in her lap and tried to look calm. "I'm not certain. He should be back any time now."

"Why do you want Patrick?" Judith asked the question she knew her friend wanted to ask but didn't dare.

Iain turned around and started for the door. "I need to speak to him before I leave."

He tried to walk outside after making that remark. Judith rushed in front of him to block his path. He was so surprised by that boldness, he stopped. He smiled, too. Her head was tilted all the way back so she could look up at him. She wanted him to see her frown of displeasure.

Before she realized his intent, he lifted her out of his way. She looked over at Frances Catherine. Her friend waved her after Iain. Judith nodded and went running outside.

"Where are you going? Are you going to be gone long?"

He didn't turn around when he answered her. "I'm not certain how long I'll be gone."

"Why did you want to speak to Patrick? Are you going to take him with you?"

He came to an abrupt stop and turned around to give her his full attention. "No, I'm not taking Patrick with me. Judith, why are you asking me all these questions?"

"Why are you acting so cold?" She blushed after blurting out that thought aloud. "I mean to say," she began again, "earlier you seemed to be in a much more lighthearted mood. Have I done something to displease you?"

He shook his head. "We were alone earlier," he told her. "We aren't now."

He tried to leave again. She rushed in front of him to block his way a second time. "You were going to leave without saying good-bye, weren't you?"

She made the question sound like an accusation. She didn't give him time to answer, either. She turned around and walked back to Frances Catherine. He stood there watching her leave. He could hear her muttering something about being damn rude, and assumed she was referring to him. He let out a sigh over her impudence.

Patrick came down the hill, drawing his attention. Iain explained his intention to take Ramsey and Erin to the MacDonalds' holding for a meeting with the Dunbar laird. The conference would be held on neutral ground, but Iain was still taking all the necessary precautions. If the Macleans got word of this meeting, they would attack in force.

Iain didn't go into detail, but Patrick was astute enough to understand the significance of the conference.

"The council didn't give their blessing, did they?" Patrick guessed.

"They don't know about the meeting."

Patrick nodded. "There'll be trouble."

"Yes."

"Do you want me to go with you?"

"I want you to look out for Judith while I'm away," Iain said. "Don't let her get into trouble."

Patrick nodded. "Where do the elders think you're going?"

"To the MacDonalds," Iain answered. "I just didn't tell them the Dunbars would also be there." He let out a sigh. "God, how I hate this secrecy."

Iain didn't expect a reply to that statement. He turned to remount his stallion, then suddenly stopped. He tossed the reins to Patrick and strode back over to the cottage.

He didn't knock on the door this time. Judith was standing by the hearth. She turned when the door slammed against the stone wall. Her eyes widened, too. Frances Catherine was sitting at the table slicing bread. She half stood, then sat back down again when Iain walked past her.

He didn't say a word in greeting to Judith. He grabbed hold of her shoulders and hauled her up against him. His mouth slammed down on top of hers. She was too stunned to react at first. He forced her mouth open. His tongue moved inside with blatant determination. The kiss was possessive, almost savagely so, and just when she was beginning to respond, he pulled away from her.

She sagged against the corner of the hearth. Iain turned around, nodded to Frances Catherine, and left the cottage.

Judith was too stunned to say anything. Frances Catherine looked at her friend's expression and had to bite her lower lip to keep herself from bursting into laughter.

"Didn't you tell me the attraction was over?"

Judith didn't know what to tell her friend. She did a lot of sighing the rest of the evening. Patrick walked with Frances Catherine and her over to Isabelle's after supper. Judith met several more relatives, all women, and all on Winslow's side of the family. A pretty little woman named Willa introduced herself. She was heavy with child, and after explaining that she was Winslow's third cousin twice removed, she asked Judith if she would please go outside with her for just a few minutes to discuss an important issue. Judith was immediately filled with dread. She guessed the issue was actually a request for help with the birthing.

She couldn't deny the tearful woman's plea, of course, but she made certain Willa understood how inexperienced she was. Willa's elderly aunt Louise had followed them outside, and she stepped forward with the promise that although she had never had children of her own and didn't have any training, she would be willing to help.

Iain was gone three full weeks. Judith missed him terribly. She didn't have time to be completely miserable, though. She delivered Willa's infant daughter while Iain was away, and Caroline's and Winifred's sons as well.

She was terrified each time. It never seemed to get any easier. Patrick had his hands full trying to soothe her fears. He was thoroughly confused by the bizarre ritual she seemed determined to put herself through. All three women began their laboring in the dead of night. Judith would be instantly frightened. She would stammer out all the reasons she couldn't possibly take on this duty, and continue ranting and raving all the way over to the birthing mother's cottage. Patrick would always accompany her, and she was usually trying to rip his plaid off his chest by the time they reached their destination.

The self-torture stopped the minute she walked through the entrance. From then on Judith was calm, efficient, and determined to make the birthing mother as comfortable as possible. She stayed composed until after the baby was born.

After the work was done, Judith would cry all the way home. It didn't matter who was walking with her, either. She wept all over Patrick's plaid, Brodick's as well, and with the third birthing, Father Laggan happened to be strolling by when she'd finished, and she cried all over him.

Patrick didn't know how to help Judith get over this torment she put herself through, and he was immensely relieved when Iain finally returned home.

The sun had already set when his brother, flanked by Ramsey and Erin, rode up the incline. Patrick whistled to his brother. Iain motioned for him to follow him, then continued. Patrick went back inside to tell his wife he was going up to the keep, but she was already sound asleep. He glanced behind the screen and saw that Judith was also dead to the world.

Brodick and Alex met Patrick in the courtyard. The three warriors went inside together.

Iain was standing in front of the hearth. He looked exhausted. "Patrick?" he called out as soon as his brother walked inside.

"She's fine," Patrick called back, answering the question he knew Iain was about to ask. He walked over to stand in front of his brother. "She assisted with three more birthings while you were away," he added. He smiled when he added, "She hates being a midwife."

Iain nodded. He asked Alex to find Winslow and Gowrie, then turned to talk privately with his brother.

Patrick was Iain's only family. For as long as either one could remember, they'd taken care of each other. Iain needed to hear now that he had his brother's backing for the changes he was going to make. Patrick didn't say a word until Iain had gone through the list of possible ramifications. And then he simply nodded. It was all that was needed.

"You have a family now, Patrick. Consider—"

His brother didn't let him finish the warning. "We stand together, Iain."

"They're here, Iain," Brodick called out, interrupting the conversation.

Iain slapped his brother on his shoulder in a show of affection, then turned to face his loyal men. He hadn't called the council together to join in. That notice wasn't missed by anyone. He explained what had happened at the conference. The Dunbar laird was old, tired, and anxious to form an alliance, and if the Maitlands weren't interested, the Macleans would do just as well.

"The council won't cooperate," Brodick predicted after his laird had given his report. "Their past grievances make any kind of union impossible."

"The Dunbars are in a tenuous position sitting between us," Alex interjected. "If they unite with the

Macleans, their warriors will outnumber us by at least ten to one. I'm not liking those odds."

Iain nodded. "I will call the council together tomorrow," he announced. "For two separate purposes. First I'll talk to them about an alliance with the Dunbars."

He didn't continue. "What is the second purpose?" Brodick asked.

Iain found his first smile. "Judith."

Patrick and Brodick were the only ones who immediately understood what Iain was telling them.

"Father Laggan's thinking to leave early tomorrow morning," Brodick said.

"Detain him."

"For what purpose?" Alex asked.

"The wedding," Iain answered.

Patrick laughed. Brodick joined in. Alex continued to look confused. "What about Judith?" he asked. "Will she agree?"

Iain didn't answer him.

Chapter 9

Patrick didn't tell Frances Catherine or Judith that Iain had returned home. He left early in the morning to go up to the keep. Judith helped her friend give the cottage a thorough cleaning.

It was a little past the nooning hour when Iain knocked on the door. Judith opened it. Her face was covered with smudges and her hair was in wild disarray. She looked as though she'd just finished cleaning the inside of the hearth.

He was so damned happy to see her, he frowned. She smiled back. She was flustered over her appearance. She tried to straighten her hair by brushing the curls away from her face.

"You're back," she whispered.

The man wasn't much for greetings. "Yes. Judith, come up to the keep in one hour's time."

He turned and walked away. She was crushed by his cold attitude. She chased after him. "Why must I go up to the keep?"

"Because I wish you to," he answered.

"But I might have plans set for this afternoon."

"Unset them."

"You're as stubborn as a goat," she muttered.

The gasp from the doorway indicated Frances Catherine had heard her remark. Judith still wasn't sorry she had said such a rude thing, because she believed it to be true. Iain was stubborn.

She turned away from him. "I don't believe I missed you at all."

He grabbed hold of her hand and pulled her back. "Exactly how long was I gone?"

"Three weeks, two days," she answered. "Why?"

He grinned. "But you didn't miss me, did you?"

She realized she'd trapped herself. "You're too clever for me, Iain," she drawled out.

"Tis the truth, I am," he agreed with a grin.

Lord, she was going to miss this battling of wits with him, she realized. God's truth, she was going to miss him.

"If you want me to come up to your keep," she said, "you should put the request to Patrick first so your chain of command will be properly followed. Do let me know what he has to say."

She was deliberately trying to provoke him. He laughed instead.

"Iain?" Frances Catherine called out. "Is the council up at the keep?"

He nodded. Judith saw her friend's reaction to that news and pulled her hand away from Iain's.

"Now you've done it," she announced in a low whisper.

"Done what?"

"You've upset Frances Catherine. Just look at her. She's worried, thanks to you."

"What did I do?" he asked, thoroughly confused. Frances Catherine did look upset, and he couldn't imagine why.

"You've just told her the council's up at the keep,"

Judith explained. "Now she's worried I've done something wrong and they'll send me back home before she has her baby."

"You gathered all that from one frown?"

"Of course," she answered, exasperated. She folded her arms in front of her and frowned at him. "Well?" she demanded when he kept silent.

"Well, what?"

"Fix it."

"Fix what?"

"You needn't raise your voice to me," she ordered. "You upset her. Now soothe her. Tell her you won't let the council send me back home yet. It's the least you can do. She's your dear sister-in-law and you really shouldn't want to see her upset."

He let out a sigh fierce enough to part the branches on the trees. He turned and yelled to Frances Catherine. "Judith isn't going anywhere." He looked at Judith again. "Have I fixed it to your satisfaction?"

Frances Catherine was smiling. Judith nodded. "Yes, thank you."

He turned and walked toward his stallion. Judith hurried after him. She grabbed hold of his hand to get him to stop.

"Iain?"

"What now?"

His gruff tone of voice didn't bother her. "Did you miss me?"

"Perhaps."

That answer did prick her temper. She let go of his hand and tried to walk away. He caught her from behind. Wrapping his arms around her waist, he leaned down close to her ear and whispered, "You really should try to do something about your temper, lass."

He kissed her on the side of her neck, sending shivers down her legs.

He never did answer her question. Judith didn't realize it until he'd ridden away from her.

The man could turn her mind into mush just by touching her. Judith wasn't given long to mull over that flaw, however, for Frances Catherine was insisting on gaining her attention.

She all but shoved Judith through the doorway, then shut it behind her.

"Iain's in love with you."

Frances Catherine sounded thrilled. Judith shook her head. "I will not allow myself to think about love," she announced.

Her friend laughed. "You may not allow yourself to think about it, Judith, but you're in love with him, aren't you? I've kept silent long enough. He never needs to know."

The last remark caught Judith's full attention. "Know what?"

"About your father. No one ever needs to know. Let yourself—"

"No."

"Just think about what I'm suggesting," Frances Catherine said.

Judith collapsed into the chair. "I wish you would have your baby so I could go home. Each day I stay makes it more difficult. Dear God, what if I *am* falling in love with him? How do I stop myself?"

Frances Catherine walked over to stand behind her. She put her hand on her shoulder. "Would it help if you thought about all his flaws?" she asked.

She was jesting with her friend. Judith took the suggestion to heart. She tried to come up with as many flaws as possible. She couldn't think of very many. The man was almost perfect. Frances Catherine suggested that was probably a flaw, too. Judith agreed.

The two friends were so intent on their discussion, they didn't notice Patrick standing in the entrance. He'd been very quiet when he opened the door out of consideration for his wife. She often took afternoon naps, and he didn't want to disturb her if she was sleeping now.

Judith's remarks caught his attention. As soon as he realized she was giving his wife her opinion of Iain, he couldn't help but smile. Judith knew his brother almost as well as he did, and when she mentioned how stubborn he was, Patrick found himself nodding agreement.

"But you're still attracted to him, aren't you?"

Judith sighed. "Yes. Frances Catherine, what am I going to do? I feel such panic inside when I think about what's happening to me. I can't love him."

"And he can't possibly love you, either," Frances Catherine asked. "You're fooling yourself if you believe that. The man cares about you. Why can't you just accept it?"

Judith shook her head. "What do you suppose he'd do if he ever found out Laird Maclean was my father? Do you honestly believe he'd still care about me?"

Years of training to control his reactions kept Patrick on his feet. God's truth, he felt as though he'd just been given a hard blow to his midsection. He staggered back outside, then hastily pulled the door closed behind him. Patrick found Iain in the great hall. "We have to talk," he announced. "I've just found out something you need to know."

His brother's expression told Iain something was terribly wrong. "Walk with me outside, Patrick," he ordered. "I would rather hear your news in private."

Neither brother said another word until they were well away from the keep. Then Patrick repeated what he'd heard. Iain wasn't surprised. "It's a hell of a mess," Patrick muttered.

Iain agreed. It was one hell of a mess.

It took Judith almost an hour to clean up. The topic of Iain kept coming up. Frances Catherine was determined to make Judith admit she was already in love with Iain, and Judith was just as determined not to admit any such thing.

"You should be helping me get over this attraction," Judith insisted. "Do you realize how painful it's going to be for me to leave? I have to go back, Frances Catherine. It doesn't matter if I want to or not. This topic is most distressing for me. I don't wish to talk about it any longer."

Frances Catherine was immediately contrite. She could tell her friend was close to tears. She patted Judith's shoulder. "All right," she said, her voice a soothing whisper. "We won't talk about it. Now then, help me change my gown. I'm going up to the keep with you. Heaven only knows what the council's wanting. There has to be trouble brewing."

Judith stood up. "You're staying home. I'll go by myself. I promise to tell you everything that happens."

Frances Catherine was having none of that. She was determined to stand beside Judith in the event of trouble.

Judith was just as determined to make her friend stay put. Patrick came inside in the middle of their disagreement. He tried to get their attention with a word of greeting, and when that didn't work, he arrogantly raised his hand for silence.

They ignored him. "You always were as stubborn as a mule," Frances Catherine told her friend.

Patrick was appalled. "You mustn't talk to our guest like that," he ordered.

"Why not? She just called me worse."

Judith smiled. "'Tis the truth, I did," she admitted sheepishly.

"Do stay out of this, Patrick," his wife suggested. "I'm just warming to this argument. I'm going to win. It's my turn."

Judith shook her head. "No, you're not going to win," she countered. "Patrick, please make her stay here. I have to go up to the keep. I won't be gone long."

She hurried out of the cottage before her friend could continue the argument. It would be up to Patrick to keep her home.

Judith knew she was probably late and Iain would surely be irritated, but she really wasn't worried about his temper. On the way up the steep hill she thought about that amazing fact. Iain was such a big, fierce-looking warrior, and his gigantic size alone should have turned her hair gray by now. She remembered feeling a little nervous the very first time she had seen him crossing the drawbridge to her uncle Tekel's home. The feeling had quickly vanished, however, and she had never, ever felt trapped or helpless when she was with him. Iain's manner was as gruff as a bear's, yet each time he touched her, he was very gentle.

Uncle Tekel frightened her. The realization popped into her mind all at once. She didn't understand why she was afraid of him. Her uncle was an invalid who had to be carried about on a litter from place to place. As long as she stayed out of striking distance, he couldn't hurt her. Yet whenever she had been forced to sit beside him, she had always been afraid.

His cruel words still had the power to hurt her, she admitted. She wished she was stronger and not so vulnerable. Then he couldn't hurt her. If she could learn how to protect her feelings, if she could learn to separate her mind from her heart, she wouldn't care what her uncle Tekel said to her. Nor would she care if she ever saw Iain again . . . if she were stronger.

Oh, what did it matter? She was going to have to go home, and Iain was certainly going to marry someone else. He would probably be very happy, too, as long as he could order his wife around for the rest of his life.

She let out a groan of disgust. Thinking about Iain kissing any other woman made her stomach hurt.

God help her, she was acting like a woman in love. She shook her head. She was far too intelligent to allow her heart to be crushed. She wasn't that ignorant, was she?

She burst into tears. She was racked with heart-wrenching sobs in a matter of seconds. She couldn't make herself stop. She blamed Frances Catherine for her shameful condition because she had prodded and prodded until Judith had finally been forced to confront the truth.

Judith moved off the path as a precaution against

someone coming along and seeing her distress, and even hid behind a fat pine.

"Good Lord, Judith, what happened?"

Patrick's voice made her groan. She took a step back.

He followed her. "Did you injure yourself?" he asked, his concern obvious.

She shook her head. "You weren't supposed to see me," she whispered. She wiped her face dry with the backs of her hands and took several deep breaths to calm herself.

"I didn't see you," Patrick explained. "I heard you."

"I'm sorry," she whispered.

"What are you sorry for?"

"For being loud," she answered. "I only wanted a few minutes of privacy, but that isn't possible here, is it?"

She sounded downright pitiful. Patrick wanted to comfort her. She was his wife's dearest friend, and he felt it was his duty to try to make her feel better. He put his arm around her shoulders and gently turned her back to the path.

"Tell me what's wrong, Judith. No matter how terrible this problem seems to be, I'm certain I can correct it for you."

It was an extremely arrogant thing to say, but then, he was Iain's brother, after all, and some of his arrogance would surely dribble down to his sibling, she supposed. He was trying to be good-hearted, and for that reason alone she wasn't irritated.

"You cannot correct this," she told him. "But I thank you for offering."

"You can't know what I can do until you explain."

"All right," she agreed. "I've only just realized how ignorant I am. Can you correct that?"

His smile was gentle. "You aren't ignorant, Judith."

"Oh yes I am," she cried out. "I should have protected myself." She didn't go on.

"Judith?"

"Never mind. I don't wish to discuss this."

"You shouldn't be weeping, not today of all days," Patrick told her.

She mopped at the corners of her eyes again. "Yes, it is a beautiful day, and I shouldn't be crying." She took another deep breath. "You can let go of me now. I've recovered."

He removed his arm from her shoulder and walked by her side up to the crest of the hill and across the courtyard. Patrick had one more errand to complete before he went inside. He bowed to Judith and started to turn away.

"Do I look like I've been weeping?" she asked him in a worried tone.

"No," he lied.

She smiled. "Thank you for helping me sort through this problem," she said.

"But I didn't—"

He quit his protest when she turned and ran up the steps to the keep. He shook his head in confusion and turned back toward the hill.

Judith didn't knock. She took a deep breath before pulling the heavy door wide and hurrying on inside.

The interior of the keep was just as cold and ugly as the exterior. The entrance was wide, with gray stone floors, and a staircase built against the wall to the right of the double doors. The great hall was on her left. It was huge in size and as drafty as an open meadow. A stone hearth took up a fair portion of the wall opposite the entrance. There was a fire blazing away, but it didn't warm the room. There was more smoke than heat circulating in the hall.

There weren't any of the aromas usual in a home, like the smell of bread baking or meat sizzling over a flame, nor was there any clutter of personal possessions to indicate someone actually lived here. The hall was as stark as a monastery.

Five steps led down into the room. Judith waited at the top for Iain to notice her. He was sitting with his back to her at the head of a long narrow table. Five older men Judith assumed were the members of the council were huddled together at the opposite end.

The atmosphere crackled with tension. Something terrible must have happened. It was apparent from the looks on the elders' faces they had received some distressing news. Judith didn't believe she should intrude on their unhappiness now. She would come back later, when everyone had recovered from their upset. She backed up a space and turned around to leave.

Alex and Gowrie blocked her exit. She was so surprised to see them, her eyes widened in reaction. The two warriors hadn't made a sound when they came inside. Judith was about to skirt her way around the big men when the doors were thrown wide and Brodick swaggered inside. Patrick was right behind him. He caught hold of one of the doors before it slammed shut and motioned for the priest to come inside. Father Laggan didn't look very happy. He forced a smile for Judith, then hurried on down the steps into the hall.

She watched the priest until he reached Iain's side. Yes, something terrible had happened, all right. There wouldn't be need for a priest otherwise. She said a silent prayer for whoever was in need of it, then turned around to leave again.

The warriors had formed a line behind her. Alex, Gowrie, Brodick, and Patrick were deliberately blocking her path.

Patrick stood on the end nearest the door. She edged her way over to him. "Did someone die?" she whispered.

Brodick found her question vastly amusing. The others continued to frown. None of them would let her leave. They wouldn't answer her question, either. She was about to tell the rude men to get out of her way when the door was thrown open again and Winslow came inside.

Isabelle's husband looked ready to do battle. He was

barely polite. He gave her a curt nod, then took his place in the line of warriors.

"Judith, come here."

Iain gave that command in such a bellow, he scared the breath right out of her. She turned around to frown at him, but it was a wasted effort on her part because he wasn't even looking at her now.

She couldn't make up her mind if she wanted to obey his rude summons or not. Brodick made the decision for her. He gave her shoulders a nudge. It wasn't an overly gentle one. She looked back over her shoulder to glare at him for being so rude.

He winked at her.

Alex waved her forward to do his laird's bidding. She glared at him, too. Someone really needed to take the time to teach the warriors some simple manners, she decided. Now wasn't the time, however. Judith lifted the hem of her skirt, straightened her shoulders, and went down the steps.

The priest, she noticed, was highly agitated. He was pacing back and forth in front of the hearth. She forced a serene expression for his benefit while she hurried across the room. When she reached Iain's side, she put her hand on his shoulder to get his attention, then leaned down.

"If you ever shout at me again, I do believe I'll throttle you."

After giving him that empty threat, she straightened up again. Iain had an astonished look on his face. She nodded to let him know she wasn't bluffing.

He smiled to let her know he thought she was daft.

Graham watched the couple and quickly came to the conclusion Lady Judith intrigued him. He could easily see why a man would be taken with her, why he might even forget she was English. Aye, she was that pleasing to look upon with her pretty golden-colored hair and her big blue eyes. Still, it wasn't her appearance that held Graham's interest. Nay, it was what he had learned about her character that had made him curious to know her better.

Winslow had told him about Lady Judith's assistance in helping with the birthing of his son, and the report had been closely followed by Father Laggan's praise over what had taken place the following day. Judith hadn't wanted to take on the duty. Winslow reported she'd been terrified. The fear hadn't stopped her from doing what was necessary, however. He'd heard she'd helped to bring three more babies into the world while Iain was away from the holding, and each time she'd been beside herself with fear and worry for the new mothers.

Graham didn't know what to make of those reports. He knew they were true, of course, but such kindness and courage coming from an Englishwoman confused him. It was such a contradiction.

There would be plenty of time later to think about this confusing issue. He could tell from Judith's expression Iain hadn't told her about the decision he'd just given the council. Graham looked at his companions to judge their reactions. Duncan looked like he had just swallowed a vat of vinegar. Vincent, Gelfrid, and Owen were in much the same condition.

It appeared he was the only one who wasn't still reeling from the stunning announcement. Of course, Iain had taken him aside before the meeting to tell him what he intended to do. Patrick stood by his brother's side. Graham had known then, before Iain had spoken a single word, that the issue was of an extremely important nature. The two brothers always stood together, united as one, on all crucial issues. Aye, he'd known it was important, but he had still been left speechless.

Graham finally stood up. He was filled with conflicting emotions. As leader of the council, he knew his primary duty was to try to talk some sense into Iain, and if that didn't change his determination, then to cast his vote against him.

Yet Graham felt another duty as well, and that was to

find a way to support Iain's decision. His reason was simple to understand. He wanted Iain to be happy. God only knew the laird deserved to find love and contentment.

He felt a tremendous responsibility for the laird. In all the years they had served together, Graham had taken on the role of father to Iain. He set out to train him to be the best. Iain hadn't disappointed him. He met every expectation, surpassed every goal Graham set for him, and even as a young lad, his strength and determination far excelled the efforts of all the others near his age and older.

At the tender age of twelve Iain became the sole parent to his younger brother, who was then only five years old. Iain's life had always been filled with responsibilities, and it didn't seem to matter how much more was heaped upon his shoulders, he easily carried the load. When it was necessary, he worked from dawn until darkness. There had been a reward for his diligence, of course. Iain became the youngest warrior ever to be granted the privilege of leading the clan.

But there had also been a price to pay. In all the years of relentless work and struggle, Iain had never had time for laughter, or joy, or happiness.

Graham clasped his hands behind his back and cleared his throat to get everyone's attention. He decided to go through the motions of arguing against Iain first. Once the other elders were satisfied he'd done his duty as their leader, he would publicly announce his support for the laird.

"Iain, there is still time for you to change this inclination of yours," Graham announced in a hard voice.

The other council members immediately nodded. Iain stood up with such quickness, the chair flew backward. Judith was so startled, she backed up. She bumped into Brodick. That startled her even more. She turned around and saw that all the warriors were now lined up in back of her again.

"Why are you following me?" she demanded in exasperation.

Iain turned around. Her ridiculous question took the edge off his anger. He shook his head at her. "They aren't following you, Judith. They're showing me their support."

She wasn't appeased by that explanation. "Then make them show you their support from over there," she suggested with a wave of her hand. "They're blocking my exit and I would like to leave."

"But I want you to stay," he told her.

"Iain, I don't belong here."

"Aye, she doesn't."

Gelfrid shouted his agreement. Iain turned to confront him.

All hell broke loose then. Judith felt as though she was standing in the center of a hailstorm. The shouting soon gave her a headache. Iain never raised his voice, but the elders were bellowing every other word.

The argument seemed to be centered around some sort of alliance. At least that was the one word that kept popping up again and again and getting the council members thoroughly riled. Iain was in favor of this alliance and the council was vehemently opposed.

One of the elders worked himself into a frenzy in no time at all. After he finished shouting his opinion, he had a fit of coughing. The poor man was choking and gasping for air. She seemed to be the only one in the room who noticed his distress. Judith righted the chair Iain had overturned, then hurried over to the serving stand to pour water into one of the silver-edged goblets. No one tried to stop her. The battle of words had escalated. Judith handed the drink to the elder, and after he had taken a long swallow, she started pounding on his back.

He waved his hand to let her know she didn't need to continue her ministrations, then turned to give her his appreciation. He was in the middle of offering his thank-you when he suddenly stopped. His watery eyes widened in disbelief. Judith thought he only just realized who was helping him. He let out a gasp and started coughing again.

"You really shouldn't allow yourself to get so worked up," she told him as she once again started pounding him between his shoulder blades.

"You really shouldn't dislike me, either," she remarked. "It's a sin to hate. Just ask Father Laggan if you don't believe me. Besides, I haven't done anything to hurt you."

Because she was so intent on giving the elder sound advice, she didn't notice the shouting match had stopped.

"Judith, quit beating Gelfrid."

Iain gave the command. She looked up and was surprised to find him smiling.

"Do quit giving me orders," she replied. "I'm helping this man. Take another drink," she instructed Gelfrid. "I'm certain it will help."

"Will you leave me alone if I do?"

"You don't need to take that tone with me," she said. "I'll be happy to leave you alone."

She turned and walked back to Iain's side. In a whisper she asked, "Why do I have to stay here?"

"The lass deserves to know what's going on," Father Laggan called out. "She's got to agree, Iain."

"She will," Iain called back.

"You'd best get on to it, then," the priest suggested. "I've got to get to Dunbar land by nightfall. Merlin isn't going to keep. I could come back after, of course, if you think you'll need more time convincing her . . ."

"I won't."

"Am I supposed to agree to something?" she asked.

He didn't immediately answer her. He turned to stare at his soldiers, willing them with his scowl to back away. They deliberately ignored his silent command. They were enjoying his discomfort, Iain realized, as every damn one of them was grinning.

"Graham?" Iain demanded.

"I support your decision."

Iain nodded. "Gelfrid?"

"Nay."

"Duncan?"

"Nay."

"Owen?"

"Nay."

"Vincent?"

The elder didn't answer. "Someone wake him up," Graham ordered.

"I'm awake. I'm just not finished considering this matter."

Everyone patiently waited. A good five minutes passed in silence. The tension in the hall increased tenfold. Judith edged closer to Iain until her arm touched his. He was rigid with anger and she wanted him to know he had her support. She almost smiled over her own behavior. She didn't even know what the issue was about, yet she was ready to stand with Iain.

She didn't like seeing him upset. She took hold of his hand. He didn't look down at her, but he did give her fingers a little squeeze.

Since everyone was staring at Vincent, she did the same. She thought the elder might have gone back to sleep. It was difficult to tell. His bushy eyebrows hid his eyes from his audience, and he was hunched over the table with his head down.

He finally looked up. "You have my support, Iain."

"I count three against, and with our laird, three in favor," Graham announced.

"What in thunder do we do now?" Owen rasped out.

"We've never faced this dilemma before," Gelfrid interjected. "But a tie's a tie."

"We'll wait to decide this alliance," Graham announced. He paused until each member of the council had nodded his agreement, then turned to Iain. "You might as well get on with it, son."

Iain immediately turned to Judith. He was suddenly feeling very ill at ease.

This meeting hadn't turned out the way he had thought it would. He fully expected everyone but Graham to vote against the alliance. The discussion shouldn't have taken up so much time, and he'd planned to have a good five minutes alone with Judith before the priest arrived. Surely it wouldn't take him longer than that to tell her what he wanted her to do.

He hated the fact that he had an audience. Brodick, true to his impatient nature, blurted out, "Judith, you aren't going back to England. Not now. Not ever. Iain isn't going to take you home."

The warrior sounded quite cheerful when he gave her his news. She turned her gaze to him. "He isn't? Then who will take me back?"

"No one," Brodick answered.

Iain took hold of both her hands and squeezed to get her attention. Then he took a deep breath. Even with his men watching, he wanted the words to be right, his declaration to be one she would always remember. It was a damned awkward undertaking, trying to think of loving words, and he had absolutely no experience in this area, but he was still determined not to muck it up.

The moment needed to be perfect for her. "Judith," he began.

"Yes, Iain?"

"I'm keeping you."

Chapter 10

Y ou can't just . . . keep me."

"Aye, he can, lass," Alex cheerfully explained.

"He's laird," Graham reminded her. "He can do anything he's wanting to do."

"It doesn't matter that he's laird," Brodick interjected. "Franklen kept Marrian and he isn't laird. Robert kept Meagan," he added with a shrug.

"I kept Isabelle," Winslow added.

"It's our way, lass," Gowrie explained.

"You didn't just keep Isabelle," Brodick told his brother, determined to set that misconception straight. "You asked for her. There's a difference."

"I would have taken her if her father had been difficult," Winslow argued.

Judith couldn't believe what she was hearing. They had all gone daft. She pulled her hands away from Iain's grasp and took a step back, away from this madness. She stepped on Graham's foot. She turned around to give him her apology.

"I'm sorry, Graham. I didn't mean to step on— He can't just keep me, can he?"

Graham nodded. "Gowrie was right when he told you it's our way," he explained. "Of course, you're going to have to agree."

His voice was filled with sympathy. Iain had given the pretty woman quite a startle. She seemed to be a little overwhelmed, but certainly thrilled with this announcement. It was the highest of honors to be chosen as wife of the laird. Aye, she was so pleased, she couldn't seem to form a coherent word of appreciation, he supposed.

Graham supposed wrong. In the space of a minute or two, Judith recovered. Then she shook her head. She might have been able to control her anger if Iain's supporters hadn't all nodded at her again.

God's truth, she wanted to kick every one of them. She'd have to quit sputtering first. She took a deep breath in an effort to gain control, then said in a hoarse voice, "Iain, might I have a word in private with you?"

"There really isn't time for chitchat now, lass," Father Laggan called out. "Merlin won't keep."

"Merlin?" she asked in confusion.

"He's a Dunbar," Graham explained. With a smile he added, "He's in need of a priest."

Judith turned to look at Father Laggan. "Then you must go to him," she said. "Is he dying?"

The priest shook his head. "He's dead, Judith. His family's waiting on mc to bury him. It's the heat, you see. Merlin isn't going to keep much longer."

"Aye, he's got to get him in the ground," Brodick explained. "He'll marry you first. The Maitlands come before the Dunbars."

"Merlin won't keep?" Judith repeated the priest's explanation and put her hand to her forehead.

"The heat," Brodick reminded her.

She started trembling. Iain took mercy on her. It had taken him days of hard thought before he'd come to the conclusion that he couldn't let Judith leave. He realized now he probably should have given her more time to think about his proposal.

Unfortunately, there wasn't any time left to consider all the reasons. After talking to Patrick and confirming his own suspicions, he knew he had to marry Judith as soon as possible. He wasn't about to take the chance that someone else might find out about her father. No, he had to marry her now. It was the only way he could protect her from the bastard Macleans.

He took hold of her hand and led her over to the corner of the hall. She stumbled and he ended up half dragging her. She stood with her back against the wall. He stood in front of her, effectively blocking her view of the rest of the room.

He nudged her chin up so she would look at him. "I want you to marry me."

"No."

"Yes."

"I can't."

"Yes, you can."

"Iain, will you be reasonable about this? I can't marry you. Even if I wanted to, it isn't possible."

"You do want to marry me," he countered. "Don't you?"

He was staggered by the possibility that she didn't want him. He had to shake his head. "You damn well do," he told her then.

"Oh? And why is that?"

"You trust me."

The bluster went out of her anger. Of all the reasons he could have given her, he'd centered on the one she couldn't argue with. She did trust him, with all her heart.

"You feel safe with me."

She couldn't argue with that truth, either. "You know I'll protect you from harm," he added with a gentle nod.

Her eyes filled with tears. Dear God, she wished it were possible. "Do you love me, Iain?" she asked.

He leaned down and kissed her. "I have never wanted another woman the way I want you," he said. "You want me, too. Don't deny it."

Her shoulders slumped. "I don't deny it," she whispered. "But wanting and loving are two different matters. I might not love you," she added.

She knew that was a lie as soon as the words were out of her mouth.

He knew it, too. "Aye, you do love me."

A tear slipped down her cheek. "You're putting impossible thoughts in my head," she whispered.

He gently wiped the tear away. His hands cupped the sides of her face. "Nothing is impossible. Marry me, Judith. Let me protect you."

She had to tell him the truth now. Only then would he change his mind about this rash decision. "There's something you don't know about me," she began. "My father—"

His mouth covered hers, effectively stopping her confession. The kiss was long, passionate, and when he pulled back, she barely knew her own thoughts.

She tried to tell him again. He stopped her with another kiss.

"Judith, you will not tell me anything about your family," he ordered. "I don't care if your father's the king of England. You will not speak another word on the topic. Understand?"

"But Iain—"

"Your past isn't important," he told her. He took hold of her shoulders and squeezed. His voice was low, fervent. "Let it go, Judith. You're going to belong to me. I'm going to be your family. I'll take care of you."

He made it sound so appealing. Judith didn't know what to do. "I must think about this," she decided. "In a few days—"

"Good Lord," Father Laggan called out. "We can't expect Merlin to keep that long, lass. Consider the heat."

"Why wait?" Patrick called out.

"Aye, he's told you he's keeping you. Get the wedding done," Brodick said.

It wasn't until that moment that Judith realized they'd

all been listening to her private talk with Iain. She felt like screaming. Then she did. "I will not be rushed into this," she told them. In a softer voice she added, "There are plenty of reasons why I shouldn't marry your laird, and I need time to consider . . ."

"What are these reasons?" Graham asked.

Iain turned to the leader of the council. "Are you for or against us?"

"I'm not overly pleased, of course, but you know I'll stand beside you. You have my support. Gelfrid, what about you?"

Gelfrid frowned at Judith while he gave his answer. "I'm in agreement."

The other council members, like dominoes, followed Gelfrid's voice of approval.

Judith had heard enough. "How can you give your approval and glare at me at the same time?" she demanded. She turned back to Iain and poked him in his chest. "I don't want to live here. I already made up my mind to live with my aunt Millicent and uncle Herbert. And do you know why?" She didn't give him time to answer. "They don't consider me inferior, that's why. Well?" she demanded in a challenge.

"Well, what?" Iain asked, trying not to smile over the outrage she was giving him. The woman was feisty when she was riled.

"They like me," she stammered out.

"We like you fine, Judith," Alex told her.

"Everyone does," Patrick added with a nod.

She wasn't believing that nonsense for a minute. Neither was Brodick. He gave Patrick a look that suggested he'd lost his head.

"But I don't particularly like any of you brutes," she announced. "The thought of living here is simply not acceptable. I won't raise my children— Oh, God, Iain, I'm not having any, remember?"

"Judith, calm yourself," Iain commanded. He pulled her up against him and hugged her tight.

"She's not wanting children?" Graham asked. He sounded appalled. "Iain, you can't allow that kind of talk. You need an heir."

"Is she barren?" Gelfrid called out.

"She isn't saying that," Vincent muttered.

"This is my fault," Winslow interjected.

"It's your fault the woman's barren?" Gelfrid asked, trying to understand. "How can that be, Winslow?"

Patrick started laughing. Brodick elbowed him to get him to stop. "She had to help with Isabelle's birthing," Brodick told Gelfrid. "It made her afraid. That's all there is to it. She isn't barren."

The council members grunted with relief. Iain wasn't paying any attention to anyone but Judith now. He leaned down and whispered, "You're right, you need more time to consider this proposal. Take as long as you need."

There was something in his voice that made her suspicious. She realized what it was almost immediately. Iain was vastly amused. "How long do I have to consider this proposal?"

"You're sleeping in my bed tonight. I thought you might want to be married first."

She pushed herself out of his arms and looked up at him. He was smiling. She never stood a chance. She realized that now. Lord, she did love him. And at this very moment she couldn't think of one good reason why.

They'd all made her daft. "Why in God's name do I love you?"

She hadn't realized she'd shouted her question until Patrick started laughing.

"Well now, that settles it. She's agreed," Father Laggan called out. He hurried across the hall. "Let's get it done. Patrick, you stand on Iain's right, and Graham, you put yourself next to Judith. You can give her away. In the name of the Father, and of the Son—"

"We're giving her away, too," Gelfrid announced,

determined not to be left out of this important ceremony.

"Aye, we are," Duncan muttered.

The scuffle of chairs interrupted the priest's concentration. He waited until the other elders had all squeezed
themselves around Judith, and then began again. "In the
name of the Father—"

"You only want to marry me so you can order me
around all the time," Judith told Iain.

"There is that benefit," Iain drawled out.

"I thought the Dunbars were your enemies," she said
then. "Yet your priest—"

"How do you think Merlin died?" Brodick asked.

"Now, son, you can't be taking credit for that death,"
Graham advised. "It was the fall over the cliff that did
him in."

"Winslow, didn't you do the pushing when he came at
you with the knife?" Brodick asked.

His brother shook his head. "He slipped before I could
get to him."

Judith was appalled by their talk. Patrick decided to
answer her initial question about the priest since no one
else seemed inclined. "There aren't enough men of the
cloth to serve up here," he said. "Father Laggan's
allowed to come and go as he pleases."

"He serves a wide area," Alex interjected, "and all the
clans we consider our enemies. There are the Dunbars,
the Macphersons, and the Macleans, and others, of
course."

She was astonished by their list of enemies. She made
that mention to Graham. She wanted to learn everything
she could about the Maitlands, of course, but there was
another motive, too. She needed time to collect herself.
She felt as though she were in a daze. She was trembling
like an infant freshly washed in cold water.

"Alex has only given you a partial list," Graham told
her.

"Don't you people like anyone?" she asked, incredulous.

Graham shrugged.

"Can we get on with this?" Father Laggan cried out. "In the name of the Father . . ."

"I'm inviting my aunt Millicent and uncle Herbert to come for a visit, Iain, and I'm not going through the council to get permission first."

". . . and of the Son," the priest continued in a much louder voice.

"She'll be wanting King John next," Duncan predicted.

"We can't allow that, lass," Owen muttered.

"Please join hands now and concentrate on this ceremony," Father Laggan shouted, trying to gain everyone's attention.

"I don't want King John to come here," Judith argued. She turned to frown at Owen for making such a shameful suggestion. "I want my aunt and uncle. I'm getting them, too." She turned and had to peek around Graham in order to look up at Iain. "Yes or no, Iain."

"We'll see. Graham, I'm marrying Judith, not you. Let go of her hand. Judith, move over here."

Father Laggan gave up trying to maintain order. He continued on with the ceremony. Iain was paying some attention. He immediately agreed to take Judith for his wife.

She wasn't as cooperative. He felt a little sorry for the sweet woman. She looked thoroughly confused.

"Judith, do you take Iain for your husband?"

She looked up at Iain before giving her answer. "We'll see."

"That won't do, lass. You've got to say I do," he advised.

"Do I?"

Iain smiled. "Your aunt and uncle will be welcomed here."

She smiled back. "Thank you."

"You've still got to answer me, Judith," Father Laggan reminded her.

"Is he going to agree to love and cherish me?" she asked.

"For the love of God, he just did," Brodick impatiently called out.

"Iain, if I stay here, I'm bound to try to make some changes."

"Now, Judith, we like things just the way they are around here," Graham told her.

"I don't like things around here," Judith said. "Iain, before we start, I want one more promise," she blurted out.

"Before we start? We're in the middle—" the priest tried to explain.

"What promise is this?" Graham asked. "The council might have need to mull it over."

"You will not mull it over," she countered. "This is a private matter. Iain?"

"Yes, Judith?"

Oh Lord, how she loved his smile. She let out a little sigh while she motioned him closer so she could whisper in his ear. Graham had to back up a space to give her room. As soon as Iain leaned down, everyone else leaned forward to listen.

They were still left guessing. Whatever she had requested of their laird had clearly surprised him, if the look on his face was any indication.

The notice naturally pricked everyone's attention.

"This is important to you?"

"Yes."

"All right," he answered. "I promise."

Judith didn't realize she'd been holding her breath until he gave her his promise. She let out a loud sigh.

Her eyes filled with tears. She was so pleased with this man. He hadn't laughed or taken insult. He didn't even make her explain. He simply asked her if it was important, and when she'd told him it was, he immediately agreed.

"Did you happen to get any of that, Graham?" Alex asked in a loud whisper everyone heard.

"Something about a drink," Graham whispered back.

"She's wanting a drink?" Gelfrid bellowed.

"Nay, I caught the word drunk," Owen announced.

"Why's she wanting to get drunk?" Vincent wanted to know.

Judith tried not to laugh. She turned her attention back to Father Laggan. "I will say I do," she told him. "Shouldn't we begin now?"

"The lass has trouble following along," Vincent remarked.

Father Laggan gave the final blessing while Judith argued with the elder about his rude comment. Her concentration was just fine, she told him quite vehemently.

She nagged an apology out of Vincent before giving the priest her attention again. "Patrick, would you go and get Frances Catherine? I would like her to stand by my side during the ceremony."

"You may kiss the bride," Father Laggan announced.

Frances Catherine was pacing back and forth inside the cottage when Judith finally opened the door and walked inside.

"Thank God you're here. I've been so worried. Judith, what took so long? Tell me what happened. Are you all right? You look so pale. They upset you, didn't they?" She paused to let out an outraged gasp. "They didn't dare try to order you to go back to England, did they?"

Judith sat down at the table. "They left," she whispered.

"Who left?"

"Everyone. They just . . . left. Even Iain. He kissed me first. Then he left, too. I don't know where everyone went."

Frances Catherine had never seen her friend like this. Judith appeared to be in a daze. "You're frightening me, Judith. Please tell me what happened."

"I got married."

Frances Catherine had to sit down. "You got married?"

Judith nodded. She continued to stare off into space, her mind centered on the bizarre wedding ceremony.

Frances Catherine was too astonished to speak for several minutes. She sat across from Judith at the table and simply stared at her.

"Did you marry Iain?"

"I think so."

"What do you mean, you think so?"

"Graham was standing between us. I might have married him. No, I'm certain it was Iain. He kissed me after . . . Graham didn't."

Frances Catherine didn't know what to make of this news. She was thrilled, of course, because her friend would never have to go back to England, but she was also furious. Her mind concentrated on that emotion first.

"Why was it rushed? There weren't any flowers, were there? You couldn't have been married in a chapel. We don't have one. Damn it, Judith, you should have insisted Iain do it right."

"I don't know why it was so rushed," Judith admitted. "But Iain surely had his reasons. Please don't get upset about this."

"I should have been there," Frances Catherine wailed.

"Aye, you should have," Judith agreed.

Another minute passed in silence before Frances Catherine spoke again. "Are we happy about this marriage?"

Judith lifted her shoulders in a shrug. "I suppose we are."

Tears filled Frances Catherine's eyes. "You deserved to have your dream come true."

Judith knew what her friend was talking about, of course. She shook her head and tried to comfort Frances

Catherine. "Dreams are for little girls to whisper to each other. They don't really come true. I'm a fully grown woman now, Frances Catherine. I don't imagine impossible things."

Her friend wasn't ready to let it go. "You're forgetting who you're talking to, Judith. I know you better than anyone else in this whole world. I know all about your horrible life with your witch of a mother and your drunken uncle. I know about the pain and the loneliness. Your dreams became your shields against the hurt. You can tell me it was just your active imagination, these dreams you now pretend aren't still important, but I know better."

Her voice cracked on a sob. She took a deep breath and then continued on. "Your dreams saved you from despair. Don't you dare pretend they don't matter. I won't believe you."

"Frances Catherine, please be reasonable about this," Judith said in exasperation. "It wasn't always horrible. Millicent and Herbert balanced my life. Besides, I was very young when I thought up such silly dreams. I was only imagining what I wanted my wedding to be like. My father was there, remember? I thought the man was dead, but I still imagined him standing by my side at the back of the chapel. My husband was going to be so happy, he was going to cry. Now I ask you. Can you imagine Iain weeping over the sight of me?"

Frances Catherine couldn't help but smile. "My husband was also going to weep with gratitude. Patrick didn't. He gloated."

"I won't ever have to see my mother again."

She'd whispered that thought aloud. Frances Catherine nodded. "You won't ever have to leave me, either."

"I want you to be happy about this."

"All right. I'm happy. Now tell me exactly what happened. I want every detail."

Judith did as she was asked. By the time she was finished with the recounting, Frances Catherine was laughing. Judith was having difficulty remembering, and she kept excusing her poor memory on the fact that it had all been terribly confusing.

"I asked Iain if he loved me," she told her friend. "He didn't give me an answer. I didn't realize that until it was over and he was kissing me. He said he wanted me. I also tried to tell him about my father, but he wouldn't let me get the words out. He said it didn't matter. I was to let it alone. Those were his very words. I did try, but I'm thinking I should have tried harder."

Frances Catherine let out an unladylike snort. "Don't you start worrying about your father. We aren't ever going to mention him again. No one's going to know."

Judith nodded. "I made Iain promise me two things. Millicent and Herbert can come here for a visit."

"And the other promise?"

"Iain won't get drunk in my presence."

Frances Catherine's eyes filled with tears. She never would have thought to ask her husband such a thing, but she fully understood why Judith would be so concerned. "For as long as I've lived here, I've never seen Iain drunk."

"He'll keep his promise," Judith whispered. She let out a sigh. "I wonder where I'll sleep tonight."

"Iain will come here to get you."

"What have I gotten myself into?"

"You love him."

"Yes."

"He must love you."

"I hope he does," Judith said. "He didn't have anything else to gain. He must love me."

"Are you worried about tonight?"

"A little. Were you worried the first time?"

"I cried."

For some reason, both women found that admission hysterically funny. Patrick and Iain walked inside, both smiling over the way Frances Catherine and Judith were laughing.

Patrick wanted to know what they found so amusing. His question only made the two women laugh all the more. He finally gave up. Women, he decided, didn't make much sense.

Iain's gaze was centered on Judith. "Why are you here?" he asked.

"I wanted to tell Frances Catherine what happened. We did get married, didn't we?"

"She thinks she might have married Graham," Frances Catherine told Patrick.

Iain shook his head. He went over to his bride and pulled her to her feet. She hadn't looked at him once since he'd entered the cottage, and that notice bothered him. "It's time to go home."

Judith was filled with trepidation. "I'll just get a few of my things," she said. She kept her head bowed and started toward the back of the screen. "Where is home?" she asked.

"Where you were married," Patrick told her.

It was safe for her to grimace. No one could see her. Then she let out a sigh. She was going to have to live in the ugly keep, she supposed, but it wasn't going to bother her. Iain lived there and that was all that mattered.

Judith could hear the two brothers talking together while she gathered her sleeping gown and wrapper and other necessary items for tonight. She would collect the rest of her things tomorrow.

She had difficulty folding her nightgown and was surprised to notice her hands shook.

She finished packing the small valise but didn't leave her little sanctuary. The significance of what had taken place today was finally settling in her mind.

She sat down on the side of the bed and closed her eyes. She was a married woman. Her heart was suddenly pounding a furious beat and she could barely catch a decent breath. She knew she was beginning to panic and tried to calm herself.

Dear God, what if she had made a mistake? It had all

happened so fast. Iain did love her, didn't he? It didn't matter that he hadn't given her the words. He wanted to marry her and he had absolutely nothing to gain other than a wife. What other motive could there be?

What if she couldn't fit in with these people? What if they never accepted her? Judith finally focused on her main concern. What if she couldn't be a good wife? She sure as certain didn't know how to please a man in bed. Iain would know she was inexperienced. It would be his duty to teach her, but what if she was the kind of woman who couldn't be taught?

She didn't want him to think of her as inferior. She would rather die.

"Judith?"

His voice was little more than a whisper. She still flinched. He noticed. He noticed his bride looked ready to faint, too. Judith was afraid. He thought he understood why.

"I'm ready to leave now," she told him in a voice that shivered.

She didn't move after making that announcement. Her valise was on her lap and she appeared to have a death grip on the handle. Iain hid his smile. He walked over to the bed and sat down next to her.

"Why are you sitting here?" he asked.

"I was just thinking."

"About what?"

She didn't answer him. She wouldn't look at him, but kept her gaze locked on her lap.

Iain wasn't going to rush her. He decided to act as though there was all the time in the world. They sat side by side for several minutes. Judith could hear Frances Catherine whispering to her husband. She heard the word "flowers" and thought her friend might be complaining about the lack of decorations at the wedding.

"Is it possible for me to have a bath tonight?"

"Yes."

She nodded. "Shouldn't we leave?"

"You're finished thinking?"

"Yes, thank you."

He stood up. So did she. She handed him her valise. He took hold of her hand and started for the doorway.

Frances Catherine blocked their exit. She was determined to make them stay for supper. Since everything was ready, Iain agreed. Judith was far too nervous to eat. Iain didn't have any trouble. Both he and Patrick ate like men who'd just completed the forty-day Lenten fast.

He didn't want to linger after the meal, however. Neither did Judith. They walked hand in hand up to the keep. It was dark inside. Iain led her up to the second level. His bedchamber was on the left side of the landing, the first of three doors along the narrow corridor.

The bedroom blazed with light and warmth. The hearth faced the door. A fire burned bright, effectively heating the area. Iain's bed was to the left of the doorway. It took up a fair portion of the wall. A quilt, made of the colors of his clan, covered the bed, and a small chest with two candles on top was next to the wall.

There was only one chair in the room, near the hearth. Another chest, much larger and taller than the one by the bed, was on the opposite wall. An ornate, gold-rimmed square box sat on top of the chest.

Iain wasn't much for clutter, she decided. The room was functional, efficient, and very like the man who slept here.

There was a large wooden tub directly in front of the fireplace. Steam filtered up from the water. Iain had thoughtfully anticipated her request for a bath even before she'd asked him.

He tossed her valise on the bed. "Is there anything else you need?"

She needed not to be afraid, but she didn't tell him that. "No, thank you."

She continued to stand in the center of the room, her hands folded together, waiting and praying he would leave so she could have her bath in privacy.

He wondered why she was hesitating to get the chore done. "Do you need help getting undressed?" he asked.

"No," she blurted out, appalled by the very idea. "I remember how," she added in a calmer voice.

He nodded, then motioned with the crook of his finger for her to come to him. She didn't hesitate. She stopped when she was just a foot away.

He was pleased she didn't flinch when he reached for her. He lifted her hair back over her shoulder, then slipped his fingers in around the neckline of her gown to catch hold of her chain.

He didn't say a word until he'd removed the chain and ring.

"Do you remember the promises you gained from me today?"

She nodded. Dear God, he wasn't going to tell her he'd changed his mind, was he?

He saw the look of panic on her face and shook his head. "I have never broken my word before, Judith, and I won't break it now." His guess had been proven correct. The fear immediately left her gaze. "If you knew me better, you never would have had that worry."

"But I don't know you better," she whispered, excusing her behavior.

"I have a promise I want you to give me," he explained. He dropped the chain and ring into her hand. "I don't want you to wear this to bed."

It didn't sound like a request to her, but an order. He didn't explain his reasons either. Judith was about to ask him why he would want such a promise, then changed her mind. He hadn't made her explain why she wanted him to promise he'd never get sotted when he was with her, and he deserved to receive the very same consideration.

"I agree."

He nodded. He looked satisfied.

"Do you want me to throw it away?"

"No," he answered. "Put it in there," he told her, motioning to the small box on top of the chest. "No one will bother it."

She hurried to do what he suggested. "May I keep the brooch my aunt Millicent gave me in here, too?" she asked. "I wouldn't want to lose it."

He didn't answer her. She turned around and only then realized that he had left the room. He hadn't made a sound.

She shook her head. She must have a talk with him about his rude habit of disappearing like that, she decided.

Since she didn't have any idea how long he planned to stay away, she hurried through her bath. She wasn't planning to wash her hair, but then changed her mind.

Iain opened the door while she was rinsing the rose-scented soap from her hair. He got a glimpse of golden skin before he pulled the door closed again. He leaned against the wall and waited for his bride to finish.

He didn't want to embarrass her. The woman was taking forever, though. He had walked a fair distance to the water basin, washed, and then walked back, fully expecting that his bride would be waiting in bed for him.

He waited another fifteen minutes, then went inside. Judith was sitting on a blanket on the floor directly in front of the hearth, diligently drying her hair. She wore a prim white nightgown and matching robe.

She looked absolutely beautiful to him. Her face was scrubbed pink everywhere and her hair was the color of pale gold.

Iain leaned against the door frame for several minutes, just staring at her. A tightness settled in his chest. She was his wife. Aye, she belonged to him now. A feeling of contentment swept over him, catching him by surprise. It all seemed so inevitable to him. Why had he put himself through the torment of trying to stay away from her? From the moment he first kissed her, he should have accepted the truth. His heart had always known he would never let another man have her. Why had it taken his mind so long to accept?

Matters of the heart were damn confusing, he decided. He remembered how he'd boasted to Patrick that one woman was just as good as another. He understood the blasphemy in that arrogant remark now. There was only one Judith.

Iain shook himself out of his foolish thoughts. He was a warrior. He shouldn't be thinking about such inconsequential things.

He turned around to go back into the hall and then let out a shrill whistle. The sound echoed down the stairs. Iain came back into the room and walked over to the hearth. He leaned against the mantel, not two feet away from his bride, and pulled his boots off.

She was about to ask him why he'd left the door open when three men came hurrying inside. They nodded to their laird, crossed the chamber and lifted the tub. They were quite deliberate in keeping their gazes away from Judith while they carried the heavy tub out of the room.

Iain followed them to the door and was about to shut it when someone shouted his name. He let out a sigh and left the chamber again.

He didn't come back for almost an hour. The heat from the fire had made Judith sleepy. Her hair was just a little damp now and most of the curl was back. She stood up, put her brush back on the mantel, and went over to the side of the bed. She was removing her robe when Iain came back inside.

He shut the door, bolted it, and then took off his plaid. He wasn't wearing anything underneath.

She thought she was going to die of embarrassment then and there. She turned her gaze to the center beam in the ceiling, but not before she had gotten a rather healthy glimpse of him. No wonder Frances Catherine had cried on her wedding night. If Patrick was fashioned anything like Iain was, and she was guessing he probably was, she could well understand weeping. God's truth, her eyes were already getting misty. Oh Lord, she really wasn't prepared for this. She *had* made a mistake after all. No, no, she wasn't ready for this kind of intimacy. She didn't know him well enough . . . she never should have—

"It's going to be all right, Judith."

He was standing right in front of her. She wouldn't look at him. He put his hands on her shoulders and gave her an affectionate squeeze. "It really will be all right. You trust me, don't you?"

His voice was filled with tenderness. It didn't help. She took several deep breaths in an attempt to calm down. That didn't help either.

And then he pulled her into his arms and held her tight. She let out a little sigh and settled down. It was going to be all right. Iain wouldn't hurt her. He loved her.

She leaned a little away so she could look up into his eyes. There was such warmth there, a little amusement, too.

"Don't be afraid," he told her, his voice a soothing whisper.

"How do you know I'm afraid?"

He smiled. "Afraid" wasn't quite the right word, he decided. "Terrified" was a far more accurate description. "You have the same expression on your face you had the night I told you Isabelle wanted you to help her deliver her son."

She turned her gaze to his chest. "I didn't want to help because I was afraid I wouldn't be able to . . . Iain, I don't believe I want to do this, either. I know it will be all right, but I still would rather not—"

Judith didn't finish her confession. She went back into his arms and rested against him.

Iain was pleased she was able to be honest with him, but he was frustrated, too. He had never taken a virgin to his bed, and he hadn't realized until this minute how important it was going to be to make it as easy as possible for her. It was going to require time, patience, and a good deal of stamina.

"Exactly what is it you're afraid of?" he asked.

She didn't answer him. She was trembling now, and he knew it wasn't from cold.

"There will be pain, of course, but if I—"

"I'm not afraid of the pain."

She'd blurted out that announcement. He was more thoroughly puzzled now. "Then what are you afraid of?" He started rubbing her back while he waited for her to answer him.

"A man can always . . . you know," she stammered out. "But some women can't, and if I'm one of those women, then I'll disappoint you."

"You won't disappoint me."

"I really do believe I will," she whispered. "I think I'm one of the ones who can't, Iain."

"You can," he told her with great authority. He wasn't at all certain exactly what she was talking about, but it seemed to be important to her, and she certainly needed his confidence now. He was the experienced one, after all, and he knew she would believe whatever he told her.

He kept stroking her back. Judith closed her eyes and let him soothe her. He was surely the most considerate man in the world, and when he was being so gentle with her, she couldn't help but love him.

It didn't take her long to get over her fear. She was still a bit nervous, of course, but she didn't think that was unusual. She took a deep breath, then pulled away from Iain. She couldn't look at him and she knew she was blushing, but that didn't stop her. She slowly lifted her gown up and over her head. Then she tossed it on the bed. She didn't give him time to look at her either. The second her gown was discarded, she rushed back into his arms.

He visibly shuddered. "You feel so good against me," he whispered, his voice gruff with emotion.

It felt much better than good to her. It felt wonderful. In a shy, halting voice, she told him so.

His chin dropped to rest on the top of her head. "You please me, Judith."

"I haven't done anything yet," she replied.

"You don't need to do anything," he explained.

She could hear the laughter in his voice. She smiled in reaction. By not rushing her, Iain was actually helping her get past her embarrassment. She knew that was his plan, and it didn't even matter that it was deliberate. His consideration for her feelings fairly overwhelmed her. She didn't even think she was blushing any longer.

The heat of his hard arousal pressed so intimately against her lower belly still worried her, but Iain wasn't being at all demanding, just gentle, terribly gentle as he slowly caressed her shivers away, and it didn't take long for that worry to seem unimportant.

She wanted to touch him. She let go of her hard grip around his waist and tentatively stroked his broad shoulders, then his back, and finally his thighs. His skin felt like hot steel against her fingertips. He was so completely different in texture and tone from her, and she found herself marveling over all the wonderful differences. His muscles were like knotted rope along his upper arms, and in comparison she was built like a weakling.

"You're so strong, Iain, and I'm so weak. It seems strange to me that I would please you."

He laughed. "You aren't weak. You're soft and smooth and very, very appealing."

She blushed with pleasure over his praise. She rubbed her face against his chest, smiling over the way his crisp hair tickled her nose. She leaned up and kissed him where the pulse beat at the base of his neck.

"I do like touching you," she admitted.

She sounded surprised by her own admission. Iain wasn't. He already knew she liked to touch him. He liked it, too. One of her most appealing traits was her desire to touch, to stroke, to hold him whenever possible. He

243

thought about all the times she'd instinctively taken hold of his hand, the way she'd caressed his arm while she gave him hell about an opinion of his she had taken exception to.

She had very few inhibitions when she was with him . . . but only with him. Aye, he had noticed how reserved she was with his soldiers on the journey here. She was very pleasant, of course, but she went out of her way to avoid touching any of them. She never relaxed in Alex's arms when she had been forced to ride with him, yet she'd fallen asleep in his arms. She trusted him completely, and that fact was every bit as important to him as her love.

And Lord, she really did love him.

"Judith?"

"Yes?"

"Are you ready to quit hiding from me?"

She almost laughed. She had been hiding from him, and he'd known that was her game all along. She let go of her hold on him and took a step back, away from him. Then she looked up into his eyes and slowly nodded.

He had the most wonderful smile. She thought about that while she stared up at him. She had the most magnificent body he'd ever seen. He thought about that while he stared at her. She was exquisitely formed, from the top of her head to the bottom of her feet, and Lord, if he didn't get to touch her soon, to make her completely his, he knew he would lose his mind.

They reached for each other at the same moment. She put her arms around his neck as he cupped her backside and pulled her up against him.

He leaned down and kissed her, a deep, devouring kiss that left both of them breathless. His tongue moved inside to taste the sweetness she offered. A low growl of satisfaction came from the back of his throat when she imitated the erotic love play and rubbed her tongue against his.

She sagged against him. Iain kept one arm around her

to keep her from falling down as he turned and leaned down to pull the covers back. She didn't want him to quit kissing her. She tugged on his hair at the back of his neck to get his attention and leaned up to kiss him when he didn't respond quick enough.

He liked her boldness. He liked the little moans she made, too. Iain lifted her into his arms and put her in the center of the bed. He didn't give her time to start worrying. He came down on top of her, separating her thighs with one of his own. He braced his weight on his elbows and let his body cover hers completely. And God, he had never felt anything this wonderful in all of his life.

Her response to him was overwhelming his desire to go slow, to take his time preparing her for his invasion. He needed to concentrate on what he was doing, to be deliberate in where and how he touched her, until she wasn't able to think, but only feel the pleasure. Judith was making his thoughtful, calculated plan impossible. She was restlessly moving against him, driving him to distraction. He kissed her again, a long, hot, wet kiss that made him wild for more. He finally dragged his mouth away from hers and moved lower to taste the fragrant valley between her soft breasts. His hands stroked, caressed, teased, and finally, when he couldn't wait a second longer, he took one nipple into his mouth and began to suckle.

She almost came off the bed. Tremors of raw pleasure coursed through her body. She didn't think she could take much more of this sweet torture. She clung to his shoulders and closed her eyes in surrender to the ecstasy he was giving her.

Iain was shaking with his need to take her. He could feel his control slipping away. His desire to taste all of her overwhelmed every other consideration. His hands stroked a path down the flat of her stomach, then lower still until he was caressing her inner thighs and slowly easing them apart. He leaned down and kissed the top of the soft triangle of curls shielding her virginity.

"Iain, don't—"

"Yes."

She tried to push him away from her, but then his mouth covered the very heat of her, and his tongue, dear God, his tongue was rubbing against her, and she became consumed with white-hot pleasure so intense, she forgot all about protesting.

Her hips instinctively rose up for more of his touch. Her nails dug into his shoulder blades. She had never known a man could make love to a woman in this intimate way, but she wasn't at all appalled or embarrassed now. She wanted to touch him the way he was touching her, to learn his taste, too, but every time she tried to move, he'd tighten his hold and make her stay put.

Iain shifted to his side and slowly eased his finger up inside her tight sheath. His thumb rubbed the delicate nub hidden between the folds, and Judith's reaction damn near snapped his own control. He'd never had a woman respond to him with such honesty or with such abandon. Her trust in him was so complete, she was free of all inhibitions. She willingly, lovingly, gave him her body, and he would die before letting himself find fulfillment first. She came before his own need . . . even if it killed him.

Loving him was certainly going to kill her. That was Judith's last coherent thought. She'd blurted it out loud, too, but she was too caught up in trying to hold on to the threads of her control to know what she was saying or doing.

She seemed to come apart inside. She cried out his name, and his own discipline vanished then. He felt her tremors and spread her thighs wider. He knelt between her legs. "Put your arms around me, sweetheart," he whispered in a husky demand. He stretched up, covered her mouth with his, and forced her to stay still by holding the sides of her hips.

He hesitated at the threshold for only a second or two, then slowly eased up inside her until he felt the barrier of her virginity.

He was hurting her, but Judith didn't think this was such a terrible pain. The way he was kissing her made everything else seem unimportant. The pressure building inside her ached, and she became even more restless in a bid to find a way to ease the sweet torment.

Iain gritted his teeth against the incredible pleasure he was already feeling and the certain pain he was going to force on her, and then drove forward with one powerful thrust.

She cried out in surprise and pain. She thought he had torn her apart. It felt as if he had. The haze of passion vanished. She started crying, and demanded that he leave her alone.

"I don't like this," she whispered.

"Hush, sweetheart," he whispered, trying to soothe her. "It's going to be all right. Don't move yet. The pain will ease. Oh, God, Judith, don't try to move."

He sounded angry and loving, and she wasn't able to understand anything he was saying to her. The pain throbbed, but another feeling, so foreign to anything she had ever experienced before, began to blend with the pain, confusing her even more.

His weight kept her anchored to the bed and to him. He took deep, calming breaths in an effort to hold on to his discipline. She was so damn hot and tight, and all he wanted to think about was slamming into her again and again until he found his own release.

Iain leaned up on his elbows and kissed her again. He desperately wanted to give her enough time to adjust to him, and he felt like the lowest of animals when he saw the tears streaming down her face.

"God, Judith, I'm sorry. I had to hurt you, but I . . ."

The worry in his gaze soothed her far more than his half-given apology did. She reached up and stroked the side of his face. Her hand shook. "It's going to be all right," she whispered, giving him the very same promise he'd given her minutes earlier. "The pain's gone now."

He knew she wasn't telling the truth. He kissed her brow, then the bridge of her nose, and finally captured her mouth for a long, passionate kiss. His hand moved between their joined bodies and he began to stroke the very heat of her.

It didn't take him long to rekindle her desire. He started to move, slowly at first, until he heard her moan of pleasure, and still he was able to hold back that thread of control he always withheld when he had been with other women, but Judith snatched that away from him with one simple declaration.

"I love you, Iain."

Passion took control of his mind and his body. He thrust deep inside her, again and again. She lifted her hips to take more of him. She wouldn't let him be gentle any longer; nay, her nails dug into his shoulders, demanding more and more of this incredible bliss.

Iain buried his face in the crook of her neck, gritting against the white-hot pleasure consuming him.

The pressure building inside her was becoming unbearable. Just when she was certain she was going to die from the intensity of the feelings flooding her senses, he became even more forceful, more demanding.

Judith kept trying to understand what was happening to her. Iain wasn't letting her. She was suddenly terrified. She felt as though her mind was being separated from her body and her soul.

"Iain, I don't—"

"Hush, love," he whispered. "Just hold me. I'll take care of you."

Her mind accepted what her heart had always known. Judith surrendered. It was the most magical experience of her life. Bliss such as she'd never known filled her. She arched her back and clung to her husband and let the ecstasy consume her.

As soon as he felt her release, Iain found his own. With a low groan he poured his seed into her. His entire body shuddered with his own surrender.

He collapsed against her with a grunt of male satisfaction. The scent of their lovemaking filled the air between them, a lingering reminder of the wonder they had just shared. Iain's heart hammered like a drumbeat, and he was so amazed by his absolute surrender to her, he couldn't move. He wanted to stay inside her forever. She was stroking his shoulders and sighing every now and then, and he wanted that to go on forever.

Dear God, he was content.

It took Judith much longer to recover from their lovemaking. She couldn't seem to quit touching him. She had at least a hundred questions to ask him. The first, and surely the most important, was to find out if she had pleased him.

She poked him in his shoulder to get his attention. He thought she was letting him know he was too heavy for her. He immediately rolled to his side. She rolled with him.

His eyes were closed. "Iain, did I please you?"

He grinned.

It wasn't enough. She needed to hear the words.

He opened his eyes, found her staring down at him. She looked worried. "How can you doubt you pleased me?" he asked.

He didn't give her time to come up with a reason. He wrapped his arms around her, lifted her to rest on top of him, and kissed her soundly.

"I f you had pleased me any more, you would have killed me. Satisfied now?"

She closed her eyes and tucked her head under his chin.

Aye, she was very satisfied.

Chapter 11

Judith didn't get much sleep that night. Iain kept waking her up. It certainly wasn't deliberate on his part, but each time he turned, she was jarred out of a sound sleep. She kept moving farther away from him. He would immediately swallow up the space until he had taken over all of the bed and she was literally hanging on to the side.

She finally drifted off to sleep a little before dawn. A few minutes later Iain touched her arm. She bolted upright and let out a startled scream. She scared the hell out of him, too. He had his sword in his hand and was getting out of the bed to defend her before he realized there weren't any intruders.

Judith was terrified of something. She was still more asleep than awake, and it finally registered in his mind that she was afraid of him. There was a wild look in her eyes, and when he put the sword down and reached for her, she jerked back.

He wouldn't be denied. He grabbed her by the waist, stretched out on his back and pulled her down on top of him. He trapped her legs by locking them between his own, and then began to soothe her by rubbing her back.

She immediately relaxed against him. He let out a loud yawn and then asked, "Were you having a bad dream?"

His voice was rough from sleep. She was terribly sorry she'd disturbed him. "No," she answered in a bare whisper. "Go back to sleep. You need your rest."

"Tell me what happened. Why did you scream?"

"I forgot," she explained. She rubbed the side of her face against his warm chest and closed her eyes.

"You forgot why you screamed?"

"No," she replied. "I forgot I was married. When you accidentally touched me, I just . . . reacted. I'm not at all used to sleeping with a man."

He smiled in darkness. "I didn't think you would be," he told her. "You aren't afraid now, are you?"

"No, of course not," she whispered. "Thank you for being so concerned."

Lord, she'd sounded polite. He was her husband and she was treating him like a stranger. Judith felt awkward . . . and vulnerable. She decided that she was just overly weary. She hadn't had much sleep at all since she'd arrived in the Highlands, and all the commotion hadn't helped.

She didn't have any intention of crying. The tears caught her by surprise. She knew she was behaving like a child, that she was being terribly foolish and emotional, but she didn't know how to stop herself.

"Judith?" His thumb brushed away one of the tears on her cheek. "Tell me why you're crying."

"There weren't any flowers. Iain, there should have been flowers."

Her voice had been so soft, he wasn't certain he understood her. "Flowers?" he asked. "Where weren't there any flowers?"

He waited for her to explain, but she stubbornly remained silent. He squeezed her.

"In the chapel."

"What chapel?"

"The one you don't have," she answered. She knew she was sounding pitiful. She wasn't making any sense to him, either. "I'm exhausted," she added as an excuse for her confusing behavior. "Please don't become upset with me."

"I'm not upset," he replied. He continued to rub her backside while he thought about the odd remarks she'd just made. What did she mean about flowers in a chapel he didn't have? She wasn't making any sense at all, but he decided he would have to wait until tomorrow to find out what was really bothering her.

Her sweet, warm body soon turned his thoughts to other matters. He couldn't touch her again, not tonight. It would be too soon for her, and she needed time for the tenderness to ease.

He couldn't stop himself from thinking about it, though. Within minutes he was hard and aching. It didn't matter. He would die before deliberately hurting her again.

Iain hugged his gentle little bride and closed his eyes. Patrick had told him that he would walk through the fires of purgatory for his Frances Catherine, and Iain remembered he had laughed over that ridiculous notion.

His brother had let all his defenses down. He'd allowed himself to become vulnerable. Iain had thought his brother was a fool. It was quite all right to care about a wife, but to let a woman rule a warrior's every action, to want to please her at every turn the way Patrick sought to please his wife, that simply wasn't acceptable in Iain's mind. No woman was going to run him around in circles. He knew he could never allow himself to become that emotionally involved. Oh, he cared for Judith, more than he'd ever intended, and now that she was his wife, he would allow himself to feel content.

He'd be damned if he'd become vulnerable, though.

He was extremely pleased that she loved him, of course. It would make her adjustment much easier.

Iain didn't go back to sleep for a long while. He continued to think about all the logical reasons he would never allow himself to be turned into a lovesick weakling like Patrick, and when he finally fell asleep, he had convinced himself that he would distance his heart from his mind.

He dreamed about her.

Judith slept most of the morning away. Iain had already left the chamber when she finally stretched herself awake. She felt stiff, tender too, and she let out a loud, unladylike groan before getting out of the bed.

She didn't have any idea what she was supposed to do now that she was the laird's wife. She decided she would have to get dressed and then hunt her husband down and ask him.

She had packed her pale pink gown and fresh undergarments in her small satchel. She took her time getting ready, and when she was finally finished, she made the bed and folded the extra plaid Iain had left on top of the quilt.

The great hall was empty. In the center of the table was a treacher filled with apples. A loaf of thick black bread was propped on one side of the treacher. Judith poured herself a goblet full of water and ate one of the apples. She kept expecting a servant to appear at any moment, but after waiting a long while, she decided they must all be outside, seeing to other duties.

Graham caught her attention when he started down the steps. She was about to call out to him, then stopped herself. The leader of the council didn't know he was being observed. His expression was unguarded. He looked terribly sad, weary too. He glanced behind him once, shook his head, and then turned back to the steps again. Judith's heart went out to the elder. She didn't know the reason for his unhappiness, and she wasn't even certain if she should intrude or not.

He was carrying a small chest in his arms. He stopped again when he was halfway down the stairs to adjust his hold on his possession, and then caught sight of her.

She immediately smiled. "Good day to you, Graham," she called out.

He nodded. She thought his smile was forced. She hurried over to the entrance.

"Would you like me to help you carry that?"

"Nay, lass," he answered. "I've got a good hold on it. Brodick and Alex are getting the rest of my things. Gelfrid's too. We'll be out of your way in no time at all."

"I don't understand," she said. "You aren't in my way. Whatever do you mean?"

"We're moving out of the keep," Graham explained. "Now that Iain's taken a bride, Gelfrid and I will move into one of the cottages down the path."

"Why?"

Graham stopped when he reached the bottom step. "Because Iain's married now," he patiently explained.

Judith walked over to stand directly in front of him. "Are you moving out because Iain married me?"

"I've just said so, haven't I? You'll be wanting your privacy, Judith."

"Graham, before Iain married me, I specifically remember you saying he had your support, that you agreed to this marriage."

Graham nodded. "That's true."

"Then you can't leave."

He raised an eyebrow over that statement. "What does the one have to do with the other?"

"If you leave, it will show me that you don't really accept this marriage. But if you stay—"

"Now, Judith, that isn't what this is about. You're newly married and you deserve your privacy. Two old men would only be getting in the way."

"Then you aren't leaving because you don't want to live under the same roof with an Englishwoman?"

The worry in her gaze was evident. Graham vehemently shook his head. "If that was my feeling, I'd say so."

She believed him. She let out a little sigh of relief, and then asked, "Where do Vincent and Owen and Duncan live?"

"With their wives."

He tried to move around her. She blocked his path. He didn't want to leave, and she didn't want to be responsible for forcing him out. The problem, of course, was his pride. She had to find a way to save that and get her way at the same time.

"How long have you lived here?" she blurted out, thinking to keep him busy answering her questions until she could come up with a sound plan.

"Almost ten years now. When I became laird, I moved in with my Annie. She died five years ago. I passed on the duties of laird to Iain six months ago, and I should have moved out then, but I lingered on. I've outstayed my welcome, I'm certain."

"And Gelfrid?" she asked when he tried to walk around her again. "How long has he lived here?"

Graham gave her a puzzled look. "Three years now," he answered. "He moved in after his wife passed on. Judith, this chest is getting heavy. Let me pass."

He once again tried to walk over to the doors. Judith rushed ahead of him. She pressed her back against the doors and splayed her arms wide. "I'm not letting you leave, Graham."

He was astonished by her boldness. "Why not?" he demanded.

He sounded irritated, but she didn't think he really was. "Why?" she asked.

"Yes, why?" he demanded again.

God help her, she couldn't come up with a single logical reason. Judith almost smiled then. She guessed that only left illogical reasons.

"Because you'll hurt my feelings." Judith could feel herself blushing. She felt like a fool. "Aye, you will," she added with a nod.

"What in God's name are you doing, Judith?" Brodick shouted from the landing above. Judith didn't dare move from the doors when she looked up. Gelfrid, she noticed, was standing next to Brodick.

"I'm not letting Graham and Gelfrid leave," she called out.

"Why not?" Brodick asked.

"I'm keeping them," she shouted back. "Iain kept me and I'm keeping them."

It was an outrageous and thoroughly empty boast, and completely ruined when Iain opened the doors. Judith went flying backward. Her husband caught her in his arms. Graham dropped the chest and reached out to catch her, too, and she suddenly found herself in a tug of war between the two men. She was blushing over her own clumsiness.

"Judith? What are you doing?" Iain asked.

She was making a complete idiot of herself. She wasn't going to tell Iain that. Besides, she was pretty certain he already knew.

"I'm trying to make Graham listen to reason," she explained. "Both he and Gelfrid want to move out."

"She won't let them," Brodick called out.

Iain squeezed Judith's hand. "If they wish to leave, you shouldn't interfere," he told her.

"Do you want them to move out?" she asked.

She turned and looked up at him, waiting for his answer. He shook his head.

She smiled. Then she turned around to confront Graham again. "You're being rude, Graham."

He smiled. Iain was appalled. "You must not speak to an elder in that tone," he ordered.

"And I mustn't hurt her feelings," Graham interjected with a nod. "If it's that important to you, lass, I suppose Gelfrid and I could stay on."

"Thank you."

Gelfrid had rushed down the steps. Judith could tell he was relieved. He was trying to glare at her and failing miserably. "We're bound to argue," he announced.

Judith nodded. "Yes," she answered.

"You won't be pounding on my back every time I get a tickle in my throat."

"No."

He grunted. "So be it. Brodick, put my things back. I'm staying on."

Gelfrid rushed back up the steps. "Watch what you're doing, boy. I won't have my chest bruised like that."

Iain tried to pick up Graham's chest for him. The elder pushed his hands away. "I'm not so old I can't manage," he declared. In a softer tone of voice, he said, "Son, your bride's a bit high-strung. She threw herself against that door and pitched such a fit, Gelfrid and I had to give in."

Iain finally understood exactly what had happened. "I appreciate your concession in giving in," he replied in a serious tone. "Judith's adjustment will take time, and I could certainly use some help with her."

Graham nodded. "She's bossy."

"Aye, she is."

"Gelfrid and I can work on that flaw."

"And I as well," Iain said.

Graham started back up the steps. "Don't know what you're going to do about her tender feelings, though. I don't suppose any of us can change that flaw."

Judith stood next to Iain and watched until Graham had disappeared around the corner. She knew her husband was staring at her. She guessed she really should offer him some sort of explanation for her behavior.

She took hold of his hand and turned to look up at him. "This is their home as much as it is yours," she said. "I didn't believe they really wanted to leave and so I . . ."

"You what?" he asked when she didn't continue.

She let out a sigh and turned her gaze to the floor. "I made a complete fool of myself in order to get them to stay. It was all I could think of to save their pride." She let go of his hand and tried to walk away. "They'll probably be talking about it for weeks."

He caught her when she reached the middle of the great hall. He put his hands on her shoulders and turned her to face him.

"You're far more perceptive than I am," he told her.

"I am?"

He nodded. "It never would have occurred to me that Graham and Gelfrid would want to stay."

"There's plenty of room."

"Why are you blushing?"

"Am I?"

"Are you feeling better today?"

She stared into his eyes while she thought about that question. "I wasn't feeling ill last night."

"I hurt you."

"Yes." She could feel her face burning with embarrassment. She turned her gaze to his chin. "I'm feeling much better today. Thank you so much for asking."

It took all his discipline not to laugh at her. Whenever Judith was embarrassed, she resorted to extreme politeness. He'd noticed that trait on the journey home, and he found it very endearing. After the night of passion they'd shared together, it was damn amusing too.

"You're very welcome," he drawled out.

He nudged her chin up and then leaned down. His mouth brushed over hers once, then once again. It wasn't enough for him. He deepened the kiss and hauled her up against him.

She forgot about being embarrassed and concentrated on kissing him back. He finally pulled back. She sagged against him.

"Judith, I left a plaid on the bed. You're supposed to wear it."

"Yes, Iain."

He kissed her again because she'd given her agreement

so quickly. Brodick interrupted them by shouting Iain's name. He enjoyed their reaction, too. Judith jumped. Iain glared.

"Erin's waiting to give you his report," Brodick announced from directly behind them. "If you're about finished mauling your wife, I'll tell him to come inside."

"I'm leaving, too," Judith said.

Iain shook his head. "You don't tell me what you plan to do, Judith. You ask my permission."

He sounded like he was instructing a child. She was thoroughly disgruntled, but hid her reaction because Brodick was watching. "I see," she whispered.

"Where did you think you were going?"

"To collect the rest of my things from Frances Catherine's home."

She decided not to give him time to give her permission. She stretched up, kissed him, and then hurried to the door. "I won't be gone long."

"Aye, you won't," Iain called out. "You will be back in ten minutes, Judith. I have need to speak to you about a few important matters."

"Yes, Iain."

Iain watched her leave. As soon as the door shut behind her, Brodick started laughing.

"What the hell's so amusing?"

"I was appreciating the fire in your wife's eyes when you told her she needed your permission, Iain."

Iain grinned. He'd appreciated her reaction, too. The woman certainly had an untamed wild spirit inside her.

Erin came into the hall then, turning Iain's thoughts to far more important matters. He sent Brodick up the stairs to fetch Graham to hear what Erin had to say.

Judith started down the hill in a hurry, then slowed her pace. It was a glorious day. The sun was shinning bright and the breeze was actually warm. She tried to concentrate on the beauty around her instead of the high-handed way Iain had told her she would have to get his permission whenever she wanted to do something. Did he actually believe she should get his approval before going to visit her dear friend? She guessed he did.

Judith knew it was her duty to get along with her husband. She was supposed to obey him just as she had promised to during the wedding ceremony. There was also the telling fact that her husband happened to be the laird. Marriage, she decided, was going to take some adjustment in her thinking.

She'd stopped halfway down the hill and leaned against a fat tree while she considered her new position. She loved Iain; she trusted him completely. It would be wrong for her to openly defy him. She would have to be patient, she supposed, until he had reached the point where he didn't find it necessary to look out for her every minute.

Perhaps Frances Catherine could offer a suggestion or two. Judith wanted to make Iain happy, but she didn't want him to turn her into a serf. Her friend had been married a long time and had certainly encountered a similiar problem with Patrick. She wondered how she had gotten Patrick to listen to her opinions.

Judith pulled away from the tree and continued on down the walkway.

The first stone caught her in the center of her back. She was pitched forward and landed hard on her knees. She was so surprised, she instinctively turned around to see where the stone had come from.

She saw the boy's face just seconds before the second stone hit her. The jagged rock tore into the tender flesh directly below her right eye. Blood poured down over her cheek.

There wasn't time to scream. The third stone found its mark on the left side of her head. Judith collapsed on the ground. If there were other stones thrown, she didn't feel them. The force of the blow to her temple knocked her into a dead faint.

* * *

Iain grew impatient when Judith didn't immediately return to the keep. He listened to Erin's report concerning the possibility of an alliance between the Dunbars and the Macleans, but his mind wasn't on the topic. Erin was telling him what he already knew, and the report was only being repeated for Graham's sake. The leader of the council hadn't believed such a union was possible, as both the Dunbar laird and the Maclean laird were too old and too set in their ways to give up any power for the sake of the other's clan. Now, listening to Erin's account of the meeting he'd actually observed, Graham was fully convinced.

And still Judith didn't return. His gut instinct nagged that something was wrong. He told himself she had simply lost count of the time. She was probably sitting at Frances Catherine's table, deep in discussion about some topic or other, and didn't realize the time. Reason didn't allay his worry, however.

He couldn't sit still any longer. He didn't announce his intention to leave the meeting. He simply got up and started for the entrance.

"Where are you going, Iain?" Graham called out. "We've need to form a plan now."

"I won't be gone long," Iain answered. "I'm going after Judith. She should have been back by now."

"She probably just lost track of time," Brodick suggested.

"No."

"Is she testing you, then?" the warrior asked, smiling over that possibility. "The woman's stubborn, Iain. She might have taken exception to your order."

Iain shook his head. His denial was vehement. "She wouldn't defy me."

Brodick abruptly stood up. He bowed to Graham and then hurried after his laird. Iain took the path down to his brother's cottage. Brodick rode his mount and took the long way around the trees.

Iain found her first. She was crumpled on the ground,

resting on her side, and the only part of her face visible to him was covered with blood.

He didn't know if she was dead or alive. And in those seconds it took for him to get to her, he was consumed with terror. He was incapable of reasoning anything through. Only one thought raced through his mind. He couldn't lose her. Not now, not when she had only just come into his bleak life.

His roar of anguish echoed down the hills. Men came running, their swords drawn, ready. Patrick had just started out the doorway with his wife on his arm when the chilling sound reached him. He pushed Frances Catherine back inside, ordered her to bolt the door, and then turned and went racing up the hill.

Iain wasn't aware he'd shouted. He knelt down beside Judith and gently turned her until she was resting on her back. She let out a soft whimper. It was the sweetest sound he had ever heard. She hadn't been taken from him. Iain started breathing again.

His men gathered in a half circle around him. They watched as their laird slowly checked Judith for broken bones.

Brodick broke the silence. "What the hell happened to her?"

"Why doesn't she open her eyes?" Gowrie asked at the same time.

Patrick shoved his way through the crowd and knelt beside his brother. "Is she going to be all right?"

Iain nodded. He didn't trust himself to speak yet. His attention was drawn to the swelling on the side of Judith's temple. He gently brushed her hair away to get a better look.

"Good Lord," Patrick whispered when he saw the damage. "She could have killed herself in the fall."

"She didn't fall." Iain made that statement in a voice shaking with fury.

Patrick was stunned. If she hadn't taken a fall, what happened to her?

Brodick answered his question before Patrick had time to ask it. "Someone did this to her," he said. He knelt down on one knee on the other side of Judith and began to gently wipe the blood away from her cheek with the edge of his plaid. "Look at the stones, Patrick. There's blood on one of them. This wasn't an accident."

It took every ounce of discipline Iain possessed not to let his rage take control. Judith came first. Retaliation could wait. He finished checking to make certain the bones in her legs and ankles were still intact, then turned to lift her into his arms. Patrick helped him.

The two brothers stood up at the same time. Iain's gaze settled on Brodick. The anguish the warrior saw in his laird's eyes was telling.

Iain didn't just want Judith in his bed. He was in love with her.

She was cradled against his chest. Iain started up the hill, then suddenly stopped. He turned back to Brodick.

"Find the bastard." He didn't wait for his command to be acknowledged. "Patrick, go and get Frances Catherine. Judith will want her by her side when she wakes up."

The vibration in his voice shook her awake. Judith opened her eyes and tried to comprehend where she was. Everything was spinning around and around, making her stomach queasy and her head pound. She closed her eyes again and let Iain take care of her.

She didn't wake up again until Iain was placing her in the center of his bed. The minute he let go of her, she tried to sit up. The room immediately began to spin. She grabbed hold of her husband's arm and held tight until everything came into focus again.

She ached everywhere. Her back felt like it was on fire. Iain quit trying to force her back down when she gave him that complaint. Graham came hurrying into the room with a bowl so full of water, some lapped over the sides with each step he took. Gelfrid followed with a stack of linen squares.

"Move aside, Iain. Let me get to her," Graham ordered.

"The poor lass took quite a fall, didn't she?" Gelfrid remarked. "Is she usually so clumsy?"

"No, she isn't," Judith answered.

Gelfrid smiled. Iain wouldn't let go of his wife. "I'll take care of her," he told Graham. "She's mine, damn it."

"Of course she is," Graham agreed, trying to placate Iain.

Judith stared up at her husband. He looked furious. His grip on her was stinging.

"My injuries aren't substantial," she announced, sincerely hoping she was right in that evaluation. "Iain, please let go of my arms. I have enough bruises."

He did as she requested. Graham placed the bowl on the chest. Gelfrid dampened one of the linen squares and handed it to Iain.

He didn't talk to her while he cleaned the blood away from the side of her face. He was being extremely gentle. The cut was deep, but Iain didn't think the injury needed to be threaded together until it healed.

She was relieved to hear that decision. She didn't relish the idea of anyone, even her husband, taking a needle to her skin.

Iain appeared to be calming down. Then Gelfrid inadvertently got him riled again. "It's a miracle she wasn't blinded. She could have had her eye plucked clean out. Aye, she could have."

"But I didn't," Judith quickly said when she saw the chilling look come back into Iain's eyes. She patted her husband's arm. "It's all right," she told him in a soothing tone of voice. "I'm feeling much better now."

She was trying to comfort him. Iain was exasperated with her. "You'll feel better after I've put some salve on your cuts. Take your clothes off. I want to look at your back."

Iain gave her the order just as Graham leaned forward to place a cold wet cloth against the swelling above her temple. "Hold this tight against the bruise, Judith. It will help take the sting out."

"Thank you, Graham. Iain, I'm not taking my clothes off."

"That blow to the side of her head could have done her in," Gelfrid remarked. "Aye, she's fortunate it didn't knock her dead."

"Yes, you are taking your clothes off." Iain told her.

"Will you quit trying to get Iain upset, Gelfrid? I know it isn't intentional, but what could have happened didn't. I'm fine, really."

"Of course you're fine," Gelfrid agreed. "We'd best watch her closely, Graham. She might be addled for a day or so."

"Gelfrid, please," Judith said with a groan. "And I'm really not going to take my clothes off," she explained for a second time.

"Yes, you are."

She motioned him closer. Gelfrid came with him. "Iain, we have . . . company."

He found his first smile. Her modesty was refreshing, and the frown she was giving him made him want to laugh. She really was going to be all right. She wouldn't be acting so damned disgruntled if the head injury had been severe.

"We're not company," Graham told her. "We live here, remember?"

"Yes, of course, but—"

"Are you seeing more than one of anything, Judith?" Gelfrid asked. "Remember Lewis, Graham? He was seeing two of everything right before he keeled over."

"For the love of—" Judith began.

"Come along, Gelfrid. The lass is about to burst with her blush. She won't take her clothes off until we leave."

Judith waited until the door had closed behind the two

elders before turning back to Iain. "I cannot believe you expected me to take my clothes off in front of Graham and Gelfrid. Now what are you doing?"

"I'm taking your clothes off for you," he patiently explained.

Her bluster of anger vanished. It was his grin, of course. She had to take time to notice how his smile made him all the more handsome, and then it was too late to argue. He had her stripped down to her chemise and was leaning over her, prodding at the bruise in the center of her back before she had time to order him to stop.

"Your back's fine," he told her. "The skin wasn't cut."

His fingers trailed a line down her spine. He smiled over the shivers his touch caused. "You're so soft and smooth all over," he whispered.

He leaned down and kissed her shoulder. "Frances Catherine is probably waiting downstairs to see you. I'll have Patrick bring her up."

"Iain, I'm fully recovered now. I don't need—"

"Don't argue with me."

The set of his jaw and the tone of his voice told her it would be useless to fight him. She changed into her sleeping gown because he insisted. She felt foolish wearing her nightclothes during the day, but Iain was in need of being placated now. He still looked worried.

Frances Catherine arrived a few minutes later. She glared Patrick out of the chamber because he'd carried her up the stairs and groaned loudly over her added weight.

Gelfrid and Graham served her supper. Judith wasn't used to being pampered. She didn't have any trouble enjoying all the attention, however. Then Isabelle came up to see how she was doing, and by the time Iain returned, Judith was exhausted from all her company.

He made everyone leave. Judith put up a halfhearted protest. She fell asleep minutes later.

She awakened a few minutes before dawn. Iain was

sleeping on his stomach. She tried to be as quiet as possible as she got out of bed. She swung one leg over the side.

"Does your head still hurt?"

She turned back to look at him. Iain was propped up on one elbow, staring at her. His eyes were half closed, his hair was mussed, and he looked ruggedly handsome.

She got back into bed, nudged him down on his back so she could lean over him. She kissed the frown on his forehead, then nibbled on his ear.

He wasn't in the mood for teasing. He growled low in his throat, wrapped his arms around her and captured her mouth for a proper kiss.

Her response made him wild. The kiss turned hot, wet, intoxicating. His tongue swept inside her sweet mouth to mate with hers, and when he finally ended the erotic love play, she collapsed against his chest.

"Sweetheart, answer me. Does your head still hurt?"

The worry was there, in his voice, and it did still ache just a little, but she didn't want him to stop kissing her. "Kissing actually makes me feel better," she whispered.

He smiled. Her remark was absurd, of course. It still pleased him. He stretched up and nuzzled the side of her neck. "It makes me hot," he told her.

She let out a little sigh of pleasure.

"Do you want me, Judith?"

She didn't know if she should act timid or bold. Did husbands like their wives to be shy or aggressive? She decided not to worry about it. She'd already started out bold, and Iain hadn't seemed to mind.

"I do want you . . . a little."

It was all he needed to hear. He pulled away from her, stood up, and hauled her up beside him. He nudged her face up so she could look at him, then said, "I'm going to make you want me as much as I want you."

"You will? Iain, you already want me . . . now?"

She didn't understand. Lord, she really was an innocent. All she had to do was take a good look at him and she wouldn't have any doubt about his desire for her. She wouldn't look, though. Her embarrassment wouldn't let her. He decided to show her. He took hold of her hand and placed it on his hard arousal. She reacted as though she had just been burned by fire. She pulled away with lightning speed. Her face turned crimson. He let out a sigh. His gentle little wife wasn't ready to let go of her shyness just yet. He wasn't going to insist.

He was a patient man. He could wait. He kissed her on the top of her head, then helped her take off her nightgown. She kept her head bowed until he pulled her back into his arms.

Then he began the appealing duty of helping her get rid of her shyness. She didn't respond the way he wanted her to when he stroked her shoulders, her arms, her back, but when he began to gently caress her sweet backside, she let out a little moan of pleasure, letting him know without words she was sensitive to his touch there.

She finally began to explore his body with her fingertips. It took her a long, long while to get around to the front of him. Iain was gritting his teeth in anticipation.

It was well worth the agony. Her hand reached his lower stomach. She hesitated, then moved lower, until she was touching the very heat of him.

His reaction made her bolder. He groaned low in his throat and tightened his grip on her shoulders. She kissed his chest and tried to move lower so she could kiss the flat of his stomach. There wasn't an ounce of fat on the man. He was all hard muscle. He flexed when she kissed his navel. She had to kiss him there again, just to drive him daft.

Iain let her have her way until she reached his groin. He pulled her back up and kissed her sweet mouth. It was a long, hard, passionate kiss. She still wasn't waylaid however. "Iain, I want to—"

"No."

His voice was harsh. He couldn't help that. Just

thinking about what she wanted to do to him made him ache to be inside her. He wasn't about to find his own fulfillment first, however, and he knew he sure as hell would if she took him into her mouth.

"Yes," she whispered.

"Judith, you don't understand," he began, his voice ragged.

Her eyes were cloudy with passion. That notice shook him. Was she becoming aroused just by touching him? He wasn't given time to wonder about it. "I understand it's my turn," she whispered. She leaned up and kissed him just to gain his silence. Her tongue thrust inside his mouth before he could take command. "Let me," she pleaded.

She got her way. Iain's hands were in fists at his sides. He took a deep, shuddering breath and forgot to let it out. Judith was innocently awkward, wonderfully unskilled, and so lovingly giving he felt he'd died and gone to Heaven.

He couldn't put up with the sweet torment long. He didn't have any idea how they got into bed. He might have thrown her there. He was so completely out of control he couldn't think about anything but pleasuring her until she was ready for him.

His fingers thrust into her tightness, and when he felt the liquid heat of her, his composure almost vanished. He moved between her thighs and let out a low growl of pure male demand.

And yet, before he moved to make her completely his, he hesitated.

"Sweetheart?"

He was asking her permission. That thought penetrated her haze of passion and tears came into her eyes. Dear God, how she loved this man. "Oh, yes," she cried out, knowing she would surely die if he didn't come to her now.

He still tried to be gentle, but she wasn't in the mood to

allow it. He eased slowly at first, until she lifted her hips up to meet him. She gripped his thighs to pull him closer, scoring his skin with her fingernails.

His mouth never left hers as the mating ritual took control. The bed squeaked from his hard thrusts. His groans blended with her whimpers of pleasure. Neither could form a coherent thought now, and when Iain knew he was about to spill his seed into her, his hand moved between their joined bodies to help her find her fulfillment first.

The fire of passion consumed him. His own release made him feel weak and invincible at the same time. He collapsed against her with a low grunt of raw satisfaction.

God, he loved her scent. He inhaled the light womanly fragrance and thought that he had surely just visited Heaven. His heart still felt like it was about to burst, and he didn't think he'd mind if that happened. He was too content to be bothered about anything now.

Judith hadn't quite recovered yet, either. That realization arrogantly pleased him. He liked being able to make her lose her inhibitions and her control so thoroughly. He kissed the base of her neck where her heartbeat pulsed so wildly, and smiled over the way that caress made her breath catch in the back of her throat.

He tried to find the strength to move away from her. He knew he was probably crushing her, but damn, he never wanted this bliss to end. He had never experienced this kind of satisfaction with any other woman. Aye, he'd always been able to hold a part of himself back. He hadn't been able to protect himself from Judith. The realization shook him, and he was suddenly feeling damn vulnerable.

"I love you, Iain."

Such a simple declaration and yet so freeing. She'd snatched his worry away before he had time to let it gain control.

Iain yawned against her ear and then leaned up on his

elbows to kiss her. His intention was forgotten when he saw the jagged cut and the swelling around her eye.

Judith was smiling until he started frowning. "What's the matter, Iain? Didn't I please you?"

"Of course you pleased me," he replied.

"Then why—"

"You could have lost your eye."

"Oh, Lord, you're sounding like Gelfrid," she remarked.

She was trying to tease him out of his frown. It didn't work. "You're damned fortunate, Judith. You could have—"

She placed her hand over his mouth. "You pleased me, too," she whispered.

He didn't catch on. He turned her attention by asking, "When you fell, did you happen to see a man . . . or a woman standing nearby?"

Judith thought about his question a long minute before making the decision not to tell him about the little boy she had seen. The child was too young to be dragged before his laird. It would be terrifying for him, to say nothing of the embarrassment and humiliation it would cause his family. No, she couldn't let that happen. Besides, she was certain she could take care of the matter. She would have to find the little hellion first, of course, and when she did, she would have a good, long, blistering talk with him. If he wasn't properly contrite, she might have to ask Iain's assistance. Or at least threaten to ask him. But that would be a last resort. And if the boy was old enough—though in truth she didn't believe he could be seven years yet—she would haul him off to Father Laggan and make him confess his sin.

"Judith?" Iain asked, prodding her for an answer.

"No, Iain. I didn't see a man or a woman standing nearby."

He nodded. He really hadn't believed she'd seen anyone, for in truth he doubted she even realized she had been attacked. The first stone probably knocked her into a faint, and her mind was simply too innocent to think about the possibility of treachery.

He leaned down and kissed her before getting out of bed. "It's already past dawn. I've duties to see to," he remarked.

"Do I have duties?" she asked as she pulled the covers over her.

"Of course you do," he answered. "Judith, why do you hide your body from me?"

She started blushing. He laughed. She kicked the covers away. Then she stood up to face him. He took his time looking at her. She stared at the mantel.

"It's all right for you to look at me," he drawled out.

The amusement in his voice made her smile. "You're enjoying my embarrassment, aren't you, husband?"

He didn't answer her. She finally looked at his face. Iain looked . . . stunned. Was her body displeasing to him? She reached for the covers to hide herself from him.

His next remark stopped her. "You just called me husband. I like that."

She let the blanket drop back on the bed. "Do you like me?"

He grinned. "Sometimes."

She laughed as she ran to him and threw herself into his arms. He lifted her off the floor and kissed her.

"You make me forget my duties."

She didn't care. She was pleased her kisses could rob him of his concentration. She went back to the bed and sat down so she could watch him get dressed.

It seemed to her that with each article of clothing he put on, he changed a bit, becoming more and more like the clan's leader, and less and less like the gentle lover she'd known a few moments before. By the time he'd attached his scaffold to his belt, he was every bit the laird, and treating her like his chattel.

Her duty, he explained, was to direct the servants in

their tasks. They didn't have a full-time cook at the keep. The women in the clan took turns supplying the fare. If she wished to take over that task, she could.

She was responsible for the maintenance of the interior of the keep. Since Graham and Gelfrid were going to continue to live with them, she was also supposed to take care of their needs.

Judith wasn't worried. From an early age she'd directed the servants at her uncle Tekel's holding. She didn't anticipate any problems she couldn't handle.

Iain seemed worried. She was very young to have so many duties thrust upon her shoulders. He made that comment to her and ordered her to come to him if she needed more help.

She wasn't insulted by his lack of confidence in her ability. He couldn't possibly know what she was capable of doing. She would have to show him she could handle the responsibilities that came with being the laird's wife. Only then would he quit his worrying.

She was eager to get started. "I'll go downstairs and begin right away," she announced.

He shook his head. "You haven't recovered from your injury. You must rest."

Before she could argue with him, he pulled her to her feet, kissed her on her forehead, and then walked over to the door.

"Wear my plaid, wife."

She forgot about her nakedness and rushed over to him. "I have a request to make."

"What is it?"

"Will you please call all the women and children together? I would like for you to introduce me to them."

"Why?"

She didn't explain. "Please?"

He let out a sigh. "When do you want this done?"

"This afternoon will be soon enough."

"I planned to call my warriors together and give them

the news of our marriage, and they would inform their wives, but if your heart's set—"

"Oh, it is."

"All right, then," he conceded.

She finally let him leave the chamber. She didn't hurry to get dressed. Iain's lovemaking had worn her out. She got back into bed, wrapped herself in the bed covers on his side of the bed so she'd feel closer to him, and closed her eyes.

Her little nap lasted three hours. She wasn't ready to leave her chamber until early afternoon. She felt guilty for wasting her time, but that didn't make her hurry. She put on the same white underdress because she still hadn't collected her clothing from Frances Catherine's yet. She tried to fashion Iain's plaid, made a muck of it, and finally went to find one of the elders to help.

Gelfrid came to her assistance. He escorted her down the steps.

Iain was waiting in the great hall with Graham. They both smiled when they spotted her.

Brodick came strolling into the hall then, drawing her attention. She turned to smile at him.

He bowed to her. "They're waiting for you, Iain," he called out. "Judith, you could have lost that eye. You're damned fortunate."

"Aye, she is," Gelfrid interjected. "I'm not understanding why our laird wants to speak directly to the women," he added then.

He wanted an explanation, of course. Judith wasn't going to give him one. She smiled at the elder and turned to her husband. He took hold of her hand and walked to the door.

"Iain, you trust me, don't you?" she asked.

He was taken aback by her question. "Yes," he answered. "Why do you ask me that now, Judith?"

"Because there is a special . . . situation, and I want to make certain before I act that you trust me enough not to interfere."

"We'll discuss this tonight," he told her.

"Oh, it should be taken care of by then."

He held the door open for her and followed her outside. She started down the steps. He stopped her by putting his arm around her shoulders and hauling her up against his side.

And then he addressed the gathering. The women, so many she couldn't begin to count, stood in front with their children by their side. The courtyard was filled, and the hills below.

Judith barely paid any attention to what her husband was telling the group. She despaired at ever finding the boy in such a crush of people, but she was determined to try. She did find Frances Catherine and was pleased to notice Isabelle stood next to her friend.

Iain stopped. "Keep talking," she whispered.

He leaned down. "I'm finished."

"Iain, please. I still haven't found him. And don't look at me like that. They'll think you think I'm daft."

"I do think you're daft," he muttered.

She nudged him in his side to get him to cooperate.

He started talking again. Judith was about to give up when her attention was drawn to one of the midwives; the one named Helen, she recalled. The midwife looked ill, frightened too. Judith's attention stayed on the woman a bit longer than necessary while she wondered why she would be so visibly upset by this marriage news. While she was watching her, Helen half turned and looked down, behind her. Judith saw the boy then. He was diligently trying to hide behind his mother's skirts.

She nudged Iain again. "You may stop now."

Iain did just that. It took a full minute for his clan to realize he was finished. Then they cheered his announcement. Soldiers who'd been standing by the side of the keep came forward to offer their laird congratulations.

"That's the longest speech I've ever heard you make," one remarked.

"It's the only speech you've ever heard him make," Patrick interjected.

Judith wasn't paying any attention to the men. She wanted to grab the boy before his mother took him away.

"Please excuse me," she requested.

She was gone before Iain could agree. She waved to Frances Catherine when she passed her, and hurried on through the crowd. Several young women stopped her to offer their felicitations. They seemed sincere. She responded with an invitation to come up to the keep for a visitation.

Helen had taken hold of her son's hand. The closer Judith got to her, the more terrified she looked.

The son had obviously confessed his sin to his mother. Judith continued on until she reached the midwife. "Good afternoon, Helen," she began.

"We were on our way to speak to the laird," she blurted out. "Then the announcement came for us to gather in the courtyard and I—"

Her voice broke on a sob. Several women were watching, and Judith didn't want them to know what was going on. "Helen," she began in a whisper. "I have an important matter to discuss with your son. May I borrow him for a few minutes."

Helen's eyes clouded with tears. "Andrew and I were about to tell the laird—"

Judith interrupted her by shaking her head. "This matter is between your son and me," she insisted. "Your laird need never become involved. My husband's a very busy man, Helen. If the matter you wished to discuss concerns the throwing of some stones, then I think we should keep it amongst the three of us."

Helen finally understood. Her relief was so great, she looked ready to collapse. She vigorously nodded. "Shall I wait here?"

"Why don't you go back home? I'll send Andrew along as soon as we've finished our talk."

Helen blinked away her tears. "Thank you," she whispered.

Iain hadn't taken his attention away from his wife. He wondered what she was talking to Helen about. Helen looked distressed, but Judith's face was turned away from him and he didn't know if she was upset or not.

Brodick and Patrick were trying to get his attention. He was about to turn to the warriors when Judith caught his attention again. He watched her reach behind Helen and take hold of her son. The little boy wasn't cooperating. Judith wasn't deterred. She pulled him forward, then turned and walked toward the slope, dragging the wailing child behind her.

"Where's Judith going?" Patrick asked.

Iain didn't answer fast enough to suit Brodick. "Should I follow her? Judith shouldn't be left alone until the culprit's found. It isn't safe."

It wasn't until his friend had asked that question that Iain understood what was happening.

"My brother can take care of his wife, Brodick. You needn't get so riled on her behalf," Patrick told him.

Iain finally turned to his brother and his friend. "There isn't any need to go after Judith. I know who threw the stones. Judith's safe."

"Who the hell did it?" Brodick demanded.

"Helen's boy."

Both warriors were stunned. "But she's with him now," Patrick said.

Iain nodded. "She must have seen him. Did you see the way she dragged him away? Oh, she knows all right. She's probably giving him hell right now."

Iain was right. Judith did give the boy hell. The lecture didn't last long. Andrew was so remorseful, and so terribly afraid of her, she ended up comforting him. He had just turned seven years. He was big, strong too, for his tender years, but he was still only just a little boy.

He was weeping all over Judith's plaid now, begging

her forgiveness. He hadn't meant to hurt her. Nay, his intent was to frighten her into wanting to go back to England.

Judith was ready to beg his forgiveness for not leaving the Highlands when the little one sobbed out his reason.

"You made my mama cry."

Judith didn't know why she'd made Helen cry, and Andrew wasn't making enough sense to give her a proper explanation. She decided she would have to talk to Helen in order to get the problem straightened out.

She sat on a low boulder with the sobbing little boy on her lap. She was pleased he was properly contrite. Since he had already confessed his transgression to his mother, she told him she didn't believe he needed to bother his laird with this matter.

"What does your father think about your behavior?" Judith asked.

"Papa died last summer," Andrew told her. "I take care of mama now."

Judith's heart went out to the little boy. "Andrew, you've given me your word you won't get into any further mischief and I believe you mean it. This matter is settled now."

"But I have to tell the laird I'm sorry."

She thought that was very noble of the child. Courageous, too. "Are you worried about talking to your laird?"

Andrew nodded.

"Would you like me to tell him for you?" she asked.

He hid his face in Judith's shoulder. "Would you tell him now?" he whispered.

"All right," she agreed. "We'll go back and—"

"He's here," Andrew whispered in a voice shivering with fear.

Judith turned and spotted her husband standing directly behind her. He was leaning against a tree with his arms folded across his chest.

No wonder Andrew was trying to hide under her plaid.

She could feel him shaking. She decided not to prolong the dreaded ordeal for him. She had to pull him away from her and force him to stand up. Then she took hold of his hand and led him over to Iain.

Andrew's head was bowed low. Iain must have looked like a giant to the boy. Judith smiled up at her husband, then squeezed Andrew's hand.

"Your laird is waiting to hear what you have to tell him," she instructed.

Andrew peeked up. He looked terrified. The freckles covering his face were more white than brown, and his brown eyes were filled with unshed tears.

"I threw the rocks," Andrew blurted out. "I didn't mean to hurt your lady, just make her scared so she'd go back home. Then mama wouldn't cry." After making his speech, he lowered his head again until his chin was tucked in his chest. "I'm sorry," he added in a mumble.

Iain didn't say anything for a long while. Judith couldn't stand to see the child suffer so. She was about to give her own defense of the child's behavior when he raised his hand and shook his head at her.

He didn't want her interference. He slowly moved away from the tree he'd been leaning against and shook his head at Judith.

He stood directly in front of Andrew. "You do not give your feet your apology," he announced. "You give it to me."

Judith didn't agree with her husband's announcement. She was the one who had been injured, and Andrew had already given her his apology. Why did he have to tell his laird he was sorry?

She didn't think now was a good time to argue with Iain, however. He might believe she was trying to undermine his authority.

Andrew looked up at his laird again. His hold on Judith's hand tightened. Couldn't Iain see how he was frightening the little boy?

"I'm sorry I hurt your lady."

Iain nodded. He clasped his hands behind his back and stared down at Andrew a long minute. Judith thought he was deliberately dragging out his torture.

"You will walk with me," he commanded. "Judith, wait here."

He didn't give her time to argue with him, but started down the path. Andrew let go of her hand and went running after his laird.

They were gone a long, long while. When they came back, Iain still had his hands clasped behind his back. Andrew walked by his side. Judith smiled when she saw how the child imitated his laird. His hands were also clasped behind his back and his swagger was every bit as arrogant as Iain's was. He was chattering away, and every now and then Iain would nod.

Andrew acted as though a heavy weight had just been lifted from his shoulders. Iain dismissed him, waited until he was out of earshot and said, "I asked you if you saw anyone, Judith. Would you care to explain why you didn't give me a proper answer?"

"Actually you asked me if I saw a man or a woman standing nearby," she reminded him. "I didn't lie to you. I saw a child, not a man or a woman."

"Don't use that lopsided logic on me," he countered. "You knew what I was asking. Now I would like to know why you didn't tell me."

She let out a sigh. "Because the matter was between the child and me," she explained. "I didn't feel the need to bother you with it."

"I'm your husband," he reminded her. "What the hell do you mean, you didn't feel the need to bother me?"

"Iain, I was certain I could take care of it."

"That wasn't your choice to make."

He wasn't angry. He was simply instructing Judith in the proper way to handle her problems.

She was trying not to get worked up over this issue, and failing miserably. She folded her arms across her waist and frowned. "Do I ever have any choices?"

"It's my duty to take care of you."

"And also to take care of my problems?"

"Of course."

"That makes me no better than a child. God's truth, I don't believe I like being married very much. I had more freedom when I lived in England."

He let out a sigh. She was saying the most outrageous things and acting as though she'd only just realized her lot in life, as a woman. "Judith, no one is completely free."

"You are."

He shook his head. "As laird, I have far more restrictions than any of the warriors serving under me. My every action is accountable to the council. Everyone has a place here, responsibilities as well. Wife, I don't like hearing you tell me you don't like being married to me."

"I didn't say I didn't like being married to you, husband. I said I didn't like being married very much. It's most restrictive. There is a difference."

The look on his face indicated he didn't agree. He pulled her into his arms and kissed her. "You will like being married to me, Judith. I command it."

It was a ridiculous order. She pulled back and looked up at him. She was certain he was jesting and his amusement would be there, in his expression.

Iain wasn't jesting however. Lord, he looked . . . worried, vulnerable too. She was surprised by that notice, and very, very pleased. She went back into his arms. "I love you," she whispered. "Of course I like being married to you."

He squeezed her tight. "And you will, therefore, like giving me your problems to solve," he announced.

"Sometimes I will," she said, refusing to give him her full agreement. "And sometimes I will solve them myself."

"Judith—"

She interrupted him. "Frances Catherine told me that you were more of a father to Patrick than an older brother. You grew up solving all his problems for him, didn't you?"

"Perhaps, when we were younger," he admitted. "Now that we're both adults, we decide together what's to be done whenever a problem crops up. I rely on him as much as he relies on me. Tell me what my brother has to do with this discussion? You do want me to take care of you, don't you?"

"Yes, of course I do," she answered. "I just don't want to be a burden. I want to be able to share my problems with you, not hand them over. Do you understand? I want to belong, to be important enough to you that you would want to share your worries with me. Could you not learn to treat me with the same consideration you give Patrick?"

Iain didn't know what to say to her. "I must consider this," he announced.

She leaned against him so he wouldn't see her smile. "That is all I would ask."

"I try to be open to new ideas, Judith."

"Yes, of course you do."

She kissed him on his chin. He leaned down and captured her mouth for a long kiss. He was reluctant to stop touching her, but finally forced himself to pull away.

Judith spotted Andrew standing a fair distance away from them.

Iain didn't turn around when he called out, "Are you ready, Andrew?"

"Yes, Laird," he called back.

"How did you know he was standing there?"

"I heard him."

"I didn't."

He smiled. "You didn't need to hear," he explained.

His remark didn't make any sense. He sounded terribly arrogant.

"Where are you taking him?" she asked in a whisper, so the boy wouldn't hear.

"To the stables," Iain answered. "He's going to help the stable master."

"Is this a punishment? Iain, don't you think—"

"We'll discuss this tonight," he interrupted.

She nodded. She was so pleased he hadn't ordered her to stay out of the matter altogether, she felt like smiling. "As you wish," she told him.

"I wish for you to return to the keep."

She nodded. She bowed to her husband and started up the hill.

"You will rest this afternoon," he called after her.

"Yes, Iain."

"I'm meaning what I say, Judith."

She realized then he expected an argument. Since she hadn't given him one, he assumed she wasn't going to obey. She tried not to laugh. Her husband was beginning to understand her.

She did keep her promise. She had a nice visit with Frances Catherine first, and after Patrick had assisted his wife back down the hill to their cottage for her afternoon rest, Judith went upstairs to her room. Her mind was centered on the ever present worry about Frances Catherine's birthing, and she believed she had finally come up with a solution. Judith didn't believe she was knowledgeable enough to know what to do if the birthing became complicated, but Helen would surely have enough experience to know what to do, wouldn't she? Andrew's mother would have to soften in her attitude toward her now, Judith thought, and perhaps if she used the correct approach, she could gain the midwife's cooperation without having to involve Agnes.

Frances Catherine was bound to have a fit. Judith would have to convince her Helen would be a help and not a hindrance.

She fell asleep praying it would be true.

Chapter 12

She slept throughout the night. When she awoke, Iain had already left the chamber. Judith remembered that she needed to hurry to begin her day. She spotted her satchels neatly stacked in the corner and assumed Iain had carried them up from Frances Catherine's cottage.

After putting her things away in the smaller chest and straightening the chamber, she went downstairs.

Gelfrid was sitting with Duncan at the table, eating the morning meal. Both elders started to stand when she entered the room, but she waved them back into their chairs.

"Aren't you going to join us, lass?" Gelfrid asked.

"I'll just take this apple with me, thank you. I have an important errand to complete."

"You look just fine wearing our plaid," Duncan muttered. He frowned while he gave his compliment, acting as though it was a painful chore to praise her.

She didn't laugh. She did smile, though. Duncan, she decided, was very like Gelfrid. He was all bluster on the outside, but full of tender feelings inside.

"Her face still looks frightful," Gelfrid remarked. "She

could have had her eye torn clean out, Duncan," he added with a nod.

"Aye, she could have," Duncan agreed.

Judith hid her exasperation. "Gelfrid, was there anything you wished me to do before I leave?"

He shook his head.

"Have you seen Graham this morning?" she asked. "He might want something done, and I would like to get my duties organized in my mind before I start my day."

"Graham went hunting with Patrick and a few of the others," Gelfrid explained. "He should be back in time for the nooning meal. They left right at dawn."

"Did Iain go with them?"

Duncan answered her question. "He and his men went in the opposite direction to have a word or two with the Macphersons. They border us on the west."

She caught the hesitation in his voice. "I'm not believing this 'have a word or two,' Duncan. Are we feuding with the Macphersons, too?"

The elder nodded. "No need to get yourself worried. It's only a halfhearted feud. The Macpherson laird is so inept, it isn't worth the trouble fighting with them. There won't be any bloodshed."

"You're certain of this, Duncan?"

"I am," he answered. "There won't be a battle."

"Aye, it's more nuisance than amusement for Iain," Gelfrid explained.

"Your husband won't be home until nightfall," Duncan added.

"Thank you for telling me," Judith replied. She made a curtsy, then turned and hurried out of the hall.

Judith was halfway down the hill before she realized she didn't know where Helen lived. She wasn't about to ask Frances Catherine for directions. Her friend would demand an immediate explanation as to why she would want to speak to the midwife. Judith was determined to talk to Helen first before broaching the topic with her friend.

She turned toward Isabelle's cottage. Remembering Agnes's boast during the horrid inquisition that both she and Helen lived close enough to have heard screams during the birthing, Judith was certain Isabelle would be able to point the way for her.

Spotting Father Laggan coming up the slope, she waved to the priest and hurried to meet him.

"Did you put Merlin in the ground?" she asked.

He smiled. "I did," he answered. "Now I'm back to give Isabelle's son a proper blessing."

"Are you always in such a rush, Father?"

"'Tis the truth I usually am," he answered. He took Judith's hand in both of his and said, "You've got a happy wedded look about you. Iain's treating you well, isn't he?"

"Yes, Father," she replied. "Will you share our supper with us tonight?"

"I would be pleased to," he returned. "And have you the time to stop in to say hello to Isabelle with me now?"

"Of course," she answered. "But first I would like to have a talk with one of the midwives," she explained. "Do you happen to know where Helen lives?"

The priest nodded. He was kind enough to escort Judith there. He knocked on the door for her. Helen was given quite a startle to find both the priest and the laird's wife waiting on her stoop. Her hand flew to her bosom.

Judith saw how worried she looked and immediately tried to put her at ease.

"Good day, Helen," she began. "Father Laggan was kind enough to show me the way to your home. He was on his way to bless Isabelle's son," she added. "And I wanted to talk to you about a personal matter . . . if you have the time. I could come back later if you wish."

Helen backed away from the entrance and graciously invited her guests inside.

The aroma of freshly baked bread filled the air. Father Laggan beckoned Judith inside first and then followed her.

The little cottage was spotless. The wooden floors had been scrubbed so clean; the slats seemed to have a shine to them.

Judith sat at the table, but the priest went over to the hearth and leaned over the iron kettle hanging on the rod above the fire.

"What have we here?" he asked.

"Mutton stew," Helen replied, her voice a whisper. She held her apron in both hands in a grip that made her knuckles white.

"Is it about ready to taste, Helen?" Father Laggan asked.

His hint wasn't subtle. Feeding the priest put Helen at ease. She ushered him over to the table and then gave him a huge helping of the mutton. Judith was surprised by the priest's appetite. He was as thin as a rail, yet ate enough for two fully grown men.

Helen lost most of her worried expression while she served the priest. It was obvious to Judith she was enjoying the compliments the priest was giving her. Judith added a few of her own after she'd eaten two thick slices of black bread covered in rich jam.

Helen wouldn't sit down, however. Father Laggan finished his meal, thanked the midwife for her hospitality, and then left to go to Isabelle's cottage. Judith stayed behind. She waited until the door closed behind the priest, and then asked Helen to sit with her at the table.

"I would thank you again—" Helen began.

Judith cut her off. "I didn't come here to gain your apologies. That problem was taken care of and Andrew has learned his lesson."

"Since his father passed away, the boy has been . . . clinging. He thinks he must stay by my side all the time to protect me."

"Perhaps he's worried inside that you might also die and he'd be left alone," Judith suggested.

Helen nodded. "There's only the two of us now. It's difficult for him."

"Are their uncles or cousins who—"

She stopped her question when Helen shook her head. "We are quite alone, Lady Judith."

"No, you're not," Judith argued. "You're part of this clan. Your son will grow up to be a Maitland warrior. If there aren't any uncles or cousins to direct Andrew, then the matter should have been mentioned to Iain. Helen, you know how important it is for a child to believe he's important." She paused to smile at the midwife before adding, "It's important for women too, isn't it?"

"Aye, it is," Helen agreed. "It's been difficult, living here. I come from the MacDougall family. I've eight sisters and two brothers," she added with a nod. "Needless to say, there was always someone to talk to, and always time for a friendly visit. It's different here. The women work from dawn to dusk. Sundays are just the same. And yet, I find I envy them. They have husbands to look after."

With Judith's prodding, Helen continued to talk about her life for over an hour. She'd married late in life and was so thankful her late husband, Harold, had saved her from becoming a spinster, she spent every waking minute trying to make his home as perfect as she could.

She admitted that, after he died, she actually enjoyed not having to scrub the floors every single day, but boredom soon caught up with her. She laughed and confessed that she was now scrubbing and cleaning just as often as she did before her husband died.

Judith was surprised when Helen admitted she missed preparing special meals for her husband. She loved to create new dishes and swore she knew at least a hundred ways to prepare mutton.

"Do you like being a midwife?" Judith asked.

"No."

Her answer was quick, emphatic. "I had already assisted with at least twenty birthings before I came here," she explained. "And I thought, after Harold died, that my expertise could be a way to . . . fit in. I won't be helping any more. After the confrontation over Isabelle, I decided I would rather find some other way to . . ."

She didn't finish. "Helen, do you believe that a woman must suffer horribly in order to please her God?"

"The Church—"

"I'm asking you what you believe," Judith interrupted.

"All birthings have some pain," Helen replied. "But I cannot believe that God would blame every woman for Eve's sins."

She looked worried after making that whispered admission. Judith hurried to ease her fear. "I'm not going to tell Father Laggan. I also believe God is more merciful than the Church would have us believe. I try not to question the wisdom of our leaders, Helen, but sometimes I cannot help but shake my head over some of the confusing rules."

"You speak the truth," Helen agreed. "We cannot do anything about these dicates, or find ourselves excommunicated," she added.

"I've strayed from my topic," Judith said then. "I would like to talk to you about my friend, Frances Catherine, and ask your help."

"What is it you want me to do?"

Judith explained. "I know you've just told me you have decided against assisting in any more birthings, Helen, but I don't have anyone else to turn to and I'm very worried about my friend. If it becomes complicated, I won't know what to do."

Helen couldn't turn her request down, not after the delicate way she had taken care of Andrew.

"Frances Catherine is afraid of you," Judith explained. "We will have to convince her you don't believe in being cruel. We'll have to keep this quiet too. I don't want Agnes to interfere."

"She will try," Helen announced. "She'll have to," she added with a nod. "It won't do you any good to talk to her. Agnes is set in her ways. She's furious with you too, for snatching her daughter's husband."

Judith shook her head. "Iain wasn't married to Cecilia," she remarked. "And Frances Catherine told me he didn't have any intention of offering for her."

Helen shrugged. "Agnes is spreading rumors," she whispered. "She's saying he had to marry you to protect your honor."

Judith's eyes widened. "Do you mean she's saying that Iain and I . . . that I . . ."

She couldn't go on. Helen nodded. "She's saying it, all right. She's hinting you're with child. God help her if our laird gets wind of her vile gossip."

"I hope he doesn't hear," Judith replied. "It would upset him."

Helen agreed. Judith tried to leave then, but Helen mentioned she was the very first company she'd had in over three months. Judith immediately sat back down again.

They visited for another hour before Judith stood up to leave.

"I've enjoyed our talk, Helen," she said. "I'll speak to Frances Catherine this evening, and I would appreciate it if you would go and see her tomorrow. Together, I'm certain we can rid her of her worries."

Judith was almost out the doorway but suddenly stopped. She turned back to Helen. "Did you know the women all take turns preparing the meals for Iain and the two elders living at the keep?"

"Yes," Helen answered. "It's just the way it's always been done. I volunteered to help, but Harold took ill right then, and there wasn't time."

"Is it a chore for the women?"

"Oh my, yes," she replied. "Especially in the winter months. There's seven women, one for each day of the week, you see, and with their own families to look after, it's most difficult."

"But you love to cook," Judith reminded her.

"Yes."

"Where do you get the food you prepare?"

"The soldiers keep me supplied," she explained. "And some of the women give me their leftovers."

Judith frowned. What Helen had just explained sounded like charity to her. "I don't know how to cook," Judith remarked.

"You're the laird's wife. You don't need to know how."

"Andrew needs direction from a man as well as a woman, doesn't he?"

"Yes, he does," Helen agreed, wondering why Judith was jumping from one topic to another.

"And you love to cook. Yes, that's the answer. It's all settled then, Helen, unless, of course, you don't want to," Judith rushed out. "It's not a favor I'm asking or an order I'm giving, and I would think about this long and hard before making up your mind. If you decide against my suggestion, I'll understand."

"What suggestion, milady?"

"To become the housekeeper," Judith explained. "You could direct the serving girls and cook the meals. You'll have all the help you wanted, of course, but you would be in charge. I think it's a sound plan. You and Andrew would have all your meals at the keep, and he'd be with Gelfrid and Graham quite a lot, and Iain, too, of course, though probably not as often. The elders are in need of someone to pamper them, and it seems to me you're in need of pampering someone besides Andrew."

"You would do this for me?"

"You don't understand," Judith countered. "We need you far more than you needs us. Still, I believe you can make your place at the keep. It would probably be easier if you live there. I wouldn't rush you on that decision. We would let Andrew get used to the arrangement of having his mama at the keep all day, and then broach the topic of moving. There's a large room behind the buttery with a nice window."

Judith realized she was getting ahead of herself and immediately paused. "Will you think about this suggestion?"

"I will be honored to take on this duty," Helen blurted out.

It was nicely settled. Judith left the cottage in high spirits. She felt as though she had just made an important change, a positive one that would benefit Helen and her son as much as it would her household.

At supper that evening she explained the request she'd made. She expected a little grumbling from Gelfrid, for she'd already decided that of all the elders, he most hated change of any kind, but he didn't give her any argument at all.

Iain walked into the hall in the middle of the discussion. He took his place at the head of the table, nodded to Graham and Gelfrid, then reached over and hauled Judith close for a quick, no nonsense kiss.

Graham filled the laird in on Judith's decision. Iain didn't say anything when the elder finished. He simply nodded.

"What do you think about the idea?" she asked.

He reached for the goblet Judith had placed in front of him and took a long drink of the cool water. "It's fine with me," he remarked.

"I'm thinking it will be a nice change," Graham announced. "We won't have to put up with Millie's supper any longer. Lord, how I've grown to hate Wednesdays."

"Is Helen a fair cook?" Gelfrid asked.

"She's exceptional," Judith replied. She turned to Graham. "As for changes, there is another I would like to make, but I'll need your cooperation . . . Iain's, too."

Graham frowned. "Is this a matter for the council?"

"No," she replied. She turned back to her husband. "I'm certain you'll think this is a minor change and not worthy of the council's attention."

"What is this change you're hinting at?" Gelfrid asked.

She took a breath. "I want Sundays."

Patrick walked into the great hall just as Judith blurted

out her request. "You might as well give it to her, Iain,"
he called out.

"What does the lass mean, she wants Sundays?"
Gelfrid asked Graham.

"I don't believe we heard her correctly," Graham
replied. "She couldn't have said—"

Gelfrid interrupted Graham. "If the lass would learn
to roll her words together, the way we do, she'd be better
understood."

Duncan came strutting into the hall then, followed by
Vincent and Owen. Judith leaned closer to Iain. "Is there
going to be a meeting tonight?"

He nodded. "We won't start until after you've explained this bizarre request for Sundays, though," he
said.

She shook her head. He raised an eyebrow. She leaned
closer, until she was perched on the edge of her chair. "I
don't wish to discuss this matter in front of the entire
council," she told him in a low whisper.

"Why not?" he asked. He reached over and brushed a
strand of her hair back over her shoulder.

She put her hand on top of his. "Because it's a private
matter you must agree to support first," she explained.

"Graham and Gelfrid were here when you—"

She cut him off. "They're part of our family now, Iain.
This private matter must certainly be discussed with
them."

"Did you hear that, Graham?" Gelfrid bellowed.
"She's calling us family."

Judith turned and gave the elder a disgruntled look for
deliberately listening in on her whispered conversation.
He grinned in reaction.

She turned back to Iain. "I will be happy to explain up
in our chamber if you could spare a few minutes."

Iain wanted to laugh. He didn't dare, of course, for his
wife would have her tender feelings injured if he showed
any amusement now. She was looking very worried, out

of sorts. Yet there was a faint blush covering her cheeks. Was the matter she wished to discuss an embarrassment of some kind? He let out a sigh. He did know that if he took her upstairs to discuss this problem, there wouldn't be time for talk. He'd take her to bed instead, and while he would find great satisfaction in touching his wife, he would also miss the meeting. Since he'd called the council together to once again discuss the possibility of an alliance, he couldn't leave them.

The elders were filling in the spaces at the table. A young warrior Judith hadn't met before carried a jug of wine over and filled each elder's goblet. Iain waved the squire's hand away when he reached for his goblet. Judith hadn't realized she'd been holding her breath. She let it out when her husband declined the drink.

Owen noticed Iain's refusal. "What's this? You've got to toast your own marriage, son," he announced. "This is our first meeting with you, a married man, advising us."

"Why does he advise you?"

Judith hadn't realized she'd blurted out the thought aloud until it was too late. She certainly gained everyone's attention. The elders were all staring at her with puzzled expressions.

"What kind of question is that?" Owen asked.

"He's the laird," Vincent reminded her. "It's his duty to advise us."

"It's all upside down up here," Judith remarked with a nod.

"Explain what you're meaning, lass," Graham suggested.

She wished she hadn't started the topic, and God, how she hated being the focus of everyone's attention. She could feel her face heating with a blush. She tightened her hold on Iain's hand, then said, "Your laird is young and doesn't have your wisdom. It would seem to me that you, as the elders, should do the advising. That is all I meant."

"It's the way it's always been here," Gelfrid countered.

The other elders all nodded agreement. Judith noticed that the squire, with Owen's prodding, had moved forward and was now filling Iain's goblet full of the dark, red wine. Her mind was centered on asking Gelfrid another question, however, and she forced herself not to overreact to the sight of her husband having a drink or two.

"Gelfrid, please don't think me insolent for asking this question," she began. "But I was wondering if you've become so set in your ways, you cannot consider making any changes at all, even if they benefit the entire clan."

It was a bold question to ask. Judith worried over his reaction. Gelfrid rubbed his jaw while he gave the matter consideration, then shrugged.

"I'm living in a household with an Englishwoman," the elder announced. "And I'm thinking that's a change, all right. I must not be too set in my ways, Judith."

She was pleased to hear this, Iain guessed, when she lessened her grip on his hand.

"Let's have our toast now, and then the laird's wife can give us her reasons for wanting Sundays," Graham announced.

"Did you hear that, Owen? Our lass is wanting Sundays," Gelfrid told his friend in a loud whisper.

"She can't be having that, can she?" Vincent asked. "You can't have a day all to your own. It belongs to everyone."

"It's peculiar," Duncan muttered.

"She's English," Vincent thoughtfully reminded his companions.

"Are you saying she's backward?" Owen asked.

"She isn't backward," Gelfrid defended.

The discussion was getting out of hand. Iain was trying not to smile. Judith was trying not to become irritated. She smiled at Gelfrid for defending her, pleased that he at least realized she wasn't at all backward.

He ruined her good opinion of him, however, when he remarked, "She's just illogical. Don't think she can help it. Do you, Owen?"

Judith glared at Iain, a silent message that he really should defend her now. He winked at her.

"Here, here," Graham blurted out to gain everyone's attention. He stood, lifted his goblet into the air, and then gave a long-winded toast to the bride and groom.

Everyone, including Iain, downed the contents of their goblets. The squire immediately hurried forward again to pour more wine into each goblet.

She edged her chair back, away from the table. It was an instinctive habit, born years ago, and she was barely aware of what she was doing.

Iain noticed. He also noticed that with each drink he took from his goblet, Judith moved a little farther away.

Her attention was centered on Graham. The leader of the council was now officially welcoming Judith into the clan.

Frances Catherine, hanging on Alex's strong arm, came into the hall then. Patrick looked both surprised and irritated to see his wife.

She waylaid his lecture before he could start in. "I wanted a breath of fresh air and a visitation with my dear friend. She lives here, too, Patrick, so you can quit your frowning. Alex didn't let me fall."

"I was going to give her a ride on my mount, but—"

"He didn't know where to lift," Frances Catherine explained. She patted her stomach and smiled up at her husband.

"Come and join us," Judith called out. "Graham just finished giving a lovely toast to welcome me into the family."

Her friend nodded. She looked up at Alex. "See? I told you there wasn't a meeting going on. Judith wouldn't be here."

"Why wouldn't I be here?" Judith asked.

Frances Catherine went over to the table, sat down next to her husband and took hold of his hand so that he'd quit frowning at her. She smiled at Judith while she pinched her husband.

She was telling him to behave himself, Patrick supposed. He found himself grinning over his wife's outrageous conduct. As soon as they were alone, he was determined to tell her that once he gave her an order, he meant it to be carried out. He specifically remembered telling her to stay home tonight. The thought of his love taking a fall terrified him. He only had her safety in mind, he thought to himself. If anything happened to her, he didn't know what he would do.

He was getting all riled up just thinking about that dark possibility. His wife turned his attention then. She squeezed his hand and leaned against his side. Patrick let out a sigh. He didn't care if it was appropriate or not. He put his arm around his wife and pulled her even closer against him.

Frances Catherine shyly asked Graham to repeat his toast so that she could hear it. The elder was happy to accommodate her. Another gobletful of wine was immediately consumed by everyone.

Again Judith moved her chair a bit farther back. She could feel the familiar knot forming in her stomach. Iain had promised her he wouldn't get sotted in her presence, but what if, quite by accident, he did get a little drunk? Would he become as mean- and surly-tempered as her uncle Tekel?

She forced her panic aside. Gelfrid was demanding her attention. "Tell us why you're wanting Sundays," he instructed.

"What in heaven's name are you doing in the corner, Judith?" Graham asked, suddenly noticing how she'd moved away from the gathering.

"She scooted herself there," Owen explained.

Judith could feel herself blushing. She took a deep

breath and stood up. "Sundays are supposed to be days of rest," she announced. "The Church says so. In England, we follow this rule."

"We do, too," Graham said. "We rest, don't we, Gelfrid?"

"Aye, we do," his friend agreed.

"All the men do."

Frances Catherine made that remark. Her gaze was centered on Judith. "That's what you're getting at, isn't it?"

Judith nodded. "I have noticed the women don't ever have a day to rest," she explained. "Sunday is just like every other day for them."

"Are you thinking to criticize our women?" Duncan asked.

"No," Judith answered. "I'm criticizing the men."

Iain leaned back in his chair and smiled. Judith had warned him she wanted to make some changes, and he assumed this was one of them. Hell, he'd been the one to suggest she change what she didn't like. He recalled the conversation they'd had in front of the cemetery. Aye, he'd made the suggestion, all right.

"Do you want us to order the women not to work on Sundays?" Graham asked.

"No, of course not. If you order them, it becomes another duty."

"Are you believing we've mistreated our women?" Duncan asked.

Judith shook her head again. "Oh, no," she said. "As fine warriors, you provide well for your wives. You cherish and protect them. In return, they keep your homes comfortable and see to your needs."

"That's what marriage is all about," Graham announced.

"Is she taking issue with marriage, then?" Owen asked, trying to understand.

Gelfrid shook his head. "It's the stones. They addled

her mind," he decided. "The one nearly plucked out her eye."

Judith felt like screaming in frustration. She didn't, of course, and tried once again to use logic to make the men understand. She turned her attention to Iain. "When do the women have time for amusement?" she asked. "Your clan never attends the festivals, do they? Have you ever seen any of the women taking their nooning meal outside so they can enjoy the sunshine while they talk to one another? I haven't," she ended with a nod.

She turned to Graham next. "Do any of the women own horses? Have you ever seen any of them ride on a hunt for game?" She didn't give him time to answer. "I would only ask that you think about setting Sundays aside for amusement of some sort. That is all I wished to say."

Judith sat back down in her chair. She was determined to keep her mouth shut now. She would give them time to think about this issue before broaching it again.

"We value every member of this clan," Gelfrid announced.

"I'm thinking it's time to start our meeting," Duncan interjected. "If the women will take their leave, we can begin."

Judith bounded out of her chair again. "The women aren't a part of this clan, for if they were, they would be allowed to bring their problems to this council."

"Now, Judith, that isn't true," Owen contradicted. "Only a few months ago we allowed Frances Catherine to come before us."

"Aye, they did," Frances Catherine agreed. "They wanted to talk me out of sending for you."

"Let's have another toast and put this talk aside for now," Vincent suggested. "Iain, you'd best have a talk with your woman about her illogical thoughts. She'll be having us obeying our women if we let her have her way."

Judith's shoulders slumped. She wasn't going to get the council's support after all.

Iain drew her attention then. He was shaking his head at Vincent. "I cannot take issue with my wife," he announced. "Because I support what she's telling you."

Judith was so pleased by his remarks, she wanted to run to him. He reached for his goblet and took a long drink. She sat down in her chair instead.

"What are you saying, Iain?" Graham asked.

"Judith was an outsider when she came to us," Iain explained. "Our way of life was new to her and she was able to see things that we have ignored . . . or accepted without question over the years. I see no reason why we cannot insist our women rest on Sundays."

The elders nodded. Graham wanted his laird to be more specific. "Do you advise us to order the women to take this day as leisure?"

"No," Iain replied. "As Judith has just said, an order becomes a duty. We suggest, Graham, and encourage. Do you see the difference?"

Graham smiled. He turned to Judith. "Now do you understand why he's laird? He gives us sound advice, Judith."

It was still upside down in her mind, but she was too happy over her husband's defense of her request to argue.

"And now, perhaps you will understand why I married him," she replied. "I would never marry an unreasonable man."

"She's scooted herself and her chair into the buttery," Gelfrid remarked in a loud whisper. "And I'm not understanding that at all."

"Judith," Iain called out. "I've ordered Brodick and Gowrie to wait outside until the meeting begins. Would you go and tell them to come inside now?"

It was an odd request to make considering the fact that his squire was standing right beside him. The boy warrior looked like he wanted to see the errand completed, but when he opened his mouth to offer his assistance, Iain raised his hand.

"I would be happy to go and get them," she said. She was so pleased by the way Iain had phrased his order, she couldn't quit smiling.

Iain watched her leave. The second the door closed behind her, he turned to Frances Catherine. "It was a false errand I gave Judith," he explained in a low voice. "I wanted to ask you something."

"Yes?" Frances Catherine replied, trying not to worry over the frown on her brother-in-law's face.

Iain motioned to Judith's chair over in the corner, then asked, "Why?"

He was asking her why Judith had moved away from the table. "The wine," she replied in a low whisper of her own.

He shook his head. He still didn't understand. Frances Catherine took a deep breath. "It's something she's always done, since she was very little . . . and learned to protect herself. It used to drive my father daft, and he finally decided not to drink at all in front of Judith. I doubt she even realizes now . . . you mustn't take exception."

"I would like to understand," Iain countered. "And I won't become insulted," he promised. "Now tell me why she moved the stool each time I took a drink. What is this lesson she learned?"

"Judith moved to put herself . . ." Iain patiently waited. Frances Catherine couldn't hold his gaze. She turned her attention to the tabletop. ". . . out of striking distance."

Iain hadn't expected that answer. He leaned back in his chair to think about Frances Catherine's explanation.

A long minute passed in silence. Then Iain asked, "Were there times she wasn't able to get away?"

"Oh, yes," Frances Catherine answered. "Many, many times."

The other elders had heard every word, of course. Gelfrid let out a long sigh. Graham shook his head.

"Why would she believe you would strike her?" Owen asked.

Iain hadn't realized until that minute how much he hated the lack of privacy in his life. "This is a family matter," he announced.

He wanted the discussion stopped before it went any further. Frances Catherine didn't catch on to his hint, however. She turned to Owen to answer his question.

"She doesn't believe Iain would strike her," she explained. "She wouldn't have married him if she thought he would hurt her."

"Then why—" Owen began.

"If Judith wishes you to know about her background, she'll tell you," Iain said. His voice was hard, determined. He stood up. "The meeting will take place tomorrow," he announced.

He didn't give anyone time to argue, but turned and walked out of the hall.

Judith stood in the center of the courtyard. She turned around when she heard the door closing behind her, even managed a smile for her husband.

"They still aren't here, Iain," she called out. "I'll be certain to send them inside as soon as they arrive."

He walked down the steps and started toward her. She backed away, though she couldn't help but notice her husband didn't appear to be muddleheaded. He wasn't scowling, either. She had counted, though, and he had had three full cups of wine . . . or had he only taken sips of the brew? She couldn't be certain. He didn't look sotted. Still, she wasn't going to take any chances. She backed up another step.

He stopped. So did she. "Judith?"

"Yes?"

"I got roaring drunk when I was fifteen years old. I remember it as though it happened yesterday."

Her eyes widened. He took another step toward her. "It was a painful lesson," he added with another step in her direction. "I'm never going to forget how I felt the following day."

"You became ill?"

He laughed. "Extremely ill," he told her. He was only a few feet away from her now. If he reached out, he could grab hold of her. He didn't. He wanted her to come to him. He clasped his hands behind his back and stared at her. "Graham fed me the ale and watched over me the next day. He was giving an important lesson, but I was much too arrogant to realize it at the time."

Her curiosity overcame her worry. When he took another step toward her, she didn't back away. "What was this lesson?" she asked.

"That a warrior who gives up his control to drink is a bloody fool. The wine makes him vulnerable, dangerous to others, too."

She nodded agreement. "Tis the truth it does," she said. "Some men would even do things they don't recall the next day. They might hurt someone and not remember. Others must be on constant guard against attack. Drunks can't be trusted."

What she was so innocently telling him made his heart ache. He was careful to keep his expression contained. "And who gave you that lesson?" he asked her in a mild, soothing voice.

"Uncle Tekel," she replied. She rubbed her arms while she explained about his injuries and how he used the wine to dull his pain. She was shivering with her memories. "After a time . . . the wine turned his mind into mush. Then he couldn't ever be trusted."

"Do you trust me?"

"Oh, yes."

"Then come to me."

He opened his arms to her. She hesitated for only the briefest of minutes, then hurried forward. He wrapped his arms around her and held her tight.

"I promised you I'd never get drunk, Judith, and you really do insult me by thinking I would break that pledge."

"I do not mean to insult you," she whispered against his chest. "I know you wouldn't deliberately break your pledge. But there will be times, like tonight, when you must drink with the others, and if the celebration requires—"

"It wouldn't matter what the reasons be," he interrupted. He rubbed his chin across the top of her head, loving the feel of her silky hair against his skin. He inhaled her light, feminine fragrance and found himself smiling with pleasure.

"Husband, you're going to miss your important meeting," she whispered.

"Yes," he agreed. He let go of her. He waited for her to look up at him, and when she did, he leaned down and kissed her sweet mouth.

He took hold of her hand and led her back inside. He didn't turn toward the great hall, however, but started up the stairs, pulling his wife after him.

"Where are we going?" she asked him in a whisper.

"To our chamber."

"But the meeting—"

"We'll have our own meeting."

She didn't understand. He opened the door to the bedroom, winked at his wife, and then gave her a gentle little shove to get her inside.

"What is the purpose of this meeting?"

He shut the door, bolted it, and turned his attention to Judith. "Satisfaction," he announced. "Take your clothes off and I'll explain in detail what I mean."

Her immediate blush told him she'd caught on to his game. She laughed, a full, rich sound that made his heartbeat accelerate. He leaned against the door and watched her battle her embarrassment.

He hadn't even touched her yet, but he was already feeling incredibly content. He hadn't realized, until she came into his life, what a bleak, cold existence he'd led. It was as though he'd moved around in a fog of duties and responsibilities all his life, never allowing himself time to think about what he was missing.

Judith had changed his life completely, of course. He found such joy just being with her. He took time to do inconsequential things now, such as teasing her to gain her always refreshing reaction. He liked touching her, too. Oh Lord, how he liked the feel of her soft body pressed up against him. He liked the way she blushed over the most insignificant things, the way she shyly tried to order him around.

She was a delightful confusion to him. He knew it had been difficult for her to plead for the women in the clan, yet she hadn't let her own shyness stop her from championing their cause for better treatment.

Judith was strong-willed, courageous, and extremely tenderhearted.

And he was in love with her.

Lord help him now, he thought to himself. She had captured his heart. He didn't know whether to laugh or roar. Judith paused in her task of removing her clothes to look at him. She wore only her white chemise now and was reaching for the chain holding her father's ring around her neck when she caught Iain's dark expression.

"Is something wrong?" she asked.

"I asked you not to wear that ring," he reminded her.

"You asked me not to wear it to bed at night," she countered. "And I never have, have I?"

His frown intensified. "Why do you wear it during the day? Do you have a special attachment for the thing?"

"No."

"Then why the hell do you wear it?"

She couldn't understand why he was becoming so vexed with her. "Because Janet and Bridget are now coming into our chamber to clean, and I didn't want either one of them to find the ring and wonder about it." She lifted her shoulders in a delicate shrug. "The ring's become a nuisance. I do believe I would like to get rid of it."

Now would probably be the perfect time to tell him

who the ring belonged to and why she was so worried someone might recognize the distinctive design and guess it was Laird Maclean's.

She put the chain and ring back in the chest for the night and closed the lid. Then she turned around to look at him. She would tell him now. "Do you remember, right before we were married, you told me my background didn't matter to you?"

He nodded. "I remember," he replied.

"Did you mean what you said?"

"I never say anything I don't mean."

"You don't have to snap at me," she whispered. She started wringing her hands together. If Iain loved her, the truth she was about to give him wouldn't destroy that love . . . would it?

"Do you love me?"

He pulled away from the door. His scowl was hot enough to burn. "You won't be ordering me around, Judith."

She was taken aback by that command. "Of course not," she agreed. "But I asked—"

"I won't be turned into milk toast. You'd best understand that here and now."

"I understand," she replied. "I don't wish to change anything about you."

Her compliment didn't ease his scowl. "I'm not a weakling, and I won't be made to act like one."

The conversation had taken a bizarre turn. Iain was getting all worked up. In her heart, she was certain he loved her, yet his reaction to the simple question was so confusing to her, she started to worry.

She watched him pull off one boot and toss it on the floor. The other followed.

"Was my question that upsetting to you?" she asked, pricked at the mere possibility.

"Warriors do not become upset. Women do."

She straightened her shoulders. "I'm not upset."

"Yes, you are," he countered. "You're wringing your hands."

She immediately stopped. "You're the one doing all the scowling," she said.

He shrugged. "I was . . . thinking."

"About what?"

"The fires of purgatory."

She had to sit down. He wasn't making any sense now. "What does that mean?" she asked.

"Patrick told me he would walk through the fires of purgatory if he had to in order to please his wife."

She went over to the bed and sat down on the side. "And?" she prodded when he didn't continue.

He stripped out of his clothing and walked over to her. He pulled her to her feet and stared down at her.

"And I have only just realized I would do the same for you."

Chapter 13

Judith walked around in a haze of happiness for two full weeks. Iain loved her. Oh, he hadn't given her the exact words, but telling her he would walk through the fires of purgatory just to please her was certainly proof enough that he loved her.

She couldn't quit smiling. Iain couldn't quit scowling. It was obvious to her he was having difficulty accepting his feelings. She thought he was waiting for her to do or say something that would confirm his suspicions that he was now vulnerable. Loving her worried him. She understood that. Warriors were conditioned to fight and protect. They spent long years training to become invincible in both mind and body. They didn't have time for the tender side of life. Iain was probably feeling trapped now, she decided. In time he'd learn to trust his love, and to feel the same joy she was now feeling.

She would catch her husband watching her when he didn't think she was noticing. He seemed terribly preoccupied. She didn't prod him to get over this foolish vulnerability, guessing he'd get all riled up if she dared to use that word with him. She kept her patience while he sorted it all out in his mind.

Gelfrid found out she was good with a needle and thread, and immediately gave her a basketful of clothing he needed mended. Graham wasn't about to be left out. He gave her his clothing, too.

She had three tall-backed chairs with soft cushions moved into the great hall and placed in a half circle in front of the hearth. Each cushion was, of course, covered with the Maitland plaid. After supper she would take her sewing over to one of the chairs and work there while she listened to the discussions going on at the table. Often Graham would call out to her to ask her opinion, and he would usually nod his agreement after she'd given him her views. She always left the hall when an official meeting was in progress, and she knew Iain appreciated her thoughtfulness in not making him have to ask her to go.

Judith learned that by pleasing the elders, she was accidentally teaching them how to please her. She remarked one morning that it was a pity there weren't any colorful banners hanging from the walls to soften the austerity of the gray stone. Graham immediately went up to his room, and Gelfrid to his, and both returned carrying beautiful silk banners they told her used to hang in their homes.

Helen assisted in hanging the banners. She was already a welcome addition to the household. With Judith's encouragement and help, she organized the kitchens and made the keep into an appealing home for all of them. The aroma of her spices, mingled with the scent of the daily baked bread, would float through the air, drawing smiles and sighs of contentment from Graham and Gelfrid.

The first Sunday declared to be a day of rest didn't turn out the way Judith expected. Most of the women ignored the suggestion they put their work aside. Judith wasn't defeated, however. She decided that the way to get the women outside to mingle was through their children. She organized games for the little ones and sent Andrew from cottage to cottage with the announcement that the following Sunday would be a Maitland festival for all the boys and girls.

It was hugely successful. Mothers dropped everything so they could watch their children participate in the games. Judith had expected that reaction. She hadn't expected the men to get involved. Some came out of simple curiosity. Others came to watch their offspring compete. Helen took care of organizing the food. Other mothers were anxious to help. Tables were carried outside and covered with trays of fruit tarts, breads and jams, and more substantial offerings such as salted salmon, smoked lamb, and fowl.

There was only one awkward moment during the entire day. An eleven-year-old girl named Elizabeth won the competition with the bow and arrow. She bested everyone, including several thirteen-year-old boys.

No one knew what to do. If they cheered for the lass, wouldn't that be a humiliation for the older boys? Judith wasn't certain how to handle the delicate situation. Fortunately, Iain had just come outside when the competition concluded. Judith went over to him, handed him one of the pretty little banners she had made for the children and asked him to award it to the winner. She didn't mention who had won.

Her husband didn't know until he looked at the target that a girl had bested the boys. It didn't matter to him, though. He praised Elizabeth for her ability while he pinned the piece of silk to her plaid. The girl's parents rushed forward. The father told everyone within shouting distance that he had taught his daughter how to use the bow and arrow and that she'd had a clever eye from a very early age.

Judith spent most of the day meeting as many of the clan members as she could. She spotted Agnes twice, but each time she tried to go to her to offer a word a greeting, the midwife would turn her back on her and walk the other way. After three tries, Judith gave up.

Frances Catherine sat on a blanket near the center of the hill, watching the games. Judith joined her for the nooning meal. Andrew followed her up the climb, and it wasn't until she'd turned to sit down next to her friend that she noticed all the other children following along.

The little ones were extremely curious about her. Although she was now the laird's wife, she was still English, and they had a multitude of questions for her. She answered every one of them, careful not to take offense over some of the outrageous things they believed about the English.

Frances Catherine told the story of how she and Judith met. The children wanted to hear more about the border festival, of course, and Judith told them all about the games. They hung on her every word. Some hung on her. One little boy, who couldn't be more than three summers, patiently stood next to Judith. She didn't know what he wanted until she removed the extra banners from her skirts. The little one immediately strutted forward, turned around, and sat down on her lap. Judith continued on with her story, and within minutes the child was sound asleep.

The children didn't want the day to end. They wanted to hear one more story, and then another and another. Judith finally gave her promise that tomorrow afternoon she would bring her sewing outside and sit at this very spot. Anyone who would like to join her was welcome, and she would tell more stories then.

All in all, Judith felt that things were going quite well. Frances Catherine was a worry, of course, and until the baby was safely delivered and her friend fully recovered, Judith knew she was going to continue to worry. Her friend had stubbornly resisted giving her trust to Helen, but she was softening in her attitude. Her faith remained in Judith, she told her, and if she thought Helen would be a help, that would be all right . . . as long as Judith was in charge.

Frances Catherine was only a week away from the birthing, if her estimations were correct. Judith thought she looked big enough to have three babies. She made the mistake of telling Patrick so. He paled considerably, and she had to hurry and explain she was only teasing. He ordered her never to jest with him again.

Iain remained distant with Judith during the days. He was very different at night, however. He made passionate love to her almost every night, and always fell asleep holding her in his arms.

Her husband had never really lost his composure or his arrogance around her until the evening she met Ramsey.

Frances Catherine had just walked into the hall to spend an hour or so with Judith. Patrick helped her get settled in one of the chairs by the hearth, ordered her to stay put until he finished an important matter, and then went across the hall to join Iain and Brodick.

"My husband's turning into a nervous twit," Frances Catherine whispered.

Judith laughed. Frances Catherine faced Iain and she noticed he smiled. A few minutes later she said something else Judith found quite amusing, and she again noticed that when Judith laughed, her husband smiled.

She thought that was terribly sweet and told Judith so. Then Ramsey walked into the hall with two other warriors.

Judith didn't notice the men. Frances Catherine did. "Do you remember my telling you about the warrior named Ramsey and how handsome he is?"

Judith didn't remember. "Have a look," Frances Catherine whispered. "You'll know what I'm talking about."

Judith's curiosity was captured, of course. She peeked around the side of the chair to get a look at the man. Then she took a sharp breath. She thought her mouth might have dropped open but she couldn't be sure. Oh,

Lord, he was beautiful. It was the only word that did the warrior any justice in her mind. To describe his appearance to someone who hadn't seen him would seem ordinary, she supposed, and Ramsey was anything but ordinary. He was perfection. He had dark, black-brown hair, brown eyes, and a smile destined to give ladies heart trouble. He was smiling now.

"Do you notice the dimple?" Frances Catherine whispered. "God, Judith, isn't he magnificent?"

How could she not notice the dimple? It was outrageously appealing. She wasn't about to admit that to her friend, however. She decided to tease her instead. "Which of the three is Ramsey?" she innocently asked.

Frances Catherine burst into laughter. The sound drew the men's attention. Ramsey smiled at Patrick's wife, then turned his gaze to Judith.

They stared at each other a long minute, she wondering how anyone could look that handsome, and he probably wondering who the hell she was.

Iain stood up, drawing her attention. He didn't look overly happy and he was staring at her.

She wondered what she had done to irritate him, and just as soon as she could manage to quit gawking at Ramsey, she supposed she would have to find out.

He wasn't in the mood to wait. "Judith, come here," he commanded in a near bellow.

She frowned at her husband to let him know she didn't appreciate his high-handed method in gaining her attention. He ignored the subtle message and crooked his finger at her.

She took her time answering his summons. After carefully folding the stocking she was mending for Gelfrid, she placed it in the basket and slowly stood up.

"I believe your husband's a little jealous," Frances Catherine whispered.

"That's ridiculous," Judith whispered back.

Her friend snorted. Judith forced herself not to laugh

again. She walked across the room, taking the path directly in front of the three guests, and came to a stop in front of her scowling husband.

"Did you wish something?" she asked.

He nodded. Then he grabbed hold of her. She couldn't imagine what had come over him. He hauled her up against his side and threw his arm around her shoulders, anchoring her there.

He was acting extremely possessive. Judith had to bite her lower lip to keep herself from laughing. Frances Catherine had been correct. Iain was jealous. She didn't know if she should be pleased or insulted.

He introduced her to the new arrivals. She was careful to give each warrior her full attention. She wanted to stare at Ramsey, but she didn't dare. Iain would notice.

As soon as the formalities were finished, Judith tried to go back to her friend. Iain wouldn't let her. She turned to look up at him. He was still scowling.

"May I have a word in private with you?" she requested.

He gave her his answer by dragging her into the buttery.

"What is it you wish to say to me?"

"Ramsey's extremely handsome."

He didn't like hearing that. Judith smiled. "But then, so are you, husband. I wouldn't walk through the fires of purgatory for him, however, no matter how loyal he is to you. I don't love him. I love you. I just thought you might wish to hear me tell you so. I would walk through the fires of purgatory for you . . . but only you."

He let up on his hold. "I was that obvious?"

She nodded. He grinned. He leaned down and kissed her. It was a gentle, undemanding kiss that left them both wanting for more.

"I'm a very possessive man, Judith. You might as well realize that."

Her smile filled with him pleasure. "I already knew

you were possessive," she whispered. "And I still love you."

He laughed. "My men are waiting," he said. "Was there anything else you wished to say to me?"

His arrogance was back in place. She shook her head. "Nay, husband."

She didn't start laughing until she and Frances Catherine went outside to gain a little privacy.

Judith hadn't made an empty boast to Iain. She would walk through the fires of purgatory to keep him safe, but she never imagined she'd ever have to actually do such an impossible thing.

Purgatory turned out to be Maclean land.

Judith was put to the test the following afternoon. Iain had left with Ramsey and Brodick to once again put down a dispute with the difficult Macphersons near the west border, and Patrick and Graham were getting ready to go hunting. Graham told her he planned to do a spot of fishing, too.

"If there be enough time, of course," the elder explained. "Patrick won't leave his wife for more than four hours at the most because of her advanced condition." He paused to chuckle. "The boy keeps taking me aside to whisper that his wife becomes overly fearful whenever he's out of her sight, and a bit later she's taking me aside and demanding I take her husband away on a full day's hunt so she can have some peace and quiet."

"He's making her daft," Judith told Graham. "He watches her every minute. She swears that when she wakes up during the night, she finds him wide awake and staring at her."

Graham shook his head. "He's making everyone daft," he admitted. "Patrick won't listen to reason. We'll all be mighty happy when Frances Catherine has her bairn."

Judith was in full agreement. She decided to turn the topic. "Are you going hunting near the falls?"

"We are," he answered. "The fishing's best there."

"Frances Catherine told me it's very beautiful."

The wistfulness in her voice wasn't lost on the elder. "Why don't you come with us today? You can see for yourself how pretty it is."

She was thrilled. She put the question to Helen. "If you need assistance today, I'll be happy to stay home."

Helen was pleased her mistress was giving her such consideration. "Now that Janet and Bridget do the heavy work, there isn't much for me to do outside the kitchens, milady."

"It's settled, then," Graham announced. "We're leaving in just a few minutes. Hurry and get yourself ready, lass. Helen, I might have some fresh fish for our supper tonight."

Judith raced upstairs. She changed into her full riding skirts, tied her hair behind her neck with a ribbon, and then went running back down the stairs.

Patrick wasn't happy to find out she was going. She understood his reason and therefore didn't have hurt feelings.

"Frances Catherine will be fine until we get back," she promised. "Helen will look in on her, won't you, Helen?"

The housekeeper quickly nodded. Patrick still wasn't convinced. Graham had to give him several good nudges to get him moving toward the stables.

It was a glorious morning. Judith took her heavy cloak along, but there really wasn't any need for the extra protection. The wind was mild, the sun bright, and the scenery every bit as breathtaking as Frances Catherine had said it would be.

They didn't reach the base of the falls, though. The Dunbars attacked before they could get there.

There wasn't any warning. Graham led the way through the thick, misty green forest. Judith was right behind him, and Patrick took up the rear. Their guard was down for the simple reason they were still well inside Maitland land.

They were suddenly surrounded by at least twenty warriors who had their swords drawn, ready. They weren't wearing the Maitland colors, but Judith was too surprised by their sudden appearance to be frightened.

"You're on our land," Graham bellowed, his fury beyond anything Judith had ever witnessed before. "You'll leave now, Dunbars, before you breach our truce."

The warriors didn't respond to his command. They were like statues now. Judith didn't think any of them even blinked.

A fair number were staring at her. She raised her chin and stared back. She wasn't about to let the enemy intimidate her. She wasn't going to let them know how worried she was, either.

She heard the sound of horses coming toward them just as Patrick nudged his mount forward. He moved to Judith's right side. He was so close to her, his leg rubbed against hers.

He was trying to protect her. She knew he would give his life to keep her safe. She said a quick prayer to her Maker that that noble act wouldn't be necessary.

No one moved until the crash of horses sounded in front of them, breaking through the thicket. Several of the Dunbar warriors turned to look then.

Five more men appeared. They were wearing plaids, too, but they weren't the same colors as the Dunbars. Judith didn't know what that meant. Patrick did. He let out a low expletive.

She turned to look at him. "Who are they?" she whispered.

"Maclean soldiers."

Judith's eyes widened. She turned back to look at the men. The leader moved his mount closer. Judith kept her attention directed on him. There was something vaguely familiar about him, but she couldn't imagine what it was. The warrior was tall, broad-shouldered, and had dark blond hair and intense blue eyes.

Graham broke the silence. "You're in league with the Dunbars, then."

It was a statement, not a question, but the Maclean warrior answered him.

"Your laird tried to prevent the alliance. He might have succeeded, too, if he hadn't had to battle you, old man, and the others who run your clan. Who is this woman?"

Neither Graham nor Patrick answered.

The Maclean warrior motioned to the men surrounding them. Patrick and Graham didn't have time to reach for their weapons, had they been foolish enough to try. The Dunbars' swords were now pointed at their necks. The warriors waited for the Maclean leader to give them their next instruction.

"I ask you again," he said to Graham. "Who is this woman? She looks familiar to me."

Graham shook his head. Judith's heart started pounding. "I will speak for myself," she called out.

Patrick put his hand on her knee and squeezed. He was letting her know he didn't want her to tell them anything.

The leader nudged his mount close to her left side. He stared at Patrick a long minute, then turned his gaze to Judith. "Then speak," he arrogantly commanded.

"Tell me who you are and I'll answer your questions," she commanded.

Patrick's hold on her knee became painful.

"My name is Douglas Maclean," he answered.

"Are you commander over these men or just the most outspoken?"

He ignored the insult. "I'm the laird's son," he said. "Now tell me who—"

He stopped his demand when he noticed the radical change that came over the beautiful woman. The color had left her face. She almost fell off her horse, and didn't even seem to notice. He reached over and grabbed hold of her arm.

She was daring to shake her head at him. "You cannot be his son."

The vehemence in his voice confused him. "The hell I can't," he replied.

She refused to believe him. A thought popped into her mind. Her father must have been married once before. Yes, that was it, she told herself. Douglas looked several years older than she. . . . "Who was your mother?" she demanded.

"Why are you asking me such questions?"

"Answer me."

The fury in her voice surprised him. "And if I do answer you, will you then tell me who you are?"

"Yes," she promised.

He nodded. "Very well," he said, his voice mild once again. "My mother was an English bitch. Her accent was very like your own. That much I remember. Now tell me who you are," he demanded again.

She was desperately trying to keep her wits about her. "How old are you?"

He told her, then painfully squeezed her arm.

Judith thought she was going to be sick. Douglas was five years older than she, and his eyes, dear God, his eyes were the same color as her own. Was his hair the exact shade, too? No, no, she told herself. Hers was much lighter.

She had to take a deep breath to keep herself from gagging. She slumped to the side of her saddle, close to Patrick's side.

Dear God, it was true. Douglas was her brother.

Patrick tried to put his arm around her. Douglas jerked her toward him, then lifted her from her mount and settled her in front of him.

"What the hell's wrong with her?" he asked.

No one answered him. Douglas growled in frustration. He still didn't know who the woman belonged to, but he recognized Patrick, all right.

"The Maitland laird will come after his brother," he told his men. "We'll be ready to give him a proper greeting. Bring them to my father's holding," he ordered with a nod toward Graham and Patrick.

The length of time it took to get to the Maclean keep was shortened considerably because they were able to ride directly there, across Dunbar land. Patrick memorized every detail on the way for future use.

Judith didn't pay any attention to where they were going. She kept her eyes tightly closed while she tried to sort out this god-awful situation in her mind.

She wanted to weep with shame over her mother's treachery. How could she abandon her child? Judith was so sickened inside, she could barely concentrate on anything but keeping her stomach settled.

As they rode, she wondered how Douglas would react if she threw up all over him.

She finally opened her eyes. He noticed. "Did the Maclean name scare you into a faint?"

"I didn't faint," she snapped. "I want to ride my own mount."

"I want you to stay here," he replied. "You're very beautiful," he added almost as an afterthought. "I might decide to let you warm my bed."

"That's disgusting."

She hadn't meant to blurt out her thought, but she couldn't keep it inside. Douglas took exception to the appalled look on her face. He took hold of her chin and forced her face up to his.

Good God, was he going to kiss her? "I'm going to be sick," she stammered out.

He hastily let go of her.

She took several deep breaths to convince him she really was having difficulty, then relaxed. "I'm better now," she lied.

"All the English are weak," he told her. "Tis yet another reason we despise them."

"English women as well as Engiish men?" she asked.

"Aye," he answered.

"I'm English," she said. "And you contradict yourself. If you hate all of us, why would you hint at wanting me in your bed?"

He didn't answer her. A few minutes passed before he spoke again. "Tell me your name."

"Judith," she answered.

"Why are you wearing the Maitland plaid?"

"My friend gave it to me. I'm here on a visitation and will return to England after my friend has had her baby."

He shook his head. "The Maitlands wouldn't let you leave. You're lying, Judith."

"Why wouldn't they let me leave?"

"You're too beautiful to—"

"I'm English." She interrupted him with that reminder. "They don't like me."

"Don't lie to me," he ordered. "Tell me who you belong to."

"She's telling you the truth," Patrick shouted. "She's a guest, nothing more."

Douglas laughed. He wasn't believing any such nonsense. His hold on Judith's waist became painful. She reached down to pry his fingers away. She saw the ring on his finger then. She let out a little gasp. Her hand flew to her bosom where her father's identical ring was hidden. "Where did you get this ugly ring?" she asked.

"It was my uncle's," he answered. "Why do you persist in asking such personal questions?"

"I was merely curious," she replied.

In a low whisper he said, "You belong to Iain, don't you?"

"I don't converse with pigs."

He laughed then. Douglas was too ignorant to know when he was being insulted. She told him so.

"It's too fine a day to take insult over anything," he announced. "I've captured Graham for my father, and you for myself. Aye, it's a fine day all right."

God help her, she was actually related to this barbarian. She didn't speak to him again for a good hour or more. Curiosity got the better of her intention to ignore him, however, and since they now rode well ahead of both Graham and Patrick, and wouldn't be overheard, she decided to find out what she could about her father.

"What is Laird Maclean like?"

"Mean."

She heard the amusement in his voice. "And?"

"And what?"

"Never mind."

"Why are you so interested?"

"It's good to know as much as possible about one's enemies," she explained. "Why will your father be pleased to see Graham?"

"He has something to settle with him," Douglas answered. "The hate goes back long years. Aye, my father will be happy to see Graham again."

They didn't speak again until they had reached Maclean land. Judith was given a few minutes privacy. She returned from the shelter of the trees, ignored Douglas's outstretched hand, and gained her own horse before he could stop her.

Patrick kept trying to get close enough to talk to her. The Dunbars weren't letting him. Those warriors took their leave when additional Maclean soldiers surrounded them, obviously intent on returning to their own holding.

Judith knew Patrick wanted her to keep silent. He didn't want the Macleans to know they'd captured the laird's wife to use as bait to draw Iain out. Douglas had only been fishing for the truth when he'd suggested she was Iain's woman. He couldn't be sure until someone who knew the truth verified it.

None of it mattered. Iain would come anyway. Surely Patrick realized that. The two brothers had always looked after each other, and Iain would come to Patrick's aid now, Judith told herself, even if she weren't involved.

There could be a bloodbath. Judith didn't have any

doubt about that. Iain wouldn't be reasonable when he retaliated, and just thinking about what would happen made her stomach ache.

She didn't want anyone to die. She didn't know what she could do to prevent the war, but she was determined to try.

She could try to get her father alone and tell him who she was. Then she would have to beg his mercy. If he proved to be compassionate, he might let Graham and Patrick leave before Iain came after them.

Judith had never begged for anything, and in her heart she doubted it would work anyway. She didn't think her father would welcome her. He hadn't bothered to come after her or her mother . . . why would he change his attitudes now?

And if she told him who she was, she would certainly lose everything. Iain would never forgive her. She couldn't blame him. She should have told him the truth, should have insisted he listen to her.

She thought about all those warm, dark nights when they had held each other close and whispered their thoughts to each other . . . oh, yes, she could have told him then.

She'd been too afraid, of course, and all because deep inside she knew he wouldn't love her anymore.

Judith's mind was so consumed by her fears, she didn't notice they'd ridden into the courtyard of the Maclean keep. She looked up, caught sight of the massive stone structure and immediately straightened her shoulders . . . and her resolve.

She gave the Maclean holding a name. Purgatory.

Douglas tried to help her in mid-mount. She kicked his hand away. He tried to grab hold of her arm after she'd reached the ground. She shoved him away, then turned and walked up the steps.

Her bearing was every bit as regal as a queen's. Graham followed her. He was so proud of her behavior, he smiled. So did Patrick. The Maclean warriors were left guessing as to why the Maitlands were in such cheerful moods. They shook their heads and hurried inside to see their laird's reaction to his son's "gifts."

Laird Maclean made everyone wait on him for over three long hours. Judith was kept at one end of the gigantic hall, and the other captives were kept at the opposite end. Patrick and Graham had their hands tied together behind their backs.

Judith couldn't sit still. She paced back and forth in front of the long table. The longer they were kept waiting, the more anxious she became. She was worried about Frances Catherine most of all. Would her friend begin her laboring when she was given the news that Patrick had been taken captive? Dear God, she wouldn't be there to help her.

Her heart went out to Patrick. He was certainly thinking the same worrisome thoughts right now.

Her pace must have been driving the Maclean warriors daft. One reached out to grab her. She was too surprised by the bold action to fight him until he pulled her into his arms.

Patrick let out a roar of fury and came charging across the hall. Douglas came running from the entrance. Judith gathered her wits before either man could get to her. She rammed her knee into the eager soldier's groin. He let out a howl of outrage—and pain, she was pleased to note—before doubling over and crashing to the floor.

She was thoroughly satisfied. Douglas caught her attention then. He grabbed her to pull her away from the soldier writhing on the floor. Patrick wasn't hindered by the fact that his hands were bound behind his back. He used his shoulder to knock Douglas away from Judith.

Douglas went flying into the stone wall. Judith went with him. She would have hit the back of her head against the stone, but Douglas's hand got there first, protecting her.

Patrick tried to slam into Douglas again. Judith was

still in his way, however. Douglas shoved her out of his way and then lunged for her brother-in-law.

"Don't you dare strike him," Judith cried out. "His hands are bound, damn it. If you want to hit someone, hit me."

"Stay out of this, Judith," Patrick roared.

"Enough."

The bellow came from the entrance. Everyone turned to see who had issued the command.

Laird Maclean stood in the center of the entrance. Judith stiffened at the sight of the big man.

The laird's hands were settled on his hips and he had a mean scowl on his face. "Get that soldier out of here," he ordered.

Douglas nodded. He helped the soldier Judith had felled to the floor back to his feet and gave him a push toward the entrance.

The laird nodded with satisfaction, then walked into the hall. He passed Judith without giving her a glance and continued on until he reached the other side of the table. He took his seat in a high-backed chair in the center.

A woman came hurrying inside. She appeared to be about ten years older than Judith. She was dark-haired, heavyset, and wore a smug expression on her face. She paused to stare at Judith before hurrying on toward the table. Judith decided to hate her.

Her attention returned to her father. She didn't want him to be handsome. He was, though. He looked a little like Douglas . . . and like her, she supposed with a sinking heart. His skin was far more leathered-looking than his son's, of course, and he had deep creases around the corners of his eyes and mouth. His brown hair was streaked through with gray, giving him a distinguished appearance.

It was apparent he didn't know who she was, but when his gaze settled on Graham, he smiled a mean-hearted, ugly smile.

Douglas walked forward. She tried to trip him when he passed her. He grabbed hold of her arm and jerked her into his side.

"I've a wedding present for you, Father," Douglas called out. "I can't be certain, but I've got a strong feeling this shrew belongs to Iain Maitland."

She kicked him because he'd called her an insulting name. Then the fullness of what he had just said penetrated her mind.

A wedding present for her father . . . no, it couldn't be. She couldn't have understood. "Your father isn't getting married, is he?"

She sounded as though she was strangling on something. Douglas turned to look at her. "Aye, he is getting married, and Lord, you really do ask the strangest questions for a captive."

Her knees went weak. Douglas had to hold her up. God's truth, she didn't think she could take any more surprises. First she found out she had a brother, and now she was learning her father was about to become a bigamist.

"He thinks he's going to marry that woman?" she asked with a wave of her hand toward the table.

Douglas nodded. The laird's companion took offense. "Get her out of here," she called out. "She offends me."

Judith took a step toward the woman. Douglas squeezed her arm. She thought he might have broken the bone. She let out an involuntary cry of pain and pulled away from him. The sleeve of her gown ripped wide.

Douglas had an appalled look on his face. In a low whisper only she could hear, he said, "I didn't mean to hurt you. Please stand still. It won't do you any good to fight."

Laird Maclean let out a loud sigh. "You will leave," he ordered his companion. "I don't need your interference."

She took her time obeying. She glared at Judith again when she walked past her. Judith ignored her.

"The Maitland laird's coming up the path," a soldier shouted from the doorway.

Judith's heart felt as though it had just stopped beating. Iain was here.

"How many ride with him?" Laird Maclean shouted.

"He's all alone," the soldier reported. "Riding up the hill as sweet as you please."

The Maclean laird laughed. "The boy's got courage, I'll give him that," he remarked. "He isn't carrying any weapons, either, I'll wager."

"Nay, he isn't," the soldier replied.

Judith desperately wanted to run outside to her husband. She tried to do just that, but Douglas caught her. He tightened his hold on her already bruised arm and pulled her close.

"You will not mistreat a woman, Douglas, no matter how much she provokes you. I'm wanting Iain, not his woman."

"For the love of God, I beg you to listen to reason, Laird Maclean. Stop this now before there's a bloodbath."

Father Laggan shouted his plea from the entrance. Judith turned just as the priest came running into the hall.

He came to a quick stop when he reached Judith's side. "Are you all right, lass?"

She nodded. "Father, did you come to listen to Laird Maclean give his marriage vows?"

"Aye, Judith," the priest wearily answered. "And to hopefully talk some sense into these men before it's too late."

Judith shook her head. In a whisper, she said, "I can promise you there won't be any wedding."

"Unhand her, Douglas," the priest ordered. "Look what you've done to her arm. The skin's already turning purple with the swelling. You're hurting her."

Douglas quickly obeyed the priest's command. Judith took full advantage of her freedom. She ran toward the doorway. Douglas caught her around the waist and dragged her back just as Iain walked inside.

He didn't even pause to take in the situation, or the numbers against him. He just kept right on coming. Judith took one look at his expression and closed her eyes. Iain was about to kill someone. She thought Douglas might very well be his target.

"Let go of me," she whispered. "He'll kill you if you don't."

Her brother was intelligent enough to do as she suggested. She immediately ran to Iain and threw herself into his arms. She buried her face against his chest.

"Are you all right?" he asked. "They didn't hurt you?"

She could feel him shaking. She looked up at him. The expression on his face told her it wasn't fear causing that reaction. Nay, it was rage.

"No one hurt me," she told him. "I've been treated well, truly."

He nodded. He gave her a quick squeeze, then gently forced her behind his back.

He walked forward to confront his enemy. Judith followed him. Graham and Patrick were given freedom to move forward. They positioned themselves on either side of Judith.

The two lairds stared at each other a long while, each taking the other's measure. Maclean was the first to break the silence. "It seems you've got yourself a problem, Iain Maitland. I've captured your woman and I'm not at all certain what I'm wanting to do with her. You dared to try to form an alliance with the Dunbars while sending an emissary to me for the same purpose. Were you believing you could play one against the other?"

"You're a fool, old man," Iain replied in a voice shaking with anger. "It was the Dunbars playing that game."

Maclean slammed his fist down on the table. "I've formed an alliance with the Dunbars. Do you call me fool now?"

Iain didn't hesitate. "I do."

Laird Maclean took a deep breath in a bid to control his rising fury. He cocked his head to one side while he stared at Iain. Then he shook his head. "You're deliberately provoking me," he remarked. "I'm wondering why. Everyone knows the store I put in family dealings. Aye, my alliance with the Dunbars made sound sense. You must know the Dunbar laird's second cousin, Eunice, is married to my brother. Aye, it was a union of family, Iain Maitland, and family comes before all other considerations. Yet you call me fool because I'm loyal? You're far too clever to deliberately goad me into killing you. You've got too much to lose. What is your game?"

Iain didn't answer soon enough to please the laird. "Is this woman your wife?"

"Her relationship to me is none of your affair."

Maclean grinned. "I might keep her and give her to one of my men," he boasted, in an attempt to get the Maitland laird riled enough to lose his composure. "Douglas? Are you wanting her in your bed?"

"I am," Douglas called out.

The outrage had gone far enough. The two lairds were like bulls, ramming heads together. Judith moved to her husband's side. "You won't keep me," she called out.

Her father's eyes narrowed. "Your boldness displeases me," he roared.

"Thank you," she replied.

Iain almost smiled then and there. He could feel Judith trembling. Maclean didn't have any idea how frightened she really was, however, and that fact pleased Iain considerably.

"You've got the voice of an Englishwoman," Maclean remarked. "And you appear to be as ignorant as your husband. Don't either of you realize your jeopardy?" He centered his gaze on Judith. "Or does the possibility of your husband's death appeal to you?"

Neither Judith nor Iain answered the laird. Maclean's patience ended. He started shouting at Iain. Iain didn't show any outward reaction to the threats his enemy was making. His expression was so controlled, it was as though it had been carved out of stone. In truth, he looked downright bored.

The laird was red-faced and out of breath by the time he'd finished spewing his litany of reprisals. "Aye, you've got a problem," he muttered. "For no one calls me a fool. No one." He leaned back in his chair, his mind made up. "I am going to kill you, Iain, for that insult alone."

"No." Judith screamed as she took a step forward.

Iain grabbed hold of her hand and forced her to go no farther.

She turned to look up at him. "I have to talk to him," she whispered. "Please understand."

He let go of her. She removed the chain from around her neck and tucked the ring in her fist. Then she walked forward to confront her father.

The hall grew silent as everyone waited to hear what she was going to say.

"You did capture Iain's wife," she began.

Maclean snorted. Judith opened her hand and let the ring drop onto the table in front of him.

Maclean simply stared at the piece of jewelry a long, long while before finally picking it up. His surprise was most evident. He turned his gaze to hers, frowning, still not understanding.

Judith took a deep breath. "Aye, you captured Iain's wife," she said again. "But he married your daughter."

Chapter 14

Her father reacted as though a blade had just been thrust deep into his chest. He lunged forward and upward, until he was half out of his chair, then fell back against the cushions. He looked furious and disbelieving. He shook his head in denial. She slowly nodded.

"How did you get this ring?"

"From my mother. She stole it from you."

"Give me your mother's name," he commanded in a voice thick with emotion.

There wasn't a hint of emotion in Judith's voice when she answered him.

Douglas rushed forward to stand on Judith's right. Their father looked from one to the other and then back again. The similarities were startlingly evident to him now. He finally believed it was possible. "Dear God . . ."

"Father, have you taken ill?"

The laird didn't answer his son. Iain walked forward to stand on Judith's left side. His arm brushed hers. She didn't know if he was looking at her or not. She was afraid to look at him, knowing he would be furious with her by now.

"What in God's name is the matter with you, Father?" Douglas asked. "You look as though you've just seen the Devil."

It was apparent Douglas hadn't heard her whispered confession. Since Iain continued to remain silent, she believed he hadn't heard, either.

Judith was determined to strike a bargain with her father. In exchange for her silence about his first wife, he would let Iain and the others go home. If he wanted to marry again, so be it. She wouldn't interfere. . . .

"Why didn't you want me?"

She flinched inside. She hadn't meant to ask him that question. What did she care if he wanted her or not? And Lord, she'd sounded like a lost little girl.

"I didn't know," he answered. He threaded his fingers through his hair in agitation. "I vowed never to return to England. She knew I wouldn't break my pledge. After she died, I never gave her another thought. I put the past behind me."

Judith moved forward until she was touching the table. She leaned even closer then and whispered. "She isn't dead."

"Good God . . ."

"If you want to marry again, I won't tell Father Laggan you already have a wife. I won't care," she added with a nod. "But you must let the Maitlands go."

She didn't wait for his promise, but backed up until she'd put some distance between them.

Laird Maclean didn't think he could take any more surprises. He was still staggered by the truths he'd just been handed.

"Father, what is going on?"

The laird tried to shake himself out of his stupor. He turned to look at his son. "You have a sister," he said, his voice hoarse with emotion.

"I do?"

"Aye."

"Where?"

"She's standing right beside you."

Douglas turned to stare at Judith. She stared back.

It took her brother a long while to accept. He didn't look very happy with the news. In truth, he looked appalled. "I don't want you in my bed," he stammered out. He was actually able to smile a little then. "No wonder you were so repelled when I tried to—"

He didn't continue, for he'd only just noticed Iain was watching him. Iain's voice was deadly soft when he asked, "Exactly what did you try to do, Douglas?"

Her brother lost his smile. "I didn't know she was your wife, Maitland," he excused. "And I sure as certain didn't know she was my sister when I tried to kiss her."

Iain didn't care what excuses were given. He reached behind Judith's shoulders, grabbed Douglas by the nape of his neck, and sent him flying backward with a flick of his wrist.

Judith's father didn't show any reaction to his son sprawled out on the floor in front of him. His attention remained on his daughter. "I'm pleased you don't look like her."

She didn't respond to that comment.

Her father let out a long sigh. "Did she turn your heart against me, then?" he asked.

Judith was surprised by the question. She shook her head. "I was told my father died defending England from infidels. He was supposed to have been a baron."

"So you lived with her all the while you were growing up?"

"No," she answered. "The first four years I lived with Aunt Millicent and Uncle Herbert. Millicent's my mother's sister," she added.

"Why didn't you live with your mother?"

"She couldn't stand the sight of me. For a long time I believed it was because I reminded her of the man she loved. When I was eleven years old, I found out the truth. She hated me because I was part of you."

"And when you found out the truth?"

"I was told you banished my mother, that you knew she was carrying me, and you didn't want either one of us."

"Lies," he whispered with a shake of his head. "I never knew about you. As God is my witness, I never knew."

She didn't show any outward reaction to his fervent speech. "If you'll only let us go home," she said again. "I won't tell the priest you already have a wife."

Her father shook his head. "Nay, I won't be getting wed again. I'm too old to wave such a sin in God's face. I'm content to let things stay the way they are."

He turned his attention to Iain then. "Did you know I was Judith's father when you married her?"

"Yes."

Judith let out a little gasp. She was quick to recover from her surprise. Iain was obviously lying to the laird and she would find out his reasons later, when they were alone. If he ever spoke to her again, she qualified. She still couldn't make herself look up at him. She wanted to weep with shame because she hadn't trusted him enough to tell him the truth.

"Then why did you seek an alliance with the Dunbars?" Maclean asked. "Or did the bastard lie to me?"

"The Dunbars approached us first," Iain explained. "I met their laird on neutral ground to discuss the possibility of an alliance, but that was before I knew my wife was your daughter."

"And when you were certain?"

Iain shrugged. "By then I knew what the Dunbars' game was. They couldn't be trusted. And so I sent my envoy, Ramsey, to you."

"Did you marry my daughter because I was her father?"

"Yes."

The laird nodded, satisfied with Iain's honesty. "Do you treat her well?"

Iain didn't answer. Judith thought she was probably supposed to. "He treats me very well. I wouldn't stay with him if he didn't."

Her father smiled. "You've got spirit. That pleases me."

She didn't thank him for his compliment. Not five minutes before, he'd told her her boldness displeased him. He was contradicting himself, and none of his compliments were ever going to ease her pain.

She noticed her father's eyes were getting misty. She couldn't imagine why.

"When did you find out about me?" Douglas asked. "Have you known since you were eleven that you had an older brother?"

Judith's composure almost snapped then and there. Her mother's treachery suddenly overwhelmed her. "I didn't know about you . . . until today," she whispered. "She never told anyone."

Douglas shrugged, trying to act as though he really didn't care, but Judith could see his vulnerability. She touched his arm in a bid to comfort him. "Be thankful, Douglas, that she did leave you here. You were more fortunate."

Douglas was moved by her apparent concern for his feelings. He cleared his throat in a bid to ease the sudden tightness there, then said, "I would have watched out for you the way older brothers should. I would have, Judith."

She nodded and was about to tell her brother she believed he would have protected her, but her father turned her attention.

"I want you to stay here with me and Douglas for a time."

"No." Iain snapped out that denial. "Judith, go outside and wait for me. I have something to discuss with your father."

She didn't hesitate. She turned around and started to

walk away. Laird Maclean watched her for a moment, then hastily stood up. His gaze was directed on her back.

"I would never break my promise to go back to England," he called out. "I certainly wouldn't have gone back for my wife," he added in a louder voice.

Judith continued to walk away from her father. She was trembling so much now, she was worried her legs would give out on her. If she could just get outside . . .

"I wouldn't go back for land, or title, or all the gold England had to give."

She was halfway across the way when he bellowed, "Judith Maitland!"

She stopped and slowly turned around. Tears streamed down her cheeks. She was oblivious to them. Her hands were gripped tightly together so no one would see how they shook.

"I would have broken my promise for a daughter," her father shouted. "Oh, yes, I would have gone back into England for you."

She took a deep breath, then slowly nodded. She desperately wanted to believe him, but knew she needed time, and distance, to separate all the lies from the truth.

Graham stood near the bottom of the steps leading up to the entrance. Two guards stood as sentries behind him. Her gaze met the elder's. The look on Graham's face took her breath away, his fury and his disdain for her so visible, she felt as though he'd just spat on her.

She was certain she was going to be sick. She ran outside, crossed the courtyard and continued on toward the privacy of the trees. She kept running until she was out of breath. Then she collapsed on the ground and broke into heart-wrenching sobs.

Judith was so confused inside. Had her father told her the truth? If he had known about her, would he have claimed her? Would he have been able to love her?

Oh God, the lost years, the lies, the loneliness. And now it was too late. She had told who she was, and

Graham had let her know, with just one hateful look, that she had lost everything. She was an outsider again.

"Iain," she sobbed.

Had she lost him, too?

Iain knew Judith needed him now. He believed he'd hurt her with his admission he'd married her because she was a Maclean. He wanted to go to her, of course, but his initial concern was dealing with her father. In his mind, Judith's safety came before her feelings.

"You used my daughter to get to me, didn't you?" Laird Maclean remarked. He tried to sound furious, but failed in his attempt. He let out a sigh. "'Tis the truth I probably would have done the same if I'd been in your position."

Iain's discipline vanished. He reached across the table, grabbed Judith's father by his shoulders and lifted him half out of his chair. Douglas ran forward to intervene on his father's behalf. Iain sent him flying backward again with the back of his fist.

"I married Judith to protect her from you, you bastard," he roared. He shoved Maclean back into his chair. "Now you and I are going to come to some sort of understanding, or I swear to God, I'll kill you."

The Maclean laird raised his hand to stop his men from attacking Iain. "Everyone out," he commanded in a bellow. "This matter is between the Maitland laird and me. Douglas, you may stay."

"Patrick stays, too," Iain ordered.

"I'm not leaving," Graham shouted.

"As you wish," Laird Maclean agreed, his tone weary now. He waited until his soldiers had taken their leave, then stood up to face Iain. "Why did you believe you needed to protect her from me? I'm her father."

"You know damned good and well why," Iain replied. "You would have married her to one of the Dunbars. I couldn't allow that."

Laird Maclean didn't argue over that possibility for he

knew it to be true. He probably would have married her to one of the Dunbars in order to make the alliance more binding. "I would have gained her permission first," he muttered. He leaned back in his chair. "Dear God, this is difficult to take in. I have a daughter."

"And a wife," Iain reminded him.

Maclean's face darkened. "Yes, a wife," he agreed. "The woman left me," he explained. "Oh, it was under the guise of returning to England to see her ailing brother, but I knew she didn't have any intention of ever coming back. I was happy to be rid of her. I felt like celebrating when I heard she'd died. If that be a sin, so be it. I've never known a woman like her," he added. "Not before, not after. She didn't have a conscience. She lived for self-pleasure, nothing more. She was so cruel to her son, I spent most of my days protecting the boy from his own mother."

"Judith didn't have anyone to protect her."

"I realize that," Maclean replied. He suddenly looked like a very old man. "She said she lived with the aunt the first four years. What happened then? Did she live with her mother?"

"Yes."

"What about my wife's brother? The drunk?" Maclean asked.

"He lived with them, too. The aunt and uncle tried to look out for Judith. She lived with them six months of each year, and lived in Hell the other months."

"A peculiar arrangement," Maclean said. He shook his head. "I can never make it up to her. I can never—" His voice broke. He pretended to cough, then said, "You'll have your alliance, Iain, if you're still wanting it. The Dunbars will rebel, of course, but we can keep them under control and behaving themselves, locked between us as they are. I have only one request to make."

"What is it?"

"I want Judith to stay here for a spell. I would like to get to know her."

Iain was already shaking his head before Maclean had finished his plea. "My wife stays with me."

"Will you allow her to come here every now and again?"

"Only Judith can make that decision," Iain countered. "I wouldn't force her."

"But you won't prevent her?"

"No," Iain conceded. "If she wishes to see you again, I'll bring her to you."

"Iain Maitland, you're making promises without authority," Graham announced in a near shout. "The council will decide any alliances, not you."

Iain turned around to look at Graham. "We will discuss this later," he commanded.

"You should be thankful my daughter spoke up when she did," Maclean bellowed. He stood up, braced his hands on the tabletop, and leaned forward. "She saved your sorry hide, Graham. I've been itching to tear you apart for a good number of years. I still might, if I hear you aren't treating Judith proper."

He paused to glare at his enemy. "Oh, I saw the expression on your face when you heard she was a Maclean. It didn't sit well, did it? It must chafe you considerably to know your laird's married to my daughter. No matter," Maclean continued in a roar. "You hurt Judith, and by God, I'll kill you with my bare hands."

"Father, what if Judith wants to stay here with us?" Douglas asked. "She may not want to go home with Iain. You should put the question to her."

Iain wasn't impressed with Douglas's burst of brotherly concern. "She goes with me."

Douglas didn't want to give up. "Will you let him take her if she doesn't want to go?"

"Let him?" Maclean found his first smile. "It appears Iain's going to do whatever he damned well wants to do." He turned his attention Iain. "You might have started out with a clever plan in mind, but you fell in love with her somewhere along the way, didn't you?"

Iain refused to answer him. Douglas wouldn't let it go. "Do you love Judith?"

Iain let out a sigh. Judith's brother was turning out to be one hell of a nuisance. "Do you honestly believe I would marry a Maclean if I didn't love her?"

Laird Maclean let out a snort of laughter. "Welcome to the family, son."

Iain found Judith leaning against a tree on the side of the trail a fair distance away from the keep. The moonlight was bright enough for him to see how pale she was.

"Judith, it's time to go home."

"Yes, of course."

She didn't move. He walked closer. When she looked up at him, he realized she'd been crying. "Are you all right?" he asked, concern obvious in his voice. "I know it was difficult for you."

Fresh tears filled her eyes. "Was he lying to me or was he telling me the truth? There have been so many lies in the past, I can't seem to find the truth anymore. It really doesn't matter, though, does it? Knowing that my father would have claimed me can't make up for the lost years."

"I think it matters to you," Iain countered. "And I believe he was telling the truth. If he'd known, he would have gone to England to get you."

She pulled away from the tree and straightened her shoulders. "I know you must be furious with me. I should have told you who my father was."

"Judith—"

She interrupted him. "I was afraid you wouldn't want me if you knew the truth." It finally dawned on her that Iain wasn't angry. "Why aren't you upset? The news must have staggered you. And why did you lie to my father?"

"When did I lie?"

"When you told him you knew I was his daughter."

"I didn't lie. I knew before I married you."

"You couldn't have known," she cried out.

"We'll talk about this later," he announced. "After we get home."

She shook her head. She wanted to talk about it now. She felt as though her entire world had just been destroyed. "If you knew . . . why did you marry me?"

He reached for her. She backed away. "Judith, I'm not going to talk about this now."

God, he sounded so calm, so bloody reasonable. "You used me."

"I protected you."

"You wanted the alliance. That's the only reason you married me. I thought, oh God, I thought because you didn't have anything to gain, that you must really just want me, that you—" Her voice broke on a sob. She was so sickened by the truth, she almost doubled over. She took another step back. Her own naivety made her even more furious with herself. "I've been such a fool," she cried out. "I really thought I could belong here. I believed I would be accepted and it wouldn't matter who my mother was or who my father—"

She took a deep breath to try to control herself. "I have no one to blame but myself for thinking such foolish thoughts. I can never be accepted here. I won't go home with you, Iain. Not now. Not ever."

"You won't raise your voice to me," he ordered in a chillingly soft voice. "But you will go home with me. Now."

He moved like lightning. She didn't even have time to run. He had both of her hands locked in one of his and was dragging her back down the path before she'd even started to struggle.

Judith quit trying to get away from him when she remembered Frances Catherine. Her friend needed her.

Iain stopped at the edge of the clearing. "Don't you dare weep," he commanded.

"You've broken my heart."

"I'll fix it later."

She almost burst into tears then and there. The crowd of soldiers gathered together in the yard changed her mind. She straightened her shoulders and rushed forward to walk by her husband's side, determined not to disgrace herself in front of the Macleans.

Graham and Patrick had already mounted their horses and were waiting to leave. Iain wouldn't let Judith ride her own horse. He handed the reins of her mount to his brother, then turned and lifted her onto his stallion's back. He swung up behind her, settled her on his lap, and took over the lead.

They passed Graham first. As soon as her gaze met his, he turned away from her. She quickly turned her gaze to her lap. She folded her hands together and desperately tried not to let any of her feelings show on her face. She didn't want any of them to know how much she was hurting inside.

Iain noticed the insult Graham had given his wife. He became so furious, he could barely control himself. Judith had become rigid in his arms. He pulled her closer against his chest and leaned down to whisper into her ear.

"You and I belong to each other, Judith. Nothing else matters. Remember that."

He didn't realize until he'd spoken the words aloud how significant they were. The tightness inside his chest eased away. Loving Judith made him feel he could conquer the world. There wasn't any problem they couldn't face as long as they were together. He remembered how she had told him she wanted to be able to share her worries with him. He wouldn't let her. And he was supposed to share his worries with her as well. Lord, he'd scoffed at the idea, arrogantly believing that he, and he alone, should make every decision, solve every problem, give every command. It was her duty to tell him what was wrong, and he would take care of it.

He couldn't imagine why she loved him. It was a miracle, that. He sure as hell didn't feel worthy. He almost smiled, for worthy or not, her heart belonged to him . . . and he would never let her go. Never.

It was as though he'd spoken the thought aloud, because Judith suddenly looked up at him. "I won't live with a man who doesn't love me," she whispered.

She expected anger, and secretly hoped for a little remorse. She didn't get either. "All right," he agreed.

She twisted away from him. Iain knew she wasn't in any condition to listen to anything he had to say. Tomorrow would be soon enough for explanations.

"Close your eyes and rest," he ordered. "You're exhausted."

She was about to do just that when she saw a movement in the darkness. She stiffened against him and grabbed hold of his arm. The trees around them seemed to come to life before her eyes. Shadows moved forward into the moonlight.

They were Maitland warriors, and so many in number, she couldn't even begin to count. They were dressed in battle attire. Ramsey led the warriors. He moved forward and waited for Iain to tell him what had happened.

Iain hadn't come alone after all. His men had obviously been waiting for his command to go into battle. Judith was thankful now she had been able to prevent a war, and wondered how many lives would have been lost if she had remained silent.

She didn't speak to her husband again until they were home. She told him she didn't want to share his bed. He picked her up and carried her there. She was too tired to fight him. She fell asleep before he had taken her clothes off her.

He couldn't leave her alone. He held her in his arms, stroking her, nuzzling her, kissing her, and in the early predawn hours he made love to her.

She was too sleepy to protest at first, and then too

consumed by his passion to make him stop. His mouth was so wonderfully hot against her own. His hands stroked her inner thighs, gently forcing them apart. His fingers thrust inside her wet heat just as his tongue invaded her mouth. The erotic love play made her whimper with pleasure. She moved restlessly against him. It was all the permission he needed. He moved between her thighs and drove deep into her. She arched up against him and wrapped her arms around his neck to bring him closer. His thrusts were slow, measured, deliberate. The sweet torment drove her wild. She tightened her legs around him and lifted her hips more forcefully to make him quicken his pace.

They found fulfillment together. He growled deep in his throat and collapsed against her. She held him tight while the waves of ecstasy swept over her, and then wept against his shoulder.

Once she started crying, she couldn't seem to stop. He rolled to his side, taking her with him, and whispered soothing words until she finally relaxed against him and he knew she'd fallen asleep again. He closed his eyes, his own surrender complete, and did the same.

The following morning Iain left the chamber a good hour before Judith awakened. The housekeeper came up the stairs to fetch her, knocked softly on the door and called her name.

Judith had just finished getting dressed. She wore her pale pink gown. At her bidding, Helen came rushing into the chamber. She took one look at Judith's clothing and came to an abrupt stop. "You're not wearing our plaid," she blurted out.

"No," Judith answered without giving further explanation. "What is it you wanted to speak to me about?"

"The elders . . ."

"Yes?" Judith asked when Helen didn't go on.

"They're waiting in the hall to speak to you. Is it true, then? Is your father . . ."

Helen couldn't seem to get the name out. Judith took mercy on her. "Laird Maclean is my father."

"Don't go downstairs," Helen cried out. She started wringing her hands together in agitation. "You look terribly pale to me. Get back into bed. I'll tell them you're ill."

Judith shook her head. "I can't hide up here," she said. She started toward the door, then paused. "Isn't the council breaking one of their sacred rules by speaking directly to me in an official capacity?"

Helen nodded. "They're probably too angry to think about their rules now. Besides, they did allow one other woman to stand before them. Your Frances Catherine. It was the talk around here for weeks on end."

Judith smiled. "Frances Catherine told me they tried to make her change her mind about sending for me. They probably want to wring her neck now. Look at all the trouble I've caused."

Helen shook her head. "You haven't caused any trouble."

Judith patted her arm. "Is my husband waiting for me with the elders?"

Helen shook her head again. It was an effort for her to get her emotions under control. Her voice trembled when she answered her mistress. "He's on his way back from his brother's home. Graham sent a messenger down the hill to get him. They won't send you away, will they?"

"My father's their enemy," Judith reminded the woman. "I can't imagine they would want me to stay here."

"But your husband's our laird," Helen whispered. "Surely . . ."

Judith didn't want to talk about Iain. Helen was getting terribly upset. Tears were spilling down her cheeks. Judith was sorry she was the cause of her distress, but she didn't know how to ease her suffering. She couldn't tell Helen everything was going to be all right, for that would be a ridiculous lie.

"I'll survive this," she said. "And so shall you." She forced a smile, pinched her cheeks to give them some color, and then walked out of the chamber.

Iain walked inside just as she started down the stairs. He looked relieved to see her. She didn't know what to make of that.

"I would like to speak to you, Iain," she called out. "I have something I want to say to you."

"Not now, Judith," he told her. "There isn't time."

"I want you to make time," she insisted.

"Frances Catherine needs you, wife."

Her entire demeanor changed. She ran the rest of the way down the stairs. "Is it the baby?"

Iain nodded. "Helen?" Judith called out.

"I heard, milady. I'll just gather a few things and follow you down."

Judith had taken hold of Iain's hand. She realized what she'd done and tried to let go. He wouldn't let her. He turned and opened the door for her, then pulled her outside.

The elders were all standing in a group in front of the table by the hearth. Iain acted as though they weren't even there.

"How long has she been having pains?" Judith asked.

"Patrick didn't say. He's so rattled, he can barely speak a coherent word."

Iain hadn't exaggerated. Frances Catherine's husband was standing in the center of the doorway. "She wants me to fetch the priest," he blurted out as soon as they came into view. "Dear God, this is all my fault."

Judith didn't know what to say to that. Iain shook his head. "Get hold of yourself, Patrick," he ordered. "You won't do her any good at all if you fall apart."

"It's all my fault, I tell you," Patrick repeated in an anguished whisper.

"Hell," Iain muttered. "Of course it's your fault. You took her to your bed—"

"It isn't that," Patrick interrupted.

"Then what is it?" Iain asked when his brother didn't explain.

"I started her laboring. We were talking about Judith's father, and she told me she'd known for years. I became a little angry she hadn't told me and I think I raised my voice to her."

Patrick was inadvertently blocking Judith from entering the cottage while he confessed his sin to his brother. Judith finally shoved him out of her way and ran inside.

She came to a quick stop when she spotted Frances Catherine. Her friend was sitting at the table, brushing her hair. She looked terribly calm. She was humming too.

Frances Catherine smiled at her, then motioned for her to shut the door.

"Hand me that ribbon," Frances Catherine asked. "The pink one by the bed, if you please."

Judith did as her friend requested. She realized her hands were shaking. "How are you feeling, Frances Catherine?" she asked in a worried whisper.

"Just fine, thank you."

Judith stared at her friend a long minute. "Are you having pains now or are you just pretending?"

"If I wasn't, I would," Frances Catherine answered.

Judith walked over to the table and fell into the chair across from her friend. She took a deep breath in an effort to calm her racing heart, then asked her what in God's name she'd meant by that illogical answer.

Frances Catherine was happy to explain. "I am having pains," she said. "But if I wasn't, I would pretend I was just to rile Patrick. I'm leaving him, Judith. No man's going to shout at me, not even my husband. You may help me pack my belongings."

Judith burst into laughter. "Would you like to leave now or after the baby's born?"

Her friend smiled. "After," she said. "I'm not at all afraid," she added in a whisper, turning the topic. "Isn't that peculiar? I've been afraid all during the months of carrying, but now I'm not afraid at all."

"Then why did you call for a priest?"

"To give Patrick something to do."

Judith didn't believe that nonsense. "You wanted to scare Patrick, didn't you?"

"That, too," Frances Catherine conceded.

"You've got a mean streak hidden inside you, Frances Catherine," Judith said. "You've deliberately terrified your husband. Now call him inside and beg his forgiveness."

"I will," her friend promised. "Was it terrible for you?"

She'd switched topics so quickly, Judith took a minute to react. "My father's a handsome man," she remarked.

"Did you spit in his eye?"

"No."

"Tell me what happened," her friend demanded.

Judith smiled. "I'm not telling you anything until you speak to your husband. Can't you hear him carrying on outside? Shame on you, Frances Catherine."

A sudden pain gripped her friend. She dropped her brush and took hold of Judith's hand. She was panting by the time the contraction faded away. Judith kept mental count of the seconds that passed during the pain.

"That one was a little stronger than the others," Frances Catherine whispered. "They're still a long time apart, though. Mop my brow, Judith, and then tell Patrick to come inside. I'm ready to hear his apology."

Judith hurried to do just that. She waited outside so that the couple could have some privacy. Iain was sitting on the rock ledge, watching her.

"I've never seen my brother so ill-disciplined," he remarked.

"He loves his wife," she replied. "He's afraid for her."

Iain shrugged. "I love you, but I'm sure as hell not going to carry on the way Patrick is when you give me my son or daughter."

He'd said the words so casually, so matter-of-factly, she was caught off guard. "What did you just say?"

He let her see his exasperation. "I said I wasn't going to lose my control the way Patrick—"

"Before," she interrupted. "You said you loved me. You acted like you meant it."

"I always mean what I say," he told her. "You know that. Judith, how long do you think this birthing is going to take?"

She ignored his question. "You don't love me," she announced in an emphatic tone of voice. "I was just the sacrifice you had to make in order to get your alliance." She didn't give him time to answer her. "The ring gave me away, didn't it? It's identical to the one Douglas wears and you recognized it."

"The ring was familiar to me, but it took me a long time to remember where I'd seen it."

"Exactly when did you remember?"

"When we were at the cemetery," he told her. "Then Patrick heard you ask his wife what she thought I would do if I found out Maclean was your father. He told me, of course, but I already knew."

She shook her head. "I don't understand," she admitted. If he knew, why did he get so angry with Frances Catherine?"

"He was angry because she hadn't confided in him."

"And so, as soon as you found out who my father was, you married me."

"Damn right," he agreed. He stood up and pulled her into his arms. "Without flowers," he whispered. "I'm sorry about that. Your safety came first. I didn't have time to make it proper for you."

Dear God, how she wanted to believe him. "You didn't have to marry me just to keep me safe."

"Yes, I did," he answered. "It was only a matter of time before one of the elders spotted the damn ring. They would have recognized it."

"I was going to throw it away," she boasted.

He let out a sigh. "You wouldn't have," he said. "You're too tenderhearted to destroy the only link you had to the man who fathered you."

She decided not to argue that possibility with him. "You don't like him, do you?"

"Your father?"

"Yes."

"Hell, no, I don't like him," he replied. "He's a real bastard," he added. "But he's also your father, and since I already knew I was going to keep you, I sent Ramsey to him to talk about an alliance. It would have been more practical to unite with the Dunbars. Their land borders ours, after all, but the Maclean laird is your father and you had a right to eventually claim him . . . if you wanted to, Judith."

"But you don't trust the Macleans, do you?"

"No," he answered. "As to that, I don't trust the Dunbars much, either."

"Do you like Douglas?"

"Not particularly."

She found his honesty refreshing. "You don't like anyone, do you?"

His smile was filled with tenderness. "I like you."

He always made her breathless when he looked at her like that. Judith had to force herself to concentrate on what they were talking about. She turned her gaze to his chest. "Why was it necessary to form an alliance with either clan? You've always isolated yourselves in the past."

"The Dunbar laird is old, tired, yet he didn't want to pass his duties on to a younger warrior. When I heard he was negotiating with Maclean, I tried to interfere before the union could be formed. The Dunbars added to the Macleans would make them invincible against us. It was a hell of a worry."

"Why didn't you explain this to me?"

"I just did."

He was hedging and they both knew it. "Why didn't you explain before?" she prodded.

"It was difficult for me," he finally admitted. "I've never discussed my concerns with anyone but Patrick before."

"Not even Graham?"

"No."

She pulled away from him and looked up into his eyes. "What made you change your mind?"

"You," he answered. "And Frances Catherine."

"I don't understand."

He took hold of her hand, sat her down on the stone ledge and sat beside her. "In the beginning, I didn't understand this bond between the two of you. You seemed to trust each other completely."

"We do trust each other completely," she told him.

He nodded. "She never told anyone who your father was, and you never worried she would."

Iain seemed to be working something out in his mind. His voice was slow, hesitant. "You in effect gave her a weapon to use against you. A man would never do such a thing."

"Some would."

"I wouldn't," he admitted. "And until I met you, I didn't believe such trust existed."

Abruptly, he stood up. He clasped his hands behind his back and turned to face her. "You've shown me you can give your friend your complete trust. I want the same, Judith. You've told me you trust me. Yet if you trusted me with all your heart, completely, you would accept without question that when I tell you I love you, I mean it. Only then will your uncertainty, your fear, your hurt go away."

Her head was bowed low. She realized he was speaking the truth. "I didn't trust you enough to tell you who my father was," she admitted in a whisper. "But I would have gotten around to it . . . someday. I was afraid you wouldn't want me any longer if you knew."

"If you'd trusted me enough . . ."

She nodded. "I did try, right before the wedding ceremony. . . . Why didn't you let me tell you then?"

"I was desperate to protect you, and the only way I knew how was to make you my wife. The council wouldn't have given the matter a second thought. If they'd learned Maclean was your father, they would have used you to try to destroy him."

"If I'd only left the ring back in England, none of this—"

He didn't let her finish. "Secrets have a way of being found out," he told her. "Too many people knew the truth. Your relatives in England might have gone to the Macleans to get their support in order to get you back." He shrugged. "They still might." He didn't seem overly worried about that possibility.

"Iain, I don't think I can stay here. The way Graham looked at me when he found out who my father was . . . He'll never accept me as a Maitland now. I'll be an outsider again. No, I can't stay here."

"All right."

His immediate agreement confused her. She thought he would at least ask her to try, and she would then be very noble and give her agreement. How could he confess his love for her and agree to let her leave?

Judith wasn't given time to make him explain. Patrick opened the door and shouted her name.

She went back inside and found Frances Catherine beaming with pleasure. Judith assumed her friend's husband had been properly contrite.

Frances Catherine didn't feel the ache in her lower back quite as much when she was walking, and so she slowly paced back and forth in front of the hearth while Judith saw to the necessary preparations.

Her friend had a hundred questions to ask about the Macleans. Judith couldn't answer any of them. When she was finally allowed to speak a full sentence without being interrupted, she told her friend about Douglas.

"I have a brother. He's exactly five years older," Judith said. "My mother left him and never said a word to anyone."

Frances Catherine almost toppled over. She became irate on Judith's behalf. "That bloody bitch," she shouted.

She was about to bellow another dark opinion of Judith's mother when she heard her husband apologizing for her outside the window. She slapped her hand over her mouth to keep her laughter contained.

"Your mother's a monster," she whispered. "If there's any justice in this world, she'll get what's coming to her."

Judith didn't believe that was true, but she wasn't about to argue with her friend now. "Perhaps," she allowed.

"Agnes got what was coming to her," Frances Catherine announced with a nod.

"Why, what happened to her?" Judith asked.

Frances Catherine seemed not to hear her. "Aye, she did. She was a fool to spread such sinful rumors about you and think our laird wouldn't hear them."

"Iain heard?" Judith asked.

"He did," Frances Catherine said. She paused to concentrate on the pain that gripped her, holding on to the edge of the mantel until it had passed. Then she mopped her brow with a linen square. "Lord, that one was a bit stronger than the last."

"It lasted longer, too," Judith told her.

Frances Catherine nodded. "Now, where was I? Oh yes, Agnes."

"Exactly what did Iain hear?"

"That you were carrying his child before he wed you."

"Dear God, he must have been furious. . . ."

"Oh, he was that, all right," Frances Catherine agreed. "You and Patrick and Graham had taken off to go fishing, and Iain came back from his duties about two hours' later. He looked in on me to make certain I wasn't needing anything. That was thoughtful of him, wasn't it?

Iain's warmed considerably since he married you, Judith. He never used—"

"Frances Catherine, you're digressing," Judith interrupted. "What did he do about Agnes?"

"I was getting to that," her friend said. "Iain went along up to the keep. Someone must have stopped him to tell him. Or perhaps one of the elders mentioned—"

"I don't care how he heard," Judith interrupted again. "I want to know what he did about it. You're making me daft, Frances Catherine, skirting around and around the way you are."

Frances Catherine smiled. "It's taken your mind off the birthing, hasn't it?"

Judith nodded. Then she begged her friend to finish her explanation.

Frances Catherine was happy to oblige. "He went directly to Agnes's cottage. Brodick told me so. He stopped by, too, just to make certain I was all right. I think Patrick nagged him into looking in on me. Anyway, another hour passed, and I went outside to take in some fresh air when I saw Agnes and her daughter, Cecilia, all packed up and marching down the hill. Brodick told me they were leaving Maitland land. They won't be back, either, Judith."

"Where will they go?"

"To Agnes's cousins," Frances Catherine explained. "They had an escort of soldiers riding with them."

"Iain never said a word to me." Judith mulled that fact over for several minutes while Frances Catherine resumed her pacing.

Helen knocked on the door, interrupting the private discussion. "We'll talk about this later," Frances Catherine whispered.

Judith nodded. She helped Helen carry in a giant pile of linens and add them to the others on the table. Winslow was right behind the housekeeper. He carried in the birthing stool. Frances Catherine promptly invited the warrior to stay for the nooning meal. Winslow was too surprised by the invitation to do more than shake his head.

Patrick wasn't in any condition to see to the chore of hanging the plaid across the beam. Winslow took care of the duty. Frances Catherine tried to serve him a beverage when he was finished.

He refused the wine and started out the doorway. He suddenly stopped and turned around again. "My wife is waiting in the courtyard," he said. "She wants to help. If you don't want her . . ."

"Please send her inside," Judith requested. "We'll be happy for her company, won't we, Frances Catherine?"

Her friend brightened up. "Oh, yes," she agreed. "She can have her nooning meal with us."

Helen paused in her task of folding back the bedding to look up. "Are you really hungry, lass? I could bring down some soup I made late yesterday. It's been simmering all through the night."

"Yes, thank you," Frances Catherine answered. "I'm not at all hungry, though."

"Then why—" Judith began.

"When it's time for supper, we have to have our supper," Frances Catherine insisted. "Everything has to be . . . usual. All right, Judith?"

"Yes, of course," Judith answered.

Isabelle came rushing inside, drawing everyone's attention. She shut the door behind her and hurried over to Frances Catherine. She took hold of her hand. While Judith stood by, Isabelle repeated all the words of encouragement Judith had given her when she'd begun her laboring. She talked about the miracle about to take place, added that yes, it was messy, but still beautiful, and Frances Catherine must remember to feel the joy in the precious duty of giving a new life to the world.

A warm feeling of contentment filled Judith. She had made a difference in someone's life. She knew she would have to leave this place, and soon, if the council had their way, but while she'd lived here, she had made an impact on someone else's life. At least one other woman besides Frances Catherine would remember her.

Helen hurried out of the cottage to fetch the soup. Isabelle had left her son in Winslow's aunt's care, and she left to tell her she'd be staying with Frances Catherine until after her baby was born.

Frances Catherine waited until the door closed behind the two women, then turned to Judith. "Are you worried about me?"

"Perhaps just a little," Judith admitted.

"Why did you have the peculiar look on your face? What were you thinking about when Isabelle was talking to me?"

Judith smiled. Frances Catherine rarely let anything get past her. "I was realizing that I made a little difference in Isabelle's life. I helped her bring her son into the world. She won't forget that. The others will forget me, but she won't."

"No, she won't forget," Frances Catherine agreed. She turned the topic then. "Patrick says Iain won't tell him what he's going to do. My husband's convinced the council will sanction both of you. He said that when he told his brother that opinion, Iain just smiled and shook his head."

Judith shrugged. "I won't stay here, no matter what happens. You understand why, don't you? I can't be an outsider again."

"Judith, all the women here seem to feel like outsiders," Frances Catherine argued.

The door burst open. "Well?" Patrick bellowed from the entrance.

"Well, what, husband?"

"Frances Catherine, why is this taking so long?"

"Patrick, you really need to get hold of yourself," Judith ordered. "This isn't going to happen any time soon."

Frances Catherine hurried over to her husband. "I'm

sorry this is so upsetting to you, but nothing's happening. I can't make the baby hurry, Patrick."

"Judith, can't you do something?" Patrick demanded.

"Your wife is going to rest now," Judith announced. "We have to be patient."

Patrick let out a sigh. "Winslow says you're twice the size Isabelle was," he remarked with a frown.

Frances Catherine didn't take exception to that comment. She knew her husband was looking for something more to worry about. "I ate twice as much," she told him. "Where did Iain go?"

Patrick found his first smile. "I was driving him daft. He's training with his men."

"You should go and help him," Frances Catherine suggested. "I'll send someone to find you when the time draws near."

Patrick reluctantly agreed to leave. He kept coming back, however, and by nightfall he was camped out on the doorstep.

Isabelle's aunt came to fetch her twice during the long day to feed her infant son, and Helen left once to make certain the elders had a proper dinner and that her son Andrew was being looked after.

Frances Catherine's contractions continued to be inconsistent until late afternoon. They came on with a vengeance then, but Frances Catherine was more than ready to take on the pain.

By midnight she was screaming in agony. She was using the birthing chair and bearing down with all her might during each long, excruciating contraction. Helen used the flat of her hands to push down on Frances Catherine's stomach, but her efforts only intensified the pain. The baby wasn't cooperating.

Something was wrong and everyone knew it. The pains were coming one on top of another, and she should have given birth by now. Something was blocking the delivery. Helen knelt on the floor in front of Frances Catherine to once again check the baby's progress, and when she'd completed her examination, she leaned back on her heels and looked up at Judith.

The fear in her eyes made Judith's stomach twist. Helen motioned her to the other side of the room.

"No whispering," Frances Catherine screamed. "Tell me what's wrong."

Judith nodded agreement. "Yes, tell both of us," she ordered.

"The baby isn't in the right position for the birthing. I felt a foot."

Another contraction seized Frances Catherine. Judith ordered her to bear down. Her friend screamed her refusal. She collapsed forward, sobbing uncontrollably.

"Oh, God, Judith, I can't do this any longer. I want to die. The pain—"

"Don't you dare give up on me now," Judith interrupted.

"I can't get my hand inside," Helen whispered. "We need the hook, Judith."

"No!"

Frances Catherine's tortured scream of denial snapped Judith's control. She was so terrified inside, she barely knew what she was doing. She tore her hand away from her friend's hard grasp, then rushed over to the water bowl. She scrubbed her hands clean. Maude's instructions were echoing in her mind. She didn't know or care that what the midwife had told her might be based on nonsense either. She would follow her procedures and trust that it mattered.

Helen stood up when Judith knelt down in front of Frances Catherine.

Her friend was hoarse from her screams. In a pitiful whisper she pleaded, "Tell Patrick I'm sorry."

"The hell with that nonsense," Judith shouted. She was heartless to her friend's agony now. "Leave it to you, Frances Catherine, to do everything backward."

"Are you thinking to turn the bairn?" Helen asked. "You'll tear her insides if you try."

Judith shook her head. She kept her attention on Frances Catherine. "Tell me when the next pain begins," she commanded.

Helen tried to hand Judith the bowl of pig's fat. "Cover your hands with this grease," she suggested. "It will make the bairn's coming through easier."

"No," Judith answered. She hadn't washed her hands clean so she could cover them with the vile muck.

Isabelle put her hand on Frances Catherine's stomach. A scant minute later she called out, "The pain's starting now. I feel the tightness building."

Judith started praying. Frances Catherine started screaming. Helen and Isabelle held her steady while Judith worked.

Judith's heart almost dropped into her stomach when she felt the tiny foot protruding from the opening. She was praying out loud now, but no one could hear her. Frances Catherine's screams drowned out every other sound. Judith gently moved the foot down and then went in search of the missing one.

God answered her prayer. She didn't have to reach far to find the missing foot. She slowly eased it down through the opening.

Frances Catherine did the rest. She couldn't stop herself from bearing down. The baby would have landed on her feet if Judith hadn't caught her in time.

The beautiful infant who had given them all such a scare was petite in size, adorably chubby, and had a sprinkle of fire-red hair covering her crown. She was extremely dainty-looking . . . and had a roar very similar to her mother's.

She was perfect.

So was her sister. She didn't give them any trouble at all. She caught everyone by surprise, though. Frances Catherine was weeping with joy, and relief, too, that the ordeal was finally over. Helen had gone outside to complete the ritual of burying the afterbirth in accordance with the rules of the Church, so that demons wouldn't attack the mother or her infant while they were in such a vulnerable condition, and Isabelle was busy cooing to the baby while she gave her her first bath. Judith was washing Frances Catherine when she suddenly started bearing down again. Judith told her to stop it. She was worried about hemorrhage. Frances Catherine couldn't stop. Her second daughter was born just minutes later. She was polite enough to arrive head first.

The infants were identical in appearance. Neither Isabelle nor Helen could tell them apart. They were careful to wrap the little ones in different colored cloths, the firstborn in white, the second in pink, before covering each with the Maitland plaid.

Frances Catherine hadn't bled overly much, but in Judith's mind the worry wasn't over yet. She was going to make certain the new mother stayed in bed a good two weeks as a precaution against complications.

Frances Catherine was finally settled in her bed. She wore the pretty nightgown Judith had made for her. Her hair was brushed and secured with a pink ribbon. Despite her exhaustion, she looked radiant, but Judith knew it was a struggle for her to stay awake.

Patrick had been kept informed of his wife's condition. He knew she was all right. Helen wouldn't tell him if he had a son or a daughter, however. That precious duty belonged to his wife.

The babies were tucked in Frances Catherine's arms for their presentation to their father. Judith smoothed the covers around the threesome, then turned to fetch the new papa.

"Wait." Frances Catherine whispered so she wouldn't disturb her daughters. Both were sound asleep.

"Yes?" Judith whispered back.

"We . . . we did all right, didn't we, Judith?"

"Aye, we did," she agreed.

"I want to say—"

"You don't have to say anything," Judith told her. "I understand."

Frances Catherine smiled. "It's your turn now, Judith. Give my daughters a friend to share their secrets with," she ordered.

"We'll see," Judith replied. She motioned for Isabelle and Helen to follow her outside. Patrick almost knocked her over as he passed her. His eagerness to get to his family made Judith smile.

The fresh air felt wonderful. Judith was exhausted, and weak with relief that the duty was finally over. She walked over to the stone wall and sat down. Isabelle followed her.

"It was a worry, wasn't it?" Isabelle whispered. "I was so afraid for Frances Catherine."

"I was, too," Judith admitted.

"She's going to need help," Helen announced. "She's had a time of it and needs plenty of rest now. She can't be taking care of those babies alone."

"Winslow's aunts will help and so will I," Isabelle volunteered. "We could take the mornings."

"I could stay from the supper hour on through the nights," Helen suggested.

Both women looked at Judith, expecting her to agree to take the afternoons. She shook her head. "We'll have to find someone to fill in," she said. "I can't promise to help because I'm not at all certain how much longer I'll be staying here."

"What in heaven's name are you talking about?" Isabelle asked, clearly astonished by Judith's remarks.

"I'll explain tomorrow," Judith promised. "Now I want to talk about Frances Catherine. I want both of you to promise me you'll take care of her. She mustn't be allowed out of bed. She isn't out of danger yet."

Judith could hear the desperation in her own voice. She couldn't control that. Exhaustion was making her more emotional, she supposed.

Neither Isabelle nor Helen argued with her. Judith was thankful for their silence. Helen let out a weary sigh. The sadness she saw on her mistress's face tore at her heart.

She decided to try to lighten the conversation. "Were you two as surprised as I was when Frances Catherine started in laboring a second time?"

Both Isabelle and Judith smiled.

"You're both looking ready to fall down," Helen said. "Go on home and get some rest. I'll stay the rest of the night."

Neither Isabelle nor Judith had the strength or inclination to move. It was so quiet, so peaceful just sitting there staring out into the darkness.

Judith heard a sound behind her and turned. Iain and Winslow were coming down the hill. She quickly turned around again and tried to straighten her appearance. She brushed her hair back over her shoulders, pinched her cheeks for color, and tried to smooth the wrinkles out of her gown.

Isabelle watched her. "You still look like hell," she whispered with a giggle.

Judith was astonished by the remark. Isabelle was such a sweet, soft-spoken woman. Judith didn't know she had it in her to tease. She burst into laughter. "So do you," she whispered back.

They stood up at the same time to greet their husbands, then leaned into each other, trying to force the other to take all the weight.

"I don't care what I look like," Isabelle confessed. "Winslow wants to . . . you know, and I don't think I should this soon. It's only been seven weeks. I think we should wait seven more . . . but some nights, I do want to . . ."

Judith wasn't certain she understood what Isabelle was stammering on and on about. She saw her blush and finally caught on. "Maude told me it's usual to wait six weeks before . . . sleeping with your husband."

Isabelle immediately tried to straighten her appearance. Judith found her action vastly amusing. Her laughter started Isabelle laughing, too.

Helen shook her head over their pitiful condition.

Iain and Winslow thought they'd lost their minds. Helen gave them the good news about Frances Catherine. Both warriors were pleased, of course, but their attention remained on their ill-disciplined wives.

"Isabelle, get hold of yourself," Winslow ordered. "You're acting like you're sotted."

She bit her lower lip to stop herself from laughing. "What are you doing up at this time of night?" she asked. "Why aren't you home with our son?"

"My aunt's there," Winslow answered.

"Is she going to stay the full night?"

Winslow thought that was an odd question to ask. "Of course," he answered. "I'll sleep up at the keep."

Isabelle frowned at her husband. He raised an eyebrow over her reaction. "Isabelle, what in God's name is the matter with you?" he asked in exasperation.

Isabelle didn't answer. Judith walked over to her husband. "Why aren't you in bed?"

"I was waiting for you."

She was overwhelmed by his admission. Her eyes immediately filled with tears. Iain put his arm around her shoulders and turned to leave. Helen bid everyone good-night and went back inside the cottage.

Isabelle had inadvertently blocked their exit through the courtyard entrance when she moved forward to confront her husband. She didn't realize Iain and Judith were standing right behind her. "I don't want to sleep with your aunt," she blurted out. "I want to sleep with you. Judith says we only had to wait six weeks, husband, and it's been seven now."

Winslow pulled his wife into his arms and out of the way so Iain and Judith could get past them. He leaned down and whispered into his wife's ear.

Alex, Gowrie, and Ramsey caught Judith's attention. The three warriors came striding down the hill. When they were close enough for her to see their expressions, her breath caught in her throat. The men looked furious.

She moved closer into Iain's side. "Why are they awake?" she whispered.

"There was a meeting," he answered. "It lasted longer than expected."

Iain didn't seem inclined to explain what had happened, and she was too exhausted, and frightened, to ask him. After tossing and turning for quite a long time, finally Judith fell into a fitful sleep.

Chapter 15

J udith, wake up. It's time to leave."

Iain was gently shaking her awake. She opened her eyes and found her husband sitting on the side of the bed. One look at his dark expression and her mind immediately cleared of sleep.

She sat up, pulled the covers around her and stared at him. "Leave?" she whispered, trying to understand. "I'm leaving now?"

"Yes." His voice was hard, his expression just as determined.

Why was he acting so cold? Judith grasped his arm when he tried to stand up. "So soon, Iain?"

"Yes," he answered. "Within the hour, if possible." He pulled her hand away from his arm, leaned down to kiss her brow, and then stood up and walked over to the door.

She called out to him. "I would like to say good-bye to Frances Catherine."

"There isn't time," he told her. "Pack only one valise. Bring it to the stables. I'll meet you there."

The door closed behind her husband. She promptly

burst into tears. She knew she was being pitiful. She didn't care. She wasn't thinking clearly either. She had told Iain she didn't want to stay here. He was simply giving her what she wanted.

Damn it all, how could he let her go? Didn't he realize how much she loved him?

Judith washed, then dressed in her dark royal-blue gown. She brushed her hair, packed her valise, and when she was finally ready to leave, she took one last look around her chamber.

Her plaid was hanging on the peg near the door. She didn't want to leave it behind. She folded the garment and put it in her valise.

She quit weeping. She quit feeling sorry for herself, too. Lord, she was fighting angry now. A husband who truly loved his wife wouldn't let her leave him. She needed to tell Iain that. He did love her. She didn't have any doubts about that. It didn't matter either that his actions were so confusing to her. She would simply make him explain what he was doing . . . and why.

She couldn't imagine life without him. Judith ran out the doorway and down the steps. Her valise was clutched tightly in her arms.

Graham was standing in the entrance, holding the door. Judith could see the huge crowd gathered beyond in the courtyard.

She tried to walk past the elder without looking at him. He touched her shoulder to get her attention. She stopped, but stubbornly kept her gaze downcast.

"Why won't you look at me, lass?" Graham asked.

She looked up into his eyes. "I didn't want to see your disdain for me, Graham. You made it perfectly clear how you feel about me the other night."

"Oh, Judith, I'm so sorry. I didn't mean to hurt you. It was just such a . . . surprise, and I was in such a fury because we'd been captured and I thought you had deceived all of us. I'm ashamed of myself, Judith. Can you find it in your heart to forgive a foolish old man?"

Her eyes clouded with tears. She slowly nodded. "I forgive you. I have to go to Iain now, Graham. He's waiting for me."

"Talk to him, Judith. Don't let him do this. We want him to stay."

The anguish in his voice tore at her heart. "He's planning to take me to England," she explained. "Then he'll come back."

He shook his head. "Nay, lass. He won't come back."

"Graham, he has to," Judith argued. "He's your laird, for God's sake."

"He isn't laird."

Judith was too stunned to mask her reaction. She dropped her valise and stared at Graham. He stooped down to pick up her bag. She tried to take it from him. Graham held tight and shook his head at her.

"Did you vote for or against this decision?"

She didn't wait for Graham's answer. She straightened her shoulders and ran outside. The crowd parted when she reached the bottom step and turned toward the stables.

Graham followed her. The other elders filed outside and lined up on the top step of the keep to watch the departure.

The crowd was behind Judith now. The stable doors opened and Iain walked outside, leading his stallion. Patrick walked by his brother's side. He was talking to Iain, but wasn't getting much of a response. Iain's face was impassive. Judith hadn't realized she'd stopped until her husband looked up, spotted her in the distance and motioned for her to come to him.

She didn't move. The significance of what she was doing hit her full force. Dear God, she didn't want to leave. She'd packed the Maitland plaid so she would have a reminder of her happiness here. She would most certainly wrap herself in the soft material during the cold winter nights ahead and try to find some comfort in her memories of happier times. What rubbish, she thought to herself. She was still going to be miserable without Iain and all the other good friends she had made over the past few months.

Her worries about being an outsider ceased to be important. She was a Maitland and she really did belong here. Aye, she had found her place, and no one, not even her husband, was going to make her leave.

She was suddenly in a hurry to get to Iain so she could explain this change of heart. She hoped to heavens she would make sense.

She picked up her skirts and started running. Isabelle stopped her when she called out.

"Judith? Will I like living in England?"

Judith whirled around to look at her friend. She was certain she'd misunderstood her. "What did you just ask me?"

Isabelle separated herself from the crowd and walked forward to stand next to Judith. She held her infant son in her arms. Winslow's aunts followed. Judith recognized the two gray-haired ladies. Both had been sitting at the table in Isabelle's cottage the day of the priest's inquisition.

"Will we like living in England?" Isabelle asked again.

Judith shook her head. "You can't go with me. You would hate living there. I don't even like England," she added in a stammer. "And I'm English."

"We'll get along just fine."

Helen called out that announcement. She hurried forward to stand beside Isabelle. Andrew stood behind his mother, holding his valise.

Judith didn't know what to make of the women. "But you can't just—"

Another woman came forward. Judith knew who she was, but she couldn't remember her name. Her daughter,

Elizabeth, had won the arrow contest the day of the festival. Her mother had beamed with pleasure when Iain presented the prize to her daughter.

"We'll be coming along, too," the mother announced.

And then another and another came forward to proclaim their intention. Judith turned around to look at Iain for assistance. Her breath caught in her throat when she saw the crowd of warriors lined up behind him.

Were they going with them, too?

She couldn't make any sense out of what was happening. Children surrounded her now, and their mothers, clutching their baggage in their arms, stood behind them.

"We'll be taking every Sunday for rest in England, won't we?"

Judith wasn't certain who had asked the question. She nodded and slowly walked over to her husband. She knew she looked stunned. Iain was going to have to talk some sense into these people, she supposed.

Her husband kept his gaze on her. His arm rested on his stallion's back. His expression was contained, but when she was close enough to notice, she could see the surprise was there, in his eyes.

She stopped when she was just a few feet away from him. She wasn't even certain what she was going to say until the words were out of her mouth.

"You know I love you, don't you, Iain?"

She'd asked him her question in a near shout. Iain didn't mind. "Aye, Judith," he answered. "I know you love me."

She let out a little sigh. He thought she was acting as though she'd finally worked everything out inside her mind . . . and her heart. She looked damned pleased with herself.

She was smiling at him now, and getting misty-eyed. "And you love me," she said then, though in a much softer tone of voice. "I remember I told you I wouldn't live with a man who didn't love me. You immediately agreed. You did confuse me, for I didn't realize then how much you did love me. I wish you had told me sooner. You could have saved me a good deal of worry."

"You like to worry," he told her.

She didn't argue the point with him. "What are you planning to do? Take me back to England? Neither one of us belongs there, Iain. This is our home."

He shook his head. "It isn't that simple, wife. I can't stand by and allow the council to make decisions based on emotion."

"Because they voted to make someone else laird?"

"We didn't vote," Graham interjected. He dropped Judith's valise and hurried forward. "Your husband resigned when the other elders wouldn't agree to his alliance with the Macleans."

Judith turned to look at the keep. The four elders were huddled together, talking. Gelfrid was waving his hands in apparent agitation.

"We aren't going to England, Judith. We're going north. It's time we left," he added with a nod toward Graham.

She took a deep breath. Then she took a step back, away from her husband.

Her bold action certainly got his full attention. "I love you with all my heart, Iain Maitland, but I'm still going to have to defy you."

He looked astonished. She folded her arms in front of her and nodded to let him know she meant what she'd just said.

The women lined up behind her all immediately nodded their agreement.

"I cannot allow defiance, Judith."

The warriors standing behind her husband immediately nodded their agreement.

She took another step back. "I really should have been able to voice my opinion before you decided to resign," she announced. "I am your wife, after all, and I should have a say in the plans that affect me. I should also have a say in our future."

Iain was trying not to smile. Each time Judith made a statement, the women nodded their support.

Judith had considered herself an outsider. Look at her now, Iain thought to himself. She was surrounded by her family of Maitland sisters. She'd won their hearts, just as she had won his.

Iain knew he wouldn't be going anywhere with just his wife at his side. Lord, the entire clan seemed determined to go with them. Patrick had already announced his intention to follow with Frances Catherine and the babies as soon as she'd recovered from the birthing. Iain had expected that, of course. He hadn't expected the other warriors' support, however.

It was humbling to know his followers were so faithful. But such loyalty put him in one hell of a position. He had resigned as laird, and no one was accepting his decision.

Not even his wife.

Iain stared at Graham now. He knew the torment the elder must be going through. His followers were deserting him. They were turning their backs on the old ways.

He tried to think of a way to salvage the old man's pride. It would be a stark humiliation for Graham if he left with the clan. Graham had been like a father to him. He couldn't shame him this way.

He couldn't back down, either. The issue was far too important.

"Judith, I can't change what has been decided," Iain announced.

"That isn't what you told me," she argued.

He shook his head. She thought he might not remember the discussion they had had the day they'd walked through the cemetery. She decided to remind him.

"I was railing against all the injustices in this world, and I specifically remember your suggestion to me. You said that if I didn't like something, I should work to change it. One whisper, added to a thousand others, becomes a roar of discontent, remember? Yes," she added with a nod. "Those were your words to me. Have you changed your mind, then?"

"Judith, it's . . . complicated," Iain said.

"Nay, it isn't complicated," Graham muttered. "It comes down to the old against the young. And that's the truth of it."

Judith's heart went out to the elder. He looked so defeated. "No," she denied. "It isn't the old against the young at all."

"Judith . . ."

She ignored Iain's warning tone of voice. She moved closer to Graham's side and took hold of his arm. The show of allegiance to the elder was deliberate, of course, for in Judith's mind Iain wasn't the one who needed his pride soothed. The warriors were all standing with him now. Graham's pride was another matter. Judith was determined to find a way to help him back down without losing his honor or his dignity.

"I believe it's experience and wisdom leading the young and strong," she told the elder. "Surely you can see that, Graham."

"There is some truth in what you say," he agreed.

Judith took a breath, then blurted out, "I would like to speak directly to the council."

A loud murmur of approval sounded behind Judith. Graham looked as though she had just asked him to slit his throat. He was rendered speechless.

"And what would you say to the council?" Iain asked.

She kept her gaze on Graham while she gave her husband her answer. "I would begin by telling the council how remiss they've been in their duties to the most important members of this clan. They've left out the women and the children. Yes, that is just how I would begin."

Graham had to wait until the women standing with Judith had quit cheering. "How have they been left out?"

"You don't allow any of us to come to you for advice," Judith answered. "Our problems should be every bit as important to you as your warrior's problems. We should also be able to voice our opinions concerning significant matters."

"Judith, every woman is important here."

"Then why can't we come before the council?"

Graham had never had anyone challenge him like this before. He rubbed his jaw while he considered his answer. "When you have a problem you wish to discuss, you should go to your husband," he finally advised.

He looked pleased with himself for coming up with his solution. He even managed a smile.

"That is all good and well," Judith countered. "Husbands and wives should always discuss their problems with each other. But what about the women who don't have husbands? Who can they turn to for advice? Do these women cease to matter? If Helen had had a problem with her son, she should have been able to come to you or Gelfrid, or any of the other elders to seek your counsel, but that opportunity wasn't available to her. When her husband died, she became an outsider."

"I would have been happy to solve her problems," Graham returned.

Judith tried to hide her exasperation. "Helen doesn't need you to solve her problems for her," she argued. "None of us do. We only want to be able to discuss these concerns, to gain another point of view . . . we want to be included in this clan, Graham. Helen has a sound mind. She can solve her own problems. Now do you understand?"

"There's Dorothy, too," Helen reminded Judith. "Mention her while you're telling him the way things are around here."

"Yes, Dorothy," Judith agreed. Helen had only just told her about the expectant mother. "Dorothy's due to have her baby in another month. Her husband died on a hunting raid just weeks after they were wed. The council should be her family now. She shouldn't be alone. Surely the elders will wish to make some changes . . . for the sake of the women and the children."

Graham couldn't help but be swayed by the valid argument. The elders had ignored the women. "We have been remiss," he admitted.

It was all he was willing to give now. It was enough. Judith turned back to Iain. It was his turn to do a little conceding. "My mother's English, my father's Laird Maclean, and I can't change that. You're laird here, Iain, and I don't believe you can change that, either."

Iain frowned. "Judith, I didn't press for the alliance simply because Maclean was your father. Tis the truth my men could take on a legion of Macleans and come out winners. They're better trained than any other unit in all of Scotland. However," he added with a meaningful glance in Graham's direction, "the Dunbars united with the Macleans would overwhelm us in sheer numbers alone. As laird, it is my duty to protect each and every member of this clan. I simply cannot accomplish this as advisor. The position is empty without power. And that, wife, is no longer acceptable to me."

"Unacceptable as it is now," she qualified.

"As it has always been," he corrected.

"Until you change it."

Iain walked over to stand directly in front of Graham. "I will not remain advisor. I want the power to act."

A long minute passed while Graham once again mulled over Iain's demand. He turned to look at the elders before giving his attention back to Iain.

And still he hedged. "Absolute power . . ."

Judith started to interrupt, then stopped herself. Men were far more delicate to deal with than women were, she thought to herself. Their pride made the most reasonable solutions difficult.

"You have to be accountable for your actions, son," Graham said. He looked haggard. Judith thought he had already decided against the change and was struggling to accept the inevitable.

And then the solution came to her. "What a fine idea, Graham," she cried out. She smiled at the elder, nodded when he gave her such a puzzled look, and then rushed over to stand next to Iain. She nudged him in his side. "Isn't it a fine plan, husband?"

He didn't know what she was talking about. "Judith, if my every decision is questioned—"

"Probably just once a year," she interrupted. "Or does your plan include giving your laird your vote of confidence more often?" she asked the elder.

Graham's surprise was evident. He finally understood what she was suggesting. He quickly nodded. He smiled, too. "Yes, once a year would do. Your actions will be accountable then, by God. You could be voted out, Iain."

He left the empty threat hanging in the air. Everyone knew that would never happen. The power had just been given to the laird. Everyone understood that, too.

"It will be a firm balance of power," Graham announced, his voice strong now with conviction. "The council will meet once a month to hear petitions from the members, of course. We'll also be giving you advice, Iain, whenever the mood strikes us."

"Will the council hear petitions from all the members? The women, too?" Judith pressed.

Graham nodded. "Aye, lass," he agreed. "Especially the women. We've kept them silent too long. It's time their voice was heard."

"Nothing has been decided until the others on the council agree," Iain reminded Graham.

"I'll go and put the question to them now," the elder said. "You'll have your vote for or against these changes within the hour."

It only took half that amount of time before the elders came outside again and announced their unanimous agreement to embrace Graham's innovative plan.

A resounding cheer echoed throughout the hills. Iain was surrounded by his supporters. There was quite a bit of pounding on his shoulder. A keg of wine was carried outside, goblets passed around and toasts given.

The elders didn't isolate themselves. They strolled through the crowd and participated in the spontaneous celebration.

When Iain was finally able to separate himself from the well-wishers, he tried to find his wife. He wanted to take her to a secluded spot and privately celebrate with her.

He spotted her walking toward the path leading down the hill and tried to get to her. Vincent and Owen intercepted him. Both men wanted to talk about Graham's clever plan. They proved to be long-winded, and Iain wasn't able to go after his wife for a good twenty minutes.

Then Ramsey and Brodick caught him just as he was starting down the hill.

"Have you seen Judith?"

"She's with Frances Catherine and Patrick," Ramsey answered. "Iain, you aren't still angry I refused to become laird in your stead, are you?"

"No," Iain answered.

"We have something to discuss with you," Brodick interjected. "It shouldn't take more than a minute of your time."

Brodick's minute turned into a full hour. Iain did quite a bit of laughing over the bizarre request, too. In the end, however, he finally agreed. He even wished them good luck.

By the time Iain made it to his brother's cottage, Judith had already left. Frances Catherine and both babies were sleeping soundly and Patrick looked in dire need of a nap as well. He was yawning when he pointed the direction Judith had taken.

He found her a few minutes later. She'd hidden herself in a cluster of trees next to the shallow stream.

She looked relaxed. She'd taken her shoes off and sat on the ground with her back against the tree. Her eyes were closed and her hands were demurely folded in her lap.

Iain sat down beside her. "Did you leave the celebration because of the drinking?"

She didn't open her eyes. She smiled though. "No. I just wanted to spend a few minutes with Frances Catherine and then find a quiet spot to rest . . . and think. It's most difficult to find privacy around here, isn't it?"

"Aye, it is," he agreed with a laugh. "You did insist on staying here."

"Yes, I did," she agreed. "Still, the lack of privacy can be irritating."

"You could go to the chapel when you want to be alone."

She did open her eyes then. "Iain, we don't have a chapel," she reminded him."

"We will have one," he explained. "By next summer at the very latest. It has to be ready on the day of our first wedding anniversary."

"Why?"

"So we can have a proper mass inside to celebrate our union," he explained. He smiled over the startle his announcement caused her, and gently nudged her away from the tree. He took her place, and as soon as he was comfortable, lifted her onto his lap. He leaned down and kissed her brow. "With flowers, Judith," he told her in a husky whisper. "They'll fill the chapel. I promise."

Her smile was radiant. "I'm married to a very thoughtful man. I don't need flowers, Iain. I have everything I could ever want."

"There will be flowers," he grumbled, pleased with her fervent words of praise.

"Why did you leave the celebration?" she asked.

"I wanted to be alone with you."

"Why?"

He cupped the sides of her face and leaned forward. His mouth covered hers. The kiss was sweet, undemanding, filled with love.

He was slow to pull away. Judith let out a sigh and collapsed against him. She didn't think she had ever known such contentment, such bliss.

Long minutes passed in silence. "Iain?"

"Yes, love?"

"What are we going to do about my father?"

"Put up with him, I suppose."

They continued to talk about her family for a long while. Judith decided she really wanted to see her father again, her brother as well, and Iain promised to take her to the Maclean holding the following afternoon.

The talk turned to the events of the day. It was a lazy discussion. Judith's eyes were closed and she was barely paying attention to what Iain was saying until he mentioned that Brodick and Ramsey were leaving on a hunt.

She heard the amusement in his voice. Her curiosity was caught. "Why are you amused?" she asked.

"They're going hunting in England," he answered with a chuckle.

"Why?" she asked, thoroughly confused.

"They haven't been able to find what they're looking for here. They're following my example."

"Iain, what are you talking about? Exactly what are they hunting?"

"Brides."

She burst into laughter. She thought her husband was jesting with her. She cuddled up against him again and thought about his bizarre sense of humor.

Iain didn't bother to explain he hadn't been jesting. Judith would find out he'd been telling her the truth when Ramsey and Brodick returned with wives.

He wrapped his arms around his sweet wife and closed his eyes.

The wind, sweet with the scent of summer, floated across the creek to swirl around the couple.

Judith snuggled closer to her husband and contemplated with wonder the blessing God had given her. She was part of a family now. She was loved, and cherished, and valued.

She was home at last.

Visit

JULIE GARWOOD

online!

For a preview excerpt of Julie Garwood's
upcoming hardcover, *Heartbreaker*, go to:

www.SimonSays.com/juliegarwood

Read excerpts from her other books,
find a listing of future titles, and
learn more about the author!

POCKET BOOKS
PROUDLY PRESENTS

Heartbreaker

JULIE GARWOOD

**Available in Paperback
from
Pocket Books**

**The following is a preview of
Heartbreaker. . . .**

It was hotter than hell inside the confessional. A thick black curtain, dusty with age and neglect, covered the narrow opening from the ceiling of the box to the scarred hardwood floor, blocking out both the daylight and the air.

It was very much like being inside a coffin someone had absentmindedly left propped up against the wall, and Father Thomas Madden thanked God he wasn't claustrophobic. He was rapidly becoming miserable, though. The air was heavy and ripe with mildew, making his breathing as labored as when he was back at Penn State running that last yard to the goalposts, with the football tucked neatly under his arm. He hadn't minded the pain in his lungs then and he certainly didn't mind it now. It was all simply part of the job.

The old priests would tell him to offer his discomfort up to God for the poor souls in purgatory. Tom didn't see any harm in doing that, even though he wondered how his own misery was going to relieve anyone else's.

He shifted his position on the hard oak chair, squirming like a choirboy at Sunday practice. He could feel the sweat dripping down the sides of his face and neck into his cassock. The long black robe was soaked through with perspiration, and he sincerely doubted he smelled at all like the hint of Irish Spring soap he'd used in the shower this morning.

The temperature outside hovered between ninety-four and ninety-five degrees in the shade of the rectory porch, where the thermostat was nailed to the whitewashed stone wall. The humidity made the heat so oppressive that those unfortunate souls forced to leave their air-conditioned homes and venture outside did so with a slow shuffle and a quick temper.

It was a lousy day for the compressor to bite the dust. There were windows in the church, of course, but the ones that could have been opened had been sealed shut long ago in a futile attempt to keep the vandals out. The two others were high up in the gold domed ceiling. They were stained-glass depictions of the archangels Gabriel and Michael holding gleaming swords in their fists. Gabriel was looking up toward Heaven, a beatific expression on his face, while Michael scowled at the snakes he held pinned down with his bare feet. The colored windows were considered priceless prayer-inspiring works of art by the congregation, but they were useless in combating the heat. They had been added for decoration, not ventilation.

Tom was a big, strapping man with a seventeen-and-a-half-inch neck left over from his glory days, but he was cursed with baby-sensitive skin. The heat was giving him a prickly rash. He hiked the cassock up to his thighs, revealing the red-and-white happy-face boxer shorts his sister, Laurant, had given him, kicked off his paint-splattered Wal-Mart rubber thongs, and popped a piece of Dubble Bubble into his mouth.

An act of kindness had landed him in the sweatbox. While waiting for the test results that would determine if he needed another round of chemotherapy at Kansas University Medical Center, he was a guest of Monsignor MacKindry, pastor of Our Lady of Mercy Church. The parish was located in the forgotten sector of Kansas City, several hundred miles south of Holy Oaks, Iowa, where Tom was stationed. The neighborhood had been officially designated as the gang zone by the mayor's task force. The monsignor always took Saturday-afternoon confession, but because of the blistering heat, his advanced age, the broken air conditioner, and a conflict in his schedule—the pastor was busy preparing for his reunion with two friends from seminary days at Assumption Abbey—Tom had volunteered for the duty. He had assumed he'd sit face-to-face with his penitent in a room with a couple of windows open for fresh air. MacKindry, however, bowed to the preferences of his faithful parishioners, who stubbornly clung to the old-fashioned way of hearing confessions, a fact Tom learned only after he'd offered his services and Lewis, the parish handyman, had directed him to the oven he would sit in for the next ninety minutes.

In appreciation, the monsignor had lent him a thoroughly inadequate, battery-operated fan that one of his flock had put in the collection basket. The thing was no bigger than a man's hand. Tom adjusted the angle of the fan so that the air would blow directly on his face, leaned back against the wall, and began to read the *Holy Oaks Gazette* he'd brought along to Kansas City.

He turned to the society page on the back first because he got such a kick out of it. He glanced over the usual club news and the smattering of announcements—two births, three engagements, and a wedding—and then he found his favorite column called "About Town." The headline was always the same: the bingo game. The number of people who attended the community center's bingo night was reported, along with the names of the winners of the twenty-five-dollar jackpots.

Interviews with the lucky recipients followed, telling what each of them planned to do with his or her windfall. And there was always a comment by Rabbi Jim Spears, who organized the weekly event, about what a good time everyone had had. Tom was suspicious that the society editor, Lorna Hamburg, had a secret crush on Rabbi Spears, a widower, and that was why the bingo game was so prominently featured in the paper. The rabbi said the same thing every week, and Tom invariably ribbed him about that when they played golf together on Wednesday afternoons. Since Jim usually beat the socks off him, he didn't mind the teasing, but he did accuse Tom of trying to divert attention from his appalling game.

The rest of the column was dedicated to letting everyone in town know who was entertaining company and what they were feeding them. If the news that week was hard to come by, Lorna filled in the space with popular recipes.

There weren't any secrets in Holy Oaks. The front page was full of news about the proposed town square development and the upcoming centennial celebration at Assumption Abbey. And there was a nice mention about his sister helping out at the abbey. The reporter called her a tireless and cheerful volunteer and described at some length all the projects she had taken on. Not only was she going to eliminate all the clutter in the attic, but she was also going to transfer all the information from the old dusty files to their newly donated computer. When she had a few minutes to spare, she would be translating the French journals of Father Andre Vankirk, a priest who had died recently. Tom chuckled to himself as he finished reading the glowing testimonial to his sister. Laurant hadn't actually volunteered for any of the jobs. She just happened to be walking past the abbot the moment he came up with the ideas and, gracious to a fault, couldn't refuse.

By the time Tom finished reading the rest of the paper,

his soaked collar was sticking to his neck. He put the paper on the seat next to him, mopped his brow again, and contemplated closing shop fifteen minutes early.

He gave up the idea almost as soon as it entered his mind. He knew that if he left the confessional early, he'd catch hell from the monsignor, and after the hard day of manual labor he'd put in, he simply wasn't up to a lecture. On the first Wednesday of every third month—Ash Wednesday, he silently called it—Tom moved in with Monsignor MacKindry, an old, broken-nosed, crackle-skinned Irishman who never missed an opportunity to get as much physical labor as he could possibly squeeze out of his houseguest in seven days. MacKindry was crusty and gruff, but he had a heart of gold and a compassionate nature that wasn't compromised by sentimentality. He firmly believed that idle hands were the devil's workshop, especially when the rectory was in dire need of a fresh coat of paint. Hard work, he pontificated, would cure anything, even cancer.

Some days Tom had a hard time remembering why he liked the monsignor so much or felt a kinship toward him. Maybe it was because they both had a bit of Irish in them. Or maybe it was because the old man's philosophy—that only a fool cried over spilt milk—had sustained him through more hardships than Job. Tom's battle was child's play compared to MacKindry's life.

He would do whatever he could to help lighten MacKindry's burdens. The monsignor was looking forward to visiting with his old friends again. One of them was Abbot James Rockhill, Tom's superior at Assumption Abbey, and the other, Vincent Moreno, was a priest Tom had never met. However, neither Rockhill nor Moreno would be staying at Mercy House with MacKindry and Tom, for they much preferred the luxuries provided by the staff at Holy Trinity parish, luxuries like hot water that lasted longer than five minutes and central air-conditioning. Trinity was located in the heart of a bedroom community on the other side of the state line separating Missouri from Kansas. MacKindry jokingly referred to it as "Our Lady of the Lexus," and from the number of designer cars parked in the church's lot on Sunday mornings, the label was right on the mark. Most of the parishioners at Mercy didn't own cars; they walked to church.

Tom's stomach began to rumble. He was hot and sticky and thirsty. He needed another shower, and he wanted a cold Bud Light. There hadn't been a single taker all the while he'd been sitting there roasting like a turkey. He didn't think anyone else was even inside the church now, except maybe Lewis, who liked to hide in the cloakroom behind the vestibule and sneak sips of rot whiskey from the bottle in his toolbox. Tom checked his watch, saw he only had a couple of minutes left, and decided he'd had enough. He switched off the light above the confessional and was reaching for the curtain when he heard the swoosh of air the leather kneeler expelled when weight was placed upon it. The sound was followed by a discreet cough from the confessor's cell next to him.

Tom immediately straightened in his chair and took the gum out of his mouth and put it back in the wrapper. Then he bowed his head in prayer and slid the wooden panel up.

"In the name of the Father and of the Son . . ." he began in a low voice as he made the sign of the cross.

Several seconds passed in silence. The penitent was either gathering his thoughts or his courage before he confessed his transgressions. Tom adjusted the stole around his neck and patiently continued to wait.

The scent of Calvin Klein's Obsession came floating through the grille that separated them. It had a distinctive, heavy, sweet fragrance Tom recognized because his house-keeper in Rome had given him a bottle of the cologne on his last birthday. A little of the stuff went a long way, and the penitent had gone overboard. The confessional reeked. The scent, combined with the smell of mildew and sweat, made Tom feel as though he were trying to breathe through a plastic bag. His stomach lurched and he forced himself not to gag.

"Are you there, Father?"

"I'm here," Tom whispered. "When you're ready to confess your sins, you may begin."

"This is . . . difficult for me. My last confession was a year ago. I wasn't given absolution then. Will you absolve me now?"

There was an odd, singsong quality to the voice and a mocking tone that put Tom on his guard. Was the stranger simply nervous because it had been such a long time since his last confession, or was he being deliberately irreverent?

"You weren't given absolution?"

"No, I wasn't, Father. I angered the priest. I'll make you angry too. What I have to confess will . . . shock you. Then you'll become angry like the other priest."

"Nothing you say will shock or anger me," Tom assured him.

"You've heard it all before? Is that it, Father?"

Before Tom could answer, the penitent whispered, "Hate the sin, not the sinner."

The mocking had intensified. Tom stiffened. "Would you like to begin?"

"Yes," the stranger replied. "Bless me, Father, for I will sin."

Confused by what he'd heard, Tom leaned closer to the grille and asked the man to start over.

"Bless me, Father, for I will sin."

"You want to confess a sin you're going to commit?"

"I do."

"Is this some sort of a game or a—"

"No, no, not a game," the man said. "I'm deadly serious. Are you getting angry yet?"

A burst of laughter, as jarring as the sound of gunfire in the middle of the night, shot through the grille.

Tom was careful to keep his voice neutral when he answered. "No, I'm not angry, but I am confused. Surely you realize you can't be given absolution for sins you're contemplating. Forgiveness is for those who have realized their mistakes and are truly contrite. They're willing to make restitution for their sins."

"Ah, but Father, you don't know what the sins are yet. How can you deny me absolution?"

"Naming the sins doesn't change anything."

"Oh, but it does. A year ago I told another priest exactly what I was going to do, but he didn't believe me until it was too late. Don't make the same mistake."

"How do you know the priest didn't believe you?"

"He didn't try to stop me. That's how I know."

"How long have you been a Catholic?"

"All my life."

"Then you know that a priest cannot acknowledge the sin or the sinner outside of the confessional. The seal of silence is sacred. Exactly how could this other priest have stopped you?"

"He could have found a way. I was . . . practicing then, and I was cautious. It would have been very easy for him to stop me, so it's his fault, not mine. It won't be easy now."

Tom was desperately trying to make sense out of what the man was saying. Practice? Practice what? And what was the sin the priest could have prevented?

"I thought I could control it."

"Control what?"

"The craving."

"What was the sin you confessed?"

"Her name was Millicent. A nice, old-fashioned name, don't you think? Her friends called her Millie, but I didn't. I much preferred Millicent. Of course, I wasn't what you would call a friend."

Another burst of laughter pierced the dead air. Tom's forehead was beaded with perspiration, but he suddenly felt cold. This wasn't a prankster. He dreaded what he was going to hear, yet he was compelled to ask.

"What happened to Millicent?"

"I broke her heart."

"I don't understand."

"What do you think happened to her?" the man demanded, his impatience clear now. "I killed her. It was messy; there was blood everywhere, all over me. I was terribly inexperienced back then. I hadn't perfected my technique. When I went to confession, I hadn't killed her yet. I was still in the planning stage and the priest could have stopped me, but he didn't. I told him what I was going to do."

"Tell me, how could he have stopped you?"

"Prayer," he answered, a shrug in his voice. "I told him to pray for me, but he didn't pray hard enough, now did he? I still killed her. It's a pity, really. She was such a pretty little thing . . . much prettier than the others."

Dear God, there were other women? How many others?
"How many crimes have you—"

The stranger interrupted him. "Sins, Father. I committed sins, but I might have been able to resist if the priest had helped me. He wouldn't give me what I needed."

"What did you need?"

"Absolution and acceptance. I was denied both."

The stranger suddenly slammed his fist into the grille.

Rage that must have been simmering just below the surface erupted full force as he spewed out in grotesque detail exactly what he had done to poor, innocent Millicent.

Tom was overwhelmed and sickened by the horror of it all. Dear God, what should he do? He had boasted he wouldn't be shocked or angered, but nothing could have prepared him for the atrocities the stranger took such delight in describing. Hate the sin, not the sinner.

"I've gotten a real taste for it," the madman whispered.

"How many other women have you killed?"

"Millicent was the first. There were other infatuations, and when they disappointed me, I had to hurt them, but I didn't kill any of them. After I met Millicent, everything changed. I watched her for a long time and everything about her was . . . perfect." His voice turned into a snarl as he continued. "But she betrayed me, just like the others. She thought she could play her little games with other men and I wouldn't notice. I couldn't let her torment me that way. I wouldn't," he corrected himself. "I had to punish her."

He let out a loud, exaggerated sigh and then chuckled. "I killed the little bitch twelve months ago and I buried her deep, real deep. No one's ever going to find her. There's no going back now. No siree. I had no idea how thrilling the kill was going to be. I made Millicent beg for mercy, and she did. By God, she did," he said as he laughed. "She screamed like a pig, and oh, how I loved the sound. I got so excited, more excited than I could ever have imagined was possible, and so I had to make her scream more, didn't I? When I was finished with her, I was bursting with joy. Well, Father, aren't you going to ask me if I'm sorry for my sins?" he taunted.

"No, you aren't contrite."

A suffocating silence filled the confessional. And then, in a serpent's hiss, the voice returned.

"The craving's come back."

Goosebumps covered Tom's arms. "There are people who can—"

"Do you think I should be locked away? I only punish those who hurt me. So, you see, I'm not culpable. But you think I'm sick, don't you? We're in confession, Father. You have to tell the truth."

"Yes, I think you're ill."

"Oh, I don't think so. I'm just dedicated."

"There are people who can help you."

"I'm brilliant, you know. It won't be easy to stop me. I study my clients before I take them on. I know everything about their families and their friends. Everything. Yes, it's going to be much harder to stop me now, but this time I've decided to make it more difficult for myself. Do you see? I don't want to sin. I really don't." The singsong voice was back.

"Listen to me, " Tom pleaded. "Step outside the confessional with me and we'll sit down together and talk this through. I want to help you, if you'll only let me."

"No, I needed help before and I was denied, remember? Give me absolution."

"I will not."

The sigh was long and drawn out. "Very well," he said. "I'm changing the rules this time. You have my permission to tell anyone you want to tell. Do you see how accommodating I can be?"

"It doesn't matter if you give me permission to tell or not; this conversation will remain confidential. The seal of silence must be maintained to protect the integrity of the confessional."

"No matter what I confess?"

"No matter what."

"I demand that you tell."

"Demand all you want, but it won't make any difference. I cannot tell anyone what you have said to me. I won't."

A moment of silence passed and then the stranger began to chuckle. "A priest with scruples. How extraordinary. Hmmm. What a quandary. But don't you fret, Father. I'm ten steps ahead of you. Yes sirree."

"What are you saying?"

"I've taken on a new client."

"You've already chosen your next—"

The madman cut him off. "I've already notified the authorities. They'll get my letter soon. Of course, that was before I knew you were going to be such a stickler for the rules. Still, it was considerate of me, wasn't it? I sent them a polite little note explaining my intentions. Pity I forgot to sign it."

"Did you give them the name of the person you intend to harm?"

"Harm? What a quaint word that is for murder. Yes, I named her."

"Another woman, then?" Tom's voice broke on the question.

"I only take women on as clients."

"Did you explain in this note your reason for wanting to kill this woman?"

"No."

"Do you have a reason?"

"Yes."

"Would you explain it to me?"

"Practice, Father."

"I don't understand."

"Practice makes perfect," he said. "This one's even more

special than Millicent. I wrap myself in her fragrance, and I love to watch her sleep. She's so beautiful. Ask me, and after I've given you her name, you can forgive me."

"I will not give you absolution."

"How's the chemotherapy going? Are you feeling sick? Did you get a good report?"

Tom's head snapped up. "What?" he demanded in a near shout.

The madman laughed. "I told you I study my clients before I take them on. You could say I stalk them," he whispered.

"How did you know—"

"Oh, Tommy, you've been such a sport. Haven't you wondered why I followed you all this way just to confess my sins to you? Think about it on your way back to the abbey. I've done my homework, haven't I?"

"Who are you?"

"Why, I'm a heartbreaker. And I do so love a challenge. Make this one difficult for me. The police will come here soon to talk to you, and then you'll be able to tell anyone you want," he mocked. "I know who you'll call first. Your hotshot friend at the FBI. You'll call Nick, won't you? I sure hope you will. And he'll come running to help. You'd better tell him to take her away and hide her from me. I might not follow, and I'll start looking for someone else. At least I'll try."

"How do you know—"

"Ask me."

"Ask you what?

"Her name," the madman whispered. "Ask me who my client is."

"I urge you to get help," Tom began again. "What you're doing—"

"Ask me. Ask me. Ask me."

Tom closed his eyes. "Yes. Who is she?"

"She's lovely," he answered. "Such beautiful full breasts and long, dark hair. There isn't a mark on her perfect body, and her face is like an angel's, so exquisite in every way. She's . . . breathtaking . . . but I plan to take her breath away."

"Tell me her name," Tom demanded, praying to God there was time to get to the poor woman to protect her.

"Laurant," the serpent whispered. "Her name is Laurant."

Panic hit Tom like a fist. "My Laurant?"

"That's right. Now you're getting it, Father. I'm going to kill your sister."